THE ELF WITCH
THE PLOT OF THE SIX SAINTS SERIES
BOOK ONE

JACQUELYN GILMORE

First independently published in the United States in 2025 by Jacquelyn Gilmore.

Copyright 2025 by Jacquelyn Gilmore.

Cover design by Beautiful Book Covers by Ivy.

The moral right of this author has been asserted.
All characters and events in this publication, other than those clearly in the public domain, are
fictitious, and any resemblance to real persons, living or dead, is purely coincidental.

All rights reserved.
No part of this publication may be reproduced, stored in a retrieval system, or transmitted in any form or by any means without prior permission in writing of the publisher, nor be otherwise circulated in any form of binding or cover other than that in which it is published and without a similar condition, including this condition being imposed on the subsequent purchaser.

A record of this book is available from the Library of Congress.

ISBN: 979-8-89546-644-5

www.jacquelyngilmore.com

❀ Created with Vellum

A COUPLE OF THINGS & CONTENT INFORMATION

Welcome to the dark and depraved Mesial Realm, where our wicked characters reside! If you didn't already know, this is a story about villains, and it can get dark at times. The tropes and trigger warnings have been updated on my website. Go to www.jacquelyngilmore.com and click "Books." Your mental health matters! They are there if you need to know what you're getting into. If you are a reader with specific triggers or sensitivities common to the dark romance/horror genre, PLEASE heed this note.

I mentioned this above, but it's worth repeating—this story is about villains and morally black characters. There will be a happily ever after, but the imperfect characters have a darker growth journey throughout the story. Characters need time to grow and evolve, so please be patient and keep this in mind while you're reading so you don't throw something in frustration when bad decisions are made! I hope you will love them as much as I do once the series is completed.

XO – Jacquelyn

"We read to know we are not alone."— CS Lewis.
To all the book lovers out there – you are not alone.

GLOSSARY

TERMS

- Breeds
Different races of humans evolved to have various types of magic and particular appearances specific to their breed.

- The Fabric
Where all magic originates. Raw, uncontrolled magic manifests as bright swirling lights like an aurora in the night sky.

- Fabric Events
Uncontrolled violent magical weather events that can come in many forms, including
ground quakes (earthquakes), acid rain, lightning storms, gravitational disturbances, etc. They are caused by pulling too much magic at once.

- Fabric Reverberations
A small outburst from the Fabric that throws magic that was cast back at the witch. It can be caused by casting magic you do not have a brand for, an unstable/broken wand, or pulling too much magic from the Fabric at once (considered a minor Fabric event).

- **The First Witch**
  A witch, chosen by the monarch, to lead the Royal Order of Magic.

- **The Royal Order of Magic**
  Governing body over witches in the Essenheim kingdom. Created to enforce the Ordinances, the Order employs and directly manages all master and archmage witches in the Essenheim kingdom. Commanded by the monarch's chosen First Witch, they ensure the laws around magic are being followed and maintain the stability of the Fabic.

- **The Ordinances**
  Laws enacted by the Essenheim monarch and the Royal Order of Magic to help people safely use magic without further destabilizing the Fabric.

- **Sigils**
  A brand on the right inner wrist signifying a person's breed in the Mesial Realm. People from both kingdoms are born with them.

Sigils for each breed of Esssnheim:
- *Norn elves: A leaf*
- *Trow pixies: A butterfly*
- *Sprite pixies: A moth*
- *Naiad nymphs: Three wavy lines stacked on top of each other*
- *Leimoniad nymphs: A tree*
- *Satyr shifters: Three vertical lines*
- *Leonine shifters: A five-point star*
- *Hobs aka Hobgoblins: breedless; people born without a sigil*

- **High Breeds**
  A person with the most potent magic typical for the breed (or none). They also physically appear perfect to the breed's expected standards, and their behavior is highly characteristic of the breed.

A triangle around a person's sigil at birth indicates they are a high-breed.

- **Common Breeds**

A person who possesses the standard magic a breed is known for (or none). Their physical looks are typical of the breed's expected standards, and their behavior is generally characteristic of the breed. Most people in Essenheim are common breeds.

A circle around a person's sigil at birth indicates they are a common-breed.

- Low Breeds

    A person with less than typical magic powers (or none). Their physical looks lack the distinctive qualities of the breed, and their behavior is less characteristic as well.

A square around a person's sigil at birth indicates they are a low-breed.

- Feeding

    When an elf absorbs part of someone's soul for energy and vitality. Feeding is required for all elves to stay alive.

- Saints

    These are mythical beings supposedly from the Upper realm who were cast out and became the Under realm's high-sentinels and monarchs. The religion that some practice in the Mesial Realm demonizes them, but no one truly knows if they exist or if the story is true.

- Heartmate

    A fated partner the Fabric chooses with both souls made from the same pieces of the Fabric. A heartmate's sigil will appear next to a person's sigil when the two touch each other for the first time. Mixed pairs are possible but uncommon. Heartmates bond to each other with three separate, specific binding spells and afterwards, they can feel each other's emotions and share magic.

- Chosen Mate

    A non-fated (non-heartmate) partner. Chosen mates bond to each other with one specific binding spell.

- Doorways

  Safe, stable portals to the other three realms (the Under, Upper and Mesial realms); they've been sealed and don't exist anymore.

- Slips

  Unstable portals to other realms that happen at random or are caused by Fabric events.

- Monarchs - King and Queen

  Male (king) and female (queen) witches chosen by the Fabric to rule the Mesial realm together as equals when the previous monarchs die. Considered the most powerful witches in the realm, these two people are chosen from the entire population to ensure the world thrives with balance, stability, and unity.

- Heir Apparent

  One person—named by the monarch—assumed to be next in line for king or queen. But until the current monarch dies and the magic passes to the next person, no one knows for certain who will inherit the monarchy's power.

- The Throne

  A magical object only the King can wield that gives him enhanced powers and abilities. It's located in the Niflheim castle.

- The Crown

  A magical object that only the Queen can wield that gives her enhanced powers and abilities. It grows from her head with plants and flowers encircling her head.

- High Sentinels

  Witches of each breed chosen by the Fabric when the previous Sentinel dies to govern and protect their territory. Considered the most powerful of the breed besides the monarchs.

- Territories

  Seven distinct districts in Essenheim, where each breed hails from and is governed by a High Sentinel of that breed. People can move and live wherever they like, though most stay within their territories.

- Coven

A group of witches who work together as a business creating and selling magic to a particular area.

- Collectors

People within covens (i.e., magic businesses) who deliver orders of magic and collect money in return.

PLACES/LOCATIONS

- Mesial Realm

The middle realm, where mortal breeds live, and atrophic and nascent magic intermingle.

- Upper Realm

The higher realm, where nascent creation magic flourishes and immortal breeds live, including the deity and angel breeds.

- Under Realm

The lowest realm, where atrophic destruction magic dominates and immortal breeds live, including the demons and satanic breeds. Souls from mortal beings also live in the Under realm after death.

- Essenheim

A kingdom in the Mesial realm.

- Niflheim

A kingdom in the Mesial realm.

- Stralas

The capital city of the Essenheim kingdom.

- Kehomel

The capital city of the Niflheim kingdom.

- Kishion
    A small port village in the southern Riverlands territory.

- Sonham
    The territory seat (i.e, capital) of the Riverlands.

- The Riverlands
    The Naiad nymphs' territory.

- The Meadowlands
    The Leimoniad nymphs' territory.

- The Plainslands
    The Trow pixies' territory.

- The Moorlands
    The Sprite pixies' territory.

- The Draswood Forest
    The Norn elves' territory.

- The Lowland Plains
    The Satyr shifters' territory.

- The Grasslands
    The Leonine shifters' territory.

CREATURES/BEINGS

- Norn Elves
    A mortal elf breed that lives in the Draswood forest territory in the Essenheim kingdom of the Mesial realm.

- Trow Pixies

A mortal pixie breed that lives in the Plainslands territory in the Essenheim kingdom of the Mesial realm.

• Sprite Pixies
A mortal pixie breed that lives in the Moorlands territory in the Essenheim kingdom of the Mesial realm.

• Naiad Nymphs
A mortal nymph breed that lives in the Riverlands territory in the Essenheim kingdom of the Mesial realm.

• Leimoniad Nymphs
A mortal nymph breed that lives in the Meadowlands territory in the Essenheim kingdom of the Mesial realm.

• Leonine Shifters
A mortal shifter breed that lives in the Grasslands territory in the Essenheim kingdom of the Mesial realm.

• Satyr Shifters
A mortal shifter breed that lives in Lowland Plains territory in the Essenheim kingdom of the Mesial realm.

• Hobs aka Hobgoblins
A mortal breedless person that lives in the Mesial realm without a territory.

• Drow Elves
A mortal elf breed that lives in the Lundr Caves territory in the Niflheim kingdom of the Mesial realm.

• Demon and Satonic Breeds
Various immortal breeds who inhabit the Under realm in different territories and kingdoms.

• Deity and Angel Breeds

Various immortal breeds who inhabit the Upper realm in different territories and kingdoms.

KEY CHARACTERS (IN ORDER OF APPEARANCE)

- Imani Aowyn
    High breed hybrid Norn elf, potential master witch

- Ara Aowyn
    High breed Naiad nymph, potential master witch, adoptive grandmother to Imani.

- Malis Oceyl
    High breed Niflheim master witch and merchant living in the Riverlands.

- Meira Aowyn
    High breed Norn elf, potential master witch, younger sister to Imani.

- Tanyl Pareias
    High breed Leimoniad nymph, master witch, Heir Apparent to the Essenheim kingdom.

- Esadora (Esa) Farawyn
    High breed Sprite pixie, potential master witch.

- Loren Ascal
    High breed Sprite pixie and master witch.

- Dialora Pareias
    High breed Leimoniad nymph, Queen of the Essenheim kingdom.

- Saevel Ilithana
    High breed Ursidae shifter, Heir Apparent to the Niflheim kingdom, older brother to Kiran.

- Kiran Ilithana

High breed Drow elf, First Witch of the Niflheim kingdom, younger brother to Saevel.

MAGIC SYSTEM

• Brands
Permanent marks on a person's skin that manifest at puberty and denote a type of magical power the Fabric has gifted them.

• Master Witch
A witch with five or more brands who works for the Royal Order of Magic; identified by a red symbol on their left hand gifted by the Fabric after successfully completing the Ascension Assessments.

• Archmage Witch
A witch with five or more brands who has successfully completed the Ascension Assessments a second time; identified by a purple symbol on their right hand gifted by the Fabric.

• Mediums
A source of natural energy that allows a person to channel their magic outward, e.g., fire, wands, water, etc.

• Draswood Wands
Wands made exclusively by the Norn elves from the magic trees in the Draswood Forest.

• Goldwood Wands
An alternative type of wand made from goldwood trees, which are extinct in the Mesial realm.

• Bone Wands
An alternative type of wand made from the bones of a person with flesh magic.

- The Drasil Wand

    An alternative type of wand made from unknown origins.

- Magic Signature

    The invisible energy of magic around a person's body that they emit unconsciously.

- The Ascension Assessments

    A three-part examination, designed and administered annually by the Royal Order of Magic, aimed at forcing the master brand to appear.

- Atrophic Magic

    Magic that destroys.

- Nascent Magic

    Magic that creates or brings something into existence.

- Flesh Magic

    A type of sacrificial, illegal magic that requires part of your body as the medium and enhances a spell to make it more potent and powerful.

- Soul Draw

    Natural magic (i.e., it doesn't require a brand) only elves possess that entrances other people and attracts them to the elf for feeding. High-bred female elves typically have the strongest soul draws, able to control another person's thoughts, actions, and desires.

- Pixie Dust

    Created by flaying the skin of Trow and Sprite pixies, it can be collected and used by anyone, without a spell. The dust from Trow pixies—Black Dust—takes away all five senses for a period of time and Sprite pixie dust—Nightmare Dust—causes terrifying hallucinations.

THE TWELVE MESIAL REALM MAGICAL BRANDS

- Alchemy

Magic that creates potions and other magical concoctions

- Alteration
    Magic that changes the physical structure of objects, people, etc.

- Binding
    Magic that enforces an agreement between two or more parties.

- Conjuring
    Magic that moves objects from one place to another.

- Defensive
    Magic that creates protective shields and wards.

- Divination
    Magic that predicts the future or reveals the present.

- Enchantment
    Magic that controls another object or person.

- Fire
    Magic that creates and controls fire.

- Healing
    Magic that heals wounds, sicknesses, etc.

- Illusion
    Magic, or glamour, that hides something.

- Terrestrial (Wind and Earth)
    Magic that creates and controls wind and earth.

- Water
    Magic that creates and controls water.

HISTORY

- First Realm War

    A war between the realms (the Upper, Under and Mesial realms) in ancient times. When it ended, the doorways between realms were sealed, never to be opened again.

- War of the Middle Kingdoms

    A thousand years ago, devastating fabric events and increasingly unstable magic caused a war between the two monarchs in the Mesial realm. The sun disappeared as storms increased in the southern parts of the Mesial kingdom, causing famine, death, and an influx of refugees escaping into the northern territories.

- War of the Middle Kingdoms Treaty

    Although the war technically never ended, fighting stopped after a treaty was signed between the two sides, forming the Essenheim and Niflheim kingdoms and permanently separating them.

PART I
THE ORDER AND THE CROWN

CHAPTER 1

With the right motivation, her grandmother could do just about anything. Imani scrunched her nose in disgust at the prison cell's dank, dark walls. Indeed, Ara could escape anytime if she wanted it badly enough.

"I hope they're treating you well," Imani said, attempting a few civil last words.

Ara's face appeared between the iron bars as she laughed in response. *Laughed.*

Imani ground her molars at the sound. They were too similar in many ways and had grated on each other for over a decade.

"You almost slit my throat the night before the arrest. You couldn't give a damn how they're treating me." Aralana tried to laugh again but started coughing instead. Her blue eyes, exactly like Imani's, glowed in the darkness, her tangled blonde hair framing her once-pretty, heart-shaped face. Who would have thought so much malice existed in such an unassuming, small person?

Imani watched silently for a minute, then said tightly, "Yes, well, I suppose the whole thing is rather humorous after what you've done to this family, especially recently. We're practically destitute with you disappearing on us these past six months. And where has all the money been going? To those old maps you brought home? To the musty books? Because we haven't seen the fruits of our labors for quite some time, you selfish hag."

Ara snickered. "Open those perfect blue eyes and look around. I saved this family after what you did. Don't waste this gift I'm giving you."

"What gift?" Imani fought the urge to reach through the bars and choke her. "Your death? Oh, no need to worry. I can't wait for you to burn tomorrow."

"Ungrateful elf," Ara snarled. With a snap, she tossed her supposedly confiscated wand at Imani. It tumbled to the grimy floor. "Stupid as ever, despite what I'm leaving you and the sacrifices I made for your life. Your parents, my heartmate, and now me. Riona, too. All dead because of you. Focus on surviving so everyone's efforts aren't wasted."

Guilt spread through Imani's chest as she stared at the wand on the ground—a wand Imani's mother made—a gift. Ara had always known how to hit everyone where it hurt. No one else could dissect a person's weaknesses and mercilessly use them as leverage. Imani secretly admired such expert manipulation, except when directed at her.

She carefully picked up the wand and slipped it into her pocket. Imani wished she could wield it. But, to her, it was a useless piece of wood without any magical brands. Still, it would be harder for Ara to escape without access to her magic through her wand.

That said, the fire itself would be a powerful medium. She couldn't help but wonder if Ara had something planned while tied to the pyre tomorrow.

Imani cleared her throat, feeling less indignant. "I'm grateful for what you've given us all these years. It was more than most. But it doesn't mean I'll forgive you for being an absolute cunt for most of my life."

"Good girl." A crooked smile spread across the old witch's face. "Leave forgiveness and mercy to the angel and deity breeds of the Upper realm."

"I wouldn't give you mercy now, even if my life depended on it." Imani's voice held no remorse because she had no sympathy for the bitch. None whatsoever. Yet, for some reason, her heart still ached all the same. She wanted to cry, sob, and beg like she had when her grandfather had died. Young people usually mourned their grandparents. Imani tried to mourn hers, too.

The emotions never came.

Ara wasn't capable of sympathy, either, or many other feelings, for that matter.

Imani brought her face directly in front of her grandmother's. "I'll make sure all of us survive, like always."

"Perfect." Ara's grin was terrifying and feral. "You'll need to be the one to make the choices no one else can stomach now, like I taught you."

Imani's lips curled in disgust. "It's what I've always done, right? You know I hate you for that, too. You said nothing when we arrived in Riverlands as children, alone and three days late! You barely showed a modicum of concern. You simply took Dak from my arms and silently waited for an explanation. When I told you our parents were dead, your only reply was, 'I see.'"

Ara nodded. "Indeed. This burden is one you'll have to carry alone."

"I hated you then, and I hate you now, a decade later."

Even if her parents hadn't died on the trip to the nymph territory of the Riverlands, Imani had terrified Sven and Saria Aowyn. After what had happened, they had been at the end of their rope and couldn't have her anywhere near the Draswood Forest, the Norn elves' territory. They had been planning to get rid of their daughter because, unlike most elven parents, Ara had no problem using a heavy hand to rein in Imani's behavior.

"You have no idea what true hate is, but you will," Ara said.

A long pause stretched out between them.

"How inspiring. I'll cherish such advice forever," Imani deadpanned, steeling herself against the familiar barbs that had marked most of her adolescence and early adulthood. Ara wouldn't miss a chance to communicate her blatant disdain for Imani even halfway to the grave.

They'd never gotten on, but Imani and Ara's relationship had further deteriorated after Imani had failed to inherit any magic. It rankled the nymph witch, who expected the whole family to earn their keep. Especially the adopted one who couldn't control her soul draw—the special compulsion magic Norn elves possessed, designed to ensnare their prey and feed on their life essence.

"We all have choices to make in life, and everyone must deal with the consequences of those choices, eventually. As wrinkled, lumpy, and uncomfortable as it may be, you made your bed. Don't you dare complain about having to lie in it, you selfish, menial piece of shit—an orphaned elf without magic. You should be grateful to have a bed at all."

Imani fought a smile at the memory of the lesson Ara had repeatedly taught her. Locked inside a cage in the back of their shop, half-starved, Ara had forced her to control her soul draw without magic. The ramification if she couldn't? Cease to exist at all. As brutal as the punishments were, they had worked.

An owl hooted directly outside the basement's narrow windows, making Imani's heart race. Imani hated birds, and they hated her right back. She hated any beasts who reminded her of Draswood, which, unfortunately, was a great many things.

"Ah … the owl." Her grandmother bared her teeth at Imani's startled face. "A symbol of death."

She composed herself and looked Ara straight in the eyes. "A good omen, then."

"No, because before we reach heaven, the saints will eat us, which means I'll be with your father shortly."

"We'll be better off without you."

"You'd be nothing without me." Ara stared back at her.

Imani brought her face directly in front of her grandmother's again. "What do you want? You called me here."

"I planned to give you more answers."

"I want absolutely nothing from you."

The old witch merely shrugged. "With power, there's always a cost. This is yours. The sooner you accept it, the easier your life will be. Starting tomorrow, surviving, despite the hatred and loneliness, will be the hardest thing you ever do. You'll need to figure out most things independently, Imani. It's always been the best way you've learned. It's why I opted for the cage all those years. Do it fast, though, because you'll be utterly alone once I'm gone."

Venom laced Imani's quiet words. "Alone? Where have *you* been? I have my siblings, and someday, maybe even a heartmate—"

"Heartmate?" A loud cackle echoed against the crumbling, dark walls, cutting Imani off. "I've met your heartmate," Ara said with a cruel smile, "and that man will hate you. In fact, he already does."

Imani froze. "What …? Wh-who is he? Have we met? What's he like?" she whispered, grasping the bars.

It was almost impossible to believe she might have met her heartmate, the one elf in the whole world made from the same piece of the Fabric as her, and therefore, her fated partner. And these days, to find him outside the Draswood Forest seemed inconceivable.

Before Imani could get more words out, Ara struck her face through the iron cage with a fist, knocking Imani's head back. She steadied herself with the bars and grabbed her nose.

"You bitch," Imani spat, her voice muffled by her hand and the blood running down her mouth.

"Get a hold of yourself," Ara said. "What I have to say about him is important." The nymph growled, frustrated, as if some memory of him suddenly enraged her. "A heartmate can be a blessing but also a nightmare. Sharing power with someone is no light matter."

Ara would know. She'd had one for decades before he had suddenly died back when Imani was still a child.

Ara's face was crushed between the bars, and her eyes looked wild. "Your father was the best divination witch I'd seen in years, and your heartmate is everything he foresaw he would be. But he's also far worse than either of us imagined. That bastard heartmate of yours sees a partner he thinks is a poor, uneducated female with no magic. You're a humiliating weakness for him, and he'll try to kill you for it. Don't you dare tie yourself to such a beast."

If she didn't know any better, Imani would have thought her grandmother was afraid of this man.

A guard yelled from the top of the stairs, hurrying them along.

With a snap of her neck, Ara's eyes suddenly burned into her.

"What that heartmate of yours doesn't know yet, and it might take him a while to realize, is you'll be the only thing to truly scare him. A weakness if you can't be controlled."

"Then he'll have to kill me because I won't let anyone, not even my heartmate, control me anymore."

"With him, you might not have a choice."

"You think, after all these years with you, I need to be loved so badly I'll let some bastard manipulate me? Don't make me laugh. I will make the life I want after you're dead, with or without him."

Imani gave Ara her back, ready to leave, but like before, a hand ripped her arm back faster than she had expected.

"You will stay and listen to one last thing I must say, granddaughter." Blue eyes hit her with sudden, chilling clarity. Ara's madness was temporarily gone. "I don't give a shit about the life you want. Do you think anyone ever asked me what I wanted? As female witches, we take the fate handed to us and do our best with it. If you want any sort of life at all, you will have to accept it and fight for what you're given. In fact, accepting everyone will soon hate and fear you will make things easier. You better start now."

Tension hung in the air.

After a long, painful silence, Imani answered in a low, threatening tone, "I meant what I said when I pressed the knife to your neck. I would have killed you if you came back. I still will. So, you better hope you die tomorrow. Drop any ill-conceived plans of saving yourself because it's over."

Ara's unreadable expression sent a shiver down Imani's spine. She let it roll through her, trying to steady her breathing. As Ara had said, people made their beds, and the old nymph was currently lying in hers. It was an unpleasant bed she found herself in.

What must it feel like to burn alive? Hopefully, quite painful. The consequences for conspiring with the enemy kingdom and using illegal flesh magic were steep.

"This conversation, maddening as usual, is over." Unsettled and with her chest heaving, Imani turned away toward the door again. Losing control right now was the last image she wanted to leave the witch with before dying.

"Goodbye, Ara," Imani shouted over her shoulder. "I'm counting the seconds until I'm rid of you."

"You aren't even close to being rid of me," Ara warned, getting in the last word before slinking back into the shadows.

Stomping up the stairs, Imani clenched and unclenched her fists a few times, letting the words sink in. Ara sat locked away, rotting without her wand. Yet, somehow, like a general to be feared, the witch still sounded triumphant. Did her grandmother truly have an escape planned?

It wouldn't surprise Imani one bit.

CHAPTER 2

Smoke and ash from her grandmother's execution began coating Imani's skin, hair, and even her mouth as the fire picked up. She tongued her teeth at the taste of the old witch.

The chalky substance coated Imani's mouth, leaving her without an ounce of guilt.

A crowd stood in impenetrable silence as the orange and blue flames licked the wooden stake, moving leisurely up the nymph's skin. While Imani waited for her grandmother to die, her focus drifted. The scent of magic hung heavy in the air for some reason. The smell set her teeth on edge, but it was why Imani bothered to come at all—to ensure Ara met her fate.

The fire grew, and the crowd flinched. But no one looked away as flames sank their teeth into Ara's skin like a wolf ripping its prey to shreds. Ara's destruction cast a beautiful glow in the drab, winter daylight of the Riverlands territory.

With each crackle of the tinder, Imani felt a terrible foreboding grow inside her. Her grandmother's death marked the end of Imani's previous life, but she still couldn't erase the eeriness that this moment was the beginning of something new, something worse.

The annoyance of having to wait proved to be somewhat of a distraction, at least. Watching someone die took a long time. The longer it dragged on, the more her eyes glazed with a detached indifference as she waited for her grandmother to leave this realm.

Startling heat blasted from the pyre, forcing onlookers back in a violent yet mesmerizing burst. Pricks of sparks hit Imani's skin, and flames danced among the circle of idiotic, wide-eyed stares. She glanced around.

He wasn't here. Ara's accuser had skipped the execution.

"You've got to give it to her. The old nymph is strong."

Imani didn't bother to try to figure out who had dared say what they were all thinking. The witch stood stock-still, silently accepting her fate, even as her skin melted. Imani couldn't look away from the gruesome sight.

Once the flames engulfed the stake at her back, Ara's eyes dropped and fixed ahead into the crowd. The witch held dominion with a simple gaze.

Soon, the flames rose to rival the height of the surrounding buildings, then the flames became Ara's hair, and that, too, whipped in the wind. It wouldn't be much longer.

Unmoving and unflinching, Ara's shocking blue irises reflected the light of the flames, flashing like a blade in the sun as they commanded a final directive to the young elf witch in the crowd.

Indeed, everything about today, she controlled, even her execution, despite her imminent death and the light dimming her gaze. Death was a mere inconvenience. Imani had no idea how or why, but if Ara made the decision not to die today, she wouldn't. It was that simple. Imani hated all the power her grandmother effortlessly exerted in all things, constantly remaining two steps in front of everyone, even when she was half-mad.

Well, *if* she was half-mad. The woman could fool the saints when properly motivated.

And still, Ara didn't move, her blue irises dimming as her life drained away.

Her grandmother spoke to her then. Those horrible eyes that looked so like her own repeated the disconcerting words she'd said only hours ago. Imani hadn't wanted to hear them last night and didn't want to listen to them now.

"Don't waste this gift," Ara had said last night.

The tingling through her limbs hadn't stopped since Ara had shared those strange words with Imani.

She rubbed her right forearm where her magical brands would have appeared if the Fabric had given her any. Imani's eyes never strayed from the pyre as her lungs breathed in the harsh smoke and she wrapped the cloak tighter around her.

Imani was magicless, and when she twisted her glamoured, pallid face into a scowl, she became so bland that no one even bothered to call her ugly. Once Ara died, any magic the witch cast, including the illusion over Imani's face and soul draw, would fall and reveal her true form. Her sister, Meira, would need to cast another at home later. It was risky for her to be out here, showing her real face, but worth it.

Another eruption of heat hit her as the nymph burned. Imani buried deeper into her cloak, not knowing when precisely the illusion would fall. It would be soon.

The nymph loosed one shrill sound, cutting through the whispers at last. She became entirely engulfed in fire, a raging inferno instead of a body, incinerating into ash while she roared.

A shudder threatened to wreck Imani's body, waiting.

With a gasp, the nymph's soul left the corporeal state.

The heat was remarkable, unbearable. What a world of pain it must be.

Finally, the witch was dead.

Imani's heart picked up speed as the tingling under her skin grew increasingly hotter, reaching a fevered temperature. Was the illusion falling?

Her grandmother's flesh had seared off her bones, ash flinging in the wind while the pyre's flames began to dim. They died quickly in the cold winter air, but the coals still radiated heat. Only the ashy figure of a woman with charred bones remained.

Imani couldn't breathe, tormented by the tingling cutting through her flesh. She fought through it, ignoring it and needing to savor this moment. Air undulated and pulsed around the burnt, grotesque shape that used to be the nymph.

She screamed an agonizing, embarrassing sound she had no

control over. Maybe it was from the physical pain, maybe from the fear of Ara leaving them without answers. Maybe both.

Exposed and alone in a city where they were outsiders trying to run a magic business, competition would be swift, with covens moving in to take the Aowyns' territory. There wouldn't be time to waste after Ara died to solidify their area if they wanted to keep their livelihoods. Especially with only one witch—her sister—to make the magic now.

It terrified Imani.

The small crowd remaining retreated. Some considered reaching out a hand to help the young elf, but in the end, strangers simply murmured their sympathies at her apparent grief.

A storm of emotions raged inside her, not the least of which included anger and no little amount of fear, but *grief*? No, she wasn't grieving one bit. She was *furious*. Furious but free.

In an act of raw hunger, rage, and impulsiveness, Imani stumbled forward, gasping and panting as she tilted back her chin, hood dropping to reveal the female Norn elf underneath. She reached out and let the spirit—no more than a wisp of smoke—wrap itself up her arm. Then she unapologetically inhaled all the air containing Ara's soul.

Blissful calm settled inside her as she devoured her grandmother's essence. Unlike the sliver she regularly took from Meira every week, this was all-consuming. It even calmed the tingling still nipping at her skin.

A smile spread across Imani's face. Prickling aside, she was invigorated and ready to claim her second helping of sweet revenge.

THE MERCHANT MALIS'S house sat on an idyllic spot along the river, and the tree-lined path greeted her with a sort of cheerfulness. Yet the peaceful scenery at twilight made her shadow menacing.

The sun dropped further, and the shade of her body danced at the edge of her figure. Odd behavior for a shadow, but Imani brushed it off as the weather. Winter rarely came this south to the village of Kishion in the Riverlands territory.

Ravens perched on the shingles, drains, and eaves. Every room in the manor remained dark except one on the first level. Imani smirked and repeated the plan to herself as she peered through the glass, looking for signs of her prey. Holding people responsible for their choices, even grown men, was something she did surprisingly well. Like most men, Malis considered himself invincible compared to women, which was probably correct in almost all other instances—females could never hit someone as hard as a male. But, like all elves, Imani still had her soul draw.

A door slammed upstairs. Imani snapped her neck to the side as the birds lifted into the air like leaves stirred by a gust. It gave her a distinct feeling of dread, of being watched.

The strange tingling slowly picked back up again. Shivering, she tried to fortify herself.

Malis had sent the servants away like clockwork. Imani assured herself it must have been the wind. Maybe she'd brought the dread from the execution and the brutal, bloody words she and Ara had exchanged. Maybe the ravens had brought some of it, too, on their feathered, twilight wings.

Imani understood one thing in the swirl of the creatures—more death awaited her.

She scurried behind the shrubs, reminding herself to keep low beneath the windows. Pleasure flooded her when she lifted her head to see him pacing in front of the glow of a hearth alone.

The tingle grew into a deep slit, cutting into her skin, burning from the inside worse than before. Imani had a fierce urge to rip her heating skin from her flesh. The illusion falling had never felt like this before, but Ara had never died before, either.

Malis stood by the windows, unmoving, as the wind picked up. It whistled through the cracks of the house.

Imani took in a ragged breath to control her body. She thought this day would have been euphoric, but seconds ticked on, turning more tiny jolts into pricks of pain streaking through her arms and hands. She leaned against the side of the house to keep her balance through a wave of dizziness. Her chance at retribution was slipping away.

Imani tugged her hair as another wave of prickling needles hit her, along with the sharp sting of weakness and worthlessness. Skin and blood caught in her nails. She ripped her hands away from her head in horror.

Veins and tendons blackened her pale skin.

Something was really, *really* wrong.

With a resigned deep breath and all the strength she could muster, Imani fled to the nearby riverbank. Nearly tripping over her feet, she half-walked, half-staggered along the dirt path. The river's current grew to a loud, dull roar. The trembling intensified, forcing her to her knees. Ignoring the overwhelming pain took all her strength. Seconds passed like hours before her belly clenched, making her slant her head.

Imani gagged violently as the contents of her stomach came up. Consuming her grandmother's soul following the execution might have been a mistake. The sickness was relentless, and she retched a second and third time until, finally, she expelled red bile and heaved a large object from her throat, nearly choking.

A powerful cough forced a small, black-scaled creature out. Rattling, the snake slipped from her lips and smacked onto the ground. It slithered in the grass momentarily. Then the animal and bile turned to ash. A light breeze picked up the remnants.

Imani wiped her mouth and watched with fascination as the ashes drifted away. She understood what the snake meant, and it made her happier than she'd ever been since coming to the Riverlands twelve years ago. Whatever flesh magic that existed inside Imani had been powerful, but the creature had turned to ash and disappeared forever. Which meant the caster—her grandmother—was dead.

She carefully dragged herself to the water's edge and peered over. With all the magic stripped, her true self stared back. Her hands were dirty from picking weeds earlier, and her long hair was tangled in a braid. Imani wanted to try harder with her appearance—she loved pretty things—but couldn't muster the energy these days. Sometimes, she even forgot what she looked like without the glamoured illusion. Did she have the same luminous blue eyes and silver hair as her mother? Did she have her father's sharp chin or bright freckles? Her adoptive father used to say they were like little diamonds sparkling in the sun.

Ara always said it was a pointless fantasy. Her father wasn't even her real father, and her parents had been dead for a long time. But Meira would say there was nothing wrong with having dreams, and Imani's shriveled heart still held some tiny hope that someday they'd be happy living in the Draswood again. Imani had plans for their magic business. Plans that might get them back into the forest soon.

Darting her eyes around, Imani panicked, but the area remained deserted. Her cloak ruffled in the wind.

"For fuck's sake," she muttered to herself, wrenching the hood over her ears, tugging it as far forward as possible to shroud the arched tips. Despite the freedom, being seen in her ethereal elven form among the naiad nymphs was unwise. In the Riverlands, Imani was more of a prisoner than powerful. Sightings of Norn elves were so rare she hadn't seen one besides her siblings since the day they had left the Draswood.

Anger ripped through her at the thought, twisting her face into something feral. Was it possible to lock someone's magic away for nearly a decade? Imani thought it probably was, but it would be a spell only the most advanced, powerful witches could pull off. Possibly even flesh magic, the worst, most atrophic, destructive kind of magic, requiring parts of the physical body as the medium to cast. Sometimes, even an entire body. Any witch could use flesh magic to enhance any spell, making it more powerful, but such barbaric, sacrificial magic was considered dark and illegal here in Essenheim.

Indeed, this betrayal went beyond simple hatred. How could her own grandmother commit such an act?

The truth was staring Imani in the face. Ara wanted another way to control her. As usual, only a fool would underestimate the woman. She had been that fool one too many times.

Walking on unsteady legs, Imani sought out the nearest tree. She felt the magic but needed to see the proof.

She tore her sleeves back on both arms. Her skin bore nine burning brands; they glimmered in the moonlight—it was a beautiful sight. One Imani wouldn't let anyone take away from her again.

Tears stung her eyes. Six, sparkling blue magical brands—alteration, alchemy, binding, enchantment, illusion, and wandlore—wrapped up her right forearm. While she only possessed the most basic power level of these abilities, the brands would allow her to use a medium, like a wand, to pull from the raw magic of the Fabric and cast specific spells related to each. Unlike destructive, atrophic magic, people with blue brands could cast nascent magic—creation magic.

Imani lifted her head as the ribbons of light danced in the sky. When the sun eventually dropped entirely, the night would light up with streaks of wild, raw magic shimmering across the stars, a source of power inaccessible to most.

In total, she had seven magical brands, denoting seven distinct magic abilities. While there were rumored to be twelve-marks out there, most witches had no more than three or four. A slight smirk tugged at her lips. Meira only possessed five brands, making Imani the more powerful sister.

While she reveled in the blue brands, the seventh, red one twisted her stomach into a horrifying knot. Only blue brands existed in Essenheim; a red brand probably meant the person could cast atrophic magic of some kind. Her kingdom didn't harbor savages or tolerate the ruinous magic they practiced in the south.

Worse, sitting on her left arm were two red stag sigils to replace the Norn's intricate leaf Imani had had before. Her mind reeled, realizing the blue leaf had been a glamoured fake. Indeed, someone had hidden her actual sigil, which had marked her dominant breed since birth. She was only half-Norn, and without a blue brand, she wasn't from Essenheim, either.

Was she from the sunless Niflheim Kingdom? How would her mother have met and mated with one of *them*? Anything to do with the southern kingdom was illegal. Imani had never even seen a Niflheim brand before—not in a book, not on a person, a painting, or in paper circulations.

The second sigil also meant she had a heartmate who was the same mysterious breed. Imani had racked her brain since Ara had mentioned him but possessed no memory of meeting a male elf before, let alone touching him, which was required for the heartmate sigil to sear into your skin. Slumping in defeat, she honestly couldn't remember this elf.

Despite the gravity of her situation, the fact that the first Niflheim brands she laid eyes on might be her own almost made her crack a smile. Realizing they had appeared immediately after the Crown had executed her grandmother for illegal magic practically sent her over the edge with hysterical laughter. Exhaustion, shock, and happiness made her lightheaded and giddy.

At least it was encased in a familiar triangle, like all high-bred elves, no matter their sigil. She didn't know what kind of elf, but she would find out.

Ara's words rang in Imani's head, sobering her.

"Before we reach heaven, the saints will eat us. Which means I'll be with your father shortly."

"We'll be better off without you."

"You'd be nothing without me."

While her magic was new and unpracticed, it didn't change anything. It *couldn't* change anything. Her heartmate's identity didn't matter right now. All that mattered was Malis had gone after the wrong family—the Aowyns—and he would soon pay for his mistake.

Imani swept her cloak tightly around her and headed back toward Malis's home.

CHAPTER 3

Rather than linger outside, Imani slipped silently through the front door. It was now or never.

Standing in the hallway, she let her cloak fall, revealing her raw form. She felt no inclination to hide anything except her illicit markings, which were easily concealed using the sleeves of her dress. This bastard would look upon her true face and see that she wasn't plain or unremarkable any longer. For the first time in a long time, Imani was powerful, with magic coursing through her veins and a plan she'd spent weeks honing.

High-bred female elves, like Imani, possessing their own magical brands and formidable, natural soul draws, were rumored to be monsters of the worst kind. They could put anyone under a spell and procure anything they wanted from your mind or body. In that case, they were an abomination too dangerous to exist.

Having lived in the forest for part of her life, Imani knew it was exaggerated. Still, she hoped Malis didn't. She hoped that seeing her like this would terrify him.

Imani approached the light flooding into the hallway from the room Malis stood in, still looking out the window with his back to her. A faint whisper murmured in her ear, sending chills down her spine. Shaking it off, she hardened her gaze at Malis. The sight of him made the blood heat in her veins.

The Niflheim merchant had stayed the same in the few weeks since their last encounter. Calloused and rough hands held a glass of dark whiskey, or scotch. His outfit appeared similar—the same black trousers and a light linen shirt untucked, with his dark jacket draped over a chair.

"I've been waiting for you, pretty little elf," Malis said without bothering to turn around.

Steadying her breathing, Imani willed herself to be calm. The air around her body thrummed with energy, as if she might jump out of her skin.

"Hello, Malis," she said, rolling Ara's wand back and forth in her pocket, appreciating the comfort of its magical signature, despite not knowing exactly how to use it.

Setting the drink down on the desk, Malis turned to face her. "You've come to kill me," he stated. Depthless eyes scanned her body like bugs crawling over her skin. His face could be considered handsome with his large brown eyes and high cheekbones, but Imani found him repulsive after what he'd done to her.

"I came for answers," she said. "Why did you ask Fen for confiscated maps of Niflheim?"

"Ah ... warming the constable's bed, too, I see." He narrowed his eyes to slits and ran his hand along the leather of the chair. "Your grandmother was guilty of every crime I accused her of before I turned her in. Not only did she steal those maps, but her list of crimes is far worse. Some of which would sicken you. She deserved to burn."

She believed him. If her grandmother wanted something, she took it. Numerous things the woman had done made Imani sick.

A menacing glint reflected in his eyes as he continued, "Did they tell you Ara admitted to traveling to Niflheim? How she was in bed with the Illithiana royals and your so-called traitor Zolyn?"

Now, *that* statement she didn't believe. "You lie."

Travel between Essenheim and Niflheim was illegal. Procuring documents like maps for the journey would be treason of the worst kind, and if Ara was also involved with the witch Zolyn, then she was a clear traitor in the Crown's eyes. It would risk everything Ara had built with their magic business. Not to mention Zolyn had been declared dead by Queen Dialora herself.

"Do I? You'll notice the authorities spared your flat from an exhaustive search. They didn't even call a master to break enchantments and wards. Why expend the resources when they had a mountain of proof, and the defendant had already confessed? Aralana hid some precious items in your flat, which I intend to take tonight."

"Like you could ever prowl around our home. It's far too protected. It's why you asked Fen to retrieve them for you." Imani itched to point the wand at him but held back. Although she had watched Ara cast spells every day and had read everything she could find about magic, she had never performed it in her life.

He shot her a withering look. "The wards fell away with Ara's death, as did the spell over your magic."

Imani dug her nails into her palms to stifle her gasp. How did he know about her magic? Oddly enough, he didn't seem to care much. Malis didn't want her dead for knowing about his illegal atrophic magic, as she'd initially thought. He wanted her grandmother's secrets and Imani out of the way. How could she be so stupid as to forget about the wards? Saints, her siblings were home!

The pressure to kill him mounted, but she wanted to keep him talking for a bit longer to learn as much as she could. "I will only repeat myself once—I want answers tonight."

"You're mistaken about who's in charge here, little elf." Malis lifted a stack of papers from his desk. "I already have most of the maps, but I want the rest and the book she hid from the throne and Crown. It's called *A History of Royal Bloodlines*, and it's hundreds of years old. While not strictly on slips and doorways, it's the only one of its kind."

Holding something even *mentioning* stable and unstable portals to other realms would be tantamount to treason, and the monarchy of Essenheim, the Crown, would ensure such a person met Ara's fate. It seemed the Throne, the monarchy of Niflheim, would do the same.

"Slips don't exist," she ground out, biting her tongue before she revealed anything else. Imani would go to her grave before she admitted that, years ago, gravity had distorted reality, forcing the ground to cleave itself open into a slip in front of her.

"Stable open doorways don't, but slips do." Malis paused. "And this is the only book I know of mentioning them both."

Imani's head spun with possibilities. Ara had believed beings in the other realms slinked around the sealed doorways, hunting for weaknesses, waiting, watching. If slips existed in more than a fleeting sense, dangers their world hadn't seen in ten thousand years could be closer than anyone thought possible.

Malis's voice slunk to a seductive murmur. Dizziness made her sway. "Have you seen the book, Imani?"

This was his compulsion magic at work, but unlike hers, it only worked on the physical body, not the mind. Her throat constricted as she tried to fight the urge to answer him. While the one tattered book she'd found inside the trunk had nothing to do with royal bloodlines or slips, there were dozens of hidden compartments she hadn't been able to search yet.

"I don't answer to an exiled beast like you," Imani managed to bite out as control of the situation slipped from her.

His stocky frame crowded her. He looked only a few years older than her, but different people aged at different rates. She had no idea his breed.

She stepped back, hitting another chair as he snarled in her face, "I'm not as exiled as you might think. Who do you think smuggled Ara back and forth? His Dark Highness briefly expressed his irritation with me when he learned the authorities had caught and killed Ara at my behest." Malis motioned to several fading bruises marring his neck. "But she's replaceable. The prince and I have come to a new arrangement."

"I would have paid to see this Niflheim prince choke you to death," Imani seethed.

He laughed. "Too bad the two of you will never meet in this realm. I'd like to watch him eat you alive." He cocked his head. "Did you think you'd slip into your grandmother's role so easily? I may not have particularly liked her, but the woman was a force to be reckoned with, and you … are not. A rival coven, like Asim's, will not let you work here unchallenged. You and your sister are no match for him."

Imani bristled. "We've owned the magic business in this area of the Riverlands for nearly two decades. The Aowyns have a claim to any spells bought or sold south of the River Meechan, and we're the strongest witches in the tri-territory area. Only the Nedalis have as much magic as us, and I can deal with that family alone." She fixed a stony glare on Malis. "Besides, if you think I won't kill Asim, you don't know me at all."

In truth, she would do no such thing. Going around killing people was terrible for business. The Aowyn family didn't murder often, but when they did, it was with meticulous planning and reason. She didn't need to kill him. She only needed to make Asim more afraid to cross her than anyone else.

But Malis? He was too dangerous to keep alive.

He scoffed. "You're alone with two young elves at home, and everyone who deals in magic around here knows you're weak."

Imani ignored the flare of anxiety in her chest, flexing her fingers slightly. "People challenged Ara up until the day she died. It might wane for a few years, but it will never end because everyone in this business is a threat." Her voice dropped lower. "I came here for answers tonight, and if I don't get them right now, so help me saints, the shipbuilder Ara beat to death last year will look merciful."

The wicked male cocked a brow at her. "While the prince demanded your sister tonight, I don't think he'll mind if I change plans. Even with the horrendous mark marring your face, you're a superior physical representation of a Norn elf and far more powerful. And unlike her, you came to me."

Imani's mind spun. What had he planned to do with Meira? How long had he known Imani was plotting against him? Her advantages quickly eroded as he backed her further into a corner. How could she have been so naïve as to think she could take this man on?

She clutched the wand tighter as a whisper urged her to call on her magic. Her breathing picked up as her eyes darted around the room for another solution, a distraction—anything.

"Why didn't your strange compulsion magic work on my grandmother when she attacked you in the shop?"

"I have no idea why it didn't work on her," he said. "Your grandmother held more secrets than anyone I've ever known."

"I should have told them *your* secret and let the Crown kill you for still wielding your magic. I should have told everyone you can still cast your atrophic magic, even without your brands." Her voice trembled as the murmuring to use her magic grew louder in her ears.

"You wouldn't have said anything." He smiled, deadly and smug. "You wanted your grandmother dead almost as much as I did."

"Who knows? Maybe they would have killed you both for your crimes," she said coolly.

"Doubtful. Without proof, it would have been my word against yours. And besides, it's natural magic like your soul draw. It's part of who I am."

She swallowed hard. His breed possessed compulsion magic, just like hers.

She clenched her jaw, desperate to keep him talking. "You're a Niflheim subject living in Essenheim. They stripped you of your magic, yet you cast some enchantment magic against her that day. What is your breed?"

"When I sought refuge, the Essenheim queen may have personally flayed my skin to the bone," Malis said as he ripped his sleeve back. His arm, covered in grotesque, rough skin, made her shudder. "But there are ways around flaying." A wand appeared in his hand, and a soft, trilling sound from his chest filled the room. "Now, down on your knees," he said in a voice not his own.

With the element of surprise gone and the threat of his magic even worse than she had anticipated, her plan continued unraveling.

No. It wasn't over yet.

Some sort of roiling began beneath Imani's skin, like water about to boil over. With her life on the line, she made a snap decision.

An unhinged cry ripped from her throat as she pointed the wand at him.

The fire went out.

CHAPTER 4

Several cuts ripped through Malis's chest in quick succession. In the darkness, Imani had no idea what spell she had cast. Her magic was alive and acting on its own instinct to protect her, but she pulled it back somehow.

The fire roared back to life. Blood seeped through his linen shirt in streaks. Strange whispers encircled her like ghosts. A tremor in her muscles clambered to dominate and destroy him, and she would let it. But Malis needed to answer her question before she did.

"What breed are you?" she repeated, putting as much power in her voice as possible, hoping the wounds would cow him into answering.

"One I'm certain you've never heard of but will haunt your nightmares. My kind isn't known for our restraint." His throat made the same abnormal noise, and he spoke to her in modulated tones, worse than before.

Imani tried to cast an enchantment to take his voice away but was caught in the web of his magic, and his transfixing spell overpowered hers. If she'd been able to look him in the eye, she could possibly have used her own compulsion to overpower him, but she'd never used it on purpose before and was unpracticed.

Her wand arm shook as dark eyes stared at her like pits in the Under realm.

"Stop moving."

Imani's body stilled.

He clicked his tongue. "Like last time, lovely Imani, you're under my spell." Glamour magic layered his voice. "Down on your knees, elf witch."

Her legs bowed as her mind shouted, *Wrong, wrong, wrong.*

His eyes glazed over. She wished more than anything that she had either used her soul draw or hidden it with an illusion, because her elf magic surged, pulling him under its spell. Soon, the soul draw would drive him to madness, wanting her to feed from him.

Female elves without magic at their fingertips were diminutive and easily overpowered, violence forcing them to feed from their attackers. She had been reckless in letting it roam free tonight.

Fear speared her chest. She panted, imagining herself in the shop with him again as her repulsion and urge to fight back had spiked. He had forced her to look at him the entire time. Over and over and over, he had slammed into her until she had turned herself into nothing but a shell. Other breeds might use physical force, but he had used his compulsion to force her to feed, and she had even less choice in the matter.

Mercifully, her mind had shut down, consciousness somewhere else until Aralana had hexed him with something dark, breaking the compulsion magic. Now, Imani spiraled into a pit of helplessness again. *Like last time, like—*

No, not like last time. Imani lived in a new world now. Her grandmother was dead, and magic rippled through her veins. It permeated her muscles and, unlike her soul draw, he didn't control her thoughts, only her body.

She threw all her mental awareness into survival.

Malis's hand snaked down her neck and caressed her breast. Imani's stomach clenched, and she tried to gag. She wanted to slip into the unknown, the void of nothing, leaving her with nothing, but tonight, she was stuck in brutal awareness.

Stifling a cry from deep within her chest, she continued screaming inside her head, begging her magic for help, although she didn't know what to command it to do.

Soft murmuring voices swirled around her awareness, but nothing happened. Still, she screamed.

Grinning maniacally over her, Malis looked like a terrifying conqueror surveying his spoils. "Look up at me," he said.

Her head snapped up as he ordered. He took her chin with his rough hand.

Imani screamed louder in her head. The whispers were now a dull roar in the recesses of her mind, something still untouched by Malis's spell. A thin tendril of darkness spread from the tip of her wand on its own, crawling and spreading from her arm and across the floor like inky fog.

"Years ago, Aralana asked for my help with flesh magic for two powerful spells." He leaned closer. "Do you know who she wanted it for?"

Imani tried to glare but still couldn't.

Malis smiled. "She wanted it for her high-bred granddaughter. Even as a child, people had considered the girl particularly striking for a Norn. Rich with the magic of your kind and outside the Draswood, she would be in terrible danger without a heartmate, or the impenetrable spell flesh magic glamour could give her when she came of age."

He stroked Imani's hair softly. Her chest constricted as she struggled to breathe. At least he was letting her breathe.

"While rare outside of the Draswood, thousands of high-bred female Norn are in Vathis. I never believed one was important enough to cast such powerful flesh magic spells, but she didn't exaggerate. Even with half your face ruined, you're such a remarkable representation of your breed. Perfect, really. And I must agree with her now. It was worth killing the hob to cast the magic."

Every person—except the hobgoblins—came into the Mesial Realm with a sigil already branded on them and a mark around it denoting the child a high-bred, common-bred, or low-bred version of their breed. High-breds were superior to others in their looks, magic, or natural talents. The closest a person could get to the definitive version of the breed was to have all three.

She almost threw up hearing the truth about Riona, their previous collector. Despite being a hobgoblin, Riona had been Imani's best friend, outside Meira. Imani had always suspected flesh magic was involved in her death, but it was still unfathomable Riona had sacrificed her whole body for a spell to hide Imani's magic.

She would never forgive Ara. Not that the old nymph even wanted forgiveness.

"Your grandmother kept your glamour locked up tight yet, for one day, you went without it around your face and soul draw—the only pieces she left untouched by the flesh magic spell—and I wonder why." Malis traced his finger down her arm. "Although, I suppose it doesn't matter. I know you provide services to several others in town."

It was true. She did. Calling it prostitution would have been accurate, but Imani never considered it that way. It didn't start as a conscious decision to service people, but rather, on a whim one night when she had stayed to catch up with a customer after delivering several spells.

"There's nothing quite like sex while a female elf feeds on you. The bliss is unexplainable. Especially a High-Norn elf like you. I will have you feed from me again before I kill you, Imani … The last time in the shop was such ecstasy."

Out of the corner of her vision, a menacing darkness curled around the room's edges. The air thickened with the smell of smoke as her magic built in the background. Imani had no idea what type of magic was brewing. The shadows appeared to be an enchantment of some kind, but enchantments required incantations and wands as a medium. Still, stronger spells overpowered weaker ones. Master witches could sense and strip away weaker illusion magic. The Norn elves' Draswood wands dominated any others.

"Stop this spell," Malis said, compulsion magic dripping from his voice. "I command you."

Imani couldn't stop. It was her fear, not words, chants, or the usual methods, which fueled the spell. His attack had no power over her emotions and thoughts.

Not even a second later, the dark swaths of shade dove at him like bats attacking prey. Massive black welts formed after slamming into his body, along with nasty purple and blue bruises. Internal bleeding, maybe?

Stumbling back, he swiped his wand overhead and growled, shouting in a language she didn't understand. His spell broke at the sound. Victory sparkled in her eyes, and a feline grin slowly spread across her face. The shadows retreated to encase her like a halo.

Imani tsked. "Those look painful, Malis."

"Nothing in this world can fight my magic."

"It seems something can," she said. "Such fascinating magic you have. I'd—"

"There is nothing!" he bellowed, arching his hand over his head. A whip of flames emerged from his wand.

Heat like her grandmother's pyre blasted her, slamming her back against the wall. She gasped as the skin on her arm seared from the burn.

A rare ability. Imani didn't think anyone in Essenheim practiced such atrophic magic, but she'd heard fire magic was common in Niflheim.

Screaming escaped her throat as she willed herself to be invisible and hit him back with more magic, flying around the room to avoid his flames. She didn't know what power poured out of her, but she acted instinctually and hit him with everything she could.

Papers on Malis's desk and the corner chair caught fire as they were swept up in the deadly dance Imani and Malis were locked in. Imani barely noticed as her body became shadows, moving and dodging fast. The adrenaline intoxicated her. Power rippled off her. The challenging magic he threw at her only fed her untamed fury.

A moment of weakness opened. Imani threw her weight into a wide hook and punched Malis hard in the jaw.

Fuck, his face hurt her fist. She fought through the pain as she pulled out the knife she kept strapped to her thigh.

The punch merely stunned him. He wasn't the biggest she'd subdued, not even close, but the man was still massive compared to her. The jarring contact caught him off guard enough to give Imani the upper hand. She ducked behind him, jumped on his back, and choked him. The move cut his airflow, strangling him.

She clamped her body around Malis, struggling for control as they wrestled. They pushed each to the limit, but Imani was desperate and knew more tricks. She growled, slid the knife across his neck, and then let go.

Blood spurted out. She missed the artery, but the cut was a good one. He would die slowly over the next few minutes.

A strange sensation took root low in her stomach. Heavy and coiled like a barbed knot of thorns, it bloomed through Imani's body until it reached her lips. The corner of her mouth twitched into a smile—into a cruel thrill, knowing the man responsible for her tears was paying his dues.

Circling him, she let his blood drip onto the floor and pointed the wand at his neck. "How perfect you look down there," she said with a maniacal grin. "Now tell me: what breed are you?"

CHAPTER 5

Flames crawled up the wall behind her, and the curtains caught fire, crackling and blazing in the background. Imani waited even as the heat roared behind her.

Malis didn't respond.

"What are you? Tell me!" she snarled.

"A better question." Blood hit the floor as he spat. "What are *you*?"

"You know I'm a High-Norn elf," she lied, her voice wavering with a mix of trepidation and confusion. "You saw my sigil when we …"

The answer to his identity hit with the force of a stoning. She *had* touched someone of another breed besides her siblings and the naiads she'd slept with for money. She'd touched Malis when he had attacked her in the shop last month.

Malis was her heartmate.

She leaned against his desk to catch her breath and steady her shaky balance. It couldn't be. *No, no, no.*

Meira would beg her to have mercy on her heartmate. Imani wished he was someone else, anyone else. In another life, she might have wanted him as a friend, if not a lover.

Imani shoved those thoughts away. Contrary to what Meira believed, Imani agreed with her grandmother regarding heartmates. Finding them could be a blessing or a nightmare. While there were rewards, including increased power and acquiring new magic to share, the risks were as significant and permanent. It was repulsive to think about tethering herself to Malis in that way.

"Don't you dare tie yourself to such a beast," Ara had warned.

Indeed, if she pulled this off tonight and followed through with the plan she had been scheming for weeks now, Imani would cherish the memory of murdering him until her dying breath.

Malis continued, undeterred by her gaping face. "You put far too much stock in the physical. You may come to find your skin has no bearing on who or what you truly are," he rasped, shutting his eyes from the pain. "Ara understood exactly what that was."

Fury overtaking her muscles, Imani shook him by the neck. "Why would she keep such a thing from me? Why did she keep *you* a secret from me?"

"Because she was a secretive, spiteful bitch." He bared his blood-stained teeth at her. "But she knew what she was doing, hiding you. The Fabric is unraveling. Magic like yours rips holes bigger than anyone in this kingdom has seen."

A pit formed in her stomach. Was her magic really so dangerous?

Her voice was softer than she had intended it to be. "Why wouldn't you mention we are heartmates? What breed are we?"

He narrowed his eyes. "*We* are nothing of the sort and never will be," he spat again, curling his lips in disgust. "But you aren't the only thing Ara kept hidden in this shithole." Malis's wild eyes glanced around the room as her shadows moved. He gave her another sinister grin. "Tell me what Ara knows about fixing the Fabric. An answer for an answer."

"Shut up," she ordered, not understanding his question. "I'm issuing the demands and questions now."

Darkness gathered around her. The shadows pulsed with each one of her breaths. It encased the room, blanketing every surface, except Imani and her prey, until the flames barely penetrated her black cloud.

Malis coughed and laughed at the same time, more blood spraying. Imani felt him slipping away; she was losing her chance to learn anything helpful.

Hitting him in his bleeding nose, she held his face and stared into his wide brown eyes. "With Ara dead, you thought to take advantage of me, didn't you? All you did was irritate me." She grabbed him by the throat with her bare hands, letting more blood gush from the wound. "If you don't give me the answers I want, I won't be merciful. I won't kill you quickly and let you drift peacefully into the Under.

"Instead, I'll seal up the slit in your throat, and you'll be locked in our shop, alive and well. Each day, I will personally rip out a patch of your flesh until you're nothing but torn skin and bones. Then, right before your body dies, you'll remember—and regret—every second you tried to take advantage of me."

He sputtered out a wet laugh. "Come find me in the Under when you're dead, and I'll answer your questions. Ara and I will wait in the deepest realm with the darkest monsters. A place where you truly belong."

"What the fuck are you? What are *we*?" she hissed into his ear.

Malis's nostrils flared, and when he tried to smile, she knew he wouldn't respond. She'd interrogated enough people to understand he was ready to die.

Insane with rage, she screamed from the depths of her chest, *"Tell me! I need to know the truth!"*

"Then it is"—he coughed blood—"my--my ... my dying wish for you not to know, pretty little Imani—"

"Don't ever call me that again!" She stood abruptly, letting him tumble roughly onto the floor, and stalked to his desk. Snatching the maps, Imani scanned each in haste. All of them were of Niflheim.

She still didn't understand what Ara had wanted with these scraps. Some were damaged and nothing but crude drawings with scribbles. A parchment practically falling apart caught her eye. It was a map of Kehomel, Niflheim's capital city. A note written in tight script at the bottom stood out. Ara's handwriting. The rest had faded too much, but her grandmother had circled a structure in Kehomel, and several words stood out—*Royal Library. Manuscript 1148. Wand Efficacy of the Second Age.* The Second Age was a millennium ago.

Under the scrap of paper lay another—a list.

Test IV. Goldwood.
Test V. Bone.
Test VI. Draswood.
Test VII. Drasil.

Draswoods were the dominant wand of the modern age, but Imani had also read about people using the first two types of wands. The fourth wand truly piqued her interest—she'd never heard of it. The Aowyns were one of the foremost wandmakers in the Draswood Forest and the Essenheim kingdom, so she considered herself well-read on the subject. It was strange she had never seen it mentioned before this crumpled document.

Stories of different wands used ten thousand years ago circulated. Some could even travel between the realm doorways. But those ancient wands had all disappeared, if they had even existed.

A final map caught her eye as she was about to toss them aside. Rolled and tied with a distinct red leather string and in far better condition than the others, it stood out. Inside, she found the most detailed map of the Niflheim kingdom she'd ever seen and dozens of other mysterious pieces of information about the magic and people immediately south of the Riverlands.

She found it strangely beautiful. What would she encounter if she crossed the river outside the manor into Niflheim? A mountain range dominated part of Niflheim's southern border, so large she wasn't sure if anything was beyond it. Handwritten notes scrawled at the bottom of the map pointed to various areas. Imani squinted, trying to make out the words.

One jumped out at her repeatedly—Drasil.

Her mouth went dry as her eyes flicked back and forth between the notes. If her reading was correct, this wand could open doorways, like the ancient wands from the stories. Not even the strongest Draswood wand wielded by the strongest monarch could do such a thing.

Turning on her heel, she waved the maps in Malis's face. "What did Ara want with these?"

His shoulders shook as blood coated and dripped down his mouth. His eyes fluttered. It wouldn't be long now.

Her vision darkened with rage. She shoved the maps into her dress pocket and, with a swift kick, slammed her foot into his gut.

He tried to laugh again, but it sounded like he was choking on his blood. Imani had never heard a sound she liked more.

It was time to finish this; Malis was already dead, and she was fresh out of sympathy for this piece of shit.

"You stole something precious from me, something I protect more than anything. Without it, I have nothing; I am nothing." She pointed her wand at him. "No one steals my freedom and my dignity like you did and gets away with it. So now, I'm going to take everything from you. Everything. Including your soul."

Imani didn't have to kill him with such ferocity, but she wanted to obliterate him for what he'd done. She needed it.

When she imagined killing him, Imani didn't hesitate, as planned. But with the whispers urging her on, she called her magic forth, wanting to be powerful.

Now.

The barriers holding back her magic fell as her control disappeared. An impenetrable, thick night exploded around them.

Magic surged through the room as a massive vacuum filled every crevice, sucking the life away and creating a void of nothing where there used to be everything. It took only a second for it to destroy his whole body.

Warm liquid sprayed her face. Blood and guts saturated the air she breathed, soaking into her lungs. She tasted him on her lips and smelled charred flesh with each breath.

Imani's magic didn't simply explode. It destroyed.

The gore didn't bother her. It meant he was gone.

A snap of cold air hit her, mixing with the heat from the flames. Imani asked the magic to return with her trembling, outstretched wand. The darkness receded, barely. A thick, peppered smell filled the air, remnants of harsh magic.

Imani's mind raced. She hadn't meant to cause such agony and destruction. What had she unleashed?

With such destruction, it had to be the red brand. She might have accidentally drawn too much power from the Fabric, using it to kill Malis.

Her panting increased, frantic at her violence. With her wand still pointed at the pile of flesh, ash, and bones, she stood over what remained of her bastard heartmate. Numb, she hardly noticed a wall from the manor had collapsed and small fires raged behind her.

Clouds gathered and swirled swiftly across the dark sky as she wandered around the desolated grounds, distress mounting at the amount of magic she'd unleashed. Atrophic magic was simply too destructive compared to the nascent magic of Essenheim. It was why everything about it was illegal here.

Swirling snow had blown in and wafted around her, making her ill. Something was wrong. She was wrong.

Malis's soul signature lingered in the air, hovering near its recently dead body. Unlike ghosts—lost beings separated from their souls and unable to make it to the Under—this spirit was still attached to its life essence, mingling with it in the first few moments after death.

A noise made her jump.

Panicking, Imani whipped her gaze around, terrified she'd find someone striding out of the nearby brush. But no one was there to see her scrape her hands down her face and silently scream.

Stumbling forward, Imani tilted back her chin. She reached out, swirling her fingers through the ethereal spirit form and letting the entire signature surround her. Bending her will and giving in, she breathed deep, taking all the air, smoke, and essence into her chest.

The entire glorious signature filled her, and Imani trembled as the bliss spread. The panic receded momentarily as she clutched her head and groaned. An invigorated feeling like she'd never felt made her shudder and collapse to her knees.

Imani wouldn't need to eat for weeks. Feeding on two entire signatures in one day was unforgivable, but at least they were already dead when she had started consuming them.

She didn't know where their souls went, but Imani was sure it wasn't to the Under. It was quite possible they still lived inside her, but she'd never found any answers because no elves ever fed on an entire signature—or at least any scholarly elves who wrote about its effects.

Twelve years ago, Imani had taken her grandfather's soul while he still lived, killing him, much to her family's horror. Such a menacing and unpredictable soul draw was the reason they had sent her to live with her grandmother, who eventually beat the urge away and taught her restraint. But it didn't mean she'd stopped wanting to do it again.

All elves received nourishment from siphoning a part of someone's essence. It was a blissful experience, but taking an entire soul was forbidden. Not every elf could even do it. Some could only take a sliver. Indeed, it was rare for a Norn to be able to take more. If they did, the consequences were dire, as Imani had learned as a twelve-year-old.

Her soul draw was deadly, and yet there was no better feeling she'd ever known.

Her trance broke as the ground shook. Loud, deafening cracks boomed one after another in the distance. Like stones skipping across a pond, the Fabric itself moved and churned above her in a sinister, foreboding swirl of black, all its normal, colorful splendor disturbed.

Imani ducked when a nasty spider web of lightning cracked across the entire sky. A reverberation, maybe even a Fabric event, rumbled above as if the whole world wanted to splinter itself into pieces from the magic taken from it. Then, in quick succession, dozens of lightning bolts hit the town's surrounding area.

A strangled cry escaped Imani's throat, watching in helpless awe as a massive one lit up the space then dropped to the ground in the nearby orchard, setting the land ablaze. The ground surrounding rumbled like it wanted to rip in half.

Unable to move for several seconds, Imani covered her mouth with a shaking hand. The house burned, flames popping and bursting with heat and noise. Chaos momentarily mesmerized her and rooted her in place.

This amount of magic would draw everyone's eyes for miles, maybe even the Crown itself.

Imani imagined the Royal Order and the queen coming for her. Her mind snapped into survival mode.

Move.

CHAPTER 6

Imani didn't have time to waste. She shivered, realizing she'd lost her cloak at Malis's house, in the fire. With the maps in one pocket and spells in the other, she hurried to the industrial lot by the river, rubbing her arms to stay warm.

Malis might have been insane, but he had been correct about Asim moving in on her family's position. She had several orders she'd planned to collect that night and needed everything to go perfectly.

After Riona had died—*was murdered*—Imani had become their collector and managed all the transactions for their business for years, taking orders for the spells then delivering the magic to the buyer while obtaining payment.

Imani needed to stay vigilant and focused on this one in particular to set the tone for her leadership moving forward.

Her magic skills were so unpracticed that she could easily see Asim taking advantage of her weakness. While the unbranded grew ignorant of her kind, other witches didn't forget, and it had only been a century ago when people killed female Norn in droves, or enslaved them. Vulnerable Norn witches were either killed or prostituted, forced to feed from customers or use their soul draw for their owners' gains.

The lot sat next to an old but well-maintained tavern managed by a common-bred naiad nymph. Common- and low-bred naiads were usually unpleasant when purchasing magic, but she preferred dealing with them over breedless hobs who were always nasty and tricky. Riona was the exception to the rule.

Imani wove between the massive barges, feeling exposed despite having cleaned off the ash as best she could and changing clothes in their tailor and seamstress shop. Her whole body trembled, but she kept moving.

A flash of light purple caught her eye. A rare fall flower peeked out of a bit of snow. It would be perfect for her sister's favorite perfume. Imani paused and pocketed the flower, putting it with Aralana's wand and the maps.

The darker it got without the familiar lights of the Fabric dancing overhead, the more fear gripped her heart. Magic was disappearing, and while they didn't have many in Essenheim, every Fabric event worsened the situation. In fact, the witches' ability to channel and cast magic could soon be gone forever. Murdering Malis was one thing, but causing a Fabric event had not been in her plans. With magic already so unstable, the consequences terrified her. She prayed it was a reverberation—a rapid slinging of violent magic back at the caster—but the signs showed it probably hadn't been.

After such an event, she was utterly unprepared to take on her new role as owner and matriarch, but now that magic and their family's business were in her grasp—the power and independence she craved—how could she let it go? She had Dak and Meira to care for, too.

Massaging her temples, she thought about how disgusted Ara and Riona would be at her failure and wished her friend were here again.

The dark, wooden tavern door groaned as Imani pushed it open. People were drunk and boisterous, enjoying the pub's warm fires and meals, despite the raging storm outside. Her ears flicked back and forth at the loud volume as she made her way toward the back.

Meira exited the kitchen, wand in hand. Worry radiated from Imani's sister, paling her perfect skin into a dull gray. Her gaze landed on Imani, and Meira rushed to her side.

"Imani? Where have you been? Why is there soot and blood on you?" Meira's eyes were alarmingly blue tonight, wide and unsettling.

Another clap of thunder boomed, and they both gasped at the sound.

Meira lifted her apron to Imani's neck, mouth thinning into a disapproving line. "This is from the burning, isn't it? I wish you hadn't gone," she muttered, dabbing the remnants of Malis's body off Imani's skin.

"Someone had to go."

"We should've spent the day together, just the three of us. Why don't we close the shop tomorrow? Let's take Dak and spend some time together by the river." She grasped Imani's hand in hers. "Dak and I might need another day," she whispered.

A day? A day of sitting around with the shop closed again? Another day so a new witch or coven could move in on their area?

The offer was tempting, especially with how tense things had been recently. Imani was exhausted and wanted to spend time with her siblings, and they deserved some kindness and reprieve after all these weeks.

But people expected products—magic and clothes—from the Aowyns, and they had money to exchange—money their family desperately needed. So, no, they would do no such thing.

Imani pointedly ignored her sister. Instead, she handed Meira one of the plants she'd found earlier. Meira picked up the stem and twirled it.

Her sister wanted to say something. "Spit it out. What's bothering you?"

"I've been thinking it's time for you to stop making these cosmetics. They don't earn us any money. It's a hobby. You must start splitting your time between the sewing shop and magic collections."

Imani wished it weren't true, but her sister was probably right. They needed to focus their efforts with three elves to feed, their modest flat to pay for, and Dak's schooling. The problem with the shop was that, even before Ara's arrest, people preferred to go to nymphs instead of the strange elves. It didn't make much income and served mainly to launder the money from their illicit magic dealings.

But Imani had plans to change their situation now.

Meira continued babbling. "Besides, I'm taking on more magic now, and I have my job here, so I won't be able to work in the shop at all."

Despite Meira's lovely, soft tone, Imani couldn't believe what she was hearing.

Even with her erratic behavior in recent months, Ara had at least done some of her own collections, and she frequently accompanied Imani on more significant, riskier transactions. Imani didn't expect Meira to go on collections at all, but she thought her sister would still put in her fair share at the shop until Imani could hire help.

"You can't leave me to run the shop without—"

"You wouldn't understand what it's like," her sister cut her off, her voice like the crack of a whip. "You've never understood. But trust me; what I do is far more tiring than making rudimentary potions."

Imani wanted to respond calmly but couldn't find the words. Meira had never spoken so harshly. After the day Imani had, the brusque tone felt like a slap to the face.

She never considered gathering herbs, weeds, and plants for cosmetics to be a substitute for magic—she would never be that insulting. All it did was offer a bit of quiet, order, and refuge from Imani's otherwise chaotic existence, and she enjoyed creating things, even if it wasn't with magic.

Meira motioned around the room, her voice a low whisper among the raucous noise of the tavern. "How can you be so uncaring? The one person who understood the burden of magic is gone," she choked out, and a quiet sob escaped her throat. "I will never find my heart-mate because we don't belong here. Now Ara is dead, so I'm performing all the magic alone, and I can't do it—I *can't*."

Her sister had always been the sweeter one, and Imani loved that about her, but this past month had taken a toll on Meira, giving her an air of bitterness.

A heavy silence fell. The sisters stared at each other as if a great chasm had opened up between them.

With a sigh, Imani broke the tension by wrapping her arms around her sister in a hug. "I'm sorry I've been so hard on you these past few weeks. When we get home, I have something important to show you, and it will improve everything."

Exactly the same height as Imani, Meira gave her a trusting look and nodded. "I'll finish up here soon, and we can leave." She framed Imani's face with her hands. "Your illusion is slipping, *ahavah*. Let me help."

Hearing the endearment elves used with loved ones made Imani's stomach knot. She hated lying to her sister.

Before Meira could cast the spell, Imani grabbed her wrist and shook her head. She was done relying on her family for her protection, not when she finally had her own magic to protect herself.

"It's fine. We'll go home after I talk to Elyon. Where's Dak? What are you doing here working, by the way?"

Meira motioned to the dining room. "He's here. Lira stopped by earlier and said they needed help. We waited for you at home, but you never came by supper."

"Saints, Meira, I didn't think you'd rush off to work a shift in the kitchens. They can live without magic for one night."

Meira crossed her arms. "We need the money, and you know it."

Unable to wait longer, Imani glanced around to confirm their privacy then rolled up her sleeve to remove the illusion over her brands. "You won't have to work here anymore, *ahavah*. Things are different now. Here, let me explain—"

Thunder rumbled closer, and the building shook again. Every boom made Imani's fists tighten, and she paused her attempt to show Meira the brands to glance around the room.

"Everyone is talking about the Fabric event. It was terrifying ..." Meira trailed off, tears filling her eyes. Imani knew all too well how terrified Meira probably felt. The Aowyn sisters witnessed one other Fabric event this close before, and it had been devastating.

Meira pointed at Imani's chest. "If you'd been home on time, I wouldn't have brought him tonight. But I couldn't sit and worry, and I was too scared to leave him home alone."

"There were so many fires. I stayed to help." The lie slipped out as Imani reached for her sister's hand. "Do they know who cast the magic?"

Meira shook her head, eyes still brimming with tears. "Fen came by to talk to me. Although the Order has yet to confirm where their master witches worked earlier, they believe our family is the only one wielding magic for miles," she said, clearing her throat.

"As far as we know."

"They can't blame this on us. He knows I was working here when it happened, and we'll admit to Fen you don't have any magic, if needed."

"They won't blame us," Imani said, not entirely believing herself.

"Could it be another fugitive, like the one who came into the shop that day? Or a visitor?"

"I'm not sure," Imani lied again.

A raucous, drunken song got louder by the bar. Stumbling footsteps followed the singing.

"Oi, Imani! Come have a drink with us," Ren, her brother's best friend, shouted.

"You know you want to," Dak sang.

Despite the heaviness weighing on her shoulders, Imani fought a smile. Dak was a terrible singer.

"You boys are sixteen years old and should be home," Imani hollered as she folded her arms.

Ren's brown eyes drank her in as he leaned his forearm against the creaky bar, more to help himself remain upright than to appear handsome.

"We won't accept no for an answer," Dak said, spreading his arms wide. His silver-blond hair was curly and messy.

Although Dak was growing from her goofy younger brother into a strapping young man, he still always made her laugh.

Ren motioned her over with a crooked grin.

Imani waved them away. "I have a collection," she explained.

Ren shrugged and walked back into the crowd, but Meira sniffled, and Dak's eyes narrowed.

He pushed between the sisters in a blur and shoved Imani's shoulders. "Are you upsetting her again? All she does is cry now because of you," he shouted, voice still slurring.

Imani gaped at her brother. He was drunk, and Dak always

protected Meira, but he would not have tried anything like this with Ara—in public. Their grandmother would have beaten him bloody for this behavior.

Pointing to the door, Imani's voice was quiet when she spoke. "Go home, Dak."

"I don't have to listen to any more orders, rules, or bullshit, especially from you." He plowed on, "Meira's right; without magic, you're nothing. *Absolutely nothing*. We are on our own."

Imani braced a hand on the wall as Dak's insults and Meira's soft crying continued.

Her siblings—her best friends—were turning against her, and she had no idea what to do. Her family was falling apart bit by bit. She had been too wrapped up in her other problems these past few weeks to do anything about it.

Grasping Aralana's wand inside her pocket, she made her choice. She pulled it out, pointing it at her brother.

"You can't even use her wand," he sneered, wrapping his arms around Meira.

Imani murmured the enchantment she knew by heart. As soon as the words escaped her mouth, Dak's voice disappeared, and Meira gasped.

A heavy silence settled around them, the only noise coming from the crackling fire and the bar. It was so crowded no one noticed them, but they were still exposed.

She flipped the wand across her fingers then slipped it back into her dress. "If you cannot respect me, you will be quiet until you do," Imani said with a pointed look at Dak. "Aralana left everything to me. I am in charge of this family and our businesses. I will run both as I see fit." Her chest heaved as she pointed between the two of them. "It simply won't do for us to always be quarreling. So, decide now." Imani paused. "Either we're together or not—there's no in-between."

Tears streamed down both Dak's and Meira's stunned faces. They both nodded.

Imani wanted to be remorseful about her harsh response, but she merely gave them a curt nod. "Dak, go home and go to bed. We'll be there soon."

He couldn't speak or even meet her eyes as he stomped away, outside the pub.

She should've remembered how the hate burned when Ara had exerted such cruelty over her, but Imani didn't have the luxury of kindness or mercy, even for her family. They were vulnerable, and avoiding hard decisions would only worsen things. Not only were they elves, but they were the grandchildren of an executed witch whose bones lay in the middle of town like a dead stray dog.

Imani turned back to Meira.

The color of her sister's blonde hair shone bright in the firelight. Pleated perfectly, her subtly pointed ears were only slightly visible. Similar to Imani, silver freckles dotted her cheeks like diamonds, as well. With her naiad blood from Ara, she was never as ideal of a High-Norn as Imani, but even crying, Meira was the prettiest Aowyn sister.

Appearing as a dramatic example of the quintessential Norn, the classic features of a high-bred elf dominated Imani's looks. Which, according to her grandmother, was "too much"—too intense, too bright, too glowing, too ethereal, too pointy, too noticeable. Some found High-Norn elves beautiful, but others considered them unsettling. Disconcerting.

Before the scarring had appeared on her cheek, and before Ara had mutilated her body parts for various punishments and flesh magic spells, Imani had imagined she might have been more beautiful than her sister in her true form. She could admit it made her jealous for years, despite loving her sister completely.

Imani didn't care much about that these days. After working for Ara for this long, she aspired to more than using looks to her advantage—she wanted *real* power, which had nothing to do with beauty and everything to do with magic.

Imani almost smiled, despite Meira's crying.

Meira's red-rimmed eyes widened to the size of saucers as she tentatively reached for Imani's wrist. "Show me," she whispered.

On a whim, Imani cast a hasty illusion over her own red sigil with Ara's wand and left Malis's. She would be honest about the other two red brands—her magic and her heartmate—but she wasn't ready to share or even accept the truth about her mysterious breed.

It wasn't a secret that Imani's mother had a chosen mate years ago, and he was Imani's real father. But her mother had found her fated mate shortly after Imani had been born, and once a person met their heartmate, there was no separating them. Imani's father had disappeared shortly after.

Everyone assumed her birth father was a Norn elf. Her mother and siblings were all Norn, and Imani appeared and acted precisely like them. Most considered her a well-bred Norn elf the moment they laid eyes on her, and she wanted to keep up the ruse, even in front of her sister.

She shoved her bare forearms toward Meira, admiring how each brand sparkled in the dim light. Meira was a powerful witch with five brands—a potential master witch—but Imani couldn't deny she enjoyed having two more magics than her sister, even if one was a terrifying red one.

"You have seven, and three are different from mine! I have divination, but you have alteration and alchemy … and this one." Meira pointed to the red brand and bit her lip. "You'll need a wand to properly channel the raw magic for any of these marks. I can teach you to use fire and water as channels for certain spells, but as you know, the wand will be the most versatile. I wish we had money to make a new one for you, but Ara's will work fine after I alter it."

Imani nodded. She didn't want a new wand—her mother had made Ara's.

"And these appeared today?" Meira's voice was filled with pure amazement.

"Yes, after Ara died." Imani's shoulders slumped. "But I suspect they've been on my arm for a long time now."

Tracing the lines of each one repeatedly, Imani tried to remember when these markings could have appeared. Nothing came to mind.

The Fabric could bestow more power to worthy witches later in life—after adversities and tests of magic and strength—but such events were rare. More commonly, the Fabric enhanced the already gifted abilities, making people master or archmage witches—far more powerful witches than normal.

"It was to protect you," Meira stated. "Ara must have decided it was too risky to have you using any magic with an illegal marking. I know you and her never got on, but she cared in her own way."

Protection was the most logical reason because they'd kill a young elf who couldn't control her magic, especially if anyone caught even a hint of the red brands. Guilt for being so angry with her grandmother swirled inside her gut. All she could do was swallow and nod.

It still didn't excuse the rest of Ara's treatment of Imani, but it explained some.

"You have more than five brands. So, you'll have to register as a potential master, like me, right?"

"Yes, I suppose," Imani muttered, hoping Meira would drop the line of questioning. Unless the urge to commit suicide hit her, Imani had no intention of registering with the Royal Order of Magic or becoming a master witch, especially with the red marks marring her skin.

She'd get a license, as all witches had to have one to perform magic, but it would be easy. Official master witches, on the other hand, were so powerful it was required the Order employ them after taking the ascension assessments if they wanted to use their magic. Imani had no desire to become one of the Order's minions, so she'd never opt to take the tests. Being a *potential* master was perfectly fine with her.

As part of the ordinances—a series of laws meant to help people safely use magic without further destabilizing the Fabric—only the Order could facilitate a witch earning a master brand. Such an accomplishment took more than practice and hard work; it took sacrifice. A board of master and archmage witches at the Order, plus the First Witch, created and administered three demanding assessments once a year, all intense enough to trigger the Fabric master brand. Intense enough people could—and did—die taking them.

Outside of accidental ascension, any witch caught wielding an unsanctioned master brand and not working for the Order would have their license to practice magic revoked. They would probably end up in jail—or, these days, worse. They'd never believe she remained ignorant of her brands with a family member found guilty of illegal magic.

"Ara would want us to continue like nothing happened. I need to go on a collection now. I'll be home shortly." With that, Imani rolled down her sleeves and shut down any more conversation. She strode into the main room of the pub, intent on her task, but a male nymph made Imani pause.

The constable was here.

CHAPTER 7

Despite Fen's incompetence, seeing the constable the night she murdered a man put her on edge. Imani swallowed hard at the sight of him. It would be stupid not to be worried.

As soon as he spotted Imani, he waved her over. She tried to ignore him, pretending she hadn't seen, but Meira wasted no time moving to greet him. Imani gritted her teeth and steeled herself for an interrogation.

Young and attractive, Fen had only been in his position for a few years. But, while Imani liked Fen, she frankly questioned how much law and order he provided their town. Living close to the border of Niflheim, fugitives frequently used their small shipping port to try to escape south. As a common-bred naiad with no magic, Fen was useless against said fugitives.

"Something we can help you with, Fen?" Meira put her hand on his arm.

He smiled at her.

Imani recognized the look in her sister's eyes.

Desire.

Blackness dotted Imani's vision as the sudden urge to feed almost overtook her body. Shocking in intensity, especially after she'd fed so much already, the force took her by surprise. She steadied herself against a chair and blinked a few times.

The constable had recently become one of her best customers, which made her want to keep Meira far away from him. Indeed, Imani hated seeing Meira acting flirtatious with Fen, but it hadn't been since her grandfather that she'd really lost control, and today wouldn't be the day she broke the streak.

She took several deep breaths, reminding herself that she did not want to kill Fen—not truly—especially for this transgression.

Growing up in a small village of nymphs meant there wasn't a large selection of friends or men to choose from, especially for elf witches. While Norn kept to themselves these days in the Draswood Forest, they still craved companionship and were naturally friendly creatures. It was why they fed the way they did—to be close to others and share intimacy. If her siblings had grown up near more people, the two would likely have many relationships beyond their immediate family.

Despite what Ara claimed, *she* might have had more friends, too—real ones, like Riona.

But now, in the Riverlands, Dak had Ren, and the girls only had each other, a few acquaintances, and casual friendships. So, Imani could hardly fault her sister for desiring Fen.

Neither of them noticed Imani's brief bout of distress, and she was able to compose herself as Fen continued talking to them.

"I'm here on constable business. We have a potential master level witch who wielded flesh magic in the area with this Fabric event. A Niflheim merchant who lived in a manor near the epicenter might be the culprit, but all we know for now is he's missing," he explained, his face drawn in a somber expression.

"So, you don't know who the witch was who cast the magic?" Meira asked.

"Do you need anything from us?" Imani asked simultaneously, her voice sounding loud and flat compared to Meira's.

"No, we don't know who cast the magic." He nervously snapped his eyes to the door then back as he leaned lower. "The event was so large, and through the network of master witches the Order employs, word has already reached the Crown." He shifted his feet, giving them a small smile.

Imani frowned. He smiled far too much, in her opinion.

"I received a raven from the Order that we're to question all witches in our territories about their activities. I'll need to talk to you again about the master witch from that day in the shop." He stepped closer to Imani. "And I'm required to do a quick search around your flat, too—"

"You can't be serious?" Imani stiffened, schooling her features into a stern expression she hoped hid her trepidation. She did not want him anywhere near their home. "We've been more than cooperative. I've already told you everything I know, and you've searched the flat multiple times this past month. Plus, you know our grandmother was executed today—it's where I was returning from when the Fabric event struck."

His face softened in sympathy. "I have no choice, Imani. Your grandmother and this potential master witch who came into your shop might have some connection to each other. She had ties to Niflheim and practiced flesh magic. We can't wait if it was related to Zolyn."

She was relieved they were looking elsewhere for the culprit, but it grated Imani to be harassed about the infuriating master witch again when that humiliating day was the last thing she wanted on her mind. In fact, Imani entirely avoided thinking about the day she had met the unregistered master nymph witch who had harassed her in the shop and had removed the glamour from her face and soul draw. In fact, *he* was the reason Malis had attacked Imani.

When Malis had entered the shop, she had no time to find her grandmother or Meira to cast another illusion, and her soul draw had taken hold of him. He'd held her down, ripped her dress, and shoved himself inside her. He had been in the midst of forcing her to feed from him when Ara had arrived. Her grandmother had attacked Malis, leaving him bleeding out in the shop, and Imani had escaped upstairs to their flat.

Ara had been arrested later in the evening, thanks to Malis, and their family had been spiraling in the month since.

Imani understood why they would search for a potential master witch practicing flesh magic as the source of the event. Magic became unstable when Niflheim legalized such barbaric sacrificial magic, causing the first fissures in the Fabric.

Although they claimed otherwise, the oppressive shroud over Niflheim's lands meant they were likely still abusing it even today.

Some blamed all magic, but *people* were the problem—greedy, destructive Niflheim breeds who took too much and cared little for the damage it racked. So, not only did the Niflheim people cause the instability, the loss of magic, and the war, but they had also caused Imani's parents' deaths and the deaths of so many others for centuries.

While the place itself made her curious, Imani hated the throne of Niflheim for letting its people run wild—a genuine, unbridled hate. Thinking about the storm raging outside, she hated herself, too. She had been careless with a brand of magic she didn't understand.

Meira interjected, "If the magic bore any resemblance to flesh magic, Fen must report it to the Crown."

Imani gritted her teeth. "I already told you everything about the male witch; again, he looked like a nymph and appeared far too young to have trained with Zolyn."

"But you don't know for a fact he was a nymph, nor do you know his age." Meira frowned at Imani, silently telling her she was being obstinate.

Fen's voice dropped lower when he moved to stand over Imani. "Maybe we could go somewhere quieter and more private? These questions might be sensitive to your sweet sister here." Fen rubbed Imani's arm in a sad attempt to comfort her. His expression conveyed genuine concern, but the desire evident in his eyes, even on the day her grandmother had *died*, lingered within.

Disgusted, she summoned all her strength to maintain a measured response. "Thank you, Fen. I understand you're merely doing your job." She paused to hold his hand tighter. Desperate to buy some time, she added in a faint whisper, "Why don't we leave here, and you both can wait in the shop while I clean up? It's been a hard day." Her eyes sparkled in suggestion.

His eyebrows shot to his hairline as he caught Imani's meaning. "Take your time."

Spinning on her heel, she walked in calm steps to hide the tension growing taut inside her. A clawing desire to hide the maps in her pockets from Fen—and find the book Malis had mentioned—grew. Imani didn't understand why she wanted to protect the items, but she listened to her instincts.

After a brief walk, she entered their building and dashed into Ara's old room. Dak would be ignoring her all night after she'd taken his voice, so he didn't even bother coming out of his room. As she tore open the trunk, a pang of guilt hit her remembering his face, but she ignored it.

She'd read everything there a thousand times, even after Ara had demanded she stop. She'd learned quickly that her grandmother would become annoyed when she chose to spend hours researching various things instead of focusing on her "duties with the magic business."

Ever since the constable's men had searched it last week, the trunk was a mess of parchment, jars, and maps, all stuffed inside with no reasonable organization. They hadn't even thought of calling a master witch and using magic.

Idiots.

Flicking Ara's wand, she murmured a spell she made up on the spot to break the wards on the secret compartments. It worked. Being around magic for so long—and transfixed with it—made using it second nature.

The locks clicked open with a puff of dust, revealing deep, cavernous storage compartments, all spelled to hold ten times more than the trunk alone.

Grabbing a thick folder, she sat cross-legged on the floor. As she flipped the frayed, yellowed paper, she found they held nothing but scribbles of irrelevant business transactions and familiar notes for spells and other magics she'd seen before.

But she came across documents she'd never read in the middle of the stack.

It was filled with illicit drawings of mysterious breeds, including elves and shifters, descriptions of illegal atrophic spells, and more lists of wands. Combined with what she had stolen from Malis, this was the most information she'd ever seen on Niflheim.

Sorting through the rest of the items in the trunk, she found a mass of crinkled papers. The parchment was practically falling apart. Another more detailed map showed a maze with an arrow leading through it. The words *"Royal Vaults and South Chamber XII"* were smudged with a loopy red script.

Gods, Aralana had been *obsessed* with the southern kingdom.

Two books on wandlore were also well obscured in the back of the cubby hole. A wrinkle appeared between Imani's eyes as she flipped through the pages. Everything was about wands. All the texts should have mentioned Draswoods, but none did. Strange. It reminded her of the lists she had seen on the maps about the alternative wands. What *had* Aralana been doing?

Her scalp prickled.

A picture formed in her head.

Ara had come home muttering and smelling like intense magic these past months, and it appeared like her grandmother was going mad. But the more Imani turned the details over, the more likely Aralana hadn't been going crazy at all. Imani reluctantly admitted she might have been working on something dangerous but incredible.

For hundreds of years, the experts agreed all they could do was slow the Fabric's degradation by controlling magic. But what had once given magic life would eventually destroy itself. The Fabric would be no more, and neither would magic. Reversing it was impossible.

Except... Aralana might have been close to finding a way.

∽

MEIRA'S FLIRTING distraction worked well enough; except for checking the spelled trunk again and a few other books on the shelves, Fen barely searched their home.

The hour grew too late for him to stay longer, and Imani breathed a sigh of relief she wouldn't have to fulfill her earlier suggestion of sleeping with him.

He paused at the door, playing with his hat, and considered his next words. "There's something else you should know."

"Get to the point, Fen. It's been a trying day," Imani snapped, her patience gone.

"Larger towns at the edge of the Riverlands are reporting an increased presence of security forces already moving in after the Fabric event, and I feel compelled to warn you." A deepening grimness swept over his features.

"About what?" Imani asked through gritted teeth.

"Queen Dialora accused the Order, including the First Witch, of letting witches go unchecked for too long, which is likely true. However, the Order accounted for all its master witches yesterday, so we can't deny the event came from a *potential* master who doesn't answer to anyone."

"But it could be any witch with five markings," Imani said. "Thousands of witches with five markings haven't ascended to master witches. How can they expect to control all potential masters? They aren't required to work for the Order."

With magic dwindling and most witches only possessing a few brands, there weren't many potential masters remaining. Still, there were enough in a kingdom of millions that this would be a problem for the Crown—and with five brands registered with the Order, Meira was one of them.

"Well, there are rumors about a new law requiring anyone registered with at least five markings to take the assessments. Anyone who passes would work for the Order," Fen stated.

Hand to her throat, Meira was unable to speak.

Imani clutched the counter in their kitchen. "Assessments kill people. They can't force witches to go to our deaths."

"They can, and they will," Fen said as he moved to leave. "I wanted you to know because it's well known your family wields magic. Of course, whether either of you have five brands is not my business. But if you do ..." He paused, backing up to the door. Tension in the air thickened, and his eyes looked apologetic. "If you do, they are coming for you."

∼

WITH THE COLLECTION Imani was supposed to go on forgotten, both sisters stayed silent for a long time after Fen had left.

The selfish, opportunistic part of Imani desperately wanted to let Meira go. Imani wanted to be saved for once and let someone take away her role as the mediocre head of a family, barely holding it together. She wanted to stay and grow the magic business she had worked so hard for all these years. She wanted to eliminate this noose of responsibility around her neck and experience real freedom.

Her sister's sobs cut through the silence. "Imani, I can't go. I can't."

The fear in Meira's words broke her heart. By nature, only the strongest witches survived to become master witches. It was what set them apart. Although harsh, parts of the ascension assessments required more than magic skills. Skills Meira didn't possess. If her sister took the ascension assessments, she would die. Imani wouldn't let such a thing happen.

A semblance of a plan formed while her sister cried, one that would send Imani to Stralas, not Meira. It splintered her heart even further to think she'd be chained again, but they didn't have another way.

Even in her head, it sounded insane.

They didn't have much time to pull the plan off, either.

Wiping her eyes, Meira watched Imani pace. "You have an idea, sister."

"I might. No one here knows the exact details of our brands, only suspicion based on what we sell. I'm not registered, but no one knows for sure. So, the people here won't know they came for you specifically, only that they came for one of us," Imani rambled.

Meira's bottom lip continued to quiver. "I hate the idea of separating."

"The last thing I want to do is leave you both," Imani whispered.

"We can ask them to spare me when they come."

"They'll take you, anyway. The Order and the Crown are serious if Fen warned us." Imani stroked her sister's hair back from her face. "When I said separate, I meant I would go to the capital and take your assessments. We'd lose the magic business, though."

Sadness overtook Imani's chest. Their magic business would be over. Everything their family worked for would be gone. Any semblance of her independence would be lost. She would be a slave to the assessments, and then to the Order.

But, for the first time in years, Imani would get to leave their small territory and explore the capital city. She'd get to learn magic, get real training and education, something denied her whole life. Despite her despair at losing everything their family had worked for, the entire world might be at her fingertips if she could escape this suffocating town. Maybe she could even meet more Norn elves there.

While helping her sister was paramount, a selfish hunger to make this work burned inside Imani.

Meira worried her lip. "But, how will we make ends meet without it?"

"Witches preparing for their assessments are still technically members of the Order, and they're entitled to a stipend. I'll send it home, and you can still work at the tavern and keep the sewing shop. It should be enough to supplement the lost income from the magic."

With the magic business as leverage in the bargain with Asim, they could receive compensation, too, and had a real chance to pull this off.

Meira sniffed. "You have three different brands than me. And I have divination, and you don't. They have records of all five of my markings."

"We will transfer your divination magic to me and use powerful magic to glamour the brands I have that you don't. If it works, the master witches at the Order won't sense anything wrong with the divination. I'll be wearing a glamour, but all female Norns are entitled to do so to temper our soul draws."

More worry lined Meira's face. "Is it even possible?"

"It is. I read about it in a book years ago." Imani didn't say that sometimes the transfer didn't work if the breeds were too different, and Imani and Meira were more different than either of them had realized.

Her sister had the magic of a High-Norn and the blue leaf sigil with the triangle around it, but Meira's features were muted in many ways, unlike Imani. Since learning her dominant breed was something else, it was even more mysterious now why Imani had inherited all the High-Norn features she had—magic, looks, and natural talents, like her powerful soul draw.

No one knew why such things happened among siblings, but like all breeds, each elf was unique.

This made the spell all that more dangerous.

"We look so similar. With your exact magic, I could easily pretend I'm you in Stralas."

"What type of magic can do this?"

Technically, flesh magic didn't fall under any ability; it enhanced already existing spells. "It's alteration."

"I only remember a few things about brands I don't possess. What is it? Like an illusion?"

Indeed, Meira wouldn't survive two hours with the Order.

"No, illusion magic simply hides something. We will be permanently changing a physical part of the world—the magic in your body and mine. You'll be losing your magic entirely and transferring it to me." It was dark, atrophic magic, and the spell would get them burned at the stake, like Ara, if caught.

Her sister braced herself on the chair and stared into Imani's eyes. A deep fear shone back at her. "Let's do it," Meira whispered. "If anyone can survive the assessments, it's you, Imani. You've been going on dangerous collections for years and have read everything you can about magic—you'll learn fast. Plus, you haven't had an incident in years. Your control over your soul draw was perfect, even when you didn't have magic. Thank you for doing this for our family."

"Of course." Nodding, Imani squeezed her sister's hand. "I won't lie; this magic is difficult. You and I will need help. The only person who might agree is another witch a few hours from here."

Now, *that* was an outright lie. When Asim, the other nearby coven leader, learned what Imani was willing to pay, he would instantly agree.

"Then we'll leave tonight," Meira said.

Pride bloomed in Imani's chest at her sister's bravery and trust. She clenched her fist, silently hoping she didn't simply kill them both.

CHAPTER 8

Blood covered every wall in the room. It stained the old sofa and the tattered chair, dripping down the windowpanes. Imani's bloodied dress lay crumpled on the floor. Blood was the last thing she remembered before she had convulsed and fainted.

Magic rocked Imani's body to its core, like lightning bolts jolting her repeatedly. She vaguely remembered someone checking her pulse then leaving. Her eyes fluttered open.

They closed again. Meira seemed to be nearby, but Imani couldn't check on her condition.

They lay in this strange in-between existence for what seemed like hours, experiencing what she hoped was Meira's magic permanently searing itself into her body.

After an eternity, the garish peeling paint of the walls at the inn came back into focus.

Imani's whispering darkness pulsed in the corners of the room. It flickered and flipped around. Her grandmother said magic was given by the Fabric but made by the caster. Brands had their different quirks. Was the divination causing this odd behavior?

The shadows were agitated and clearly linked to Imani's moods.

Imani stared at the cracks in the ceiling and held her sister's hand for a minute. Then, with shaking arms, she pushed herself to her knees and brushed strands of wet, messy hair off her face. Whether sweat or blood soaked her head, she couldn't be sure.

She swayed when she stood but took a deep breath and called the darkness back before Meira awoke. The walls moved, and the ceiling swirled like an impending storm—hallucinations. She fumbled again against the wall, using it to walk to the window. Imani's eyes took in the street below—it was dark still.

Good.

Grabbing her clothes, Imani padded to the sofa. The floor was soggy, black, and sticky. Asim must have left hours ago, not even bothering to see if they had lived. Not that she had expected much from such a bastard.

He'd practically salivated when Imani had told him she would give up their whole territory in exchange for two powerful flesh magic spells—an alteration and an illusion—and modest compensation.

She gingerly sat down to examine the long, deep cuts marring her naked body. The gash across her collarbone needed stitching. Enchanting a needle and thread from her dress pocket, she sewed herself up while trying to remember what had happened and determine if the magic had taken.

Two fingers on her left hand and two toes had to be severed. But the magic from the sacrifice had exploded in the room, and Asim had expertly latched onto it. While she'd been silently screaming in pain, an invisible veil had tightened around her chest and limbs. Indeed, she could feel it now, vibrating under her skin.

Her brands had changed. The blue leaf Norn sigil was back, all the red brands were gone, and Imani's blue alteration and alchemy marks appeared invisible. The only magic her sister didn't have was now essentially gone, and Meira's divination symbol shone on her arm like a black and blue bruise. Whether or not it worked was another question, but there wasn't time to test or worry about it. They had been awake nearly all night but still had work to do.

Imani didn't know the spell Ara used to glamour and restrict her magic; she only knew how to mask the brands. She would need to be careful when using the hidden magic and exercise complete control. Any slipup revealing she wasn't truly Meira could be deadly.

Good thing all Ara had done was teach Imani to control her impulses and temper.

He was only a four-mark, but she might've been impressed if Asim weren't such a smarmy piece of shit.

Getting dressed was a pathetic affair of shaking limbs, clenched teeth, and hisses of pain.

Imani ambled over to her sister. "Meira, wake up."

"Did it work?" Meira croaked, rubbing her eyes as she let Imani help her stand.

Once upright, Imani displayed her forearm.

Meira sighed in relief as she squeezed Imani's hand.

Panic flooded Imani, and an image burst into her mind.

Jewels dripped from around her neck, the folds of a rich dress swimming around Meira's feet. Her sister collapsed to the floor. Blood dripped from her nose and mouth and from around the crown of her head. Her face—wiser-looking but not aged—was slack and pale, eyes big and lifeless, and covered in more blood. A chalice tipped on its side as it fell from her hand.

The premonition disappeared as fast as it had come. Imani didn't recognize the images, but a hollowness opened in her chest all the same. Her heart ached as the slice of the future hit her—her sister's death, to be exact.

Meira's divination magic worked inside her, after all.

~

Dawn came, but the sun didn't rise. A sinister quiet had settled over Kishion overnight.

Throwing open the curtains at home, a foreboding fog greeted Imani. Nothing permeated it except a mournful mist, lightning flashes, and the arid stench of smoke blowing into the Riverlands.

Fear spread—fear their skies would darken permanently. It hadn't yet cleared, so the shaken villagers sequestered themselves in their homes. While some carried lanterns as they made their way to work, many storefronts remained empty and dark, with oil lamps as the only light. People peeked out their doors. They shivered as the night charged at them like a wild beast and hugged them in cold, chilling discomfort before slamming them shut again.

Imani squinted her eyes to the south. Night had spread like a disease across the horizon there and never left. Everyone agreed—except the branded and people familiar with magic—that it was a problem of the *other* kingdom—repercussions they'd received from the deity breeds of the Upper realm for their lawlessness and brutal culture.

Indeed, before today, most people in the Essenheim Kingdom shook their heads, refusing to look, even as smoke blew into their lands, carrying the smell of magic and death.

As if sensing her thoughts, booms of wicked thunder rumbled far in the distance over the Niflheim Mountains. A mesmerizing orchestra of lightning lit up the enormous dark cloud, flashing in random sequences for a minute.

After years spent watching this same Fabric storm over Niflheim, Imani found it difficult to believe such destruction wouldn't eventually spread here. Abused and chained into submission for far too long by witches, the Fabric always took something in exchange for magic, and no one escaped payment. Even here in the sunlight, Imani knew dozens of those who'd already paid.

She'd been one of them with the Fabric event her parents had died in, and the price was almost too great to comprehend. Some days, with Ara, she'd also wished she'd gone to the Under with them.

A warm hand fell on Imani's shoulder, making her turn her head.

"I wanted to talk to you about something before you leave," Meira said quietly.

"How's Dak? Still angry with me? I gave him his voice back an hour ago, but he hasn't said a word."

"He'll get over it, like always," Meira assured her.

Imani nodded. "You should be resting. I'll say goodbye when they get here."

"I can't rest. I can't stop thinking about it …" Meira trailed off, rubbing Imani's fake blue leaf sigil. "I'm worried about how you're going to feed there. You could revert and lose control … another accident could happen."

Defensiveness stiffened Imani. They never talked about what had brought them to the Riverlands in the first place—the reason Ara had hated her so much.

"I haven't had an issue in years," Imani muttered. She would never mention what happened in the pub earlier with Fen, or the fact she'd let herself feed from Ara's and Malis's souls.

The invisible chasm between them got bigger. Meira hugged herself. "You're right. You haven't had any issues in years. I know you're wary of getting too close to people because of what happened with grandfather, but maybe you should try to make friends in Stralas."

Make friends? Imani dreamed about it sometimes since Riona had died. Like being unglamoured with her family in the Draswood, she imagined having a real friend who wasn't a customer or a family member.

But Ara's voice sounded in her head.

"Please, as Riona's friend—" Imani had begged, *in tears as she hugged the hob's urn against her chest.*

"You think you can have friends?" Ara had cut her off, looking at the window. "Don't make me laugh. You can't trust anyone enough—including yourself—to let them get too close."

"I'm not like that anymore."

"You are, though—a murderer," Ara had stated matter-of-factly. "And once people learn more about your inclinations and base needs, they will want to use you for them—or they will be terrified."

Meira pointed to Imani's wrist. A flare of jealousy sparked in her sister's bright blue eyes. "What about *him*? Your heartmate is real and could help you, and us. Feeding from him wouldn't be dangerous at all. You can't kill each other. How did he not feel the brand burning? Do you have any idea who he is?"

A twinge of horrible happiness sparked inside Imani. For once, she had something her sister wanted—something powerful. Yet Imani hated herself for the emotion and shoved it down.

"The block on my magic must have stopped the burning. I have no idea who he is, and I don't want to. We'd both be killed if anyone found out the truth about us, anyway—two red and blue sigils—an illegal mixed pair. I'm a Norn, and he's something else. I'd say it's a good enough reason for him to stay away," Imani stated flatly.

She had no idea if illegal mixed pairs even existed—she and Malis certainly weren't a mixed pair with both their red sigils—but the lies kept coming out. Since she hadn't told her sister that she wasn't a Norn elf, and Asim had glamoured over her red brand, it would be the same as Meira's sigil. As far as Meira knew, they were a mixed pair.

Meira gave her a look that said, *Don't be so wretched*, and then smoothed Imani's braid. "How could he not want you, *ahavah*? There must be a good explanation for keeping you apart ... You'll be more like yourself there. Even slightly glamoured, you're still going to be the most beautiful person in every room. Like always."

Imani almost laughed. Yes, she'd hide her scars and mutilated fingers as well as mute her soul draw, but the situation was so much more complicated than Meira could comprehend. Could she trust herself to let someone close enough for her to feed like heartmates would? Imani only did it with her sister after years of practice. Could she find someone similar in Stralas? Hope bloomed in her chest at the thought.

But Aralana's words came back to her again. *"That man will hate you. You're a humiliating weakness for him, and he'll try to kill you for it."*

Indeed, he tried to kill Imani as Ara had predicted.

Her heartmate had been a sadistic monster who deserved to die, which Imani had been more than delighted to help him do.

Heartmates fit perfectly together—their souls made from the same piece of the Fabric—and as a result, Norn heartmates fed from each other perfectly. She didn't know if she'd find anyone else who could come close to replacing him.

However, she'd try.

"I'll find someone else. Forget about him, Meira."

"I can't. Think of all the other elves who never find their heartmates and struggle to have children. Don't be so selfish," she snapped. A hint of nastiness imbibed Meira's voice.

Imani stared, open-mouthed, as Meira wiped her eyes.

"I'm sorry. I hate myself for being envious of you. You deserve happiness and children as much as me."

Without returning to the Draswood, the chance of either sister having their own children was nearly impossible, and the Aowyns couldn't live there because of the murder Imani had committed.

Meira could never learn Imani had killed Malis, too. Imani's heart was already cracking in two, knowing how much Meira wanted children of her own, and if anyone deserved to be a mother, it was Meira. The truth about Malis would destroy what little they had left of their small family.

"If I could give up mine to ensure you get yours, I would." Especially since Imani wasn't keen to share her magic as she knew heartmates did with each other.

"I know you would," Meira said, wrapping her arm around Imani. "No one has ever been able to tell you what to do, and I certainly have never been as clever or brave. I know you'll prioritize our family while I take on the responsibilities here. I'm scared, but I trust you. We can do this together."

Something had changed in Meira since yesterday—a maturity that hadn't been there before. Her sweet sister was still there, but Meira's eyes no longer held the usual innocence.

Imani squeezed their clasped hands in a silent promise.

Meira nodded before packing Ara's old trunk with Imani's belongings, and Imani let her. Her sister needed to fuss, and there was nothing else to say about heartmates.

Meira pulled out a few books and blew the dust off them. "Did you want to take anything from inside the trunk, or should I clean it all out?"

Snatching the books from Meira's grasp, Imani studied them momentarily. None were *A History of Royal Bloodlines*, but Imani thought they could still be significant. "I want all of it. Leave nothing behind."

Meira tilted her head but put the books back in the trunk without a word.

Curiosity burned through Imani seeing the wandlore book again. She cleared her throat. "Meira, did Ara ever mention a wand called a Drasil? Maybe when she trained you in wandlore magic?"

Face scrunched in confusion, Meira folded a dress and tucked it into the trunk. "I don't remember any wand with such a name. Is it a type of Draswood?"

"No." Imani picked up one of the ratty old maps. "I think it's a wand from a different tree altogether. From Niflheim, maybe."

Meira narrowed her eyes at the map. "You should drop it, Imani. I know your obsession with learning everything about magic, but you need to focus on finding someone to feed from in Stralas and passing the assessments. Being tangled up in this same mess is what got Ara killed."

"I never said I was going to get tangled up in it," Imani bit out.

Guilt gnawed at Imani with the lie she'd told her sister. How could she stop finding the most powerful wand in the world?

Even if she couldn't go to Niflheim, there would be answers in Stralas about the Drasil. Something about the wand waited for Imani there, and she was going to find it.

∼

THEY CAME for her at what would have been sundown. Carriages holding potential master witches and two dozen soldiers on horses rolled into the village like a storm.

A hard pounding on their door made everyone but Imani jump. Soldiers clad in stiff uniforms greeted her. They were out of place in the dismal, rundown hallway.

"We have records of a potential master residing here named Meira Aowyn. Is she here?"

Imani nodded. "I'm Meira."

"By decree from Her Radiant Majesty, Queen Dialora, and the First Witch of the Royal Order of Magic, you are ordered to come with us. As a potential master witch, the Order officially employs you. Follow me."

The real Meira helped Imani don her new cloak, but the sisters and Dak said nothing. She hugged them both, relieved when her brother squeezed her back.

Outside, a foreboding winter wind whipped by, rustling the vibrant leaves on the uneven cobblestones. The same townspeople who had attended the execution now stood at their windows. More soldiers surrounded the building, and their horses whinnied and shuffled nervously. It was overkill, but potential master witches, even small ones, could be dangerous.

Flanked by the soldiers, they led Imani toward a carriage at the front of the line. Each step made her missing toes throb, but she held her cloaked head high.

They stopped in front of the most oversized, ornate carriage. A soldier opened the door, and a male witch stepped out.

Impeccably dressed and young, the master witch symbol shone brightly on the golden skin atop his hand. His dark blond hair was tied back, and his beard was freshly trimmed, framing a solid, masculine jaw. Imani couldn't determine his breed. He could've been a pixie, a nymph, or a shifter; all she knew for certain was that he wasn't an elf.

Desire emanated from him while hunger curled in her belly.

Towering over her, he cocked his head in evident surprise. "It's not often you see a High-Norn elf outside the Draswood," he murmured. "Especially an unmated female."

"Yet, here I am," she said demurely.

The man's eyes sparkled at her like she was something to possess. He referenced a piece of parchment, one that presumably stated every known potential master witch in Essenheim. Meira's name was on there, near the top.

"You can call me Master Grey, Lady Aowyn. Now, let's see your arms, please. I'll be confirming your brands and checking for deceptive magic."

She wrenched up her sleeves, and he reached for her wrist.

An image slammed into her. Another vision of death. It only lasted seconds.

"You are a fucking traitor," someone said with a wand against his throat.

Grey's face was wrought with fear. Invisible magic strangled him until his eyes turned glassy.

He steadied her with his arm. "Lady Aowyn? Are you all right?"

"Y-y-yes ... yes, I'm fine," she stammered.

"I sense a light glamour on you," Grey whispered.

"Female elves tend to attract unwanted attention." Imani momentarily lifted her cloak off her head and loosed part of the illusion.

"It's been a long time since I've seen a female of your kind," he whispered. "But why are you still glamouring yourself so much?"

"My illusion isn't only for my elven magic. I have"—she trailed off and glanced around—"disfigurements that make people uncomfortable."

After she had warned him, she let the rest of the glamour fall.

Lingering on her face for longer than polite, it was as if he saw through her to her bones. Did he sense the flesh magic hiding her brands? Could he feel the strangeness in the divination magic? Imani gritted her teeth, heart hammering.

An arrogant, skeptical gaze stared down at her. For one long second, Imani's chest constricted.

"You have unique brands. I think you're still hiding something, and I intend to figure it out, Meira." A ghost of a smile tugged at his lips.

Was he teasing her? Complimenting her? She couldn't be sure.

With a swish of his cloak, he turned back to his carriage, but before disappearing inside, the master witch looked over his shoulder. "I suggest you drop the illusion spell permanently. Unwanted questions are far worse than unwanted looks at court."

Drop the illusion *entirely*? Her soul draw would drive unmated males insane with the compulsion to feed from her. Not one female High-Norn left the Draswood without some form of an illusion.

She stared at the closed door, unsure if he was ignorant about her kind or if he didn't care.

Imani's hands trembled slightly, but there was no going back now. She had to pull this off.

Pointedly ignoring his suggestion, she restored her glamour and tucked herself into an open coach door before craning her neck to peer at their flat, to see her siblings one last time.

The window remained empty.

Imani let her head fall back against the seat, ignoring the sharp pang of hurt as they set off into the night to Stralas.

CHAPTER 9

Much to her relief, the sun rose, even over the Riverlands, as things returned to normal.

The carriage rocked back and forth along the rough dirt road that ran across the boggy terrain. A sharp wind blew in from the approaching sea and whistled through the coach's cracks. The Neshuin Coast and the capital were close.

Cold, tedious, and with everything jostling about, Imani couldn't do much but stare out the window. Indeed, she could barely think.

At least they planned to give her a traveling companion at their final stop in the Moorlands, where the sprite pixies lived. Something inside Imani hoped maybe she might be friendly with this person.

But a pang of anxiety stirred her gut, remembering Ara's words. Meira had been correct; feeding would be more complicated for Imani here. And lately, with her shadow magic, she'd been having a more challenging time with control. The shadows had a mind of their own.

In the past three days, their company had traveled swiftly through all the territories and picked up each of the breeds living there. Imani was homesick for the tall trees and roaring tributaries of the Riverlands, and she could admit she was nervous about living in Stralas. It was the opposite of her provincial town.

Stralas and the Neshuin Sea belonged to the Crown. All breeds were welcome to live and work there. A bustling metropolis, it offered excitement Imani had never experienced. She might even see some Norn elves there.

Imani knew she should be trying to make a friend or two among the group of apprentices for feeding, but she kept to herself. Half would die taking the assessments, anyway, perhaps more.

Still, she needed to find *some* allies.

Yesterday, they had passed by her home territory and didn't stop. Despite many elves possessing powerful magic, none of her kind was with them. It disappointed her more than she wanted to admit. The Crown would never travel into the Draswood without an invitation, let alone barge in and demand Norn witches.

They weren't fools.

She spotted the edge of the forest from the carriage's window. Dark inside, the Draswoods towered to the sky and blanketed the flora and fauna underneath in their shade. She only caught one look before they moved on.

Around midday, she sensed Stralas's magic long before she could see it, like a collective buzzing over her skin. The wards protecting the city stood far outside the perimeter.

Imani kept her gaze fixed on the horizon, heart hammering in anticipation. Finally, shadowed outlines of the great walls came into focus as they made their way up the craggy coast. Structures rose on the peninsula in the distance, too. As the massive capital of the Essenheim Kingdom grew more prominent, their company hushed.

An hour later, they stopped at a crossroads. They were still in the Moorlands, and while Imani had been keen to see the cityscape from this view, a sense of unease hung in the air. Even she could tell this was a different route into the city.

Their caravan halted entirely, and she whipped her head out the door to catch a glimpse.

Immediately, the wind, which smelled like the sea, ruffled her cloak and hair, reminding her of Master Grey.

Soldiers shouted indiscriminate orders down the line, calling them back into the carriages. A scuffle caused Imani to sit up straighter. She creaked open her carriage door, and more people shouted. Something was happening outside.

She cast a quick invisibility illusion over her body, hopped down, and scurried to hide behind a tree near the dirt road.

The breeze spun through the cotton grass in a field ahead, tousling the blue hair of a diminutive woman pointing her finger at the soldiers. Delicate, translucent, moth-shaped wings snapped out and fluttered with surprising force.

Imani's brows shot up.

While Norn elves only *seemed* elusive, pixies were truly rare. Only a small number remained after their populations had been decimated years ago by several Fabric events, not to mention those taken captive by the more ruthless covens for their dust. Like the Norn elves, people rarely spotted trow or sprite pixies in their larger forms outside the safety of their home territories of the Plainslands and Moorlands.

Imani wanted to get her hands on some pixie dust of any variety, one of the most coveted magic items. According to rumors from Fen's bed, some versions of Niflheim pixie dust could raise the dead, but the same dust also made pixies powerful and dangerous.

Blue hair shining, the fierce sprite pixie arched her wand over her head and summoned a shield of defensive magic. An invisible wall shimmered into existence, ensconcing the pixie.

A pang of jealousy hit her. Defensive magic was invaluable in physical combat. It produced all sorts of shields and wards to keep a person safe from other witches' magic or even push the same magic back at the witch, hurting themselves with their own spell.

The ground shook as the pixie cracked a deep hole using another powerful spell—terrestrial magic—which bent water, dirt, plants, and even the weather to a witch's will. One soldier fell inside, which Imani immensely enjoyed—it served them right for treating all the potential master witches on this trip like prisoners. Recently, Imani had seen many roughed up for not willingly following the new laws.

Soldiers tried to create a perimeter around this tiny beast, but the pixie roared and cut two more down, killing them.

Whoever she was, Imani immediately thought this witch would be worth keeping tabs on.

A dozen soldiers surrounded the sprite pixie now. Imani flinched as another blast sent more dirt flying.

The pixie flung enchantments and terrestrial and defensive magic at anyone who came close. Indeed, she possessed enough magic to take out at least five men alone and was adept at wielding it.

All delight faded from Imani's face when Master Grey approached in the periphery. Everyone's eyes tracked him staring down the formidable witch.

Shrugging his cloak off his broad shoulders, he appeared calm and amused. Grey was handsome, whatever his breed, and he was likely aware of this fact. But he looked less put together today, and with a longer beard and windswept hair, traveling showed on him.

As he approached the pixie, his dark, crimson master witch robes swirled around him from the breeze she'd created. Then, ten feet away, Grey stopped.

The soldiers scattered behind him like children hiding in their mother's skirts. His lips pulled into a slight grin, and he pointed his wand at the pixie. Dull clouds above swirled while the wind picked up. He also possessed terrestrial magic, but he was a master, and this pixie was not.

"We must do our part for this kingdom, including you, pix. So, you're coming with us. One way is painful; the other is easy. I don't want to hurt you, little one."

Imani glared at him for his demeaning words, having been called the same many times. But the female smiled unforgivingly, staring the master dead in the eye.

"Call me little again"—her voice boomed loudly—"and I'll shove my wand so far up your ass you'll be shitting your snide attitude out of your nostrils for months."

With another snap of her wand, the ground wrenched open further, crumbling toward Master Grey. In perfect control, she stopped the crack mere inches from dropping him to his death and laughed.

Oh, Imani liked her.

To his credit, Master Grey didn't even flinch. Instead, a savage, unkind grin darkened his face.

Thunder rumbled in the clouds above, answering the master. A vertical swipe with his wand called rain and a lightning bolt down from the sky, blasting through the pixie's barrier ward. Lightning was terrestrial magic and impossible for anyone but a master to wield.

A crackling current filled the air. The pixie's blood-chilling scream rattled Imani's chest.

Dust rose and swirled in response to the impact. When it cleared, the pixie fell onto her back, struggling against invisible ropes. No match for a lightning strike, she snarled and snapped her teeth, practically feral, while Master Grey watched on.

A longing wrapped around Imani's heart after witnessing the command of magic they both possessed. How far behind would she be from the other apprentices?

Master Grey approached slowly and inclined his head, as if debating whether to squish a bug he'd captured. With a flick of his hand, the soldiers surrounded her again and struck.

Beating the pixie wasn't fair, but they delivered it enthusiastically, anyway. Eventually, they carried her away.

Invisible, Imani retreated, as well. Heat crept down her spine, and she froze.

Cocking his head to the side, Master Grey narrowed his eyes in her direction. Despite the illusion spell over her body, he sensed something from her. She held her breath.

He stared for far longer than she was comfortable with before eventually striding away.

~

Frigid air blasted Imani, and her head snapped to the right as someone flung the coach door open. She'd only returned moments before and blinked, gaping at her new companion.

Crawling into the seat opposite Imani, the pixie sat back and sighed loudly.

Imani stared unabashed, overcome with the curiosity at seeing her first pixie. Although her true form was measured in inches, not feet, this one appeared in her larger body today, which was not much bigger than a Norn. With the typical blue hair of a pixie cut blunt around her chin, frazzled by the wind and lightning, her features were severe but pretty.

Almond-shaped eyes with a violet hue and sharp cunningness glanced around at her surroundings. "So, this is what it's like to be in a gilded cage, marching to your death," she muttered, shifting her weight and hugging her cloak tighter. A deep gash on her cheek gleamed bright red.

Based on how the pixie carefully sat back against the plush seat, Imani guessed she had bruises and scrapes on her back, too. She should offer to help her. It would be kind, something Meira would do.

"I don't have healing magic," Imani said, studying her more, "but if you let me, I could perform a numbing enchantment."

Suspicion swept over the pixie's face. "I know better than to touch one of your kind," she said, raking her gaze over Imani's body from top to bottom. "Besides, when they look at me, I want them to remember not everyone is going quietly to their execution."

The pixie was wrong about the touching. All Imani had to do was stare into her eyes, but she didn't correct her.

Silence fell for several minutes. The pixie's eyes locked onto her, observing.

In Imani's opinion, unlike others in their company, the pixie wouldn't have to worry about surviving the assessments. Imani pressed her mouth into a thin line, unsure what to make of her.

"Let me guess, you've never seen a Norn elf before?" Imani asked, desperate for the staring to stop.

"No, I've seen a few. Even High-Norn females, if you can believe it." The pixie settled her gaze out the window. "I'm having a hard time believing they braved the Draswood to retrieve one creature like you. Even if you are a potential master witch."

Imani bristled. "I'm not a *creature* easily retrieved, I promise you."

"Let me see your markings then." It wasn't a demanding or sneering tone but a challenge.

Swallowing hard, Imani regarded her for a moment. Witches kept their brands close to their chests. The impolite request made her nervous.

Before she could change her mind, Imani loosed the glamour and revealed a bit more of her true form. While she kept her disfigurements hidden and a light illusion on her soul draw, Imani imagined her features sharpening, her eyes widening, the blue of her irises brightening, and her skin glowing.

Shoving her sleeves up, Imani thrust her arms forward. The markings sparkled even in the dim light, showing her sigil and legal Essenheim brands. The rest remained perfectly undetectable, as far as Imani knew. She waited to see if the pixie could sense them.

Mumbling, the pixie was careful not to touch. She took her time examining them all then looked back up. "Yes, retrieving you against your will might be harder than expected." She narrowed her eyes at Imani. "Without healing magic, you're pristine. Not a scratch on you. I don't believe for a second the Norn let a young, unmated female go without a fight, especially a high-bred one. But, even if they did, let's be honest—your kind never leaves the Draswood without your special magic cunt so heavily glamoured no one spares you a glance. Yet, here you sit, in all your High-Norn glory with merely an illusion on."

"It seems some of us do."

In truth, parts of Imani *were* heavily glamoured, but not with the magic most people expected. Yet her companion still didn't sense any of it, which meant her flesh magic illusion spell was more powerful than the pixie witch.

The pixie clearly didn't think it was possible. *Good.* Thank the saints for flesh magic.

Sitting back with a heavy sigh, the pixie stared at Imani. "So, how did you come to be here?"

"I haven't lived in the Draswood since I was a child. I'm from the Riverlands."

"You lived with the naiads? That's ... that's strange." The pixie paused and gave Imani a once-over. "You come from excellent breeding. Not only are you physically perfect, with a powerful soul draw, but you have a wandlore brand. Why did you leave the Draswood?"

"My family died. My naiad grandmother raised me."

Another pause.

"You're a strange elf witch, and there's nothing naiad about you."

Despite the innocent comment, Imani's stomach twisted into knots. The pixie was bright, and although she hadn't figured her out, she sensed Imani was hiding something. Like Master Grey, how many people in the capital would perceive the same? Although being a High-Norn elf would draw some attention, she would be in trouble if she couldn't stay somewhat inconspicuous.

Imani averted her eyes from the window before replying. "I'm nothing special. I have more nymph in me from my grandmother than you would think." Lies, but all valid for her sister. "The soul draw is affecting you when I let my glamour loose. Per your request, by the way," Imani added.

"Possibly. Fucking elves." She rolled her eyes. "People wouldn't love you half as much without your soul draw."

"I certainly hope someone who talks like you has the markings to match the attitude," Imani said snidely.

"I do." The pixie tugged back her sleeves and revealed seven markings and a circle around her blue moth sigil. Imani sensed an illusion over the brands. The pixie was hiding something—or someone.

CHAPTER 10

The pixie didn't deign to say anything about her magic or sigils as she pulled her sleeves back down, and Imani didn't ask.

After a long pause of silence, she gave Imani a sly smile. "What's your name, elf witch?"

"Meira Aowyn."

"Esadora Farwyn. But call me Esa—"

A commotion outside made them both startle. In the next instant, they clambered out of the coach.

Up ahead, Master Grey climbed onto the coach's roof with the grace of a predator. Pushing out his palm, he cast with a methodically practiced form.

"What is he doing?" Esa whispered after another minute. "Those shields are miles long. There are at least a hundred spells, some older than the Order, and most can't be fully disabled by one witch, nor should they need to be. There are easier ways to enter the city."

Imani suspected the same. Swallowing hard, she gave Esa a sidelong glance. "He's not disabling them, though. He's smashing a hole."

"But why? The power it will take to hold it open for us to pass, then to fix the wards again..." Esa trailed off.

Only a master could. The city had been well protected for centuries because of it.

"Saints alive," Esa muttered. "It would be easier for us to go through the main gates instead of pulling on the Fabric and sending someone out here to repair the damage. Why are we entering this way?"

Imani agreed it was odd. "I've heard that no one passes the wards and goes into Stralas without the Order and the queen's knowledge."

"It's true," Esa said.

Unease passed between them as they silently came to the same conclusion—the Crown had planned this roundabout entrance. They were to enter through a back way, and the damage had been sanctioned to ensure the witches arrived in relative anonymity.

"Maybe they want to avoid creating large crowds coming out to see us? Witches are a rarity," Esa whispered.

"It's possible. Or is this way somehow faster?" Imani questioned.

Esa shrugged.

It didn't appear the others had put the pieces together. Heads peeked out of carriages with excitement, and people pointed in awe like fools. But Imani and Esa stood frozen, confused. A sense of wrongness swirled inside her, and Imani seriously questioned what the apprentices were here for and why.

A massive cracking sound, like thousands of trees being torn down, stunned everyone into silence.

Master Grey clenched his outstretched hand, and more magic poured out of him. Bright red and orange sparks rained above and beneath the canopy of the trees, using terrestrial and defensive magic to cut an arch through the invisible shield. They lit up the dull gray afternoon as he tore through the tranche of spells making up the massive wards surrounding the city. The disruption caused the shrubs and trees beyond to ripple, their leaves blurring together and swirling wildly in distortion.

Imani's hands trembled while he decimated the shield in minutes, melting a hole straight through. Desire reared its head deep from the recesses of her mind. A low growl threatened in her chest. She didn't know if she wanted him or his power. Maybe both.

Another push of his free hand sent energy ropes shooting out as he attacked all the weak spots with enchantments of some kind. The shields broke and fell away in quick succession. He'd used at least three different magic abilities simultaneously—an impressive feat.

With a jerk of his chin, still holding tight to the magic, the witch signaled to his guard.

This one appeared to be in charge. His uniform was decorated with more regalia than anyone else's, but unlike the others, Imani sensed he wasn't a complete idiot and worked closely with Master Grey. One time, they smiled and laughed together, giving her the distinct impression the two might be friends.

The two women swiftly slid back inside their coach as it lurched forward, passing through the tunnel the master held open.

When they approached the threshold, Imani blatantly stared at him. A thick, burned scent hung in the air—the aftereffects of his magic. Low humming and a crackling noise emanated from the tunnel, surrounding them as they drew closer. Only a tiny wrinkle across his strong brow hinted at his concentration. Nevertheless, the magic appeared to be well within his range.

Even if the Order had given him the knowledge to break through, to wield such taxing, physically demanding magic, it impressed her. He must be an incredibly apt witch.

A knot tightened in her stomach. Imani had a mountain of secrets to hide from the powerful magic wielders here, of which this master witch was only one.

Bright, piercing gray eyes whipped her way, and he locked gazes with her momentarily. A smile almost slipped through. It was anything but friendly. On the contrary, the look said, *I have my eye on you.*

Heat shot through Imani's spine, but warning bells went off in her head. She held his eyes until the angle was too great to stare at him without craning her neck.

~

"OUR MASTER PREFERS ELVES. But who doesn't, right?"

Imani pursed her lips, uncomfortable at Esa noticing the exchange. "I doubt it. We've hardly spoken."

Esa shrugged. They fell back into silence. Was she jealous? Probably not, but Imani had just met her.

Once inside the city's outer limits, the apprentices were herded into smaller groups, splitting off to take different roads leading to various entry points into Stralas.

Even on the outskirts, it got louder. The streets were narrower, with neighborhoods, shops, and buildings growing more extensive and crowded. Stealing a look outside, Imani gripped the edge of the window. She couldn't take her eyes off the bustling streets as they painstakingly entered the city's confines. Their pace slowed as their party was hemmed in by milling people, carriages, and livestock.

Imani lost herself in the cacophony—markets, crowds, shouts, bleating sheep and goats, and rickety carriage wheels—as they jostled toward the peninsula's highest point. They climbed higher, and the homes and buildings became more opulent and elegant.

A regal palace stood tall over the endless Neshuin Sea as they halted at the base of the hill.

Guards perched at their watches, high in several of the many towers lining the walls of the gates, idly glancing at the handful of new Order witches approaching. These appeared to be a more severe caliber than the ones accompanying them, their gazes steely and unflinching.

A guard leaned out of a tower and shouted to another to let them in. The gates creaked loudly as they obliged.

"Keep the gate open!" another guard shouted down. "The prince approaches from the south!"

Imani and Esa whipped their heads toward the other window, hoping to glimpse the heir apparent.

"Ah ... it took two damn hours to get up here. Extra royal security for the spoiled arsehole." Esa glanced at Imani. "What do you know about him? Rumor has it only the truly hedonistic can run with the prince's inner circle. Staying up all night, gambling away all his mother's money, and bedding anyone." Esa's eyes were amused.

"Lies," Imani shot back wryly, a smirk tugging at her lips. "One person can't gamble away all the queen's money. There's far too much for one person to spend in their lifetime."

"Well, the bastard is trying."

"I heard he's also actually a talented master witch. At sixteen, he was one of the youngest to pass the assessments."

Esa played with a string on her dress. "Well, some say the queen is concerned the prince isn't powerful enough. His mother thinks another kind will inherit the monarchy after her death."

The Pareias were an old high-bred leimoniads nymph family from the Meadowlands, who had shocked the kingdom forty years ago when Queen Dialora broke a three-hundred-year streak of various shifters being in power.

Nymphs hadn't held the Crown in centuries.

"Where did you hear all these rumors?"

"I've visited the court a hundred times to see my brother. You hear things."

So many questions arose in Imani. A hundred times? Her brother? Esa wasn't the most powerful witch they'd collected, but she came close. With seven markings and a circle around her blue moth sigil, the only creature more powerful ended up being a nine-mark high leonine shifter. Imani had seven marks, of course, but had to pretend to have five.

"Did you train here? With your magic?"

"No. My brother taught me."

"He must be talented. Most people here don't know much beyond their own breeds or abilities." Most people were like her sister.

"Was. My brother *was* talented. He had eight markings." Facing out the window, Esa's face remained unreadable. "He died taking his assessment."

Silence fell. The gates closed as they entered the palace grounds with Imani's mind reeling.

A trained eight-mark *died*? Esa's assertion they were marching to their death wasn't so dramatic anymore.

FEMALE WITCHES each had their own rooms. Esa entered hers without a goodbye, but the whole palace distracted Imani too much to notice.

The gleaming white walls towered over the rest of the buildings, standing right on the end of the peninsula over the sea with a maze of gardens and courtyards surrounding it. Imani's apartment was more incredible than any she'd ever seen, even for the *east wing*, which Esa made sound barely nicer than the stables. Servants brought Imani's belongings. Maids helped her bathe and prepare for sleep.

Although exhausted, she woke repeatedly throughout the night, drenched in sweat. Dreams of her sister sobbing, more real than any dreams she'd had before, clenched her heart tight. Every time she shut her eyes, the pain shocked her limbs, and she, too, had tears running down her face. All night, she'd feared she'd let them both down, that something was gravely wrong with Dak and Meira.

But they were only dreams.

In the morning, they were all but forgotten as a knock on her door slammed her back into reality. A steward stood outside.

"Lady Aowyn, your presence is requested before the others. I'm to escort you as soon as possible."

Several maids filed in without waiting for a response, bustling about to get her dressed.

Standing in her robe, she crossed her arms. "This early? As you can see, I've only just risen. I'm not ready."

The servant cleared his throat. "I must insist, my lady." He handed her a piece of paper and crossed his white-gloved hands behind his back.

Unfolding it, one sentence in a looping script greeted her.

Time to answer some of those unwanted questions.

It was signed, *Master Grey*.

The servant bowed then quietly went into the hall to wait for her.

No one had ever bowed to Imani. She liked it more than she should.

CHAPTER 11

Sweat covered her palms at the conversation ahead, but she wanted to get this over with, to assuage Master Grey's suspicion.

After a long, winding walk, where people stared openly as if she were a circus animal, they entered the Order's wing.

Dust coated everything, making it less polished than the rest of the palace. The carpets were frayed in some places, less decor hung on the walls, and paint peeled in various corners. Its remote location in the court was odd, as if the queen had tried to shove the distinguished Royal Order of Magic into the attic and forget about them.

The servant took her to one lone door and opened it.

She stepped past him and found herself in a large open room where two men engaged in a rather intense but clearly friendly duel.

Furniture sat piled off to the side. Half a dozen tall windows lined the outer wall, exposing the green gardens. One man, a broad-shouldered pixie, shot some enchantment and slammed the other man into the wall. The pixie's sleeves were in ribbons, and he had a massive slice visible down his lean abdomen.

Her back stiffened in surprise as the other, a nymph with short, dark blond hair, sent one of the chairs flying across the room and smashed it into his companion. Unlike the pixie, the nymph had somehow lost his shirt entirely, and sweat glistened on every inch of his golden skin as he braced his hands on his knees, panting.

Both snapped their gazes toward her.

When she met the nymph's discerning eyes, recognition shot through her.

With her hammering heart at the sight of Master Grey, she carefully held the paper between two fingers. "I was summoned here."

"Lady Aowyn," Master Grey greeted her with a lazy smile.

She crossed her arms, about to unleash a snarky comment about him putting a shirt on, but she held her tongue. Meira wouldn't say anything so crass.

Imani dropped her confrontational mask, given the circumstances.

The male nymph ran a hand through his messy hair and motioned to the door. "Lore, I have business to attend to."

The pixie named Lore gave Master Grey a slight bow then left.

They were alone, and the master loomed down at her.

He strode over, slipping his shirt on. He had shaved and cut his hair short, and without his robes and shirt ... well, he appeared vastly different. Younger and more relaxed.

"You have questions for me." Imani's voice sounded quiet and formal.

"Indeed. I reported to my colleagues you're glamouring yourself constantly."

"Is there some rule against it? I'm not trying to hide but rather blend in."

"No, there's not a rule against it. But it's uncommon," Master Grey said, his white teeth catching at his lower lip in the prelude to a grin. For a moment, his face was heart-stopping boyish. His smile faded. "Most people don't bother. It's generally seen in poor taste when someone tries to make themselves more attractive using tricks most of us see through."

Her glamour had never been a matter of vanity—Imani had none. It was a waste of time and none of her concern. She had hid all her life to mask her soul draw and hid now because, without the glamour, it revealed a weakness Imani didn't want anyone to know.

"I'm not trying to make myself more attractive."

He cocked his head to the side in amusement. "I told them that, as well."

She stood her ground. Everyone should be allowed to control their appearance, deciding what people see and when without others being suspicious.

She let her primary glamour disappear entirely. He had already seen her without it.

The curtain lifted, and she turned back to him. "People are uncomfortable when they see me, High-Norn or not."

Blinking a few times, he moved closer. "How did you get a mark like that?"

Nobody outside her family and heartmate had seen the marking before, but she had expected this response and let the prepared lie slip out. "Birthmark."

In truth, she hadn't been born with the black veins and marred skin disfiguring half her face. Yet no one understood where she'd gotten it or why. It had appeared slowly, growing over the years until she came of age, stopping around the time when her brands were supposed to have appeared.

As a young child, Imani would disobey her family, often escaping to play in the Draswood alone. Children commonly roamed and explored around the city's edges, but inside the forest, it could be dangerous, even for elves. All the plants and creatures possessed magic. Ara had said everyone's best guess was Imani had encountered something there. Her family had glamoured it when the mark started showing up and had never said a word.

Master Grey swallowed, now even more suspicious.

She forced her expression to soften. "Please," she whispered, imploring the nymph. "I don't know if you have much experience with my kind, but I'm a female elf witch alone here. Without a heartmate's magic to share, I'm exposed. Let me blend in more. No female elf in her right mind would leave the Draswood without some form of protection. I haven't been seen unglamoured by so many people since I was a child, and even then, they were all Norn elves. Do you know any Norn elves, Master Grey?"

"At least one," a male voice sounded from the doorway. A large frame with a discerning expression darkened the doorway.

Her heart almost stopped.

The first male Norn elf she'd seen in years looked like her adoptive father, or what she imagined he'd be like if he were still alive.

Silver hair, although shorter, was the same as she remembered, and the elf's complexion appeared older but shone with a similar luminosity. It gave the master witch an iridescent magic signature surrounding his body.

For some reason, she immediately liked him.

"Lady Aowyn, I must admit I was so very pleased to hear about your arrival. Training a young Norn witch to join the Order is a thrill I haven't experienced in decades." He ambled forward and, without touching her, greeted her in a formal elven fashion she hadn't seen since childhood—two fingers on the forehead and a deep bow.

She stumbled through her response but managed.

"Meira, meet Master Selhey, the only High-Norn master witch to serve here in Stralas."

Master Selhey ignored Imani's gaping mouth. "I've vehemently argued you have the right to keep your glamour for unpleasant reasons you know all too well. You're a female elf alone here and have a right to any protection necessary."

Imani didn't know what to say to his statement, but a surge of affection rose inside her for this stranger.

He held up his wand. "Many, including myself, regarded your parents as the best wandmakers in centuries—your father made this one."

Sven and Saria Aowyn *had* been the best wandmakers in centuries.

Clutching her own, an unbearable sadness came over her, missing both her parents. Not many people knew she wasn't entirely an Aowyn, and her adoptive father had never treated her any differently. Although her parents had been terrified of her after what had happened with her grandfather, they'd always treated her with love before that day.

Master Selhey put his wand away and folded his arms across his chest. "Your parents died young in a Fabric event near the border of the Plainslands and Riverlands, did they not?"

Emotion clogged her throat. All she could do was nod.

"It was a particularly horrific event. Strong enough that Niflheim could've called the treaty void if they had known about it," he muttered with an edge to his voice. "The area there still hasn't fully recovered. It's a miracle you survived."

Imani had to agree. It *was* a miracle.

Images from the day flashed in her eyes. Black, burning rain had poured from spliced pockets of the world, as if two realms had smashed together, fighting to exist in the same plane. The ground had disappeared underneath them, gravity and time had shifted as the world tilted, and her parents' bodies had been caught between the two, effectively breaking them into pieces.

Parts had been strewn here in this realm, while others presumably went ... elsewhere.

Master Selhey turned to Master Grey. "Elves are different from the others in this kingdom in almost every way—our appearance, magic, and emotional needs. All the more reason she should be able to keep the illusion."

"She's not even close to the most powerful witch here. I don't see the point."

"I don't think you quite understand the magic a female's soul draw has on others, nor the distraction her ... other looks would bring," Master Selhey tried to explain patiently.

Glaring, Imani faced the nymph witch head-on again. "I want to learn here. I want to be taken seriously for my magic, not for being an unmated female elf with a strange birthmark. People see this"—she motioned up and down her body—"and they forget everything else. They ask me who I'm feeding from—"

"Who *are* you feeding from?" Master Grey's voice came out rough as he interrupted with a familiar longing she'd seen before.

Her cheeks heated in frustration to see her magic at work, and she wanted to put her illusion back on to hide from his attention. Much to her chagrin, it occurred to Imani that she found this male nymph painfully attractive. Hunger bit at her insides, but she forced herself to remain impassive.

That was a problem for another day. Or week.

Such irritating stirrings—his desire was all fake. It made her want to show him what it was like to have a piece of furniture thrown at him.

Again, Meira would never do anything so rude, and he didn't deserve it. She hated the soul draw sometimes.

Before she could respond, Master Selhey interjected, "*That* is none of your business, Master."

Master Grey had the decency to look affronted, at least, and relented. "I'll tell the other master witches and the First Witch you can keep the spell. We'll likely be the only ones who will sense it, anyway."

"Thank you." Imani meant it.

The male nymph gave her a final dubious once-over. "Come; we'll take you to the other apprentices."

They made their way out, but Master Grey whipped around to stare at her, forehead furrowed in concentration. "You're still hiding something." His voice dropped low. "It would be a mistake to be dishonest with the Crown or the Order. As a witch with only five brands, you're far from the most powerful, but they are rare enough brands for us to notice, so we'll be watching you. That much, I can guarantee."

Tension mounted in the room, and while Master Selhey's eyes narrowed, he said nothing.

As they stepped into the hallway, both master witches murmured to each other softly. Imani's ears flicked back and forth as she listened closely to their conversation, her elven hearing kicking in.

"This is the last favor I do for you until you can answer me about the divination spell," Master Grey said.

"I will give you the same answer I gave your mother—the spell is notoriously difficult to cast. The future is constantly changing as witches are born and die. Given this, it's impossible to discern the truth until the moment it happens."

"Other master witches have managed to divine the heir apparent with a spell before."

"Then they lied to appease their monarch. The divination mark is one of the rarest in this realm, giving the caster dangerous abilities many people desire but few possess. Many don't understand it."

"It seeks to reveal the truth or the future; what's not to understand?"

Their conversation was cut short when they entered the main hall.

Dozens of gazes fell on her. Some apprentices stepped back in surprise, and others stared in confusion. Esa's brows shot so high they practically touched her hairline.

Puzzled, Imani met their expressions, daring them all to look her in the eye. With her glamour back on, she had nothing to hide. She had never *met* most of these people, yet hostility wafted through the air.

Four master witches stood in crimson robes and black attire at the front of the room. Master Grey approached, and the others bowed to him.

Each of them murmured in low tones, "Your Highness."

The shock made her jaw drop. He was the *heir apparent?*

All Imani could do was breathe as the scene unfolded.

"I spoke with Master Selhey and Lady Aowyn. It's my opinion, as the heir apparent and a master witch with this Order, we should let her retain the glamour. It's innocuous. We haven't had a Norn witch study here in fifty years, but I promise it will prove helpful in eliminating distractions for everyone."

One master witch voiced his disagreement.

The prince's gaze darkened, along with her own. It was, quite frankly, *astounding* how ignorant people here were about her kind. She had expected it from common breeds in other territories but not educated high-bred witches in Stralas.

"Furthermore, I don't think High Sentinel Ellisar would be pleased if she were mistreated in any way. Which means my mother wouldn't be pleased, either," the prince added.

Imani almost scoffed. She didn't even know the high sentinel of the Norn. Like the monarchs of the Mesial Realm, high sentinels were chosen by the Fabric once the other died. Many were the most powerful of their breeds and oversaw their people in each territory while also sitting on a council to advise the queen. Imani assumed it worked similarly in Niflheim, but she wasn't sure.

High-Norn female elves, like her and Meira, were rarer and rarer these days, but thousands still lived in the Draswood.

Ellisar wouldn't even spare her a glance.

Still, she appreciated the lie.

All the witches turned to watch the male standing the farthest away. With a purple marking on the top of his hand—an archmage—he must be the First Witch, the only known witch in Essenheim with such a brand. There could be others, of course, but they were nearly impossible to earn.

"Yes. We agree that displeasing Ellisar and your mother would be most unfortunate." He bowed his head. "Please inform her of your successes this past week. We'd hate for the queen to think we are not entirely supportive of the new laws."

The prince gave a curt nod. "Of course. The queen looks forward to a stronger partnership between herself and the Order for a stronger Crown."

The First Witch murmured, "Magic to magic."

"Truth to truth," the prince said. Then, without sparing another glance at her, he strode from the room.

Practically shaking from learning the young master witch was the heir apparent, she turned on her heel and marched to the back of the group to stand next to Esa. Everyone continued to level her with blatant stares, but she kept her countenance neutral.

Esa glared. "What exactly were you doing with Prince Tanyl this morning?"

Imani brushed her off. "Nothing. He had some questions for me about my magical training."

Esa arched a manicured brow.

Luckily, there wasn't time for any more questions. The First Witch waved his hand, and the sconces lining the walls of the room brightened, somehow silencing everyone at the same time.

"Witches, welcome. I am First Witch Savus. I'll get straight to the point—you're here because you possess the potential to wield incredible magic. A power only earned and bestowed by the Fabric itself."

Firelight washed over his strong jaw and stunning golden skin. The First Witch was a satyr shifter whose magic signature seeped into the air around him. Even from a distance, it moved in a formidable caress.

With his pale eyes, he scanned the room. "The ascension assessments are an honored tradition as old as the Essenheim Kingdom itself, and we are bound to its ancient rules and structure. However, we recognize most of you have not volunteered. The world is changing, and we must change, too, to ensure our control over magic. However, we do not view our role as controlling. Instead, we view it as a partnership, protecting and enforcing the law by ensuring balance. Master witches serve the Crown and the people of our kingdom first. Therefore, we have always respected our power and protected those who can't wield it."

With a tug on his sleeve, Savus revealed his ten brands for the room. A shock rumbled through the crowd at his boldness as he displayed his forearm, brands gleaming.

"As you know, there are twelve magical marks the Fabric bestows upon witches from the Mesial Realm—binding, illusion, alteration, alchemy, enchantment, wandlore, divination, conjuring, healing, fire, terrestrial, and defensive—and as potential masters, you all possess five or more. You'll be divided into groups to train for each of your abilities, and the assessments will allow us to show us your mastery of your magic as a whole."

At this point, more master witches strode into the room, all wearing traditional red and black cloaks. The same brand flashed on the tops of their hands, identifying them as master witches.

"Here, at the Order," Savus continued, "some will die during the ascension assessments. Only a select few of you will survive and gain a place among us as master witches. The rest of you will be given honorable deaths. To die in the pursuit of magic is a death we should all hope for." His gaze landed on Esa. "Bow today," he declared.

"Rise tomorrow." The echoing words rose from the witches like a haunting melody.

A faint magic signature hit Imani as Esa's anger rose—not everyone agreed with First Witch Savus.

"If you survive"—Savus motioned to the crowd of apprentices—"you will receive magic only most can dream of, and we do not take this gift lightly. It's a lethal responsibility, and we demand you achieve specialized expertise in your branded abilities. We will challenge you to properly draw power from the Fabric that no other wielders can, and we'll start today. Your instructors will break you into groups now."

"This is sanctioned extermination and enslavement. The Crown will either kill us or force us to work for them," Esa said through gritted teeth, cracking her knuckles. "And no one here gives one shit about it."

A bout of nausea hit Imani at Esa's words. She'd suspected something suspicious about how all the apprentices had gathered, and she was starting to agree with her that it was with malicious intent.

CHAPTER 12

"*Did you use magic to fix this?*" *The man glared, snatching the cloak from her hands. "There are rumors about the elves who own this shop—nothing but trouble. You should be locked up with the other Order witches—too dangerous to have any magic around us," the customer sneered.*

She felt sick but stayed silent behind the counter.

"The other shop couldn't mend anything for another week. They've been so busy. I had no choice but to come here," he grumbled.

Tears welled in her eyes. "I promise you, sir, I barely used magic to mend your cloak. A simple enchantment spell is all." They needed the business, but more customers had been suspicious of the elves who owned the tailor and sewing shop.

"People are talking, saying you're hiding markings, and they've seen you perform master-level magic. This shop should be shut down." He grabbed her wrist painfully. "Show me your markings."

Crying out in pain, it was all she could do to stay calm.

Imani woke with a gasp. Tears ran down her face, and a bruise gleamed around her wrist. *Was it a dream?* Flashes like this happened more to her, even when she was awake. It was like she *was* Meira in them, and she was confident it had to do with the divination brand.

Imani wiped her eyes and tried to catch her breath, unable to shake the feeling her siblings were in trouble. Worse—she'd only received one letter from Dak and Meira to temper her concerns. They were supposedly doing well, but she was cut off from her family and missing them. Something wasn't right, despite the words on the paper.

A cramp in her stomach caused her to hunch over and grasp her side. This had also been happening more often—her hunger gnawed at her. Imani hadn't fed since her sister. She needed to feed soon, or these fever-like waking and sleeping dreams might intensify. Elves who starved themselves of affection and connection went insane. Feral.

Unable to sleep, she dressed slowly and trekked to the library. It was empty at such a late hour. The clock on the royal library wall chimed—it was well past midnight.

Imani scrubbed her hands down her face. The search for the Drasil remained at a frustrating standstill. Weeks of researching in the palace library had yielded nothing.

Massive stacks of books and parchment surrounded her like buildings in Stralas, and she could smell the old, musty papers and ink as she made her way to a table in the corner. It was marvelous, but she was too frustrated to appreciate it.

Confident she was alone at this hour, Imani laid out everything she had on the Drasil. First, she unrolled the map of Niflheim with the words *"Royal Vaults* and *South Chamber XII"* next to a circle around a structure in Kehomel, the capital of Niflheim. This was her most specific, profound clue about where a Drasil might be. It might be here in this chamber, in this vault, but if so, it was entirely out of her reach. She had no idea where these chambers were, and to go to Niflheim would be dangerous—a suicide mission without help. Help like Ara had had from the Niflheim royals, and help that had gotten her killed for working with them.

Going to Niflheim was out of the question. She needed to find another Drasil here in Essenheim.

Imani pulled out the scrap of paper with the list of wands and the words *"Royal Library. Manuscript 1148. Wand Efficacy of the Second Age"* scribbled underneath.

Nothing she dug through talked about the manuscript, and she hadn't found one hint of *A History of Royal Bloodlines* book or the Drasil, either.

Meira wanted Imani to focus on returning to their family, but the more she read and reread everything she had, the more Imani's mind fixated on the Drasil. Finding it—no, *possessing* it—was all she thought about most days. The idea of losing her magic choked her with fear. With her duties and choices never her own, magic was the one semblance of freedom she'd ever had in her whole life. If the Drasil could save magic and free her from her chains of responsibilities, she needed it.

She would find one even if it killed her.

Working for the Order for the rest of her life sounded like a death sentence. Meira would understand once Imani used the Drasil to repair the Fabric.

She sighed and let her forehead fall against the table, trying to think of anywhere else she could search tonight, but there was nothing.

At this point, Imani had read everything she could think of in meticulous detail, tried every combination, and grabbed any book looking remotely relevant. It was clear the manuscript and the book were located elsewhere.

There was one more place here in Stralas that possibly held the answer. Indeed, she had a gut instinct it did—the master witches' restricted library. If it didn't, she would find a way to the Draswood. Their library housed the most prolific history of wands in the realm, and despite being exiled, she would find a way.

This search wasn't over yet.

Standing up, she made her way toward the back, like she had every night recently, at the same time and place. The library's massive size meant weaving through a maze of shelves to the far corner.

Her mind buzzed with more possible workarounds as she made her way to the cordoned-off area of the library, almost too distracted to hear the whispers from between the stacks.

Once she did, she stopped, her heart pounding.

Imani hid among a row of manuscripts and peered through an opening. Her eyes widened, recognizing the heir apparent with Esa.

Esa glared up at Prince Tanyl, who shook his head while she unbuttoned his pants. He removed her hand, shaking his head once more.

Oh? They honestly thought they were alone. A sigh of relief escaped Imani's lips.

They weren't precisely arguing. Yet, judging by Tanyl's exasperated expression and Esa's defiantly lifted chin, they disagreed.

Imani narrowed her eyes. Esa hadn't exactly lied, but she knew Prince Tanyl far better than she had let on.

Imani strained to hear more.

"I told you. It was fun before, but I'm not interested in continuing," Tanyl said.

"What's changed?" Esa shot back.

A long, tense moment passed, but he didn't reply.

Esa let out a string of curses. "I can't trust the bastard with *anything*. He told you, didn't he?"

"Lore is a friend, and I'm not an idiot. I figured it out on my own. It's all too complicated now."

"It's not. He and I are nothing. And this"—Esa motioned between them—"doesn't have to be anything, either."

He grabbed her, towering over her diminutive pixie frame. His voice was a harsh whisper. "In case you haven't noticed, this place has become a tinder box. It's too risky to sleep with *anyone* right now. I can't. You shouldn't, either."

"I don't believe you. If not for *your friend*, we wouldn't even be having this conversation; we'd both be getting off, as we need."

"Don't be difficult. Accept my decision—"

"Can I take this to mean you've gone celibate? Ceased all dalliances and turned into some pious prince waiting for your *heartmate*?" she sneered.

"Please. Whores are one thing, but my relationships with other court females, even discreet ones, are done. Things have changed—*are* changing. I need to start thinking about my future, and so do you."

Scoffing, Esa shoved past him, heading toward another row of books. He crept after her, and their voices dropped to a mere murmur not even Imani could hear before ceasing altogether.

Seconds later, the door shut with a faint *click*, and Imani was alone again.

Unable to take the chance at getting caught, she waited five minutes. Then she crept closer to the master witches' section. Silence greeted her at every turn in the dim library, but she padded as softly as possible.

When she approached the door, it appeared ordinary, yet it was covered in thick, invisible magic, and a faint humming buzzed in her ears. Scanning the room, paranoid, she confirmed the library was deserted again.

She grabbed a pen from a collection of enchanted items in her bag. Most wards couldn't keep out inanimate objects. Dropping it as if on accident, it rolled into the ward.

The pen hit the invisible wall and shot back, air rippling and vibrating with the force of the shield. Holding back a frustrated growl, Imani tried five more times with multiple items. After half an hour, she gave up.

These wards were beyond her skillset to break. Like the ones around the city perimeter, they were a thick tranche of complicated spells layered upon each other so they couldn't be easily tricked or dismantled.

Grabbing everything she dropped and dumping it back in her bag, she turned to walk past the first row of books. Fine hairs on her neck stood up.

Imani stopped, glancing to her left. Her nostrils flared at the pixie staring her right in the face.

～

FOR SEVERAL SECONDS, the two simply watched each other. Imani didn't want to be the first one to speak. She wanted to know what Esa had seen.

After a moment, Esa finally broke the silence. "I'll get straight to the point. You tried to break the wards around the master library. I'm sure you know the penalty for even an *attempted* breach is steep. So, what are you searching for that's worth the risk?"

Imani deliberated. Esa had seen something she shouldn't have, but so had Imani.

She tilted her head to the side. "It was fascinating to see you with the prince, and my, what a little liar you were, acting like you didn't know him before. Lovers' quarrel?"

Running her hands absently over the books on a shelf, Esa stepped closer. "If you saw us, then you know we are nothing. So, go ahead and shout it from the rooftops. Besides, if sleeping with the heir apparent were as serious a crime as breaking the Crown's wards, they would hang half the city."

"It didn't sound like nothing. Are you in love with him?"

Esa chuckled. "Let's stay focused on the matter at hand. Not only will I keep your little illegal activities up here a secret, but I can get you into the library. For my help and my silence, I want two things from you in exchange."

"How can you get me in? Because you're sleeping with the heir?"

"How doesn't concern you." She drew herself up to her full height and stared at Imani, eye-to-eye. "I may not be in Tanyl's bed anymore, but I have his ear more than you. Are you interested, or do you want me to start blabbing?"

"I'm interested in your silence. What do you want?"

With a meandering gaze, Esa regarded her for a long time. "You're mediocre at physical magic in combat, so you lose a lot but hate losing. I can see the red in your eyes when you've had enough, and then you fight dirty—without magic. It's well-practiced street fighting, but street fighting, nonetheless. It's the only thing keeping you right in the middle of the pack—exactly where you want to be, from what I can tell."

"You're wrong," Imani lied. Truthfully, she *had* held back, trying to stay inconspicuous, but she didn't dare admit it to Esa. She didn't need more eyes on her.

A low laugh sounded from Esa. "Am I? You don't know much about pixies, do you? I immediately noticed you carry yourself like a low or common breed. I bet a low of some kind taught you, maybe even a hobgoblin."

Genuine surprise made Imani flustered. "Good guess. It was a hob."

"I knew it," Esa said with a nod.

Exposed, Imani crossed her arms.

Esa pressed on. "I'm going to be blunt—these new laws, all of us being brought here against our will and immediately forced into training for the assessments—you know *something* is wrong."

"I agree it's odd. But I'll be blunt, as well. I'm ignorant about politics, nor do I care. All I want is to pass the assessments and find a way to return to my siblings." A lie, but another necessary one.

The pixie tsked. "High-bred females in the capital with competitive magic are in a dangerous position. People like us are at the top of the execution list. The Crown will murder you and call it an accident before you return."

A pit formed in Imani's stomach. "Did something similar happen to your brother?"

"Don't speak about my brother here," she hissed, eyes blazing.

Imani backed off and held up her hands. "I'm sorry."

Esa smoothed out her hair. "You and I need allies, and help. I want to train with you."

Imani's heart skipped a beat.

Assessments occurred in the spring, in a little over a month. Despite adoring her studies with the master witches, especially wandlore with Master Selhey, her nerves danced on a knife's edge these days. There was so much to learn, and while she was progressing faster than anticipated, Meira's magic veered more toward utilitarian rather than combat. The assessments would assuredly require her to be more physical than her sister's magic allowed her to be.

"Why would you want to train with someone like me? I'm mediocre at magic."

"I'm blackmailing *you*, so *why* I'm doing it is irrelevant." Esa stared down her nose at Imani. "But everyone has some friends, even among enemies. Unlike elves, pixies have never been well regarded, and we don't have anywhere near the same loyalty as your kind or shifters. So, when I look around at my choice of allies here, there are few."

A memory surfaced from her last night in the Riverlands, when her sister begged her to make friends, and Meira's words whispered in her ears.

"Bare is the back of the friendless."

Imani gave Esa one nod to continue.

"You're intelligent and driven. You may be ill-trained and inexperienced, but you have undeniable potential to actually pass the assessments. And as much as you try to stay in the shadows, I'm not the only one noticing." She paused. "Do we have an accord?"

The silence gave Esa her answer. The training was a good idea, especially since Imani *did* want to survive the assessments. While she didn't plan on enlisting Esa's help with the wards, she'd agree to almost anything right now to ensure her business remained unnoticed by anyone else.

"Excellent," Esa said. "Now, I promise the second bargain will be easier for you to agree to."

Imani furrowed her brows.

A wicked smile spread across the pixie's face. "You'll come with me to the Neshuin New Year party."

"Only master witches and nobles get invites."

"You're a High-Norn elf, and even with the glamour dulling the typical luster of your kind, you've got your magic cunt. I mean, *really*? You're a fool if you're not using it to its full advantage."

Imani bristled. "I'm not having sex with anyone for you, Esa."

"You don't need to sleep with anyone for me … unless you want to, of course. I already have someone to go with, but his friend is dragging his feet. My date won't go without him." Her smile widened. "If I offer you up, I'm *sure* he'd be interested."

"You fought tooth and nail when summoned here to Stralas, and now you want to go to a party with everyone?" This didn't seem like an event Esa would be interested in, but again, Imani barely knew her.

"I don't like my choices taken from me, especially by my government," she said. "But if we're forced to be here, we might as well have a bit of fun." She fixed her eyes on Imani. "And I plan on having as much as possible while I still can." Esa paused. "Agreed?"

While Imani didn't like it, she had a soul draw for a reason. This could be the perfect solution to her hunger problem.

"Yes, agreed," Imani answered right away. "Do you want to make this binding?"

"Well, you'd have to cast it since I don't have a binding brand, so absolutely not, elf." Esa huffed a laugh.

It was true. Imani had the advantage in a binding deal without a third party to administer it.

"Fine. But if, at any point, you want to drag more favors from me, think again."

"Don't mistake this as a soft spot for you. Just because we're helping each other doesn't mean I trust you. You're up to something, and I don't particularly care what it is. Keep your head down, train with me, and come to the bloody party."

With those final words, Esa turned on her heel and disappeared around the corner, leaving Imani more hopeful than she had been in weeks.

CHAPTER 13

"We're late," Esa grumbled, increasing her steps as they strutted quickly down the hallway. Equally matched with each other, they'd lost track of time earlier, training nearly all afternoon inside Esa's suite.

"Late is perfect," Imani stated. "Let everyone look their fill when we enter." Diminutive females needed all the power they could get in this court of vipers, and Imani wanted to feed tonight. She had loosened her glamour, wanting attention. Half-starved, she needed to ensnare someone as a means to survive. Still, she assumed they would blend in with all the glitz and festivities.

She assumed wrong.

Groups of courtiers milled around, stealing glances while servants and other staff openly watched, too. Watched *her*. Their eyes fell on her delicately pointed ears and red velvet, form-fitting dress.

Esa and Imani were both curiosities. Imani should have known better, but such hunger tore through her insides that she deemed this worthy of the risk.

Even fixing her gaze straight ahead, she couldn't help but notice muted colors were the court's fashion this winter. Women wore boxy dresses, all in some drab shade. Unfortunately, they made elves look like corpses with their pale complexions. Unlike the shapeless fashion the courtiers wore, Imani's dress cut a crimson slash through the crowds and hugged every curve down her body. Meira had made all her dresses and, in Imani's opinion, had sent her to Stralas like a monarch.

Despite Esa's gown conforming to the current fashion, she was anything but drab. Pinned up flawlessly, her hair sparkled like a sapphire, and her violet eyes shone bright and big. But it was the wings drawing everyone into her orbit. Usually tucked tight against her back, the startling moth wings gifted to her particular breed of pixie—high sprites—were spread wide. They were stunning enough to be a topic of conversation on their own.

Imani pursed her lips at the scrutiny. The cautious thing to do after tonight would be to toss out all the dresses her sister had made for her and glamour her face more to blend in, but for the first time in years, she was free and now had magic to protect her. So, instead, she held her head high with every right to be there. Meira *was* a registered High-Norn elf, and Imani would wear her real face and the clothes her sister had made for her no matter how much they stared.

Trying to ignore the stares, Imani focused on the luxury around her. Everything they passed appeared gilded in gold or marble, and she gaped at the paintings, vases, rugs, and ornate sconces lighting the vast hallways.

The leering eyes thinned when they moved down a winding, carpeted staircase.

Downstairs, standing on the sumptuous black carpet, Imani allowed herself to gaze around the atrium. Her head tilted back as she took in the gleaming, glass-painted windows. Excited energy hummed around the room, which was already filled with guests enjoying drinks and aperitifs.

An usher announced the arrival of a high sentinel and her mate, then another, and another, until Imani wondered if she stood in a room with all nine of the high sentinels of the Essenheim Kingdom.

But only a few pixies stood around and no elves except Master Selhey, so it couldn't be true.

Power and prestige moved over her skin as if they seeped into the air she breathed. Anywhere she laid her eyes, money, money, money looked back at her. Females and males of all breeds mingled, smiling and laughing.

Longing to belong in this world of power and magic hit her. It was a frivolous desire, but at least, for one night, she would pretend she was in charge of her own choices and destiny.

Despite the smaller crowd downstairs, people's eyes widened, and some whispered amongst each other, making no secret they were gossiping about the unusual pair—an elf and a pixie. For a fleeting moment, insecurity rose inside her. But with one glance at Esa—all assured sexuality and confidence with her gorgeous blue hair and wings—Imani squared her shoulders and continued holding her head high as they strode toward their waiting group.

"Sideòs," Esa purred, kissing his cheek in greeting. "Let me introduce your date, Meira Aowyn."

Imani recognized him immediately as Tanyl's friend and guard who had helped collect the apprentices from around the kingdom. The black waistcoat and boots made the captain of the guard's dark hair more noticeable. The jacket he should be wearing was draped over his shoulder.

"Pleasure," Imani murmured in greeting, trying to hide her surprise at the high-ranking identity of her date.

When he took her hand and offered it a kiss, a vision overtook her senses but lasted only seconds.

Sideòs was on a battlefield. Chaos and confusion surrounded them as he backed himself into a tree, mouth bared in a snarl with his sword held high. A massive roar sounded, and a giant creature swiped its arm forward, ripping Sideòs's head from his body.

The sight dissipated, but Imani had to work to get her breathing under control. So horrified, she could barely meet his eyes.

"Meira? Are you all right?" He held her hand tighter.

Nodding, she took a few shallow breaths. "Yes, thank you, Sideòs."

"Please, call me Sid."

Esa turned back to Imani. "This is Aiden, whom I know is *dying* to meet you."

"The enigmatic elf witch, we meet at last." The shifter beside them raked his gaze down her, slow and deliberate, not caring how boldly his eyes took in her body. He gave her a lazy smile, but she thought his eyes held a note of suspicion. "I've been curious to meet the only witch to gain a private audience with the prince."

His death vision came on slower when he took her hand. A roar dulled the noise around her as Aiden came to mind.

He wrestled on the ground with someone, and a shocked expression took over his face before a massive bear of a man approached him.

"It was an accident. Things got out of hand, but—" Aiden sputtered as the larger male grinned and grabbed him by his throat with one hand.

"Thought you could get away with it, huh?"

Imani wanted to wince at the sound of bones crunching and flesh ripping.

Dead, his body hit the ground with a heavy thud, *a massive hole gaping in his chest. His heart followed, falling onto the dirt with a sickening* smack.

The vision faded, and the room grew into clear focus again. She remembered he'd asked her about her audience with Tanyl.

"Oh, it was nothing," she said with a dismissive wave. Attempting to redirect the conversation, Imani motioned to the woman beside Aiden. "And this is …? Your hair is perfect, by the way."

"Nida, my heartmate," Aiden said.

Even as he pressed the female shifter closer to his side, the desire for Imani sparked from him. While she wanted to be noticed tonight, he must've been a real bastard for her soul draw to affect him, despite being heart-mated. Such magic was supposed to be subdued after completing the heart-mating ritual.

A vicious urge to wrap her shadows around his throat and suffocate him slowly rushed through her. It took everything in her to resist as she forced a fake smile, knowing his death would be far, far worse.

"Lovely to meet you," Imani said with her teeth tight. She turned to Esa. "Where's your date?"

Grabbing a glass of wine as a server slid by, Esa rolled her eyes. "No idea. But, unfortunately, he'll probably be along soon," she muttered dryly. No love was lost between Esa and her date, whoever he was.

In a whoosh, the room hushed. Several of those already seated rose to stand out of respect.

The most influential female in the Mesial Realm breezed into the room.

Petite and unassuming, with delicate, fair features, an ideal representation of a high leimoniad nymph, Queen Dialora certainly didn't appear imposing. Imani barely detected a signature surrounding her body. Her power merely tickled Imani's skin, raising the hairs on her arms.

Dazed, Imani's eyes were locked onto the queen.

Small leaves and flowers fluttered from the branches on the crown growing from her head. Vines twisted intricately together with stems and roots. Alive and a part of Dialora, it constantly flowered. Buds and petals embedded themselves within her skull, protected by thorns. There was something familiar about it, but Imani had only seen it depicted in art over the years.

Its size and beauty surprised her. Yet, for all its power, the Crown of Life appeared understated and utterly seamless, a part of the queen's body as much as her arms and legs.

Imani often imagined how uncomfortable something so foreign and immovable must be for the queen. But, seeing it now, it didn't bother her more than her hair. Even if it did, the burden of the Crown would be a small price to pay for being queen, the most powerful female witch in the realm.

An air of reserved poise and magnetism remained even after the female nymph moved into the ballroom in a swirl of smiles and greetings with other nobles.

Voices picked back up in soft murmurs. Esa and Sid roped her back into another trivial conversation. Grabbing her drink, Imani offered a few comments while Esa lightly touched the captain of the guard's arm, laughing. Despite Sid being her date, Imani was anything but offended. Instead, she sipped the wine and enjoyed her friend's shameless flirting.

Imani lost herself in the moment, imagining she could be friends with these people. Had her sister been right? Ara's voice still echoed in her mind. So, Imani listened and observed rather than engage.

While flirting, Esa's attention subtly shot across the room every few seconds. Despite her warm smiles for the captain, she kept tabs on something—or someone—else.

Following Esa's gaze, Imani thought it was the heir apparent for a moment, who stood speaking with several master witches. But hawk-like eyes from the witch standing next to Prince Tanyl kept darting over to their group too many times to ignore.

Imani tilted her head to the side, recognizing the high sprite pixie who had sparred with the heir apparent on her first day at the palace.

The *male* sprite pixie. His name was Loren, if she remembered correctly.

Imani regarded him now with fresh eyes.

Physically, he was quite different from Esa. His broad shoulders and rugged looks made him strikingly attractive, unlike Esa's diminutive form and delicate features. Even in his perfectly tailored formal wear, he exuded the brutal aggressiveness sprites often possessed.

Leaning up to say something to Tanyl, Lore clapped him on the shoulder then promptly walked away. Weaving through the crowd, he strode forward with an intense yet alluring purpose.

Esa intercepted Lore with a hand on his chest, excusing herself at the perfect time. She didn't seem happy.

Everyone was oblivious to the two pixies. Only Imani had picked up the exchange.

"Lore," she greeted him coolly.

"Esadora." His response was clipped. Although no bigger than a male nymph, Lore's frame towered over Esa's petite one.

Her friend's back stiffened, ramrod straight, but she didn't shy away from his nearness. They stared at each other for a long minute, both tense, hackles raised, arrogance glowing in his eyes and a deadly look of contempt in Esa's.

Imani half-expected her friend to let out some biting remark, dismissing this presumptuous arse outright, sending him on his way. But, after an intake of breath, she speared him with daggered eyes, muttering something like, "What is your problem?" and grabbed his arm, pulling him away.

Imani's mouth gaped at the sight of the two pixies. Who was this man to Esa? Unlike her tryst with the prince, there was *nothing* casual about this relationship.

Prickles of awareness tingled down her spine.

Even while he conversed with others across the room, Tanyl watched her. For a horrifying second, she thought he was about to come over. She tightened her hold on her soul draw a bit, hoping to get a reprieve from the attention before dinner.

But it did nothing.

Irritated at his continued attention, she gave him a slight nod before returning to the captain.

～

The tension in the room set Imani's teeth on edge as they sat down to dinner. Her hunger kept growing, and not for food.

"Well, this should be an entertaining exercise in boldface lying for both the Order and the Crown," Esa said out of the corner of her mouth, careful to keep her expression pleasant as they sat down. "Bloody sycophants," she added as an afterthought, giving her date a vicious sidelong glance.

Loren ignored her entirely, his attention on two other female master witches.

"Isn't this night supposed to be a celebration?" Imani bit into a piece of warm bread as more than one courtier fidgeted in their chairs.

"This night is a bloody warning," Esa whispered. "Dialora and the Order have had a contentious relationship for years, but she's bringing it to a head with these new laws."

The queen pinned her gaze on Master Selhey, and every person at their table visibly leaned closer when she spoke.

"Fascinating article in the most recent Order publication. I commend your persistent efforts and passionate beliefs. Such an inspiration to stand up for what you believe in, despite being in the minority."

"I wasn't aware I was in the minority, Your Majesty. So many vehemently agree these anomalies could be reversible if we study them properly."

"We've studied them enough to know magic is the cause. We confirmed casting before every single recorded event." The queen's face was a frozen mask of frigid, ethereal beauty framed by billowing branches and flowers flowing like rippling water around her temples.

Master Selhey didn't relent. "Yes, but we don't have enough data. What if we restrict magic even more, yet the problems persist? With all due respect, my passion for this subject is unmatched, and there are few things for which the answers cannot be found, Your Majesty." He bowed his head slightly.

"There's sufficient evidence also to suggest this is simply an organic process. Natural phenomena."

"Natural phenomena? Does anyone seriously believe *that*?" Imani interjected.

Heat crept up her neck as everyone's attention shifted, including the queen's.

All at once, the queen's faint signature flared out in a spear of challenging power.

Imani's shadows whispered loudly in her head, demanding freedom, responding to the threat. She wrung her hands in her lap and swiveled her head around the room, biting back the urge to rip Dialora's entire soul from her signature. Her control hadn't been this unhinged in years.

It took considerable effort, but Imani tried to appear innocent. She was more like a disgusting insect next to a powerful, elegant bird compared to the queen.

A dangerous smile formed on Dialora's lips. "It's the position of the Crown *and* the First Witch that the Fabric instability theory is unreliable without more evidence. But the fact remains, we've let magic run unchecked for too long."

Tanyl took a sip of his drink. "The longer we wait, the lower the chances of fixing this decreases because we're losing magic faster than ever. Our witches' numbers are less than half what they were a century ago."

Imani's respect for Tanyl shot up.

"Coincidence," the queen said flatly, her eyes like cold stones. "We're all concerned that we haven't been blessed with as many branded, but who are we to question the gods of the Upper? This is their will."

As if they have anything to do with it, Imani thought bitterly. Worshipping the beings of the Under and Upper realms—supposedly inhabited by the mighty demon, angel, and deity breeds—was for uneducated fools. For all they knew, these other realms were destroyed when the doorways had been sealed. Besides, even if they did exist, they were probably filled with the same power-hungry people as here.

Yet, as Imani surveyed the others, an alarming number of nobles nodded their agreement. If such an insane religion was taking hold here in the capital, it did *not* bode well for witches, especially dwindling breeds like pixies and elves.

The tawny prince let three beats pass, ignoring his mother's glare. "Restrictions might treat the symptoms, but they're not a cure. It's our responsibility to find a way to fix it, not ignore it. Or it'll mean more loss of magic"—he gave his mother a grim smile—"and lives."

The queen's mouth thinned while she pierced her son with a severe expression, as if saying, *How dare you?*

Being the heir, Imani assumed he was comfortable defying her in public, but she got the sense he'd be paying for it later.

"The danger to our citizens is all that concerns me." Dialora paused. "Bow today."

"Rise tomorrow," the rest of the table murmured. The queen waved her hand dismissively, signaling the end of the discussion.

But Imani couldn't get it out of her head.

CHAPTER 14

*E*verything around them gleamed as the aristocracy ushered in a new year.

Enduring the party's meal made her sick, and her *other* hunger raged. In fact, Imani's arms shook, and her heart raced. None of which were good signs. She needed to feed soon and would find someone at this party to lure in.

She had no idea where Sid had wandered off to, so Imani lingered alone at the edge of the room, hiding from everyone.

Aiden and Nida danced together. With her arms up, Nida tipped her head back and shut her eyes, dancing as if she didn't care about the assessments or her bastard of a heartmate. The nymph synced perfectly with her heartmate, and moonlight from the windowed ceiling gleamed off her green gown. She was gorgeous. Why wasn't half of Stralas already in love with her?

A sense of being watched caused her to stiffen. With a quick sidelong glance over her shoulder, she stifled a groan.

Tanyl stood behind her, his face contemplative.

The last thing she needed was more of his attention on her, so she didn't say anything in response.

While she needed to feed, he was too suspicious of her, too smart. She couldn't be so intimate with him.

Imani knew little about Tanyl outside of his persona as Master Grey, which she learned while researching in the library was his middle name, and his rakish reputation. But tonight, a part of the contradicting rumors had come out. He stood on dangerous ground with his sovereign and defended magic. His fortitude to stand up against such ignorance from his powerful mother was something she couldn't take without snarling, but he'd argued with her like a king.

What lurked beneath the surface of the seemingly superficial, arrogant prince?

Maybe nothing. Maybe Tanyl was simply an incapable, spoiled child trying to sit at the adult table. None of it meant she was interested in answering more of his suspicious questions.

After letting him wait a moment, Imani faced him with her hands clutching the folds of her dress, unable to hide her skepticism at his actions. The weariness and weight lingered in his eyes, and he lifted his chin toward the stairs.

"*Come*," he mouthed silently.

Could she deny the heir apparent? Perhaps. But curiosity got the best of her.

He led her up the grand staircase to the railing overlooking the atrium without speaking. The second floor was dark and nearly empty of people compared to the crowd below.

A star vaulted across the sky when Imani leaned over the railing and tilted her head up. Explosions of light brightened overhead like stars shattering. The glass ceiling shone brighter and closer than any she'd seen before.

Unlike the destructive mess of lightning that erupted with the Fabric event, these eloquent, multicolored stars exploded, danced, and volleyed across the sky in beautiful, dream-like movements, captivating her.

Imani's breath lodged in her throat as the massive display kept bursting.

"You seem more interested in the show than dancing," he murmured. "And there's a much better view of the fireworks up here."

As if on cue, several more went off overhead.

Imani craned her neck more to gaze in wonder, with a flare of warmth filling her chest. Tanyl probably wanted to get her into bed, and only a fool would think otherwise, but the kindness still tugged at her a bit.

"Fireworks," she whispered to herself, committing the name to memory. "Shouldn't you be down there, basking in adoring attention? A bit scandalous for you to be seen up here with me alone."

"If anyone is receiving adoring attention tonight, it's the only female High-Norn elf in attendance." Desire painted his features as he stared, letting his eyes roam over her low-cut dress.

Imani could see her magic wrapping around him, like she'd planned. Without it, he'd likely be paying her no mind, but she couldn't find the energy to care.

"Your mother's attention was the opposite of adoring," she said, returning his gaze with her own perusal. Away from any audience, his face had a boyish charm she appreciated.

"I must confess"—he dropped his head closer to whisper in her ear—"I want to steal you from your date."

"He's your friend, no?"

"He is, but I find myself unable to stay away."

Hunger tore through her. She didn't care if he was the heir apparent—she wanted him.

But before Imani could respond, the entire floor trembled.

Stumbling, she braced herself against the railing.

The glass shattered overhead, sending shards raining down. Tanyl shouted for her to get down, and they both crouched, covering their heads.

The shaking rocked Imani down to her bones, but Tanyl shot up.

"Stay here," he shouted.

She would do no such thing. Imani made an incredulous face and scrambled up, running out to the terrace to try to follow him outside. The balcony went out over the grounds, and the wind whipped her hair as the destruction unfolded below with a chilling familiarity.

Esa and Sid rushed forward and stood beside her, open-mouthed and wide-eyed, while the entire palace and grounds rumbled.

Dozens more people joined them, and someone yelled as the ground in the gardens opened up, splitting into a great chasm.

A flash of light caught her attention below. The prince and two other master witches had crawled onto a fallen statue or fountain, now reduced to a pile of stone and rubble, with their wands pointed forward.

The movement and roiling of the ground continued to spread out before them across the gardens.

Glimmers of magic shot out of their wands like ropes, and attached themselves to the rocks. The ground responded to the magic. Dozens of ropes spread out, and Tanyl's neck cords tensed as he gripped his wand with two hands now. The magic tethers grew hot and glowed red, trying to stop the chasm from growing wider.

Tanyl cried out in pain when his wand overheated with the power, barely audible over the screams and rumblings. The other two masters were too absorbed in controlling their magic and couldn't stop.

She didn't think. Imani ran to the gardens despite people exclaiming that she should turn around.

When she got to the prince's side, miraculously, their surroundings stilled. An unearthly silence fell, but she could still hear his wand humming with magic. It could reverberate the spell back into his body if he were still holding onto an unstable wand.

She quickly surveyed the miniature canyon now cutting through the center of the gardens. The damage terrified her, but she swallowed it down.

Panting, she yelled at the prince, "Let go of the wand!"

Tanyl glared down at her.

"Now!" she screamed.

A line appeared between his brows, but he let the wand fall onto the crumbled marble floor like it burned him. It probably had.

Wandlore magic was her most substantial ability; maybe from natural talent, an inborn interest, or both. Master Selhey had taught her more about it in the past month than she'd learned her whole life, and she knew what to do. This was a spell she and Master Selhey had been working on constantly—how to adjust a wand's inner magic for optimum use and stability and how to stop it from casting magic entirely.

Whispering to Tanyl's wand, Imani dropped to her knees and took out her own, waving it over his. It was a Draswood and communicated back to her, telling her all about the magic within. The prince's magic murmured inside, a replica of his brands. Magic, like fingerprints, had its own signature in wands and around people's bodies.

Inside, elemental terrestrial magic flashed as the strongest, Tanyl's most potent abilities. Binding and alteration magic vibrated oddly underneath, the flaring heat telling her the wand hadn't been configured correctly to wield that power. Deeper, enchantment, illusion, and defensive magic swirled together—all normal. Alteration simmered faintly close to the core. It flickered in and out. How could Tanyl even wield such magic?

Imani used her power, channeled through her wand, to force the layers inside to meld with another spell, calming them into an ember of muted power. The boundaries of the wand cracked still, struggling to pull magic from the Fabric to fight the Fabric. It didn't want to attack itself but was trying to all the same.

So strange.

She whispered more spells, coalescing the magic further into a dying ember.

Her hand trembled, but the wand was cool when she picked it up. Standing, she carefully handed it to Tanyl.

People wandered around in the background, pointing and some crying. Imani barely registered any of it as she regarded the heir apparent. Tanyl's eyes were wild, and his chest still heaved. Dirt and sweat covered his dark gold hair as he pushed it back off his face.

"What did you do to it?" His voice was accusatory.

"Weakened the magic into fewer layers so it won't reverberate your own magic back at you, which, as I'm sure you know, would be your end. Your wand's magic wasn't properly imbued into the wood. The layers were all uneven, and some barely attached to the core. It's too dangerous to cast anything. It won't work for you until you have a master reconfigure them—"

"That could take weeks," he muttered.

"Actually, it could take *months*," she snapped. "It might never wield complicated magic again."

He studied her cautiously. "Why is your face so bloody?"

Confused, Imani lifted her hand to her temple. It was sticky with blood, but it didn't hurt.

She didn't let him change the subject. "How did you break through the wards with your wand? It wasn't configured properly to handle such intense alteration magic."

"Your concern is noted, but it wasn't intense." Toying with his wand, he sounded casual, yet a flicker of defensiveness swept over his eyes. "Quite the little know-it-all with magic, aren't you?"

"When it comes to wand magic? Yes, I am."

"You don't know as much as you think you do because it wasn't alteration magic. Although alteration would work, too," he said, slipping his wand back into his pocket. "It was a shockwave enchantment spell. I used it to strain the barrier and cast gravitational terrestrial magic to create a hole in the weak spot."

A thrill raced through her. If alteration worked, too, then Imani had all those abilities. Which meant she might be able to break down the powerful master level wards.

Off to the side, Sid shouted for the prince.

Tanyl tousled his hair, bits of dirt and glass falling free. "Go back to your room, little elf. I'm needed elsewhere."

Clenching her jaw, she let him walk away without arguing further. *Ungrateful, spoiled prince.*

It also didn't pass her notice that he had lied to her. He *had* used alteration magic with his wand when he had gone to retrieve Esa and tied invisible ropes around her.

What was Prince Tanyl hiding?

CHAPTER 15

The main room of the master library was empty hours before midnight when Imani finally entered.

Few people ventured out at night anymore, and since the ground quake a week ago, a subdued perturbation had permeated the usually vibrant halls of the palace. It was a Fabric event, but no one said it out loud, and the queen used it as an excuse to pass new laws.

Tanyl's wand concerned her, too. Abilities evolved, and the Fabric branded more to witches over time, but something about the configuration bothered her. He had to be lying. His wand had performed alteration magic, yet the power inside the layers was wrong. It was as if some magic had been added later, which would be odd unless he was given more magical abilities after coming of age. But none were correctly done, and as a prince, he would have the best wandmakers adjusting his wand.

Then there was the binding ability she'd detected. His wand had barely noticeable binding magic inside—a light layer, at most. Not enough to cast binding spells.

The wand was performing magic Tanyl didn't possess; magic added to its initial configuration. But why would he risk such a thing?

Wielding magic a witch didn't possess a matching brand for always ended in death. The wand might trick the Fabric for a while, but to take from it when the witch didn't have the Fabric-given ability went against the laws of nature and would eventually end in a reverberation, likely killing the witch.

She bit her lip in confusion but shook away the thoughts. An arrogant prince playing with magic he didn't understand wasn't her problem.

Pushing Tanyl aside, she slipped into the back recesses of the library, making her way to the staircase leading to the higher floors. The walk always felt long when she tried to remain unseen.

Eventually, she stood staring up at the restricted library door above. Lifting her steady hands, she worked the spell she'd created earlier. Energy thrummed through her palms and wand. Imani would go soliciting help from Esa if this didn't work, but only then.

Streaks of bright magic from her shockwave enchantment cracked through the transparent wall surrounding the door. In the center, a tiny hole buzzed with energy, straining the barrier.

With her arm outstretched, she wasted no time attacking the weak spot. But gravitational alteration proved vastly more complicated. The muscles in her forearm strained. For a terrifying moment, she thought her bones might break. Gripping it with her other hand, she reinforced the pull and hissed in pain.

The overtaxed ward glowed and crumbled further until the hole was large enough. Putting her wand in her mouth, she dropped to her knees and crawled through it. Inside the breach, the magic sensed an intrusion. Agitated sparks burned her skin, and the air was thick like syrup. She hoped the caster couldn't feel her enter either. Depending on how the wards were set up, they might be able to. It was also possible they had been in place so long that the witch or witches who had cast the spell were far from the capital.

She was willing to take a risk, and the wards let her pass.

Pushing herself up, she leaned against the wall. The only sounds were her labored breaths. Sweat covered her face, but she shoved loose strands of hair away and tried to keep calm. Imani couldn't stop, and she couldn't panic.

Cracking her neck, she took a deep breath. Then she strode to the shelves like she belonged, frantically perusing everything.

While organized in a simple alphabetical order, the languages and dialects made identifying the material more difficult. Imani didn't understand any older languages beyond their common tongue.

An excessive amount of time passed. Imani's frustration grew, and she cursed her general lack of language skills and education. Ara hadn't let Imani attend much school, like Dak and Meira had.

The room warmed the longer she searched.

She would only have this one possible chance. Once the Order learned someone breached the wards, they'd shore up defenses again.

One, old, tattered book caught her eye. The word *sangris*, an Elvish word for *blood*, stood out. She carefully pulled it so the book stuck out further on the shelf and tried to decipher its full title. It was in bad shape, yet this could be something.

Her breath hitched. She opened the inside of her cloak to drop it inside, but a second later, the glass entrance door shattered.

Smoke filled the entire room. A spell ripped apart her own magic. Her wand slipped from her hand as she glanced down at her now visible body.

"There she is," the guard said, wand pointed at her. He turned to another master witch next to him. "Grab her wand and check the upper levels. Ensure everything is intact."

His smile was the last thing she remembered before everything darkened.

~

SILVER HAIR FELL in a curtain around her as she tried to lift her head. Everything hurt.

A ticking clock was the only sound in the room. It moved past two in the morning, and she shivered a bit. No fire burned in the hearth. Faint light shone from two chandeliers.

Her vision sharpened, and she found herself in a lavish room. It was far more elaborate than her own and, luckily, not a jail cell, as expected. Still, nothing about this situation boded well for her.

Imani turned her head around the room three more times.

Escape wasn't possible. They had tied her hands and feet with tight ligatures to a chair. Her wand had disappeared. Her best option was probably talking her way out, but she had no idea who'd caught her. If she did, she might be able to find a quid pro quo to help her out of this predicament.

The creaking of a door opening made her jump, and then the heir apparent walked into the room.

Imani fought a grin. *This* she could work with.

Despite tallying several intriguing traits from the prince, including powerful magic, handsomeness, and shrewdness for court politics, the prince still lacked the stomach for certain things, and she didn't perceive him as particularly manipulative. He was somewhat kind underneath the arrogance. His kindness and honesty were weaknesses for her to exploit, or at least try to.

He wore a perfectly fitted shirt and waistcoat with a dark formal jacket. His hair fell against his forehead, a bit messy, and he smelled like smoke and other magic. Imani guessed he'd been gambling and whoring and had come straight from Kesen Street.

Her heart rate increased with hunger pangs. Had he been with a female? She gripped the restraints and kept her face neutral while imagining it.

Taking off his jacket, he placed it on the back of a chair before calmly turning back to her. He continued remaining silent, taking his time.

Imani's muscles tensed while she tried to lessen her shivering. He narrowed his eyes at her and, using the kindling in the hearth, enchanted them to light a fire. Warmth filled the room, proving her assessment of his gentlemanly sensibilities correct.

But she stayed quiet. She wanted to get Tanyl talking and give herself as much time to formulate a plan.

He rolled up his sleeves and ran a hand through his hair, raising his brows in arrogance. "My, my, my, isn't this a surprise? The pretty little Norn elf caught red-handed. I guessed it was you when my guards reported a breach."

Imani blinked at him. What did Tanyl want? What could she give him to sway him?

"Do you know the punishment for stealing from the Order?"

Silence.

"Death. Execution," Tanyl confirmed.

"Good thing I didn't steal anything then," she said coolly.

"While it's true you were caught before you could steal the book, breaking a ward of the Crown and the Order is no minor crime," he added.

"Tanyl," she purred, "I made a silly mistake. Surely, you don't want to punish a young witch so harshly. There must be *something* we can work out together."

His eyes went glassy at her magic subtly drawing him in. "Really? What are you offering?"

Imani paused, debating her offer—a risk—but she wanted to go for it.

"My wandlore magic, it's a rare ability. Outside of storming into the Draswood, which we both know is impossible, you only have one master witch here who can perform it."

"Impossible? I can enter any one of Essenheim's territories—they belong to the Crown."

Imani let her head fall back and laughed. "Walking uninvited into the Draswood? Demanding magic from the Norn elves' master witches? Gods, Ellisar would be furious." She let her smile fall. "Go ahead. I dare you."

He paced and studied her surreptitiously.

She tilted her head to the side. "Hmm. You don't have many options for repairing your wand."

He crossed his arms but still didn't respond. Imani almost smiled again.

"Furthermore," she pressed, "your wand is irregular—someone tampered with it. Maybe experimented. I'm not entirely sure. But I wager discretion is of the utmost importance to you. Which is why you haven't sought out Master Selhey." If that had been the case, Imani would have been called to assist him in a lesson.

A glint flashed in his eyes. The look alone told Imani she'd nailed it.

"Tell me. How are you so qualified in wandlore? You might know a bit about it, but you're untrained. You said it yourself—you're only a young witch."

"Only a fraction of Norn elves can practice true wand magic, and I happen to be a high breed who grew up living and breathing it. My entire family was expert wand workers—ask Master Selhey. Later, even when we lived outside the Draswood, I practiced. I read everything I could on it and studied independently," she explained, embellishing a bit. "I might be young, but if anyone can help you fix your wand quickly and quietly, it's me."

He stayed silent, weighing her words.

She wanted to snarl at his stalling and proximity when he kneeled in front of her. Instead, she bit her tongue. His pupils were large, as if he weren't quite clearheaded, either from her magic or something else.

"Who are you feeding from here?"

"None of your business," she bit out.

"It wasn't before, but now, it seems it is."

She narrowed her eyes. Of the two options she had at her disposal, she should have known sex would trump magic, especially when she'd let her feeding draw wrap around him earlier.

"No one," she said tightly, hunger rearing its ugly head.

The prince smoothed back her hair. "Even with such a hideous mark disfiguring you, you're a mesmerizing elf," he murmured.

Gritting her teeth, she allowed his intrusive touch without protest.

After a moment, he stood, clasping his hands behind his back. "Lady Aowyn, I will allow you to remain here and forgive your crime. As such, only three people are aware of it, including me. The other two are part of my private royal guard. It will be our secret."

"How magnanimous. What do you want in return?" she sneered. Imani guessed what it would be, and truthfully, the price was fine for her. Sex in exchange for getting away with this crime? She'd agree to that deal any day.

"Your wandlore magic was an appealing offer, but I want your help with something else ... besides repairing my wand."

Imani hid her surprise. Enlisting her help with the wand had always been the more intelligent and respectable choice for her over whoring herself out. Her admiration for Tanyl increased.

He crossed the room and picked up the book she'd attempted to steal from a table. His slate eyes danced with excitement as he dropped it in her lap. With a wave, the restraints lifted, and she rubbed her wrists, eyeing him warily.

"*A History of Royal Bloodlines* is ancient—a rare and mostly dull book written in Elvish. I think the pages you will be most fascinated by are halfway through in the section on doorways. At least, those were the ones I found interesting."

Imani lightly traced her fingers over the ragged cover. "How can you be sure this is even the book I sought? Maybe I pulled this out only to find it was wrong."

"You didn't pull out any others, and why would you? You're searching for a Drasil wand. This is the only book in the entire library mentioning it."

CHAPTER 16

It took considerable effort to mask her sheer terror and shock at his words.

"How could you possibly know such a thing?" Her voice was barely a whisper.

He kneeled again and handed her back Ara's wand. "I'm searching for it, too."

A storm of butterflies exploded in her stomach. She met and held his gaze, grasping the Draswood tightly. "Why would a prince—the heir apparent—waste his time?"

"Besides the obvious fact that it would be the most powerful wand in the world?"

"Besides that."

He sighed. "My mother. You already know her views on magic are growing more radical, all while magic disappears as the Fabric grows more unstable. Instead of protecting and increasing our magic, she wants to kill two birds with one stone by pooling all magical power with a select few."

"It's why she continues eroding the Order's power," Imani said.

"Yes. Fewer magic wielders, less instability is my mother's public reasoning. But it also means she can severely limit competition for the next monarch."

"How convenient it also happens to give her vast powers over everyone then," Imani said. "Where do you stand regarding your mother's plan?"

"Controlling and restricting magic the way she wants will be disastrous for the kingdom." He tightened his hand over hers. "I want to save it and build up our magical forces, not reduce them."

Imani turned over this information and the deal he offered her. For all his passionate idealism, Tanyl knew what he was doing—because whoever controlled magic and the Drasil? They held the doorways, and whoever controlled those ruled the realm.

Imani wanted the power for herself.

He searched her face while she sat thinking. "Why would a little elf be searching for it?"

She let out a calming breath, stalling to think of a lie. Searching for the Drasil had gotten her grandmother executed, and Imani needed to distance herself from Aralana in Stralas.

"I came across it in my research on slips and doorways. My parents died in a Fabric event, and I've been researching it for years." She shrugged. "And you said it before—it would be the most powerful wand in the world. I want that power."

"To be clear, you would give up the power to me. But, from what I've read, only a monarch will be powerful enough to wield the Drasil, anyway. What have you learned about where one might be located?"

Wands didn't work like that, so he was testing her. Or he didn't know much about it. She kept her mouth shut.

"I don't have a location yet," she confessed. "My strategy is focused on learning about its uses and history in hopes the information reveals some hint about who might still possess one or where one disappeared."

"I agree. You're smart." His eyes sparkled with a secret.

"Stop being coy. What do you know about a potential location? If you don't tell me, then there's no agreement. Put me in jail or execute me. You can search on your own."

"Calm down, elf witch." He stood with his palms facing her in placation. "I've read the book a dozen times, and the only mention of the Drasil is during the Norn chapters."

Imani didn't quite believe that was all the book had to offer. Malis had been quite adamant he wanted it for the information on slips and doorways, but she stayed mum.

Tanyl continued, "One part detailed how the Norn used wands to eradicate a disease killing the Draswood trees. Being elves, they tried hundreds of wands, each with varying degrees of success, so there were many details to review. As a result, I didn't think much of the excerpt."

"Don't tell me they used a Drasil to heal the trees," Imani murmured, remembering the scrap of paper she found listing the "tests" and the names of wands.

"If it were so easy, I would've entered the Draswood already," he scoffed. "They did list a handful of wands they did *not* try. But tucked away in *that* list, under a group of what they termed 'alternative' wands—"

"Wands not made from Draswood trees," Imani finished for him, her mind reeling. She knew exactly what list he was referring to, but again, kept that information to herself.

"Precisely. There were several types of wands listed. In addition to the Draswoods, there were several goldwood wands, a few bone ones located in various territories of the realm, and one Yggdrasil wand, which had the word 'Nereids' next to it."

Imani stiffened. He must have had more of the list than her scraps of paper—all those wands were on it and more. They had to be related.

"What does 'Nereids' mean?"

"I don't know. It's not a word in the common tongue or any current elvish dialect. It's probably a thousand years old, or older. Likely a dead language, as well." His eyes were earnest and hopeful, but the weight of disappointment crushed her.

While learning the Drasil's full name—an Yggdrasil—was interesting, it was practically *nothing* compared to what she had. She'd been coming up empty-handed here, even in Stralas, and while it didn't mean there wasn't information to be found here, especially in the royal vaults, the dozens of maps of Niflheim combined with Ara's fragmented notes gave her a better lead. If she could somehow get to the Niflheim Kingdom, explore their library, and speak with the other wand-making elves there, Imani could piece more clues together and learn more, maybe even find a Drasil.

Despite the kind heart that she could sense from him, could she trust Tanyl with this knowledge? It was a desperate hope. She badly wanted a confidant in this search, yet she had to be smart about what details she revealed and when.

"These wands were made maybe ten thousand years ago. The fact someone mentioned it even a thousand ago is a miracle," Imani said. "If we can learn what the word means, we might have a solid lead."

"I casually asked Master Selhey if he was aware of any other wand materials, including the Yggdrasil. But, even as a wandlore expert, he knew nothing about it and assumed it was inferior to Draswoods, like all alternative wands. Since it wasn't part of their history, I wondered if Norn elves could even adjust a Drasil."

He was incorrect. "Any breed with a wandlore brand can adjust any wand, likely even a Drasil." Imani fidgeted, curious as to what he was keeping from her. She was keeping quite a bit from him, too.

A beat of silence passed as Imani considered her words. "Over the years, I've read everything the Norn have written about wandlore, and my family was expert wandmakers. I'm nearly certain Norn elves had nothing to do with creating these wands. Whoever did simply has the same wandlore magic."

"Yes, it is odd only one Essenheim breed possesses the brand today. It stands to reason many more used to practice the craft."

"Indeed. It's also possible the Drasil trees—these Yggdrasils—don't grow in Essenheim or even this realm."

"If we were to find a Drasil wand, could you ensure it worked properly for me?"

He already knew the answer.

She let out a deep breath. "Anyone with wandlore magic would be able to study the Drasil. Norn elves never use the other materials you mentioned, like goldwood, as they're vastly inferior to the Draswood, yet they can still make them. I assume an Yggdrasil is a more powerful tree from which to create a wand than all those materials."

He put his hand over his mouth, thinking.

"How did you learn about any of this?" she asked, hoping to steer the conversation away from wandlore.

"A children's story my mother told me when I was young," he said, "about a lost city under Menlone Mountain."

"Menlone. Where Niflheim's capital city Kehomel sits?" Imani asked, her heart beating wildly at the mention of the Niflheim Kingdom. What did he know about the Drasil being there?

"Yes, the old city of Zorah was there when Niflheim and Essenheim were still united as one kingdom with a king and queen. It was famed for its beauty, and travelers from all the realms made it their home. However, a great war broke out—"

"Between Essenheim and Niflheim?"

"No, this was thousands of years before the War of the Middle Kingdoms."

"You're talking about the Great Realm War."

Tanyl nodded. "When the Upper gods won and ended it, they sealed the doorways as punishment to the Under and Mesial realms. Time passed, and with people living in peace, they had no use for Drasil wands. My theory is that most disappeared over time. Now only monarchs can manipulate the slips, and the doorways are … unusable."

"But what does this have to do with Kehomel?"

"They say the first recorded Fabric event was when the original city of Zorah went into the depths of Menlone Mountain during a ground quake. They rebuilt the Court of Darkness on top of it."

"Didn't the ground quake destroy the buildings?"

"Oddly enough, they say it miraculously sank into the mountain, simply making it impassable and impenetrable. With the mountain as protection, if anyone were to find it, it would be as beautiful and untouched as before. So many foolish explorers have tried, but none have lived to tell if they found it. But it's only a children's story to teach a lesson about greed." He crossed his arms. "We have a better chance of finding a Drasil here in our kingdom than chasing after legends in others."

Imani had a lot to consider. She met his gaze head-on. "What exactly are the terms of this deal you want with me?"

"We're going to do a binding using your ability. In exchange for the pardon of your crime, you'll agree to help me find the Drasil. We'll search for it, research it, and if you find it, you'll hand it over to Essenheim—"

"You mean to hand it over to *you*," she clarified.

"Yes, to me. And I'll need you to fix my other wand."

Enter a binding and agree to give up the Drasil to him? This would be a considerable sacrifice, and Imani couldn't lie to herself—*she* wanted the Drasil.

But Tanyl's lack of knowledge about wandlore remained an advantage for her. Imani knew more about the Drasil from Aralana's research, and she likely understood its capabilities far better.

Imani fought a grin, realizing this binding would be meaningless. Tanyl would never even hold the wand unless he found one first. Like how powerful master witches could sense and remove magic cast by lesser magic wielders, the Drasil would overpower weaker magic, even a binding. It would be the most powerful magical object in the realm.

Moreover, he never mentioned her agreeing to modify the Drasil for him. Maybe he assumed handing it over to him meant she'd also configure it for him. He thought wrong. He'd never be able to use it properly without his magic trying to destroy him unless he specifically stated she was to modify it—which she, of course, wouldn't do.

He might ask another elf for help, but the chances were slim. Something like the Drasil, he couldn't entrust to simply anyone.

Imani would modify it so that it only worked with her magic.

Another example of the world's ignorance concerning her kind—Norn elves were notoriously tricky regarding bindings.

Agreeing too quickly might tip him off, and Imani hesitated to push her luck. But the pull to ask was too irresistible. "Between fixing your current wand and searching and handing over the Drasil, you're asking for a lot. I want something else."

He waited for her to continue.

She cleared her throat. "I'm a strong witch. I'll pass the assessments. I'll work for the Order, but when you're king, I want to be named the First Witch." Her aspirations went much higher, but it would be unwise to overplay her hand now. Tanyl might be a spoiled prince now, but she surmised he would be a good, noble king when the time came. However, unlike his mother, he would never prevail at cunning schemes or ruthless decisions.

Imani would happily play the role for him as his chosen mate and queen consort, but she wasn't going to press her hand on it yet. She'd settle for the First Witch for now.

The prince didn't hesitate. "Done."

~

"What are you staring at? It's over."

Tanyl said nothing. His massive pupils bore into her as she struggled to sit up. The euphoric, disorienting effects of magic were still potent.

"I can't stop thinking about you."

"How unfortunate," she said while trying to get control of the dizziness.

"It's devastating."

"You'll get over it." She winced, trying to wipe off the dried blood from her hands, marveling at how Tanyl had demanded a flesh-magic binding.

"Doubtful. You don't want to know how many people I've slept with to get you out of my head, imagining they're you."

"Very sorry for your situation, Tanyl. Truly abhorrent how much sex you've had to have in my name." A wave of dizziness forced her to lie down again.

The high of the flesh magic coursing through her, and the accompanying waves of hunger, were hard to ignore.

"Meira," he breathed, brushing her hair off her face. "I've met only a few female Norn elves before, but you are different."

His scent wasn't arousing to her. It was consuming.

Hunger shot through her. She wanted to devour him.

She shifted onto her side and shuddered at the force it took to stop.

"Meira." A dreamy smile tugged at his mouth, somehow making

him younger but more handsome. He propped his chin on his arms. "You're magnificent."

Could she open herself up to him? Feeding relaxed elves reduced their inhibition and made them feel safe and close to their prey. She had so much to hide. What if she accidentally corrected him and called herself Imani? She had always planned to pick someone safer, more inconspicuous, less suspicious of her.

Her magic was working hard on him.

Invisible bugs crawled over her skin, sensing the soul draw pulling him in and taking hold. Before her magic, the sensation would have meant she was in danger. This meant the prey was ready to be ensnared.

She wasn't afraid, merely entranced at how his eyes glazed over with unnatural desire. She stared directly into them and used her illusion magic to temper the draw a little to lull him into a calmer yet still malleable state. She was in his head.

"You want to sleep with me." Her eyes locked onto his, voice sounding lilting and soft. It was a demand as he was under her spell, and he'd say yes.

"Yes," he breathed. "But I should stay away from you. I can't get tangled up with another female at court, not with my mother watching," Tanyl said in a quiet voice, moving closer, their heads almost touching. He moved his mouth closer to hers and continued stroking her hair. "But when you remove your glamour for me, even with the marking on your face, you are quite literally the most beautiful female I've ever seen." He ran a finger down where the scarring was invisible.

Her first instinct was to jerk away, but a tiny, screaming part of her also wanted to lean in. Was she attracted to the prince? Or was she simply starving? She hardly knew anymore.

She was too greedy to worry about any of those questions or explain to Tanyl how his desires weren't natural. Her magic had trapped him with a trick to get what she needed to survive.

He probably wouldn't even care, making it even worse when she grabbed him and crushed her mouth to his.

CHAPTER 17

Imani paced alone in Tanyl's rooms, peering at the clock every few minutes. It was unusual for him to keep her waiting this long.

Feeding from the heir these past few weeks had made her normal again, despite the grueling training they put the apprentices through. It had put her in an amiable mood to confide in him, which she did on many subjects about magic. Unlike her sister, Tanyl could talk about magic for hours, and while he was more educated than Imani, she could keep up. They might have even been friends in a way, especially when they teamed up to research the Drasil, though they were no closer to finding it. Imani's best lead was still to travel to Niflheim.

Being true friends out in the open was impossible since Tanyl hid her from everyone, keeping their dalliance a secret from the court and her to himself. Being a secret and a dalliance were both fine—she didn't need any more attention on her.

His apartment exuded relaxation and quiet, but something in the air increased her unease. Usually, she'd take this opportunity to snoop, but servants bustled around in the other rooms.

Voices murmuring in the hallway caught her attention.

She crept closer. Easier for an elf, Imani much preferred eavesdropping over snooping regarding secrets, especially since she was already likely in the silencing charm Tanyl had placed on his rooms, which meant she could listen without detection.

"An argument with my mother about a precarious situation with our navy kept me," Tanyl said, sounding bitter.

Confused, Imani bit her lip. She hadn't known Essenheim had a navy.

"The enemy gutted our reinforcements. Less than half returned. Fighting the Lochheim breeds decimated us, even with the extra leonines we sent."

Lochheim? Imani only knew of the Essenheim and Niflheim breeds. Were they from another realm? She made a note to research these new breeds in the library.

With a silent gasp, an unbidden image of Meira running from something came into view. Imani grabbed the wall for support. Someone yelled, but Imani didn't understand, and her sister tripped and cried out. Imani placed a hand on her temple, gritting her teeth and willing the vision to stop.

The divination brand was a menace. Lately, they had come on more frequently when she was awake. Flashes of strange places with Meira and Dak, or only Meira—places she never recalled ever being. It was never clear enough to understand full conversations—only snippets—yet she felt the heat of the fire and smelled the laundry, which convinced her something about the visions was real.

A heaviness had settled on Imani's shoulders recently, as though someone always pushed her down. She couldn't shake the feeling that something terrible might happen.

Eventually, the vision dulled, and Tanyl's voice grew louder as her head cleared.

"We have double the number of high sentinels they do, and we're more powerful with a monarch on our side. But we can't take any more breaches. The border skirmish out on the Neshuin Sea was the worst yet. My mother sealed the slip, but it's only a matter of time before it becomes a rift."

Slips usually happened during Fabric events and led to uncontrolled breaches in the Fabric that split open the world, making it possible to enter either the Upper or the Under realms. Slips were dangerous and volatile, unlike doorways, which were stable, safe portals into the other realms. After witnessing one herself, Imani'd had no idea they could be sealed, but she supposed it made sense; otherwise, creatures from the other realms would be entering theirs.

"We're getting concerning news from the outer territories, too. Unfortunately, more seals are weakened, and we discovered a handful of new slips across the kingdom. Whatever is happening in these other realms means these other creatures desperately want to make this their new home," Sid said.

Her heart beat faster. So, other realms were trying to enter theirs? With the doorways closed for ten thousand years, these slips would be the only way.

Ara had been right about the creatures slinking around the openings.

"We need more armed forces."

"From where? The number of branded declines every year. You know this, Sid."

"Then tell your mother—"

"You think she listens to me? Essenheim has always depended more on witches to defend us over brute strength, but now, she'd prefer to exterminate the wielders in favor of selling us out for alliances elsewhere. Anything to protect her power."

Alliances elsewhere? Where?

They fell silent. Imani waited.

"Our position grows more precarious by the day. The Illithianas' activity around our southern borders also concerns me," Sid muttered. "Our days of peace between them are numbered."

"Tell it to my mother. She and I only recently agreed on a plan to buy us time. Although it's certainly not why she acquiesced to a deal regarding the treaty."

The captain sighed. "You know it will weaken our position against them in the short term. So, how did you get her to agree?"

"My relationship with my mother is complicated. But the Niflheim Kingdom's breeds are far more aggressive, far more lethal than ours, and they have a standing army that would bring us to our knees right now with our forces split at sea. I need more time."

"Who are they sending? Will the king come?"

Tanyl let out a low laugh. "You remember the last time Dialora and Magnus breathed the same air?"

"I remember them fucking for a day straight," Sid replied.

"Well, that ... and they nearly killed each other."

"Right. A bloody mess." Sid paused. "If the heartmate theory is true, we need to focus on finding yours. Dialora has been deteriorating for a year now."

"Nonsense. An unproven theory at best. *When* I become king, I won't go mad without my heartmate. Dialora could rule for the rest of her life, another hundred years. Magnus would live even longer as a shifter."

Something tugged at her chest, hearing about Tanyl finding his heartmate. Imani would be out of the picture if that happened.

Her hand curled into a fist as the image of her strangling a faceless woman surfaced in her mind. Taken aback by her own violent imagination, Imani pushed the image away, shaking her head. Yet, the feeling lingered.

How far would she go to become queen consort? She wasn't sure, especially since she'd killed her own heartmate without remorse.

Imani couldn't wrap her mind around the king and queen in the same room, either. No monarch of Essenheim or Niflheim had spoken in a thousand years, not since the treaty had been signed. Imani surmised the Crown likely had backchannel contact with the Throne, but the citizens had no such knowledge.

"I hope you know what you're doing."

A long, painful pause stretched between everyone.

"I do," Tanyl eventually said.

"Good. Because if we're fighting at both borders, Essenheim will fall," Sid said.

A shiver ran down her spine.

"I would *never* let such a thing happen," Tanyl returned, incensed.

After a long pause, the main door to the hallway opened then closed. She moved to the chair, knowing Tanyl might enter at any moment.

The door opened, but the prince barely acknowledged her. He

undressed and tugged his jacket off with a loud sigh. A tense silence cut through the air.

With a slow approach, Imani stood in front of him. "What kept you?" she asked casually.

In an instant, his expression softened. He brushed the hair off her face. "Court business. Difficulties with my mother."

Even at his most irate, Tanyl couldn't hold onto his anger. He was far too idealistic and kind. In some ways, she understood why the queen thought him too weak to be king. That, and he was far too handsome.

She ran her hands through his hair then down his broad chest. "I can help you forget for a bit," she murmured, undoing his pants and kneeling.

His gaze flashed to her with heat. "You're a goddess," he moaned, lowering his head as a boyish grin played on his mouth.

As she took him in her mouth, she wondered if he realized how much of his soul she was devouring simultaneously.

∼

Chanting and shouting from the streets traveled up to the east wing, loud enough to wake Imani at dawn. Dim sunlight streamed into the room when she flung open the curtains. Her apartment had no view, but a disturbance was near the palace.

A firm rap on her door startled her.

"It's Esa. Open the door now."

It was far too early for them to practice magic together.

Imani waved at the door with her wand, and it unlocked.

Esa barged in and promptly stood beside her by the window, glancing outside, antsy. "What did the prince say about the announcement? You share his bed these days. I knew he couldn't resist you if you showed up at the Neshuin New Year's party."

It was a good guess by Esa, but Imani wouldn't deny it. Tanyl probably wouldn't have liked it, but she enjoyed being able to confide in someone about her relationship with the prince.

"He never mentioned an announcement."

"We're resuming diplomatic relations with our southern neighbor after a thousand years." She put her hands on her hips. "You're telling me he said nothing about the Niflheim Kingdom? Not even a whisper or a hint? The queen announced it this morning."

Imani's mouth fell open. Tanyl *had* mentioned Niflheim.

Imani recovered quickly and schooled her face into an impatient scowl. "We're having sex, not confiding in each other about matters of state and security." She pressed her fingers to her nose. "But he was in a horrendous mood last night," she muttered.

"I'm sure." Esa snapped her eyes to Imani then back to the window. "I would have killed the queen if I were him."

"People must be terrified and enraged at opening the borders, even to select dark breeds and their magic."

"There's protesting in the streets as we speak." Esa motioned to the window.

"Did the queen give a reason?"

"The public explanation is we're opening the borders again in a limited capacity for the growth and prosperity of the economy."

A wrongness twisted in Imani's chest. "Unbelievable. What other explanations have you heard?"

Esa regarded her for a moment. "I heard the Niflheim Throne and the Essenheim Crown have been in talks for some time. It's all whispers and secretive, but they say the king reached out first, accusing us of abusing the Fabric and breaking the treaty. He threatened to invade the Riverlands."

Imani's mouth went dry. "But it would be an act of war."

"Indeed. However, it's where the Fabric event originated. Niflheim has us by the balls under the guise of preventing further damage."

"I'm from the Riverlands. It's fine. It was nothing."

"Night lasting for days in Essenheim is not *nothing*. And unlike the past events we hid from the king, this was massive and beside their border. Queen Dialora and the First Witch blame a Niflheim refugee, a merchant. He's disappeared, and they think he murdered someone, as well—bones were found at the scene."

"But an invasion? Surely, the queen wouldn't risk it," Imani choked out, forcing her body through sheer grit to get a hold of itself, thinking about that night.

"No, but I guarantee she saw this as an opportunity to further her agenda, even at the expense of what's best for Essenheim. But, of course, the public must be told one thing, so you won't hear any mention of any escalating conflict."

Imani swore under her breath and squeezed her eyes shut, remembering what she had overheard about Essenheim's lack of armed forces. "Tanyl never mentioned any of this directly to me."

Esa crossed her arms, the accusation blatant on her face. "So, he *indirectly* mentioned it? You're not merely fucking him then. He may not confide in you, but you hear things."

Was Esa jealous of her and Tanyl?

No. The sprite was no such thing. She proved it by plowing on without sparing it one more thought.

"As part of the 'diplomatic strengthening,' they've negotiated a deal," Esa continued. "In exchange for the king not attacking us for breaking the treaty, they're demanding their pick of our witches, including high sentinels. By further distributing magic wielders across the Fabric, they're spreading the magic evenly, so we aren't pulling too much from one area, like the Riverlands incident."

"In other words, controlling us."

"Exactly." Esa's face was an emotionless stone.

"How will they pick?" Imani could barely breathe.

"They'll put any witch they choose through their own assessments."

"And kill hundreds of our most powerful witches?" Imani's voice sounded shrill.

Esa nodded. "At the end, they will take at least fifty who survive back to Niflheim to work for them indefinitely to prevent future events."

"It's sanctioned murder."

"It is, and in preparation for the arrival of the princes, the Order called all master witches back from their postings around the kingdom, including our high sentinels."

"They can't take the high sentinels away along with so many of our other branded," Imani said, panic rising at the thought of her siblings. "It would leave everyone in those territories incredibly exposed."

"They can do whatever they want because it's either this or war," Esa stated.

Border territories, like the Riverlands, would be especially vulnerable to attack without magical protection from their high sentinel and master witches.

"Niflheim has had this plan ready for years, I'm sure," Esa muttered. "It's ingenious. Wait for a large enough Fabric event, which was inevitable, and use the breach of the treaty to gain access to our kingdom. Kill our most powerful weapons with their ascension assessments before imprisoning the others under their control."

Mind racing, Imani was already thinking past the assessments to what came after for the survivors—they would be granted passage to Niflheim.

This was her opportunity. She could still return money to Dak and Meira while searching for the Drasil.

"When is this happening?"

"The heir apparent and his brother, the youngest prince, will arrive in two days."

"Two *days*? If all our master witches are here by then, they must have known about this weeks ago."

A smile spread across Esa's face. "Now you're starting to get it. Dialora and the Niflheim king have been working on this bargain the second they learned about the Riverlands event."

It was crazy enough to be accurate, and Imani believed her.

"How do you know all this?"

"You're not the only one warming the bed of someone important." Esa shot her a sidelong glance. "You might be useful to our cause if you'd like to be on the right side of this looming war. Unless you don't want to be allies anymore."

Imani did want to be allies—she'd already considered Esa more than an ally at this point.

"Me? Why?"

"Let's say they are *extremely* interested in who you have between your legs. So, keep Tanyl happy."

"And they want to meet with me about Tanyl? Why?"

Imani had to admit she was interested in making the acquaintance of the influential person Esa was sleeping with, especially if they had intimate knowledge of Niflheim and these assessments. If Esa trusted them, having more allies at court, especially powerful ones, might be helpful.

"Ah, something for us to discuss at another time. If you're interested?"

"I am. But this is the heir apparent we're discussing—it better be worth my time."

Esa nodded, as if expecting no less. "I'll be in touch." She strolled to the door and let it slam loudly behind her.

PART II
THE ASCENSION ASSESSMENTS

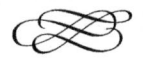

CHAPTER 18

A heavy, apprehensive silence passed between Imani and Esa as they made their way to the palace's grand entrance following training. Wringing her hands in the folds of her skirt, Imani tried to rein in her trepidation at what lay ahead.

Sleep had evaded her, and she had barely even eaten for the past two days. Instead, she'd pored through everything in the trunk about the Niflheim Kingdom.

A family of shifters had ruled Niflheim for half a millennium. The current monarch, Magnus Illithiana, had become king forty years ago and had six sons—all shifters, as far as Imani could tell. None of it was helpful or interesting, but one fact stuck out to her: curiously, power had transferred to the king less than a year after Dialora had inherited the Crown, after Zolyn, the First Witch at the time, had murdered the last monarch of Essenheim.

In another book, Imani had learned that, since the first recorded monarchs, the fates of the king and queen were tied together in inexplicable ways. There was always one male and one female, one king and one queen. When one died, the other's time would soon follow.

She found no explanation beyond these tidbits of unconfirmed theories. No other books or writings existed on the subject of Niflheim, which was unsurprising since they'd all be illegal. As far as she could tell, the neighboring land was filled with rain, darkness, ashes, and death.

Rumors, on the other hand, were more readily available. Everyone buzzed and gossiped during mealtimes about the Niflheim Kingdom. Most of it sounded horrifying and too violent to be true. In their desperation without the sun, the Niflheim king funded violence and genocide against its breeds for their types of magic while trafficking elven witches to further control the Fabric's power. The worst magic ever created came through their slips, bringing monstrous breeds with it. It forced the Throne to create labor camps of massive demon armies. An unstable economy built on a police state perpetrated terrifying political crimes against citizens.

Imani had no idea what to believe. It was all quite outlandish.

The crowd jammed themselves onto the terrace overlooking the garden. Minutes went by. Still, the princes hadn't arrived.

The sun beat down on the crowd, and birds squawked overhead. Everything inside Imani tensed. Her heart hammered against her chest like someone was watching her. Lifting her head, she flanked to her left, and that fear sank into her gut.

Ravens. Six of them were perched atop the stone pillars and archway, and all their heads were turned to peer at her with their beady, black eyes. Ara's taunting words forced her to stay strong. *"You fear the crows, owls, and ravens, Imani, but you're a fool. For a small bird makes a small catch, and the hour of our doom is set."*

There was an eerie inevitability to her grandmother's insane ravings at the end of her life that Imani was only starting to comprehend.

Esa grabbed her arm, tearing her attention away. "They're here."

The ravens took flight all at once, soaring up into the air. Imani immediately wished she hadn't come, but a relentless instinct that she couldn't escape, even if she wished it, made her plant her feet.

Voices stilled into an unsettling silence, the birds cawing above the only sound beyond an errant cough.

Traveling with more security forces than she'd seen in one place, Imani's senses tingled as they neared. Unsurprisingly, the Crown considered them more dangerous than all their apprentice witches combined.

The caravan slowed in front of the majestic main entrance and gardens. Murmurs intensified.

They'd spared no expense making the palace immaculate, even after the ground quake. Servants were ordered about, with the Essenheim royals standing to greet them first.

Neither Niflheim prince was visible yet, but their presence crackled in the air when the carriages stopped. People were dead silent as a footman opened the door. Another bird cawed, and Imani almost rolled her eyes at the drama. But, in truth, she was equally ravenous to glimpse these mysterious shifter breeds.

Servants moved to the side, and a man stepped out. There could be no mistaking him. He held himself like a regal king, commanding all the attention around him. He didn't need to prove himself or flaunt his power to earn respect. His jaw worked as he took in the crowd. One weapon sat on his hip—a black wand.

His magic signature encircled his head in tight, faint swirls of power, and while he didn't have as much magic as she imagined an heir would possess, he had to be well-trained.

Tanyl and the queen strode forward, exchanging formal greetings and bows, conversation too faint for even Imani to hear.

When the Niflheim heir apparent smiled and laughed, the image of him in Imani's mind cracked more. His eyes didn't match his genial countenance. She'd hoped for a hulking brute with little training and no brains to step out of the coach. He *was* a hulking brute, but the easy smile he offered and the predatory way he inclined his head hinted at his true cunningness.

Imani chewed her bottom lip, trying to hide her unease.

While the royals exchanged pleasantries, another person slinked behind the carriage. No one else noticed him. He was a primarily faceless man in the shadows, recognizable only by the sinister curiosity emanating from his serpentine smile of arrogance and venom. But he tugged on her awareness, demanding her gaze.

Her shadows whimpered and writhed, needing, wanting, and projecting a visceral, raw flurry of yearning around her. They were frenzied. Her magic built, and it was as if an invisible force in her chest rapidly spread down her midsection like fire. An aching need twisted inside her core, tightening low and deep.

Brushes of silken magic spread around her, circling, murmuring a hello, a warning, or a promise. More alarming, it pulled on her signature. "Impolite" didn't even begin to describe this intrusion; she was certain it came from this man.

A final, delicate stroke of power caressed down her signature. Then an unsettling sense of completeness instantly settled in her, and the shadows stilled.

It unnerved her to have her signature manipulated. But the ease of her subjugation at his soul draw scared her most of all.

In theory, all kinds of elves likely possessed compulsion magic since all elves needed to feed off someone's life force. But she didn't know about other elves besides the Norn and her and Malis's mysterious breed.

"Is he some member of the Niflheim court?" Imani asked Esa through a clenched jaw.

Esa tore her eyes from the Niflheim heir apparent. "Oh, him? He's the youngest Niflheim prince. Sixth born. Or maybe seventh? I can never remember."

Show yourself, she said silently in her head, already knowing what breed she'd see when he did but needing to see it, anyway.

The man moved from the shadows to greet the queen. Immediately, she could see the two princes were related. Both had the same black hair, golden skin, and graceful demeanors. They even stood the same.

Although she'd expected it, Imani blatantly stared at him. An elf was still a rare sight indeed.

His stoic profile swept over the crowd with chilling indifference. The opposite of his charming brother, he didn't bother with the feigned smiles.

She had no idea how he remained inconspicuous and aloof for the entire exchange with Queen Dialora. He was a powerful witch. Strong enough that she almost missed the illusion he had used to hide his appearance. A layer of spells surrounded him—a glamour—and she had to assume it was what made him unobtrusive to everyone here. Yet she had sensed him right away.

He was tall like an elf but broad-shouldered like his shifter brother, and handsome. More striking than any man Imani had ever seen.

The prince raked his hand through his tousled, beautiful hair, and a few inky strands fell across his forehead. But, while silky and full, he kept it parted to the side and brushed it back off his face. Well-tamed and perfectly controlled, except for the few waves rebelling—wildness fighting for freedom. Another swift movement of his hand put them back.

The habit told her this supposed savage took care of his appearance. Interesting.

Several soldiers dismounted around the Niflheim princes, surrounding them.

"What must it be like to be a prince constantly relegated to the shadows?" Imani murmured to Esa as people exited around them.

"A bunch of fools rule this kingdom. I'd sooner give King Magnus access to our witches over Prince Kiran."

Blinking in surprise, Imani instantly found him vastly more remarkable than his brother. If Esa considered him more dangerous than one of the most powerful men in the world, Imani took notice.

Until now, people had only referred to the youngest prince as the Snake Prince, the Mad Prince, or some variation. She'd brushed him off like others did. Hearing his name for the first time, she seared it into her mind.

Esa moved inside, but Imani remained rooted to the balcony.

Kiran trailed behind his brother, utterly unassuming, his face still a blank mask. Overshadowed by his brother's presence, he all but disappeared, walking in measured steps with his hands clasped casually behind him. His existence exuded power and dominance, demanding attention as much as the Niflheim heir apparent. So, why was he hiding?

The imperceptible way his eyes shifted and his movements conveyed a subtle but calculated approach. This prince acted with purpose. Doing nothing by accident, he stood exactly where he wanted to be—in the shadows.

Prince of Snakes, indeed.

The Niflheim heir apparent removed a black obsidian circlet and ran his hand over his hair, exactly like Kiran had earlier. The circlet was a symbol, useless compared to the crown Dialora wore. But as the heir walked inside, Imani thought about the Throne. What power did it give the Niflheim monarch? From the rumors about King Magnus, it must be formidable.

Off to the side, Prince Kiran lingered. With a wrinkle on his forehead, he raised his head at the birds while the servants and soldiers bustled around him. Unlike the blank stares from the mindless soldiers around him, Imani *sensed* a storm of thoughts in his head. He was thinking constantly.

No one paid him any mind at all.

Low in the sky, several crows circled above the royal caravan, scouting and scenting their next meal, likely a rodent in the gardens. The birds flew mere yards from the crowd, and the strange prince spared more than a glance for the beastly animals—more than he did for the queen and Tanyl. Perhaps his kingdom was so void of light that birds were rare?

The crowd thinned further, exposing Imani's presence. She wanted to move, but she couldn't tear her eyes away, needing to understand him. Although she'd fed from Tanyl earlier, she found this prince intriguing.

His eyes snapped to her for the first time, widening a minuscule amount. A terrifying jolt shot through her entire body at the connection. She'd surprised him. That much was obvious. Maybe this unmated male hadn't expected an unmated female elf.

The bastard didn't look away like most people would when caught staring. Instead, he studied her more with an unreadable ghost of a smile creeping over his face.

Unwilling to break contact, Imani clenched her jaw and held his gaze. As the female, Imani was the only one able to get into his head, but both their soul draws swirled around each other. Tugging. Pulling. Playing.

Everything about him was perfect except for his disturbing, unnatural eyes. Like his brother's, one shone bright mossy green, reminding her of rolling hills, of trees, and life. The other was pure, unyielding black. Not only was the iris discolored, but his entire eye was black with no white. Dead. He had to be half-blind. And there was something dangerous in the depths. A genuinely dark magic emanated from it—a magic she didn't understand.

What caused such horrendous disfigurement? Kiran had given her no reason to yet, but something deep inside her said she should fear this man.

He finally let a small smile free, but it did not last long. In the next second, he broke contact and strolled inside.

The wild gleam of amusement in his eye and the dance of a smirk on his lips unsettled Imani. She had no idea why he'd had such a strong effect on her.

Whatever kind of elf he was, it was wicked.

CHAPTER 19

Inside the palace, Imani found Esa talking to Sid at the bottom of the stairs. She tried to slip away unnoticed, but much to her dismay, Esa gave him a curt goodbye and fell in step beside her.

Still spooked, a conversation was the last thing Imani wanted right now. Too many things had taken her off guard in the brief introduction to the Niflheim royal family. She should be steadfast in staying far away from these princes.

Esa eyed Imani's trembling hands. "You seem nervous."

Imani swallowed hard. "The princes are not what I expected."

"What did you expect?"

"Savage shifter breeds, not smart enough to tell their head from their arse."

Esa snorted. "I'm sure it's what they want people to think. Or, at least, they're not interested in proving it wrong. Only a fool would underestimate them."

"Both are strong with magic," Imani said. "I heard a rumor most Illithianas lack brands for a ruling family."

"I heard the same. Saevel has enough, though—enough to be named the heir apparent, anyway. But Kiran, he's powerful. Especially as a half-breed."

"Interesting," Imani hummed. So, Kiran was half-shifter and half-elf, but Imani was sure his dominant breed had to be his elven side.

"His magic behaved strangely." Imani rubbed her chest. "It's like he could influence my signature."

Esa's brows rose in genuine surprise. "Someone said Kiran has ways of controlling people and influencing them. There are so many rumors, but it wouldn't surprise me if he could compel magic signatures—rare, but it's possible. Could have something to do with him being a half-breed." Esa glanced around before continuing with a grave expression as her voice dropped. "Many people highly suspect Kiran is a twelve-mark."

Tension passed between them. A day ago, Imani would have laughed at such an outrageous statement. But now she didn't know what to believe.

He might be.

"What else do you know about the Niflheim princes?"

Once they rounded a corner toward their rooms, Esa continued, "Kiran's father despises him. He wanted his last child to be a female elf."

"What could be *that* awful about him having a male elf instead?" Imani asked, incredulous at someone ever despising their twelve-mark child.

"Any son whose dominant breed isn't a shifter is a disgrace—weak comparatively. The king has plenty of sons but no daughters. A female elf would have made a beautiful—and useful—addition to his brood," Esa explained.

"Weak is the last word I'd use to describe the man I saw outside," Imani muttered.

"He's well-bred, to be sure, but with his elven side more dominant, even a twelve-mark would be an unimpressive shifter, at best. Worthless offspring in the king's eyes."

"That's ... that's insane."

"Runs in the family, I guess." She shrugged. "Magnus and his sons aren't known for their restraint, and Kiran is the maddest of them all."

"But with a powerful father, he should still be able to shift into *something*. Half-breeds get powers from both parents, even if his dominant breed is his elven side."

"Yes, they say he's a serpentine shifter whose snake form—rumors claim—is a true horror to behold. Hence the title of Prince of Snakes. But it's *nothing* compared to his brothers' and the king's shifted forms."

"I thought the name was because he was a slippery bastard."

"Well, that, too." Esa paused. "But the Serpent Prince is smart. He knows the king won't kill him as long as he uses his cock often enough and controls their magic."

Imani scoffed. "Why is it worth anything to the king?"

"Ah, well, the king still wants a well-bred female elf. For decades, they've needed to strengthen ties with their elf populations, and things are only worsening. A granddaughter would help make alliances."

"I'm sure Prince Kiran is more than happy to oblige," Imani mumbled. "I assume he hasn't been successful?"

"Not for lack of trying, or at least pretending to try for his father's sake. But he probably needs his heartmate to have children, like most of your kind. Who knows? This is all gossip and pure speculation." Esa waved her hand dismissively.

"Does Saevel have a mate?" Imani asked, referring to the Niflheim heir apparent, trying to remain nonchalant.

"I have no idea. No one's mentioned one," Esa said carefully, shooting her a sharp sideways glance. "Even if he found his heartmate, it's rare for an Illithiana to bind to one, as it requires sharing power *and* being monogamous."

They walked quietly for a few moments.

Pretending to be Meira put her on dangerous ground, but she might need to do something out of character and sleep with one of the princes to get what she wanted.

As if reading her mind, Esa broke the silence.

"I would be cautious about getting into bed with either of them, if it's what you're thinking about," Esa said when they reached their rooms. "Both princes have enjoyed whores since crossing the border. Nasty stories from this past week are circulating. They like it rough."

Imani glared down her nose at Esa. "I can handle rough." She didn't care that Meira wouldn't have said anything of the sort. Imani's desire to get to Niflheim was overwhelming; she'd do almost anything.

Grabbing her arm, Esa stopped them both. "Sleep with them if you want. I'm the last person who'd make the mistake of underestimating you, but this 'diplomatic honor?' You should avoid being chosen for the ascension assessments. They are a death sentence." She paused. "If you know what's good for you, you should stay away from them altogether."

Her friend would be disappointed.

"If you were desperate for something, and they could give it to you, would you stay away?"

Esa cocked her head to the side, thinking. "Exactly what I thought you'd say, and we understand each other perfectly. A summons will be waiting in our rooms to be ready at dawn when the Niflheim princes will choose their witches for the assessments. They want the most powerful specimens to participate, and it won't only be your magic and markings dictating who they pick."

Turning on her heel, Esa left Imani alone in the hallway, confused. How did she know so much about tomorrow's events?

～

IMANI ONLY SLEPT ABOUT HALF the night and spent the early morning hours restlessly perfecting her appearance.

Her chest and stomach ached with the tug of hunger, the need. She'd slept with Tanyl, but being around the Niflheim princes yesterday had woken something inside her. Maybe it was simply being around an unmated male elf, but she'd never felt this way before.

Her guilt also worsened by the hour.

She read and reread Meira and Dak's last letter repeatedly as the sun rose. They loved and missed her and couldn't wait for her to return. The shop wasn't doing well. Meira had to pick up more shifts in the kitchen. She hoped Imani would soon be home to help train

Dak. His magic had begun to manifest, and she was too overworked to do much about it herself. On top of it, Fen had taken a chosen mate, and while she didn't mention it beyond the one sentence, Meira was devastated.

We aren't a family without you, Meira had written.

Guilt shredded Imani's insides, thinking about those words.

To be chosen by the Niflheim princes would be a betrayal of the worst kind to Meira, but she couldn't let this chance slip away. Imani was *desperate* to find a way to the Drasil. Besides, finding the wand would do more to help her family than simply returning home.

Esa and Imani walked silently to the main ballroom. The guilt intensified into a pang of pressure pressed down on her chest. She rubbed between her breasts, where her cleavage was on display to its fullest in the emerald dress her sister had made for her. She was racked with guilt and on edge about being chosen *and* passing the first assessment, which was set to take place immediately.

Conversation filled the room. If she thought there were a lot of apprentices in the capital before, it was nothing compared to all the thousands of master witches of the Essenheim Kingdom filling the room now. Many of them knew each other, too. All of them were there to compete in the assessments. The master witches had already passed their assessments, but they could be retaken by those wishing to become archmage witches.

Esa kept her eyes ahead but leaned closer to Imani. "Of course, you wouldn't listen to me. You're trying to get chosen, aren't you?"

"We both want the same thing."

"Indeed, we do. I have business in Niflheim." Esa's tone brooked no more conversation on the subject.

Imani was curious to know what business, but Esa's secrets were her own, as Imani's were hers.

Esa gave her a pointed once-over. "You look good—really good. I'm glad you let go of some glamour. You *feel* like a High-Norn female for the first time since I met you. Gods, you even smell different." The pixie paused. "You're being smart. We're not going to survive this with our raw magical talent. I am curious about the first assessment today."

Imani agreed and was glad she'd trusted Esa's advice. Her entire appearance this morning was on purpose, and her illusion was the lightest it'd ever been since she had come to the palace. She wanted to appear like the perfect High-Norn. While she kept her soul draw simmering low, she was prepared to let it out in full force if she needed to manipulate the Niflheim princes.

The mystery of the first assessment lingered in her mind and made her jittery. She could rely on her physical combat skills as a collector, but magical combat was a different story, and she wasn't remotely prepared for it, even with the progress she'd made with Esa and the Order. Worse still, keeping her shadows and alteration magic in check under pressure would require intense focus. She couldn't allow any slipups if she wanted to continue the Meira ruse, especially with her shadows as unpredictable as they were.

"I don't see Ellisar or Gorre anywhere," Esa muttered darkly. "It seems my sentinel and yours aren't interested in obeying the Royal Order or the Crown."

No surprise there.

More than a hundred thousand High-Norn elves lived in the Draswood, but the likelihood Imani would meet any remained low. As expected, they'd deliberately chosen to ignore this mandate.

Elves living in the Draswood enjoyed the freedom, safety, and protection the Aowyns never had in the Riverlands. Practically as magically powerful as a monarch, the high sentinel of the Norn elves ruled his territory like an independent kingdom.

Until yesterday, Ellisar was the only other witch alive rumored to be a twelve-mark, and the Draswood city of Vathis was as impenetrable as Stralas itself, especially to uninvited outsiders. Imani spent the first decade of her life in the massive city in the center of the forest and knew firsthand how treacherous and disquieting the woods surrounding Vathis could be.

Only the Norn understood the Draswood's secrets, a powerful magical entity on its own. But it didn't mean it was less dangerous to them. Her fingers instinctively brushed over the hidden black scarring on her cheek.

Attacking and invading the Norn elves would be utterly foolish of the Crown with the escalating southern conflict.

Imani didn't know about the high sentinel of the sprite pixies. If Gorre was like Esa, he had probably laughed when they had summoned him. But he couldn't offer the same protection as Ellisar. Hundreds of pixies were in the room.

Nervous energy thickened the air. People shuffled their feet back and forth, some wringing their hands. Even experienced, powerful witches' eyes flicked around, taking in the competition.

The First Witch instructed them to arrange themselves by breed, then low, common, and high-bred. There were few low and common breeds, as most magic was gifted to the high-bred. Almost everyone was a high breed of some kind.

The two shifter groups—the leonines and satyrs—took up half the space in the center of the room, with the two nymph breeds—naiads and leimoniads—assembling behind them.

Both pixie breeds—sprites and trow—were scattered around the room's edges, including Esa. Most sprite pixies had moth-like wings, beige with bold, russet accents and black-tipped edges, while the trow pixies looked delicate and rose-colored, shimmering with pale green dots at the apex.

Some kept theirs tucked up tight against their backs, but others, like Esa, left them out, floating effortlessly behind them as the edges furled and unfurled. With a *whoosh*, a sprite pixie released her wings. Though not as vibrant or lively as a trow's, their softness and the graceful way they danced in the air made them entrancing to watch.

All had blue hair, and none were friendly to each other. Indeed, it appeared to be a veritable glare fest. Imani remembered Esa had said pixies were aggressive and had no loyalty to each other like other breeds.

Lore and Esa ignored each other but stood close. Before Imani lost them in the crowd, the male pixie pressed his hand to her back and moved her closer to him. Esa let him without a word.

After a turn around the room, Imani finally spotted three male elves standing in the back with severe expressions. Imani assumed at least Master Selhey would be there, but her mentor wasn't with them. It struck her that this was the most she'd been around her kind since leaving home.

The men narrowed their gazes as she approached. They didn't bother to hide their surprise at the sight of her.

The male elves were far taller than Master Selhey and strikingly masculine compared to her form. Yet, with silver hair, blue eyes, and shimmering pale complexions, they were unmistakably her kind. Magic rolled off their signatures, and when they reached her, the closeness of her kin made her want to cry.

Still, Imani could sense an undercurrent of worry emanating from all three men. Worry for *her*.

Desperate to end the uncomfortable moment, Imani pressed her hands together on her chest and bowed a formal greeting.

They responded similarly, and then one moved closer and murmured a question to her in rapid Elvish.

Grasping the basics of Norn Elvish still, some familiar words jumped out to Imani.

Was she here alone?

It wasn't accusatory. He was genuinely concerned and shocked to find an unmated female elf alone here. Now their reaction made sense. They could probably smell she was unmated.

Nodding, she switched to the common tongue and explained how she had grown up in the Riverlands.

Their concern lessened, but a swell of confusion, sympathy, and sadness emanated from them.

Imani bit back a snap. She didn't need pity and especially didn't want it in front of the Niflheim princes. She had her magic to protect her and wanted to appear strong in front of them.

Meira would keep her composure, and Imani would, too. She smothered those emotions back down to where they belonged.

They accepted her explanation, so she told them about her home and how her grandmother had been a high naiad witch from a southern border village in the Riverlands.

For a few moments, the conversation flowed easily. Each of the other elves lived outside the Draswood, as well, with their non-elf heartmates. It made Imani realize how rare a female elf sighting was these days when she'd only met four Norn elves since leaving home, and all of them had been males.

In a breath, one elf jerked his chin toward the open door, whispering to another. While Imani didn't understand the words, they relaxed.

With confused, pleading eyes, the leader approached her. "Our apologies for our response earlier. It was our mistake we assumed you were alone."

"Oh, I am alone …" Imani trailed off as a hush moved through the room. She whipped her head toward the door, and her mouth closed mid-sentence. Except for a few murmurs, it was deadly silent.

The Niflheim princes were here, and Kiran's eyes were nearly luminous with his fury as they stared directly at Imani and the other elves. His magic signature snaked out toward them threateningly.

And the male elves took several steps back from her.

CHAPTER 20

What did he have against Norn elves? And why did he keep staring at her?

Confused, and more than a little defensive, Imani couldn't tear her eyes away from him.

Kiran eventually looked elsewhere but didn't relent entirely, his hardened eyes glancing over to her occasionally. Maybe it wasn't simply Norn elves he hated then. Perhaps it was *her*. She cracked her neck, trying to calm down.

She needed to be chosen; if he hated Norn elves, it would not be in her favor.

The two Niflheim princes roamed the room like cruel hunters set on punishing their helpless prey. Their choices revealed little about their methods or strategy.

While he pointed at people, Saevel deferred to Kiran. The latter merely whispered in his brother's ear.

While his fierce magic signature from the palace entrance had quelled, Kiran still aimed a darkly amused expression at all the witches, sweeping his gaze around the room from time to time.

Esa had said their choices would not be entirely about magic prowess. Those deemed worthy based on some unknown criteria were directed outside to the courtyard near the training field and stables to prepare for the first assessment.

Her soul draw pressed against the restraints she'd put on it, and her signature grew increasingly agitated at the sight of the princes. A flare of magic burned through her chest the longer she stood and stared. An elf didn't have the sense of smell like shifters, but it was heightened compared to other breeds, and if the prey was exciting to them, they sometimes tracked it on instinct, which she did to Kiran now. It distracted her, and she needed to be in complete control.

Minutes passed. Esa was picked, but Lore was not, and he was furious, his face irate as Esa left with the others.

The Niflheim princes had nearly chosen their allotment when their attention fell on the four Norn elves.

Tanyl refused to even look at Imani, directing his attention to anything else in the room but her. Saevel was amiable and inquisitive. His eyes roamed down to her breasts, and he openly stared.

A smirk curled her lips seeing him do precisely what she wanted, but Kiran's lack of reaction irritated her. Somehow, he still appeared sly and amused, despite his horrifying, disfigured eye. It was more grotesque this close and revealed few emotions, unlike his brother. She glared at it and sucked in a deep breath as something pulled on her core. The kind of warm tug that made a female stand up and take notice. She pressed a hand to her navel, willing the compulsion of his magic to go away and glaring at Kiran for not putting an illusion on his soul draw.

Despite positioning himself in his brother's shadow again, and his muted elven features, more females than yesterday gave Kiran curious, appraising attention.

Princes who were rejected or mad clearly didn't want attention from women, especially when they had magic like soul draws.

Something about the Serpent Prince's magic was catching, too. It moved from his signature to hers, creeping up from her fingers to her chest, where it burst into vibrations of restless energy. He still hadn't paid her a glance.

Not being able to catch his attention, especially after his glaring earlier, made her feel off-kilter. She wanted to pull her hair, to run around cackling and casting errant magic to catch his attention.

Madness.

Another part of her wanted to simply slit his throat and roar while her shadows danced on his corpse—the more reasonable part of her.

One thing was sure. She couldn't deny this prince, and his magic fascinated her.

"Only one female? Enchanting creature. What's her name?" Saevel asked, his voice deep and husky.

Imani tipped her face up at him, keeping her expression blank but her chin held high. His movements were graceful for someone so large.

"Meira Aowyn. A young female and incredibly untrained." Tanyl cleared his throat and glowered at her. For all his easy smiles and handsome charm, the moment Tanyl's face darkened, his dangerous side came through.

Tanyl's protectiveness continued to irk her. She clenched her hands.

"What do you think, brother?" Saevel motioned to Imani.

Lazily, Kiran turned his head to his brother in question as if he didn't hear him.

Saevel rolled his eyes. "The female Norn; what do you think of her?"

The youngest prince finally let his gaze fall on her form, and she stared right back. An inexplicable warming spread through her chest at his eyes on her, leaving her greatly unsettled.

Kiran hadn't said a word until now. The sound of his voice took her by surprise. She had expected it to be unpleasant. But it wasn't at all.

"She's perfect," he said without an ounce of emotion, letting his voice slide over her skin like silk. It made her shiver. He blinked and pierced his odd gaze at her again. In that instant, with his full attention on her, she was oddly less irritated. "But isn't it the point of her breed? So, really, she's not special."

All at once, her annoyance rushed back.

"Rare to observe a female like her without a heavy illusion outside the Draswood, though," Prince Kiran said to Tanyl and looked around in mock confusion. "Surely, this can't be all your high-bred elves? I'd hate for us to begin without what we agreed, Tanyl."

Imani noted the use of the prince's given name. The animosity between the two men was palpable.

"They were delayed," Tanyl said. *Liar.* "I'll bring word to you as soon as they arrive."

Kiran pinned his eyes on Tanyl in warning, making her shiver again. "Good."

"Yes," Saevel agreed. "I'm interested in meeting more of your elusive Norn elves. However, this one is incredibly diminutive. I've never seen such small hands before." He laughed. "And if she's untrained, we might as well not bother."

With a curt nod, Tanyl moved to the other Norn witches, pulling their attention away from her.

All three princes spoke to each other in tense, low whispers, darting looks at all the male elves, not indicating they wanted to choose her. She didn't understand their selection process—it must have something to do with size—but probably more about power. And she wouldn't get chosen by standing around, acting pretty.

When they were about to overlook her, Imani panicked. She let more of her soul draw out, and tingles shot down her flesh. She fought a smile. The thrill of releasing it made her magic pulse and ripples subtly rolled off her body.

Gods, it felt *incredible*.

Tanyl narrowed his eyes slightly, and both Niflheim princes turned to her. She stared Saevel dead in the eyes and let the full force of the draw hit him. *Choose me. You want me,* she said in her head as his eyes glazed almost imperceptibly. "I'm not as untrained as most people think," she purred out loud.

Imani doubted anyone would question the magic unless they, too, were elves. Her illusion magic tempered it to the perfect amount. Female Norn compulsion magic naturally pulled vulnerable people in, so, unlike Kiran's draw, the magic would feel instinctive, not intrusive. Subtle but lovely.

However, without illusion magic, hers would run wild in the

room. It would cause frenzied chaos as males bore down on her for a chance at her feeding. She needed to keep it highly controlled using her glamour, directing it to only one person.

The combination of magic and the ability to influence thoughts and actions made females of her kind more dangerous than men. Indeed, she could sense the unmated males in the room drawing closer, their interest piqued. All she'd need to do was stare them in the eye and they'd be under her control.

Kiran wouldn't be able to control them—*maybe* influence them. But make demands they'd be forced to obey? No.

She played with fire.

Something akin to anger—perhaps suspicion—flashed across Kiran's face. More magic snaked off him to meet hers.

Her stomach dropped. Did he guess she was manipulating Prince Saevel with her soul draw? Probably.

Still, she held firm, refusing to be cowed from his posturing. He might be an advisor, but Saevel made the final call in whom to choose.

Kiran's magic backed off.

Shifting to watch Kiran for a moment, he gave her a knowing smirk with his arms folded over his chest, as if he wanted to both strangle and laugh at her. He knew what she'd done, no doubt. But he tilted his head toward Saevel as his brother moved to whisper in his ear. Kiran slit his eyes but didn't say anything. Saevel let out a low chuckle.

Another inhale of breath passed, and finally, Saevel pointed at Imani lazily. "Her. The female High-Norn elf. She can go with the two other High-Norn elves on the left."

At those words, she immediately stiffened. Trying to move as little as possible, magic and energy contracted back inside her, and she let out a quiet, deep exhale. She slowed her heaving chest after pulling her soul draw back inside.

Smug and victorious, she sauntered past the three princes, not sparing any of those arrogant bastards a glance.

Kiran's strange magic trailed after her for longer than she liked.

IMANI PRETENDED to cast a few spells outside while warming up with the others, but her real intention was to observe Tanyl and Kiran in the corner.

A smile tugged at her mouth as they stood off to the side together. Two outrageously arrogant princes who hated each other attempting to converse? Either Tanyl was stupid, or he honestly thought he could get under Kiran's skin. Imani didn't know him, but she wagered few people rattled Kiran.

Imani tilted her ears to listen more.

"Do drow elves have the same feeding needs as our Norn, Prince Kiran?"

Imani's ears flicked back and forth, hearing Kiran's breed. She needed to learn as much as possible about drow elves.

Black and green eyes slid to Prince Tanyl with acute disdain. Then Kiran quickly slipped his mask of boredom back on. Unblinking, the prince stared at the witches and took his time responding.

When he did, there was a lilt to his words she hadn't noticed at first, a slight accent pleasantly riding his speech. "All elves feed off the essence of others," he said. "Each breed is different, but make no mistake—all elves are predators. More so than shifters in many ways."

The wind ruffled Kiran's thick, dark hair, which was perfectly cut on the sides and slightly mussed on the top. His expression was unreadable as his eyes were locked on Imani. Tanyl noticed, too.

"An exaggeration," Tanyl said with a cutting look.

Kiran canted his head to the side, amused. "I'm vastly curious. Why would you even care about *my* needs?"

Tanyl leaned back against the wall. "I'm nothing if not an attentive host, and I didn't see you arrive with any females of your kind. Surely, you didn't come here alone."

"Your concern for my well-being is noted. Rest assured, there are plenty of volunteers for my sustenance. Elves have a penchant for drawing people close," Kiran said wryly, and for a moment, he stared right at Imani. She kept her eyes focused straight ahead as his voice dropped lower, slinking over her skin seductively. "I couldn't help but notice your lone female High-Norn elf is unmated."

Imani's face heated, hearing them talk about her. But she hid a smile, pleased she had an audience.

Throwing her old strategy of being inconspicuous out the window, Imani figured if she was interesting enough, she might make it through these assessments. Yes, she had secrets to hide, but they were secondary to passing the brutal assessments she was sure the princes had planned.

Tanyl's jaw worked. "Why would she interest you?"

Kiran rolled his eyes. "Don't be an idiot, Tanyl. Even in Niflheim, there are rumors about unmated Norn female elves, and she is extremely well-bred. A genuine rarity to spot in the wild, and I've always been curious to experience their feeding."

"We can procure more experienced female Norn elves than her if you'd like."

"Please. Have you seen her? None of those whores would compare. With both our needs, she and I might be able to reach a mutual agreement."

How did drow elves feed?

Her hunger surfaced instinctively, and she imagined for even one moment what Kiran suggested—her meeting his needs. The sensation in her chest said to look at the elf, pulling her toward him. It was an inconvenient moment for her hunger and magic to surface.

Damn his draw. Whatever kind of elf a drow was, he certainly didn't lack one.

Tanyl didn't admit they were sleeping together, but a satisfied grin spread across his face. "I'd love nothing more than to see you try. She'll never agree to anything with you."

She thought a dark emotion swept Kiran's face after the last comment. It disappeared too quickly for her to discern its meaning.

A moment later, Kiran found the entire exchange amusing again. "Are you *protecting* her?" There was a mischievous gleam in his eye.

Tanyl ignored him. "High-bred females like her are impossible to find, but I can get you female Norn elves. You're right; they're not high-bred, but there's no comparison to the beauty of a Norn elf woman, no matter her sigil," Tanyl said.

"Yes, even among my kind, we call them the *nakir archones*—"

"Silver angels. I speak some of your dialects," Tanyl cut in. "Fitting name as our Norn descended from the angel breeds of the Upper realms." He leaned closer, lowering his brow. "Protecting her has nothing to do with it. I'm merely informing you she's just a shade of a true Norn. She has some nymph blood and an unsightly disfigurement—"

"A disfigurement?" Kiran asked casually. "And she's shown you this part of her before?"

"Yes. Here." Tanyl motioned to the side of his face. "Not to mention her powers are unpracticed, at best. I'm sure you noticed the illusion she wears to hide her true form and enhance her beauty." He picked absently at his nail. "I'm shocked your brother picked her. She's not ready to pass any ascension assessments yet."

It took considerable effort for Imani not to storm over and punch Tanyl for trying to protect her by discrediting her. But it would mean revealing how good her hearing was compared to the others and the extent of her powerful magic. She wanted to keep them guessing. She had to give them just enough to keep choosing her and passing the assessments but not enough to reveal all her secrets.

The comment wasn't entirely unexpected. Tanyl wanted her to remain here, sleeping with him for selfish reasons. Yet, somehow, it was still a betrayal. Most of all, it was sloppy because it was evident he *was* protecting her, and she didn't need it.

She was *not* casting an illusion to make herself more beautiful, and Kiran fucking knew it. She was confident Kiran understood how elves and their illusions worked, unlike Tanyl.

"As it happens, I've encountered a High-Norn female once before." Kiran's eyes glazed with a faraway expression. "And indeed, she was exquisite—perfect, in fact."

Surprise—and a bit of jealousy—made her eyes widen. She tried to see more of Prince Kiran's expression out of the corner of her eye. He watched her with a mix of curiosity and amusement.

Prince Kiran wanted to feed from her, which might be something she could work with later. But could she betray Tanyl? Maybe. He'd just betrayed her by making her seem weak.

These assessments proved to be far more complicated than anticipated.

"I can't imagine she paid a sixth-born prince like you any mind," Tanyl said impatiently.

Something like hurt flickered in Kiran's expression. The change was so subtle Imani might have imagined it because, in the next moment, his mismatched eyes were wild as he pushed off the wall. "Time for you to leave, precious Prince. I have work to do, and I'd hate for the sixth-born bastard to embarrass you."

"You're ordering me around in my kingdom? In my own home?"

"You'll find I do pretty much whatever I want," Kiran said coolly, winking at him. "And you know there are no Essenheim guards, staff, or royals during our assessments."

"Shouldn't you ask Saevel's permission to even talk to me?" Tanyl lifted a brow. "You're a pathetic lapdog to your father and brothers."

"Better to be their lapdog than your mother's, right? My leash appears to be much longer than yours," the Serpent Prince chirped, clapping him on the shoulder. Kiran moved to walk away, laughing to himself, but stopped abruptly and turned back.

"Honestly, your lovely elf is probably *starving* with the selection here." Cocking his head to the side, Kiran gave Tanyl a lopsided smile. "So, I might take my chances on the rejection you're so sure of with her."

With his hands in his pockets, he lazily made his way over to his brother.

CHAPTER 21

As Kiran moved to stand by his brother, the *aenils* bells in the palace steeple chimed, their rich song spreading through the courtyard and over the gardens in a synchronized, booming melody. With the sun full in the sky now, it was a call to prayer to the Upper realms—a concerning new tradition the Crown was perpetuating. But that was a worry for another day.

Imani returned her attention to the princes, her face emotionless and stern. She had seen violence before. In fact, her whole life had been filled with violence once she had gone to live with Ara.

I can handle this.

Tanyl had already left with his royal guard. Kiran had been correct; they weren't allowed near the assessments. The witches were now alone with Saevel and Kiran in the vast training field and courtyard.

While both princes were far from the savages she had anticipated, they were as cold but more calculating than she'd expected. Fear mingled with anger inside her. If they demanded a display of exceptional physical magic, she would surely disappoint, and probably die. She had trained and practiced independently well but was still primarily driven to cast magic on instinct. Her control, something she'd struggled with for a long time, faltered. She needed control if she hoped to hide her shadow and alteration magic.

It also ate at her heart that so many talented witches would meet their demise, as they already had so few.

What a waste.

"Kiran," Saevel said.

Not needing to raise his voice to summon him, the elf wandered over, unhurried but obliging.

It was strange how power shifted around the two princes. Despite Saevel being the more muscular of the two males, he appeared smaller, somehow, as Kiran meandered forward.

Once at his brother's side, Kiran lifted both hands. His silently murmured incantation took hold instantly.

Immense magic erupted from his signature. It ripped ribbons of power from the Fabric before flinging a vast ward overhead. The ward moved outward until it encased the courtyard in an invisible dome, and Kiran layered additional defenses to fortify it further.

The shields spread until they shuddered with one final pulse then stilled. Residual power from his magic rattled Imani's chest.

Lowering his hands, the spell was complete. No one would be able to pass without Kiran's permission. They were effectively in the Niflheim Kingdom's domain now.

"Your monarch declared you'll serve your kingdom for the greater good, a diplomatic and honorable service." Saevel angled his head. "That's a lie."

No one spoke, not even a whisper.

Saevel continued, "Make no mistake. This is a reaping meant to administer punishment to your kingdom, and you are all guilty. Why we picked you to participate is irrelevant. You have gone unchecked for far too long, and now we're going to give you a choice in how you pay for the crime. If you survive our first ascension assessment today, you'll move on to the next. Or you'll die. That's it. Those are your choices, and we start right now."

"Not all of us are going quietly into slavery." A leimoniad nymph pointed his wand at Saevel.

A maniacal smile overtook Kiran's face before he flipped his wand upright. "I hoped *someone* would put up a fight."

Barely moving his wand, Prince Kiran unleashed a spell at the defiant witch in the crowd.

Fire burst forth, encasing the man in his inferno.

Everyone flinched, ducking and covering their heads. Imani kept her eyes locked and unblinking at the gruesome sight. The Serpent Prince lived up to his name. Positively feral, his magic warmed her face from fifty paces back. Malis's fire had been a fraction.

Before Imani could take another breath, Kiran withdrew the spell back into his body and sent a gust of wind through the remains with a flick of his wrist.

Ashes coated the crowd.

It raised the hair on her arms. Imani was now sure he was a twelve-mark.

Prince Kiran held too much power, and likely abused it, because the magic was like nothing she'd encountered before. Not even a dozen Essenheim master witches would be enough if they went against him.

Worse—a deep, deadly force, one bordering on insanity, fought for freedom inside the elf. The man would be magnificent if not for the raw insanity rolling from him in startling waves. His eyes held a haunted viciousness that spoke of imbalance, and it told her more than she ever needed to know about the Mad Prince. It was more acute than when he'd used his magic to cast the wards. Maybe the other Norn and their keen elven senses felt it, too, but no one else did.

While her own magic made her half-insane, this terrified her.

As a collector for a decade, Imani had lived in society's shadows long enough to become an expert on spotting danger. This witch would kill or had killed without batting an eye, and he was smart— brilliant, probably. All Imani's instincts said to run, and while he fascinated her, she wasn't too prideful to admit he frightened her, as well. A simultaneously horrifying nightmare and a transfixing dream.

"Does anyone else want to choose now?" Saevel asked, arms out, inviting. "My brother and I would be happy to—"

Two others pointed their wands and shouted as they ran forward.

A brutal blow to their bodies awaited, but this time, it was Saevel. He roared, and Imani stared in shock as his body tore into a bear's form. Standing on its hind legs, the bear eclipsed the witches, stretching over fourteen feet tall.

Rearing up and veering around, its maw opened in an untamed snarl, showing off long, pointed teeth.

The witches hit him with powerful magic, but it did nothing. Its paw swung around in defense, and the magic dissipated.

People in shifter form could still be hurt by magic, but rumors circulated that the powerful royal shifter family in Niflheim was impervious. She had incorrectly found it too unbelievable even to consider it valid. Sinking defeat settled in her chest.

Stalking toward the first man, the animal's massive claws slashed across the witch's body. The bear gutted the man, dumping blood and insides onto the dirt. The other witch pummeled more magic at Saevel, trying to stop him. He couldn't.

The witch screamed, his back arching and thrashing while the bear ripped him apart. Bones crunched as he crushed both witches. Their blood and guts smashed into the gravel. Over and over, Saevel batted their bodies, destroying them into the ground. It was like he'd smashed them with a thousand bricks.

Crunch, crack. Blow, crack. Saevel didn't stop.

Outside of Malis, Imani had little knowledge about Niflheim breeds, but Saevel's shift reminded her of an animal she'd read about in a book—werebeast shifters. Such monsters populating Niflheim made her stomach churn.

With another fierce growl booming in the courtyard, Saevel's body blurred again, swirling with his shifter magic. A second later, he stood, panting. The sweat gleaming on his forehead was the only sign he'd changed forms.

Saevel curled his lip in distaste as he motioned to the remains. "Clean it up," he said to his brother, eyes promising violence if Kiran didn't.

Kiran merely shrugged, obeying like a good little lapdog.

"All of you, on your knees," Prince Saevel ordered.

Everyone shuffled to the ground but one.

Imani looked over her shoulder to see a satyr shifter still standing. He was an eight-mark but not a master.

Kiran sighed dramatically. "As much as I'm enjoying the challenges, we'll kill them all by the end of today at this rate," he muttered, too low for most breeds to hear.

"He bends the knee or dies," Saevel snarled.

"Well, you heard your future king." Kiran pointed to the ground with a flourish. "Let's go, horse face."

The satyr shifter didn't move.

Impatient, Kiran motioned again, snapping his fingers. "Down, boy. You'll get to die soon enough. Today will be *such* a bore if you force me to do it now."

After hesitating for a second, the shifter dropped to his knees.

Kiran clapped loudly, his face a giant grin again.

Saevel crossed his arms. "Now that you're all bowing to your true sovereign, my brother is going to bind you to take our assessments."

∼

With people already dead and the rest bound in agreement to serve the Throne, the princes wasted no more time getting the first assessment started.

The rules of their ascension assessments were simple—fail or attempt to resist completing the three tests in any way, purposely or otherwise, and the binding would kick in. Any survivors were bound to serve King Magnus and the Niflheim Throne.

Unease blossomed inside her at the idea of servitude for the rest of her life, away from her home and siblings. But she had to believe it would afford her the opportunities she needed to search for the Drasil.

Then she could free herself forever.

Their abilities were evaluated for hours. Several other master witches from Niflheim helped run the assessments. The candidates were grouped repeatedly in every way imaginable—by breed, sex, height, physical magic, spiritual magic, elemental magic, functional magic, and on and on.

The princes didn't speak once throughout the ordeal, but Imani sensed their judgment, not missing any detail. Especially Kiran. Although, blessedly, he didn't show any sign of detecting her flesh magic.

When the sun set, the Essenheim witches were sorted into two, long parallel lines, an air of finality permeating. They were split evenly down the middle, staring at each other. Most kept their gazes averted, shifting nervously. Except Imani. She fixed her eyes on the brothers, not wanting to waste precious time observing them.

"The left half is dead as we speak. You've been chosen to lose today," Kiran said.

"Those on the right," Saevel said, "will execute the person across from you. As far as you're concerned, these are now enemies of Niflheim, and we expect total compliance from our vassals."

Imani was on the right. She would advance to the next assessment if she could murder the person across from her. It was a horror, but if she wanted to live, she'd need to complete the task.

Those bastards, she thought, thinking about all the dead witches standing on the opposite side.

Murdering people was a perfect assessment. Magic capable of killing required immense control to wield without unintended consequences. People killed themselves if they couldn't cast correctly. It also ran a spectrum of abilities, requiring the same demanding task from everyone while allowing witches to showcase their individual powers.

Both princes knew it was the perfect assessment, too, because smug satisfaction showed on their faces. Why worry about killing the Essenheim witches when they'd kill each other? With permission, the princes eliminated nearly a quarter of the most potent magic wielders from their enemy's army.

Still, she was anything but nervous. Her anger made anxiety impossible, and she bristled at them making her complete such a task. Imani didn't murder innocent people on a whim, especially witches, but the binding made disobeying impossible. Her fist tightened, imagining it slamming into one of the princes' faces.

"And if we refuse?" a nameless witch called out from the far end.

Kiran chuckled.

Imani narrowed her eyes at the sound.

Saevel gave the nameless witch a withering look. "Then you failed to keep your vow, and the binding ramification will kill you." He waved his hand at him, irritated. "You've volunteered to go first."

Kiran gripped his wand tight in one hand and raised his other. Ropes appeared out of thin air and tied themselves around the shaking, crying candidates across from Saevel. Kiran forced them onto their knees with a smirk. When some let out wails of pain, he swiped his wand and silenced them with a spell all too familiar to Imani.

Kneeling on the ground, the first victim shook so violently Imani thought the woman might fall over.

Seconds passed as the victim and executioner stared at each other. No one moved, enraptured by the atrocity about to inevitably occur, no matter the choice.

Backing away, the master witch shook his head. "I can't. I won't murder this woman—"

Before the words left his mouth, he grabbed at his throat as the air left his lungs. He swayed and fell on the gravel, his body contorting and jerking in every direction.

Saevel's and Kiran's faces didn't shy away while the witch scratched at his throat and choked for air that would never come. It took him several minutes to suffocate but, mercifully, he stilled.

Afterward, no one refused, and like the Niflheim princes, Imani never averted her eyes from the carnage. With Tanyl and anyone from Essenheim barred from viewing the assessments, the Niflheim princes were free to commit any atrocities they deemed appropriate for the assessments. Sandpaper coated her mouth as she looked on.

She'd have to participate like all the others, but such indiscriminate killing of witches infuriated her. Nevertheless, she refused to show weakness in front of the princes. It was the only way she could survive such cold-blooded cruelty.

To their credit, those playing the executioners tried to ensure a painless passing. Body after body fell, and Kiran didn't even let their families keep the remains—he burned the corpses with detached efficiency. The wind carried them away, all remnants gone in seconds. Thrown into the skies, they ceased to exist here anymore.

Esa sucked the air out of the lungs of her victim, and with the next, blood spilled from a slit throat. Unlike the rest of the victims, the two souls hovered above their bodies, lingering, tempting Imani to feed. And indeed, it *was* tempting. She wanted the strength, the vitality it afforded, and the blissful feeling. But it would be impossible to get away with it right now, and when she refused the spirits, they disappeared, presumably to start their journey to the Under with the others.

Heads whipped toward her, signaling her turn.

Imani stole a brief glance at the Niflheim princes. The piercing darkness of Kiran's eyes tore through all the voices, people, and commotion to find hers. An illicit shiver of fear jolted her at the unexpected intimacy. Kiran's snaking magic coiled around his body and rolled off him in prominent waves, as if he read her and she'd failed some sort of test.

Imani would not let this serpent know how much his stare and assessment rattled her. Slipping out her wand, she ignored how he made her heart pound and stomped forward, quickly closing the distance between her and the victim. Kiran's stare burned into her spine.

Once she stood over the man's trembling, kneeling form, she didn't hesitate. Gripping her wand overhead, she cast a spell, slicing her victim's head clean off.

It rolled on the gravel, and the body collapsed. Blood spurted from his severed neck. Like the others, his spirit rose above his body, and Gods helped her, she almost gave in to her hunger to devour his being. Instead, Imani tilted her head and examined the bleeding, headless corpse. *That was it?*

Her own ruthlessness surprised her. She had expected to feel more than hunger, but a cold, vacant stare hardened on her face. Sacrifices had to be made to pass the assessments, she supposed, one of which might be her soul.

Without a crack in her mask, she strode back to her spot on the grass.

The final two finished, and one remained—the one the witch whose executioner refused to kill her.

Saevel pointed to Imani. "You, elf witch, finish her off," he ordered with gleeful malice at making her complete the task twice.

Despite the Niflheim heir's barking, Kiran's magic bore down on her, threatening again—a warning for her to obey.

Their gazes snapped together, and an impish smile tugged at his mouth. He'd been staring at her for several minutes, maybe more, but now he took his time with his close-up view, probably searching for signs of weakness.

He would find none. She'd dressed the part today, after all. She would prove she belonged in these assessments, at least for today.

Imani moved forward in measured steps, unhurried. Others might have interpreted her slowness as hesitation, but hesitation had nothing to do with it. She simply wanted Kiran to see the obstinate detachment on her face.

You'll have to do better than this to rattle me. The thought was clearly visible on her expression before she separated the last victim's head from her neck.

Acceptance liberated her mind.

She'd done her fair share of immoral acts and had never defended her actions. A large part of her found some satisfaction, especially when someone wronged her or stood in her way.

A line existed she'd never crossed before. One where people committed atrocities for no other reason than they enjoyed them. In this instance, it simply needed to be done, but how close would Niflheim's assessments bring her to that line?

CHAPTER 22

*P*laying with Esa's note in her pocket, Imani made her way upstairs.

East Wing. Top Tower. Midnight.

Today, she'd survived despite the weight of the witches' lives lost, but she anticipated the rest of the assessments would be far more brutal for her. Dominated by physical magic wielders, these Niflheim princes came for blood. By keeping her alchemy, alteration, and shadow magic unused and thus hidden, Imani needed to give herself any advantage.

Which made making a deal with Esa's contact more attractive.

It crossed her mind to let her magic out, anyway, accepting the consequences. But she hadn't officially trained to use her alteration magic, and alchemy was practically useless in combat. Not to mention the way Malis's home had been utterly destroyed, Imani feared the shadow magic would get out of control. It would be a death sentence for her and probably any others in the vicinity when she let it out, and she had her siblings to think about.

The irony of finally having such powerful magic to protect herself and being unable to use it wasn't lost on her.

She massaged her temples as the constant whispering grew louder, signaling a headache coming on. The shadows speaking to her were growing worse. However, outside of being annoying, it didn't concern her. Her illusion was nowhere near as powerful as Ara's had been since her grandmother had sacrificed a life, but it still held firm against everyone so far. Even Kiran.

Servants scurried past as she made her way up the stairs. On the wing's top floor, several men guarded each end of a long hallway with only two doors. No one spared her invisible form a glance as she quickly slipped past them.

Imani darted her eyes around to be sure she was alone then knocked on the door as softly as possible.

No answer.

She knocked again, louder.

No answer.

Smothering a frustrated noise, she tried to open the door.

Locked.

She took out her wand, but none of the lock-picking enchantments worked, and her temper flared. After this day, her patience had run out.

Unlock it, Imani ordered her shadows.

A black tendril of wispy smoke curled from the Draswood and flowed underneath the door.

A faint clicking noise made a grin tug at her lips.

The wards skimmed over her body as she walked inside, stripping her weaker illusions away, but they let her pass. Imani did a frenzied check to confirm her flesh magic illusions were in place—they were—before making her way further inside.

The decor and furniture were far more opulent than her quarters.

Who lived here?

The hallway flickered with elegant sconces. Faint murmurs drifted toward her from the main room, and Imani padded closer to the orange glow emanating from the fire, forgetting she stood entirely without glamour.

Leaning against the wall, a male stood with his shirt unbuttoned and a much more petite pixie in his arms. His muscular body pressed into hers.

Esa.

A pool of something heavy and unpleasant stirred inside Imani.

"Kiran—"

He cut her off with a kiss. The pixie moaned into his mouth, wrapping her arms around his neck.

A strange nausea-like sensation roiled Imani's stomach as she pictured Kiran inside Esa. Heat surged in Imani's veins, jarring in its suddenness and strength. A sick sort of possessiveness she didn't understand surfaced. Was she being instinctively territorial over the only other unmated male elf here? Imani had never been around one, so she couldn't be sure.

Shadows dimmed the room in a rush, teetering close to darkness as Imani's magic demanded to be freed.

Stiffening from the shift in the light, Kiran and Esa whipped their heads toward where Imani stood rigid with her wand out.

With merely a thought, Imani extinguished the sconces for a few seconds, not caring if they witnessed her magic. Let loose, the hearth flickered from her darkness, cowing at its presence.

"What is the elf witch doing here, Esa? Is *she* the one you've been working with?" He appraised Imani's tense posture yet made no move to untangle himself from the pixie.

Biting her lip, Esa pushed Kiran away from her. "I've spent months ensuring she met every detail. She might not be who you had in mind, but frankly, a rare High-Norn female like her is even better than you wanted. Now"—Esa stood—"I honored my end of this deal. I expect you to honor yours."

The words out of Esa's mouth stabbed Imani's skin. If Imani read between the lines correctly, Esa had taken advantage of her breed and manipulated her for this prince. Exactly why or how, she didn't quite understand yet, but with Esa's words, there was no doubt she'd somehow tricked Imani. How could she have considered this woman a friend?

Tears stung the corners of her eyes, but she held them back as best she could. A few stray drops still fell down her cheeks.

The Niflheim prince had been Esa's source of information about the treaty breach, no question. Imani assumed Esa's source had *ties* to

Niflheim, but she never imagined such a betrayal—that he would be a Niflheim breed, let alone a *royal* one.

While she wanted access to Niflheim, being entwined with a prince in the Illithiana family wasn't what Imani wanted, especially after Ara had been executed for the same treason.

An image surfaced of her shoving Esa away from him and suffocating her with a nearby pillow. She had to grit her teeth to stop herself from acting on it. Despite her possessiveness and anger at being set up, she would take the high road and let the pixie leave without assaulting her.

Stepping further into the room, the heat from the fire lit up the murderous expression on Imani's face, black scarring and all.

Esa's mouth gaped at the sight. "Your face ... it's—"

"Yes, this is my real face. You're always complaining how I'm hiding something. Well, here I am—the real me." Imani spread her arms wide with a nasty, unhinged smile. "And I echo the prince's question—what the *fuck* am I doing here? I suggest you explain yourself quickly."

"Don't act so surprised about this arrangement—an arrangement *you* wanted, by the way," Esa sneered. "I've never hidden the type of person I am from you, and don't act like you wouldn't have done the same for something you desperately want. Just because I lied and manipulated you into sleeping with Tanyl doesn't mean we both can't benefit."

She *what?*

Esa had deliberately set her up with Tanyl in a bid to make a deal with the Niflheim princes. At the revelation, Imani changed her mind about hurting Esa. If Imani couldn't crawl into a ball on the floor and cry in shame, she'd draw blood.

She struck like a predator with her teeth bared, landing a hard punch across Esa's face. The force knocked the pixie to the ground.

Imani barely paused, wrenching Esa back by the sleeves and yanking the pixie up, only to take another swing, smashing her fist into her face again, and again. Red spots hit the carpet.

Imani grabbed a chair—for a desk or something—and smashed it against Esa's shoulder, splintering it all over the carpet.

Rage simmered in Imani's blood. It scared her how aggressive she was, but it felt *good*, and she didn't have any inclination to stop. With both of them growing up fighting scrappy, each had a point to prove by not resorting to magic, especially since Esa performed physical magic better than Imani. It would be a cop-out if she used it, and Imani didn't want to risk provoking her shadows. If they fought with magic, she might be unable to control them.

Traitor, she thought, landing another punch in Esa's gut. Then another, and another, beating the little pixie bloody. She'd thought this female might be her friend, but Imani had been played—manipulated—and there was nothing she hated more than being made to feel powerless, lied to, taken advantage of, and used. If only she had the Drasil, no one would be able to pull one over so easily again.

She glanced back at Kiran. The arrogant bastard sat as relaxed as ever with a slight smile on his handsome face.

Esa elbowed Imani hard in the side. A perfect hit, knocking the wind out of her.

Groaning, Imani couldn't help but question again where Esa had learned to fight.

It went on and on, each of them trying their best to kill the other without actually killing each other, fighting and struggling on the floor like savages. Finally, Esa managed to back Imani into a corner and pointed a wand at her. The fight would end soon, with magic or sheer physical prowess.

Imani pretended to hesitate, keeping the pixie comfortable and unafraid while drawing her in. Then, once Esa was close enough, using surprise and speed, Imani slammed her elbow down onto her arm, breaking it. Esa screamed.

Imani gripped the pixie's throat with both hands, cutting off Esa's air firmly, then shoved her into the wall.

Black clouded Imani's vision. Before this, Esa had been careful not to touch Imani for long, but Esa's death now slammed into Imani's mind.

Esa stood on the steps of a pyre, letting the wind play with her longer blue hair. With her hands tied behind her back and her wings cut off, she had to walk sideways up the steps. Behind her stood Lore, his hands tied behind his wingless back. Both were resigned, grim, while they were tied to the stakes. The fire started to crackle.

Esa collapsed onto her knees, choking and coughing as Imani dropped her. Green eyes narrowed up at the elf witch, angrier than a storm.

Imani shook her head to get the image out of her mind and glared down at Esa on the floor. "I won't be so merciful next time."

Both fell into silence, trying to catch their breaths. After a minute or two, Esa stood.

Despite the catharsis of fighting and winning, Imani silently seethed. The pixie had executed a masterful manipulation, knowing her vulnerabilities and weaknesses as an unmated female Norn. Not to mention her accurate suspicion Imani was hiding something. A small part of her admired Esa, but the risk had been immense. This type of treason—working with the Niflheim royals—was breathtaking. What did Esa so desperately want from Prince Kiran?

"Why me?" Imani's voice sounded raspy.

"Same reason anyone uses female elves—your magic cunt. Tanyl wouldn't sleep with me, so I had to pick someone he couldn't resist. I suggest you learn from this valuable lesson in naïveté and start protecting yourself more."

Imani made a sound of disgust, but the pixie held up her hand to silence her.

"I am not your friend, but I'm not your enemy, elf witch."

"Are you willing to throw away our potential alliance for some *Niflheim* breed?"

"Are *you*?"

"If you have an agreement with someone, keep it," Imani snarled.

"If you're going to be a criminal, do your homework first," Esa shot back.

Imani's wand was already pinned to Esa's throat. "You utter one more word, and I will slit your throat then drink your blood. You think you know me and what I want, but you don't. You have no idea what I'm capable of." Imani reached out and pushed down on Esa's bruised ribs. An anguished cry tore from the pixie. "Now leave so I can chat with my new acquaintance," Imani said loudly, pretending to sound confident about the prospect.

The pixie was about to argue but, instead, gave Kiran a slight nod before limping toward the exit, cradling her broken arm.

CHAPTER 23

Imani found herself alone with the prince. Tension filled the room like a vise around her throat. She took a deep breath, waiting for him to speak.

Instead, he stared. Sitting up straighter and bending a knee to prop his elbow on it, his head rested in his hand. He studied her with a mixture of confusion and manic interest.

An odd sense of time slowing came over Imani. A blip of chilling pressure awakened a minuscule crack inside her, leading somewhere vast and profound; a place she didn't want to even think about for too long. She ignored it, but the emotion lingered.

If he sensed it, too, he gave no indication.

"Hello, little elf witch," he murmured politely. His grin grew. "I didn't expect you to be the one Esa would bring here tonight, darling. It's rare when something, or someone, takes me by surprise." He clasped his chin, where a shadow of dark facial hair had grown. "How did you get inside? I placed the wards myself."

Her soul draw was on full display, although she wasn't sure it worked on another elf as strongly as it did on other breeds. If this conversation turned problematic, it was her only defense against a powerful witch like Kiran. Though she disliked using it—and it generally being more of a problem than a solution—the draw might help her tonight.

He put his fingers to his mouth and studied her, thinking. His eyes met hers, and she stared back, testing to see if her soul draw would affect him as his did her.

Kiran's disfigured eye was like a hole with no bottom—endless black. His green one was beautiful—a bright, verdant color sparkling in the firelight. For some reason, it reminded her of the nymph witch she'd met in their shop before Malis had attacked her. She'd never forget those eyes, but the man had had two.

"Again, why am I here?" she asked in a lilting voice layered with her elf-witch magic.

One of his eyebrows flicked up, but he remained clearheaded. "I wanted to see who and what we're dealing with before discussing a potential partnership."

Something about his black eye tempered her hold on him. In her raw, true form, even with the black marring her face, such an unnatural reaction bothered her. Kiran clearly enjoyed the company of females, yet Imani couldn't find any hint of the usual hunger.

With her scar, she wouldn't be as beautiful as the other female Norn he'd met.

It doesn't matter, Imani admonished herself. Her appearance and soul draw were superficial powers; they had always been tricks rather than real magic. Yet she couldn't deny her disappointment. Controlling such a powerful witch, especially when bargaining with him, would have been a boon for her. But it wasn't an option.

Kiran leaned closer. "Your illusion keeps your magic well hidden. You're stunning without glamour, and I can't tell you how much it pleases me."

"I couldn't care less about pleasing *you*. I want to speak to your brother."

Kiran laughed again, a musical sound making her toes curl. "What a little liar you are," he purred. "Of course, you care about pleasing me. My brother isn't making any decisions here without my counsel." Walking forward, he loomed over her, although she supposed it wasn't too hard to do with his considerable height and broad shoulders. With his thumbs, he skimmed the skin beneath her eyes. "Even these perfect little eyelashes sparkle without the glamour." His face became concerned. "But this soul draw of yours will be a problem, one I didn't anticipate with the security measures in place."

"What security measures?"

"The room is warded against illusion magic," he said with a sly glint.

She felt like a bird caught in a cage but kept her composure. Not many witches could pull off such a spell. Kiran's defensive magic impressed her.

Someone else entered the suite.

Kiran positioned himself between her and the door, hiding her from view behind his large body.

Without her powerful illusion, Prince Saevel sensed her. He canted his head to the side in a predatory way, and his pupils enlarged, rapacious in their penetrating stare.

She wouldn't call Saevel handsome. He looked far too much like an actual bear to her. Yet, like yesterday when he'd exited the coach, he displayed an undeniably regal, lethal grace—magnificent but utterly alarming.

Peering around Kiran, Saevel paced—no, stalked—toward them. "What are you hiding, brother?"

Her instincts from her collecting days kicked in, and the longer Kiran didn't respond, the more dangerous the room became. Still, she wanted the Drasil too badly to try to leave yet.

"I said, what are you hiding?" Saevel's voice sounded light, but his eyes had the familiar glaze. He would attack if they locked eyes, and she had no illusion magic to temper his desire by controlling the soul draw.

The day in the shop with Malis came rushing back to her. Would Kiran protect her if Saevel overpowered and forced her to feed from him? If not, her shadows might come out.

Kiran must have sensed her rising panic. With his hands still at his sides but a bit behind, the elf shifted to block her more subtly, making it impossible for her to run.

Prince Saevel moved closer to the two elves. He glared at Kiran. "Is this her?"

Kiran's voice was quiet but no less threatening. "Yes, but we have an unexpected issue. My contact did her job well since we are trying to ensnare a prince in the bedroom."

"Then what's the issue?"

"Our new friend is a female Norn elf, which presents a problem for us right now," Kiran said matter-of-factly.

The air swirled with charged, heightened dark energy from Kiran's signature and the promise of violence. All her senses elevated. Her magic sensed the danger from earlier growing.

"I'm not in the mood for your games," Saevel murmured. "We always promised we'd do this together. No more secrets, remember?"

"It isn't a game. Unfortunately, once I learned who we'd be meeting with tonight, I had little time to put a plan together, so you need to trust me."

Each particle of her body was acutely aware of how closely he stood. A buzzing energy vibrated between them. Kiran kept tracing slow circles against her skin, calming her while inching ever closer. But it wasn't in comfort. It was a warning, telling her to stay put.

"You're pissing me off, and after this fucking day, I'm not in a trusting mood. So, why should I?"

"Since I've spent months planning this for you, we can't risk anything, including *you*, ruining it. And you know we can't have privacy *and* illusion magic in this room. So, unlike this morning, she will be in her true form. Now, you either agree to a binding not to touch her while we have this arrangement so we can do this together or leave and let me handle this alone." Kiran's voice dropped to a whisper. "Finding your heartmate would make these conversations—conversations you'll have to have as king—far easier."

Kiran's calm voice and touch did something to her. Now, so close to her, his soul draw made Imani want to shut her eyes and drop her forehead to his back. But she resisted and refocused on the matter at hand.

"You only remind me every day," Saevel groaned, rolling his eyes.

"You are not immune to her, brother," Kiran said. He held her tighter to his back until his body entirely obscured her. "Females of her kind are the most dangerous elves, and this one is more beautiful than most. Do you want to lose control because of her?"

"Get out of my way," Saevel stated, his voice deadly.

"Stay away from her." Kiran's voice came out as a low rumble, and by the saints, he sounded … terrifying. Lethal. Dangerous.

Whipping his wand out and pointing it straight at Kiran, a force from Saevel tugged at his brother. Kiran didn't budge. With a growl, Saevel slashed his wand in a line. A sharp gust of wind pushed Kiran over, and he landed on his knees with a grunt.

Saevel's command of magic was better than Imani had anticipated.

Exposed, Imani found a pair of startling green eyes glaring at the jagged, black vein-like mark running down her face. She knew each detail. The mark spider-webbed and cracked in imperfect slashes across her cheek and around her forehead. She must have looked frightful with her true form exposed, bruises and splotches of dried blood covering her arms. But her Norn magic had him ignoring it all.

"Lovely. Who marred this perfect face with such a vicious injury?" Saevel murmured.

"Some bastard who threatened me." The lie slipped out, and she gave him a saccharine smile. "I killed him."

They locked eyes, and his green ones went dark as he succumbed to her magic. "I can't stop imagining how to shut that perfect mouth up."

"I'd sooner cut off my arm and beat you with it than get in bed with you. Now back up." Her voice carried the weight of the power the soul draw gave her.

A wicked grin spread on the shifter's beastly face, but he obeyed. "We'll see."

"The only person you'll be fucking is yourself," she hissed back, pressure building inside her. Her shadows wanted out.

But before anything could happen, Kiran pushed her away, putting himself between them again.

She peeked around him. Saevel's huge eyes were still locked on Imani, but he still stayed back, like she'd ordered. The Niflheim heir apparent was strong, but Saevel couldn't fight it. So far, no one could, except maybe Kiran.

While she was in control now, it wouldn't last. The soul draw ran wild and built. Soon, it would make Saevel crazed, and he would attack. Without her magic to protect her, she'd be at his mercy.

At least Imani wasn't alone.

A menacing sound came from Kiran's chest, so deep and predatory it startled her and made Saevel back further away.

Saevel narrowed his eyes. It was an unmistakable challenge. Then, without even thinking, Saevel attacked. Like a beast, he lunged quickly—quicker than she'd thought possible for someone his size. Kiran's arms had banded around her like iron earlier. He was strong, but Saevel grabbed the front of Kiran's shirt, yanking him away and pressing him hard into the wall. Pieces of the plaster fell to the floor under the force.

Afraid, shadows slammed against the wall of her control.

She tried to anchor her focus by training her eyes on Kiran. Much to her surprise, he appeared unconcerned with his current situation, pinned against the wall. Instead, he met his brother's murderous gaze with a raving half-smirk.

Subservient but completely insane at the same time, he said, "Remember the last time you attacked me, Saevel? Are you the beast Father thinks you are? His pet beast, huh? Are you turning into him?"

Saevel's temper burned hot and fast.

Kiran emitted a violent edge, too, but his was more calculated and sharp, like a knife rather than a hammer. His stillness sent shivers down her spine. Magical power filled a vast chasm inside him, ready to explode, but his restraint astounded her.

What would happen if Kiran let go?

Imani envied his skills, but there was something wrong. He wasn't as in control as he led people to believe, and it scared her.

"I'm *nothing* like him, and you forget your place," Saevel shouted, his voice booming. "How many times do you need to learn this lesson?"

"At least once more, I suppose," Kiran said, emotionless.

Yanking the wand from Kiran's hand, Saevel sent it tumbling

across the floor to the other side of the room. He then snapped his fingers, ordering his brother around like a servant. "Kneel in front of your heir."

Kiran made no move to obey, the wild gleam in his gaze brightening.

"Is today the day you want to die, brother? Do you think anyone would care if you no longer existed? Father would thank me. Most people would. But the choice is yours." Saevel punched his brother straight in the mouth.

Kiran didn't react, not even a wince, although the force of Saevel's fist made him stumble. "You think Father hasn't done exactly this to me before? I thought you were more creative than him," Kiran said, wiping blood from the corner of his mouth.

Imani's fear of his loss of control increased. Another fierce jolt of her magic rose.

Kneel, you idiot, she silently pleaded, impatient for this argument between brothers to end before she did something stupid. If she were threatened, her shadows would obliterate everyone and everything in this room.

Prince Kiran didn't spare her a glance. His gaze fixed on his brother as he sat on his knees but not kneeling. A tiny muscle flexed in the male elf's defined jaw. Imani's eyes widened as he struggled not to laugh. Was he *enjoying* this little defiance?

Another punch landed across Kiran's face. "I don't need to be more creative than Father. I only need to be stronger."

More blood trickled down Kiran's face and neck, and his laughter hinged on maniacal as his head fell against the wall. Blood shone on his white teeth, but his smile didn't reach his eyes—because something beastly hid behind his arrogant mask.

Born inside the Draswood, Imani understood animalistic predators more than most. Seeing his face made more terror build inside her. She did not want to see the monster freed to take on her own magic.

Scared, Imani took in erratic breaths. The shadows vibrated inside her, and no matter how hard she tried to hold them back, magic started turning her fingernails black, like a slow seeping of liquid, spreading under her skin.

Kiran's eyes were unfocused for a moment, but he stayed silent. Blood from his nose or mouth covered his shirt. Somehow, he'd managed to right himself and stare up at his brother, but it had to hurt. How could it not?

If she was honest, it impressed her how Kiran had remained conscious after taking two punches to the face from someone like Saevel.

With a look of ire, Saevel prepared to strike Kiran again, and Imani watched in terror as her shadow magic spread through the veins in her hands. Tiny streams of smokey magic escaped her fingertips until the magic covered the tops of her hands entirely. Imani wiggled her fingers, trying to call them back, but nothing would stop the dark mist when it exploded. Her control was even more tenuous when her fear was this high.

Prince Kiran's eyes flicked to hers as a sense of doom set in. Imani had been extremely careful not to use her shadows in front of most people, especially powerful master witches. No one noticed it unless it seeped out. Even when it affected the lights or the fire in the room, people brushed it off.

Kiran would be powerful enough to see this display—there was nothing she could do about it now—but she desperately didn't want him to know the full extent of her secret.

He tilted his head to the side, his gaze sliding back to his brother with resignation. A wave of relief fell over her.

The room froze for one second before he kneeled as a chill shuddered through her. His mask lifted like a lightning strike, illuminating what was always hidden in the dark. For one moment, she glimpsed a part of Kiran's madness. It had a face—it took *over* his face. An unbridled, raw hatred churned beneath Kiran's skin.

Its eyes snapped to her. Both eyes were pitch-black now, with no green to be seen, but they weren't empty and cold like a dead spirit's. They were equally troubling, however.

Endless and heated, those all-black eyes made her tremble. For a few moments, she stopped breathing. A nightmare permeated her mind, some being who shouldn't exist there.

Or anywhere.

An acute sense of horror seeped into her body, and something menacing and evil reached out and grabbed her soul, shaking it. Never in her life had a sensation so disturbing struck her. It terrified her as nothing had before.

Did it feel the same when she forcibly took someone's soul from them while they lived?

A scream like nails on a chalkboard no one else could hear but her filled the room. She wanted to crouch down and cover her ears.

A mere second later, it stopped. The being disappeared so fast Imani thought she'd imagined it. She hoped she had. A dark creature with Kiran's deep magic well at its disposal? Was it his snake form? The thought made her physically sick. Indeed, what Imani felt from him then truly scared her.

He bowed, his tense jaw the only hint of his obstinance.

She rubbed her hands, pushing the shadows back inside. The darkness receded, leaving her skin unharmed and perfect again.

Kiran jumped up, straightening his shirt and trying to fix his disheveled hair, but he did not bother to clean up his blood. Her heart slowed as he moved to stand close to her again.

His voice cut through the tension, irritated but calm, as if nothing had happened. "Are you done thinking with your cock?"

Running his hands down his face, Saevel took a deep breath, trying to focus. "I'm sorry, Kiran. I got out of hand." Saevel motioned to Imani. "You were right about her. This is inconvenient."

"Yes, but her being an elf couldn't have worked out better for our needs. No one can resist wanting her, including you and Prince Tanyl." He pointed at his brother's chest. "I told you this was important, and I meant it. We need leverage. You must trust me if we want this to work."

"I know." Dragging a hand through his hair, Saevel looked over at Imani. "How does the little whore's draw not affect you, then? Huh?"

"Oh, it does." Kiran's voice was so low she almost didn't hear. "But all elves have the same compulsion magic, to some degree, and it's somewhat easier to manage. Otherwise, we'd all go mad living together." He paused. "So, you either agree to a binding to avoid her soul draw controlling you or leave."

"It is not your decision, brother. There will always be a hierarchy in this relationship." Saevel glared at Kiran, and his magic flared in the room. A command.

She braced for another confrontation, but Kiran surprised her.

"Of course." Kiran bowed his head to his older brother.

Seeing this powerful witch so subservient unsettled her again. There was something inherently *wrong* about it.

Any malice from Saevel dissipated, and he nodded at his brother with utmost trust in his eyes. "Fine. I'm sorry I lost my head for a bit. You were right about the soul draw. If you say it's important, then it is," he agreed calmly. "I'm tired. Let's get this over with now."

Despite losing his temper, Saevel's response surprised her. Not only did he trust Kiran as an adviser—the one most people despised, mistrusted, and avoided—but he also knew when to listen and when to take advice.

Maybe he would become king after all.

CHAPTER 24

They sauntered back into the room minutes later.

Imani crossed her arms, grateful for the coverage of her long sleeves, as her true form—minus her flesh-magicked brands—was displayed without the illusion glamour.

"I'm regretting that binding." Saevel paced around her. Kiran's spell prevented him from getting close to her.

"Stop stalking her," Kiran said, his voice low and threatening. He pointed to a chair by the hearth several feet from her. "Sit."

With a grumble, Saevel gave up and dropped heavily into the chair.

"What do you want from me?" Imani wanted to get this over with as quickly as possible.

"A mutually beneficial agreement," Saevel explained.

Her back straightened. Would they offer to take her to the Niflheim Kingdom without passing the assessments? It would be too good to be true.

She considered her words carefully. "I'm not stupid," she said evenly. "What are you offering for my access to Tanyl?"

Saevel waved a lazy hand at his brother. "Do you have what you need to finish this up?"

"I don't, but I will soon." Prince Kiran's voice sounded cold.

Detached. He pushed off the wall. As he moved closer, she flinched, pulling back from his touch.

"I need you to show me all of your markings," he said, the tone of someone accustomed to getting their way as a pulse of magic spread around him.

"You saw them earlier when you examined them at the assessment," she argued.

"We both know you wore an illusion."

"For my soul draw, like all female Norn," she hit back.

But Kiran merely waited. "I hate repeating myself," he added, entitlement embodying his every word.

Imani disliked his lethal, calm tone. The gentle softness and words now only increased his danger.

"You've already seen them," she lied through gritted teeth.

The brothers exchanged a knowing look that batted unspoken words between them.

Her heart rate quickened. Imani was a lying liar. Somehow, he knew because his teasing grin turned wolfish.

A beat passed before he let out a low laugh, mirth dancing in his eyes as he grabbed her arm.

Terrified he'd see through the flesh magic, she jerked back, hissing at him. "Don't touch—"

He cut her off by ripping up her sleeve again, this time even further, revealing all her markings.

Imani scowled as a tingle of awareness slid up her arm. Every time he touched her, it happened. Did her body recognize something in him?

Stealing a glance down, she let out a breath. Her illicit brands remained hidden, still invisible under the powerful flesh magic. But Kiran's gaze narrowed in on the divination one.

She'd tried to hide the bruise-like appearance with a lighter glamour, thinking no one would notice. But without any illusion, it was different than her other marks.

Kiran tapped his finger on the divination brand, the wickedness in his gaze returning. "Hmm, let's start with the fact that you're not the High-Norn elf named Meira," he stated, dropping her wrist and any pretense of gentleness. "Do you mind if I call you Imani when it's only us, little elf?"

Imani's heart pounded. "You have me confused," she rasped, vowing to keep the ruse going until she absolutely couldn't anymore.

A faint smile tugged at Kiran's mouth as he gently brushed the hair strands loose from her braid. "While you're fooling the rest of the sheep, I know with complete certainty you're Imani Aowyn. You could never be Meira in a million years."

"How …? How could you know this?" Imani's voice was a shaking whisper. If he couldn't sense the flesh magic—and she was still unsure if he could—then he shouldn't have known her name. They didn't know each other.

He grinned. "The divination brand doesn't belong to you, and who do you think your grandmother worked with in Niflheim before she died? It was a guess that you had an illusion over your brands. I doubted you both had the same magic, even if you are sisters."

Imani couldn't help but suck in a quick breath. *It was him*. He hadn't known who she was immediately, but she'd been familiar, and *that* was why he had watched her since arriving. He was the prince who had strangled Malis. He was the one Ara had admitted to conspiring with.

"Why are you here, masquerading as Meira?" Kiran's voice dropped to a whisper. "I suggest you stop lying. Otherwise, I'll have to sort this confusion out with your brother and sister."

"If you do anything to my siblings, I don't care who your father is or how powerful you are—I will end your existence," she spat, drawing herself up as tall as she could. She wished more than anything she could use her soul draw on him.

Kiran fought an incredulous laugh. *"End my existence?* You're delightful."

Her glare darkened, but she dropped the charade, letting the truth spill out with as much venom as she could muster. "Meira would never survive here. The Order would eat her alive, and my grandmother kept my magic unregistered, unlike hers."

"So, you switched places with her. How noble." Kiran's voice was flat.

"What else are you hiding, I wonder?" Saevel said smugly.

Imani lost the little control she had. Wrenching herself away from Kiran, she found a large dagger on the table nearby. It was the size of her forearm, but she didn't care. She picked it up and flew at Saevel in a rage. "You have your *leverage*," she snarled. "Now, tell me what you want me to do for you!"

"Calm down, darling." Kiran snaked his arm around her waist, holding her back from attacking his brother again, her back to his chest. "Feral little thing, aren't you?" He set her down in front of him and grabbed her wrist, which held her wand. "Let me be clear, elf witch. You are mine. You can't walk away, not with a family relying on you for survival. I reveal you're a traitor and a liar to your queen, and they will make an example of you. And where would it leave your siblings? Hmm?"

The light in the room flickered as the vision arrived. It was unavoidable after the prolonged touch.

Kiran's face contorted, frantic, as if he couldn't breathe. His eyes closed in blatant agony from a pain in his chest. He kneeled on the ground in the forest and, with one smooth motion, shoved a dagger into himself. With a grimace, he pushed harder with the knife, its blade fully lodged in his stomach.

He gritted his teeth but stayed silent, gripping the bloody dagger with one hand before he fell onto his side, reaching for someone's hand while shutting his eyes in pain. He held it tight, murmuring something she couldn't understand. Blood ringlets spread everywhere, dripping onto the snow and dirt. Red blossomed across his chest now. He rolled onto his back. Each breath he took sounded labored as he bled out.

A gasp escaped her mouth when it ended. She landed back in the present, trembling. Too many questions. Too much blood. A whirlwind of emotions wrapped around her heart. The other deaths had been different—softer and duller. But his death vision was in full color, and the red from the blood was so bright she whipped around to face him.

Kiran appeared uninjured, aside from the fading cuts on his face. A breath of relief escaped her.

His hands fell to his sides. "What's wrong?"

It was clear that people had no idea she had these visions, and she wanted it to remain as such.

"Nothing," she breathed, blinking to get control back. In one smooth motion, she pointed her wand at his chest.

"Going to try to hurt me, too?" The glint in his eyes became slightly wild.

"What would you do if I did, Prince?"

"There's nothing you could do to hurt me. I have awe-inspiring magic skills. Don't you agree, Saevel?"

"There is very little magic you can't do," his brother admitted.

Kiran gave her a predatory, warning smile. "Now, stop this nonsense, and we'll explain what we want from you."

She dropped her wand and shut her eyes, waiting.

"We all know you're sleeping with Tanyl. Esa set that up beautifully," Kiran explained bluntly. "So, you'll deliver me reliable and usable intelligence about Tanyl. In return, we'll keep your little secret and give you information to prepare for the next two assessments—a trade of sorts."

"You'll help me cheat?"

Kiran brushed his thumb over the center of her throat in a slow, soothing pattern. "Call it whatever you want. I'm ensuring you continue providing value as long as possible."

"You didn't need to learn my identity to get me to agree," she seethed. "I would have said yes in exchange for information on passing the assessments."

"We needed extra assurance you'd keep quiet about our arrangement. After all, you are sleeping with the heir apparent. What stops you from being righteous and double-crossing us by tattling to him?"

She glared. "What information do you want?"

"Anything to do with his plans for the Order and anything you learn about his relationship with his mother. *Anything.* Understand? Seemingly irrelevant details could be important—where he goes, who he talks to, his moods. If he gets his fucking feelings hurt by his mother, we want to know about it. When your information pleases us, you'll get the details of the next assessments in exchange. Before it happens."

"You're asking too much. I might hear a thing or two, but he doesn't tell me anything important. You're essentially asking me to fuck the heir apparent for vague pieces of gossip."

His mouth didn't change, but his eyes warmed. "Oh, Imani, darling, don't act like it offends your delicate sensibilities," he crooned. "I've been whoring in courts before you even understood the word. I know my own kind, and vague pieces of gossip can be more helpful than you know."

Imani was so angry at being exposed, at being trapped. She wanted to smash his head into the stone floor and tell him she was nothing like him. She imagined herself doing it, over and over, his brain matter sticking into the grooves.

He was right. It didn't offend her. Not in the slightest. And frankly, Kiran could have said much more with what he had on her and how badly she wanted to pass the assessments.

"You think you know me because you watched me for two days and knew my grandmother?" She met his wild stare with one of her own. "I want a binding," Imani said.

"Absolutely not." Kiran huffed a laugh.

"Agree, or I'm walking away."

More laughter, now from both Niflheim brothers.

"You're asking me to do all this without a binding? Why should I trust either of you to keep your word?" Imani said.

"Because you have no choice," Saevel said, still laughing.

Her stomach sank. The three stared at each other for another moment, and she knew when she'd lost.

CHAPTER 25

Imani lifted the knife over her shoulder before throwing it at the target. She'd been practicing for over an hour in the setting sun. Despite her shaking limbs, it hit the center with a loud *thwack*. Riona had taught Imani about throwing knives, among other things. While she didn't know what it was yet, with the second assessment approaching, she didn't want to get rusty.

She sighed and wrung her hands together then walked to retrieve the knife, glancing around the crowded area where others sparred and practiced magic. Her eyes caught on a tall figure at the entrance to the practice field.

Tanyl stood in the archway. His hair was longer than usual, a couple of errant strands curling against his forehead. He scanned the field with a stern look on his face. When his eyes locked onto hers, he inclined his head for a moment, and she was sure he would come over.

But with his hands in his pockets, he broke the contact and sauntered away. Walking toward the back edge of the grass, the breeze ruffled his hair as he disappeared into the gardens.

Although they were never seen in public together, the exchange made her more than anxious. Something was wrong with Tanyl; three days had passed, and he hadn't called on her. It made Imani nervous so close to her first meeting with the princes. Did he suspect her betrayal?

She needed more information to give the Niflheim princes if she was going to get the details she so desperately needed. Tanyl barely revealed anything to her as it was, and she needed as much time as possible with him to gather any scraps she could.

Normally, she wouldn't go to Tanyl's rooms without being summoned, and because he'd been silent, Imani had stayed away.

Today, she needed to seek him out.

With a flip of her knife, she stashed it against her thigh and followed him through the shrubs. The tall bushes made the gardens challenging to navigate, but as she turned a corner, something grabbed her dress and ripped her backward.

Esa flipped Imani around and pressed a finger to her lips. They backed away slowly.

With her superior elvish hearing, eavesdropping was easy for Imani; it was one of the most potent tools in her arsenal. But Esa had saved her from passing through the silencing ward, which would have alerted the caster. She had slipped through Kiran's similar defenses for some reason—maybe like called to like with dark magic—but she wasn't sure if it would work with Tanyl's.

Instead, Esa pointed to the bushes, and they ducked down behind them. The thick brush hid the petite females as they waited for Tanyl to exit the gardens so Imani could follow him. If he caught them, Imani was sure her chances of hearing any new information would die.

They waited a good five minutes. Then footsteps broke the silence. Two pairs of leather boots moved swiftly across the stones.

"I think we should move up the timeline," a man who sounded like Sid, the captain, said.

"Do we have enough support?" Tanyl sounded desperate.

"We have the Order, minus the First Witch, and I command our forces. They're loyal to me, not the Crown."

The implications of such a statement were treasonous, and it was all Imani could do to keep her mouth from gaping. She crept around the corner to confirm if the man speaking was Sid, a breeze blowing her unbound hair around her face. The silver must have glinted in the disappearing sunlight and caught the guard's eye.

"We aren't alone," Sid whispered through clenched teeth.

Tanyl whipped around, and Imani bit her tongue so hard the taste of copper dripped against her cheek. She held it there, crushing it between her teeth, biting, biting.

Striding forward with ire in his eyes, Tanyl wrenched her from the shadows and into the small courtyard. Esa must have shrunk to her minuscule pixie size because she was nowhere in sight—another reason she couldn't be trusted.

Imani held up her hands in defeat. "I only came around the corner seconds ago. I didn't want to interrupt, nor did I hear anything."

Tanyl shot her a once-over, clearly not convinced. Then the prince turned to Sid. "We're done here. I'll take care of this situation."

Sid nodded then turned in the opposite direction without a word.

Gripping her by the elbow, Tanyl stared straight ahead as he dragged her through the maze. "Come on; we're going to my rooms to have a little chat."

He did not speak on the walk there or glance at her once they'd entered his suite. He poured himself a glass of wine and didn't offer her any. Without turning to meet her stare, he said, "What did you overhear?"

"All I heard was there was a timeline that needed to be moved up," she stated.

"Liar." He paced the room like a large animal trapped in a cage.

She fidgeted with her hands in front of her as she exhaled. "Tanyl, I didn't hear anything else. It was too windy today, and I had only been there a few seconds—I swear it." Her lies continued to pile up around her as she tried to play it off as unimportant. "Besides, you couldn't have been talking about anything important. Who would be so stupid to do so in such a public place without being inside a silencing enchantment?"

"I tolerate your mouth because we have fun together, Meira. Tread carefully, or you might cease to be amusing." His voice was hard as he locked eyes with her for the first time since they had entered his rooms. The harsh tone took her aback.

She shivered, and all she could do was nod and acquiesce in response. "I understand." The last thing she wanted to do was to get kicked out tonight. She had little time left. Imani wanted a night of passion with him—*needed* it—to convince him everything was fine.

The prince did not appear to feel the same. He prowled over to the fireplace and leaned against the mantel. The flames flared and writhed before him.

Out of choices, she had one last trick up her sleeve. It made her feel guilty to use such power on him, but with his cold demeanor, she wouldn't be getting anything out of him using her typical methods. It was dangerous, and she was low for using it on him, but desperate times and all that.

Despite being practiced at hiding the draw—Meira and Ara made sure of it before Imani had left home—she was less practiced in using it. However, she'd been getting more proficient since coming to the palace.

Imani loosened the illusion on her soul draw. It felt incredible to take control of this magic that had controlled *her* most of her life.

Like the other times she'd used it, Imani imagined her skin glowing slightly, her eyes widening, and their blue color deepening. Her scent filled the room, subtle enough to catch his attention but not noticeable enough for him to sense the manipulation. Her illusion magic kept the feelings even and steady.

Come on; look at me, she said silently.

Finishing the glass of wine with a flourish, he scooped up the silver decanter to refill it for a second time. He lifted his head and put it on the table. His gaze flicked up, eyes snagging her focus. His pupils seemed more prominent, and his eyes had no visible gray. How he looked at her was like … like he had no idea who Imani was, as if he didn't see her. His throat worked as he stared.

"I didn't hear anything," Imani murmured, her voice distorted with her enchantment magic while she tentatively moved closer to him. He would believe her now. She'd *made* him believe it.

She gently reached out and cupped his face.

Tanyl didn't shy away for one second. He didn't even blink. There was a hardness to the line of his jaw as he stared at her, and when he spoke, there was a roughness in his voice that hadn't been there before. "I have to be able to trust you, Meira ... I shouldn't even be doing this with you. I have a mountain of responsibilities on top of me right now. You're a distraction."

"You can trust me with anything ... Now, what were you and Sid talking about?" Her voice was still layered with her enchantment magic. He would trust her moving forward.

"The elves are not coming," he stated. "Ellisar killed every man we sent to the Draswood and sent them back in pieces. We shouldn't have used so much force."

"It wasn't your call, though. The queen is growing more brazen." Imani shuddered at the thought of Dialora receiving the mangled soldiers back.

A deep sigh was Tanyl's only response as he rubbed his eyes. He sounded utterly exhausted, his weariness palpable. "The Niflheim princes won't take this lightly. They continue to ask about the elves, knowing some of our most powerful witches are Norn."

"We can't risk provoking them right now. We may need to make another bargain to appease them."

"I know." Tanyl ran a hand through his hair.

"How far into the Forest did they make it?"

"Barely to the outskirts. Ellisar has the Draswood locked up tight. He's going to be a problem, eventually. We need to start understanding how to make him an ally. My mother has not put enough effort into it. She either ignores him to rule the Draswood alone or deals with him with outright force. There must be a better way."

Imani tilted her head back. Her lips touched his as she said, "You'll find it."

"You're so damn beautiful," he whispered. His voice was thick. "And so damn unexpected." He adjusted himself to rub his cock against her center. The friction sent pleasure rushing through her. "Have you ever used your soul draw on me?" His voice held a tone of vulnerability in it.

She kissed him, murmuring against his lips again in her enchanted voice, "Never on purpose. You can trust me." The words felt like a perversion as Imani forced them out. Her lies disgusted her, but she had to remember she was playing a longer game, one leading her to the power and independence she craved—the Drasil.

It was worth it.

"I know," he groaned, giving her the answer she had manipulated out of him, making him truly believe it as he tightened his arm around her waist and drew her closer.

Imani felt him, hard and thick against her. Gripping his arm, tension coiled inside her.

They fell into bed, a tangle of arms and legs, and the passion absent from him earlier came rearing its head.

Imani let him do whatever he wanted, enjoying being back in his good graces. As much as she was lying to him, she *liked* Tanyl. Probably a little too much, considering their precarious situation.

The last thing Imani remembered was lying face-to-face with Tanyl, him toying with her hair.

A sleepy, pleased smile tugged at her lips.

CHAPTER 26

Two days later, she broke into the Niflheim princes' rooms again for their first meeting.

Despite the thicker magic coming off it and a nasty heat signature warning people away, at her command, it rushed around her like a broken dam, stripping away the glamour over her appearance. But again, not the flesh magic.

She smiled to herself as she stepped over the threshold in her mostly true form.

A man's voice drifted down the hall. "She gave us everything. All the proof, ready to go."

As she approached, the orange glow from the fire lit the room up, including the three men standing together near it. The sight made her freeze.

A million scenarios for why the sons of the high sentinel of the naiads were here ran through her mind, and none were good.

"If you bring this evidence to the queen, she'll have to take it seriously," the other said.

"The magic was—" the first man cut himself off, staring at Imani. He glanced at her and back to the prince. A slow, wicked smile spread across his nymph face. "Well, well, well, Lady Aowyn."

Her grandmother had met with the men's father on a few occasions years ago—all business—and on more significant transactions, she and Riona had always accompanied. So, while they'd seen her years before with her glamour on, he still recognized her.

Imani stood firm, unflinching despite the weight of their heavy stares on her unglamoured form.

"What a nice surprise, Imani," Kiran deadpanned in a tone suggesting the opposite before he turned to the brothers. "I wasn't aware either of you personally knew Lady Aowyn." The prince's face remained impassive, but a muscle in his jaw tightened. She shouldn't have let herself inside his rooms.

In no way did Imani personally know the sons of the high sentinel of the naiads, but she kept her mouth closed in a thin line.

"I wasn't aware you did, either, Kiran," Selwyn said smugly. "My, she's certainly more grown up than she was all those years ago." He lowered his eyes to her breasts with heat banking in his electric-blue gaze. "I always thought you'd be pretty; never *this* pretty." He tsked. "Except for the horrible scarring. It's hideous."

Her lips parted, breathing short and shallow. Still, she stayed silent.

The younger brother, Maelon, leaned against the wall and studied her curiously. She suspected her magic had taken hold of him already and chastised herself again for her carelessness and arrogance in barging in here.

He shook his head, stepping closer to Imani. "Hmm, indeed. It's a shame the prince here is planning to kill off—"

He didn't get to finish because Kiran slammed his fist into the second man's face. A sound like crunching bones and a muffled groan echoed. The body fell onto the floor.

Kiran stared for a moment at what used to be the high sentinel's oldest son. His boot slammed into his head, knocking away his wand and forcing the man onto his back.

Selwyn opened his mouth to protest, but the prince didn't let him, grabbing him by the hair and smashing his head against the marble above the hearth.

"What part about not talking about *anything* did you not understand? Let"—he smashed his head—"me"—another smash—"remind you!" Kiran yelled, hammering the man's head against the fireplace mantel. Stone crumbled onto the floor, mixing with the blood.

Yet, Kiran didn't stop.

"You don't talk about my business to anyone." Smash. "You don't mention me—ever." Smash. "And you sure as shit don't call me anything but *Your Highness*."

Crush. Slam. Smash. The prince didn't hold back, and she cringed each time.

Imani exhaled when he finally released Selwyn's head, now covered in blood and flesh. Utterly destroyed.

No emotions showed on Kiran's face as he let the body fall to the ground. He had likely died after the first two hits into the wall, but the prince had wanted this nymph's head to come off his neck.

Rolling his shoulders, Kiran paced. With a choked laugh, he tugged on his hair with both hands like he was working on composing himself. His muscles tensed with his unhinged gaze dragging over the room. His chest was heaving, covered in blood splotches, scrubbing his hands down his face, looking both devastating and positively insane.

Actually, without a doubt, the man *was* positively insane. It didn't take a master witch to see that.

She fought a crazed urge to close the distance between them—a sick, despicable notion. But he intrigued her to no end.

Brushing his hair off his forehead and wiping blood off his face, Kiran stared at the bodies around him.

Another fool stepped into the room. The unknown nymph instantly stilled, his mouth dropping open at the gore.

Kiran rolled his eyes. "Are all naiads this stupid?" he asked no one in particular, reaching for his wand as the nymph tried to turn and run. Kiran sliced off his legs with one swipe, and the nymph fell.

The prince strolled over and cocked his head to the side at his sobs and screams. Kiran laughed again and winked at him. "I did warn you not to make this deal with me if you couldn't keep your mouths shut."

Kiran blasted a hole through the man's face with his magic, and again, blood splattered onto his cheek. He groaned in irritation once more at the mess before turning to Imani.

She'd seen scenes like this before. It didn't happen often, but violence was unavoidable if you sold magic. However, her current situation with the princes was far more dangerous than she wanted to admit. It made her afraid. Not because she was afraid to die at their hands—she wasn't scared to die—but because of the sheer power their kingdom was up against.

The fact Kiran had made a deal with the sons of a high sentinel then murdered them seemingly on a whim in his room in Essenheim's palace told her how little the Crown threatened them and how deep the Niflheim Kingdom had infiltrated.

Two choices were laid out in front of Imani now: tell Tanyl and expose herself or keep quiet and let the Niflheim Kingdom continue tightening the noose around their neck. Neither of which sat well with her.

Ripping off his bloodstained shirt, the elf prince continued ignoring her, even while she crept closer and openly studied the multitude of binding markings and scars over his entire body. They surprised and mildly shocked her. It was difficult to predict how and where a binding brand would show up, and unless the spells were permanent, they'd disappear if they weakened, the caster died, or the terms were fulfilled. But he was absolutely *covered*.

Over the years, Imani had seen all kinds of low breeds working for the large covens, and most had bodies like Kiran's. Witches who sold magic collected scars and binding brands all over their bodies the longer they were in business. Saints, even her own body had more binding brands and scars than most high-bred females, but he was a *prince*.

"Still breaking into our rooms, I see." His voice shattered the strange silence between them.

The warning slithered over her. A logical response would have been to stay still, give Kiran the information he wanted, and try to get out of there quickly. She could hold this over his head, threatening to tell Tanyl what had happened.

With a pause, she took in the bodies of the high naiad males—the high sentinel's sons.

It was then Imani understood threats would get her nowhere

regarding Kiran. If someone was in his way, he simply killed them. Outside of the monarchs and his brothers, there weren't many people Kiran couldn't cut down.

To survive around people like him, a person always needed to ensure they were more valuable alive than dead. She needed to find something he desired badly enough to hold absolute power over someone like Kiran. And she wouldn't be able to do it if she left and told Tanyl about what had happened.

Without a thought, she drew herself up to her full height, as insubstantial as it was, and let her magic signature surround her before sauntering to stand before him.

Those mismatched eyes stared down at her intensely, sending shivers through her spine. Despite his madness, despite what he'd done, she wanted him to come down from whatever insane precipice his mind was on.

Her hands lifted to run up and down his arms of their own accord to calm him. "Who are you planning to kill, Your Highness?"

His expression flickered to one of curiosity. "Maybe *you* for breaking into my rooms. I've killed people for less."

"You're not going to kill me. Not when I came here to share what I've learned this week." She tilted her head to see his reaction. "Besides, you have your hands full with the rest of these bodies. What will Tanyl say when he learns what you've done?" she tsked.

Madness still shone in his gaze as he slid his eyes shut for a moment. His body relaxed under her palms.

Warmth spread through her at his soft inhale as she touched his chest. It felt right and so natural, even while none of this seemed natural.

He made that sound again—the rolling rumble—and her entire body shuddered.

Such power she held at this moment. It was an effort to prevent her hands from roaming further to coax more sounds like those from Kiran.

He stood incredibly still as he stared down at her, like a predator who had sighted its prey and was about to pounce. Her heart hammered while he traced his fingers down the column of her neck, his voice lowering. "All three of those witches were participating in the assessments," he rasped. "Once I dispose of the bodies, it's my word against yours about what exactly happened. So don't even think about telling anyone about this little transgression."

Kiran controlled all the Essenheim witches participating in his assessments. He would say they died while taking the assessments, and no one would question it, especially since there would be no bodies left to examine.

Before she could say anything else, he placed his hand over hers, stopping it. "I might still kill you. I'm a savage, remember? Anything's possible when I sense a threat." He dropped her hands and picked up a lock of her hair, wrapping it around his finger as if he couldn't stop touching her. "I always knew I'd have to kill those nymphs—they all have big mouths. Am I going to have to kill you, too? Are you going to go blabbing what you saw here today?"

Pressure clamped down on her chest. She couldn't move but finally managed to shake her head.

He smiled and let her hair loose from his finger before tucking it behind her ear.

"I should cut all my hair off and give it to you since you're so interested in it," she said, her voice more breathless than she'd intended.

An emotion too brief to name passed over Kiran's face. "I'm interested in every part of you, Imani."

Her name on his lips made her tense. The strange sense of recognition settled in her bones again, horror and delight all at once.

With a sobered expression, he pulled back. "But no, I won't kill you tonight." He turned in a silent directive for her to follow.

Trailing Kiran into the next room, Imani discovered Saevel and two female nymph witches waiting for them—naiads, by the look of them. One was an older, gorgeous female who twisted a wand in her hand. Another was younger, also pretty, lounging half-naked on a chair.

The fire cracked awkwardly when no one spoke.

Imani narrowed her eyes at the women, not at all amused about the situation.

Saevel lazily unbuttoned his pants in greeting.

Across the room, Kiran's face was unreadable, his disconcerting eyes glinting under half-closed lids. For once, the ever-present cocky smile was gone. Instead, he kept watching her.

She lifted her chin, refusing to hide from him, but she felt exposed, like he was peeking into her mind. What was he thinking?

The nymph witch with the wand sauntered over to Kiran and whispered in his ear. He gave the witch a grim smile and nodded.

Kiran abruptly turned to his brother before she could assess their relationship. "I have a situation to take care of." Then they both left.

Blinking a few times, not knowing how to respond, Imani stood there like an idiot as he walked away. Who in the saints was the witch whose counsel *Kiran* heeded? The brothers had brought a dozen of their own master witches as advisers, so it was possible she was one of them. Such an enigmatic relationship intrigued her, but she couldn't worry about it now.

Imani motioned to the whore. "What is this? I have a report to give you."

"And you will. I'm busy, and you'll find I multitask *extremely* well."

She was about to watch Saevel have sex with a whore, a blatant display of power meant to irritate her soul draw, meant to control her, meant to demean and mock her. Fury burned her chest.

CHAPTER 27

The whore studied Imani. "This is a female High Norn."

"Indeed. Quite observant you are," Saevel said blandly.

"I've never seen a high-bred female elf before, Your Highness," the whore murmured, eyes widening with surprise before turning back to him. Without glamour, Imani tried to reign in her emotions, but her blood steadily heated at the scene that was about to unfold. Her hunger didn't have rational responses. It had been two days since she'd fed from Tanyl. Imani had gone three *weeks* when she'd first arrived, but now she was ravenous.

Caught in her thrall already, the whore didn't wait for a response before pinning her gaze back on Imani. Clad in nothing more than a dressing gown, the woman surveyed her with a demure smile. She let the robe fall, pooling on the floor, and sauntered closer. Imani noted her sigil—a common-bred naiad.

"I want to touch her. She's as beautiful as they say, even with—"

"Get away from me," Imani snarled and tried to shove her. She had nothing against this woman personally, but she hated feeling out of control without her illusion magic to temper her soul draw.

Saevel grabbed the whore by the arm and ripped her back. "I said, don't talk to her," he growled.

The whore nodded as if clearing her head and dropped to her knees.

The prince stood towering above the female shifter, and Imani couldn't help but explore his form.

Again, she was struck by how beastly he was—not her type at all. But a strange desire and disgust tangled inside her all the same. Damn her hunger. Depending on the prey, feeding was usually tied to sex. With family members, it simply made you closer to them, but with unmated males, it heightened arousal. Exactly as Saevel had planned, she was sure. Starved and agitated, her shallow breaths deepened.

Regardless of her feelings, she'd conduct herself with dignity.

Narrowing her eyes to slits at his audacity, Imani despised Saevel right then.

An even greater hunger rose in her as he rubbed his hands up and down the female's bare waist, forcing a gasp out of Imani. She bit her lip. She wouldn't give him the satisfaction of ever letting him see her internal conflict.

"I'm waiting for your report, Imani," he said over his shoulder while holding himself hard in his hands. His movements were languid, like he had all the time in the world.

Fighting her own hunger, she wrenched her eyes open with a quiet growl.

"Open your mouth." Saevel grabbed a fistful of the shifter's hair and pushed her head down. "I'm going to fuck it."

"Do we trust her to hear this information?" Imani asked, her voice tight.

With his hand pressed at the back of her head, holding the woman in place, Saevel turned to Imani. "There is no *we* here, but I promise she won't remember anything after I finish." Memory spells and potions were tricky. But if anyone could wield them, she guessed Kiran could.

He pushed the woman forward with a jerk of his hand, and she whimpered.

"Try not to choke yourself," he advised, guiding himself into her mouth. His eyes narrowed down. "I like it deep." He shoved himself into her—*hard*. He was choking her with his dick.

Crossing her arms, Imani talked and didn't stop. Saevel wanted her blushing and averting her eyes, but she would give him the opposite.

When the shifter blinked a few times, Saevel grabbed the woman's chin. "I want you to watch."

As punishment, he thrust his cock into her throat. For a horrifying moment, Imani thought the woman might vomit, but Saevel lodged himself so deep she couldn't even throw up. Despite the lack of air, the woman obeyed and took him in her mouth, grabbing his hips. She even made a small moan of pleasure.

In a blur, Saevel pushed away, leaving her gasping for air and trying not to collapse onto the floor.

The whore's eyes darted between Imani and Saevel. Desire passed over her features. "She's—"

"Shut up." Wrapping her hair around his hand, Saevel ripped her head back. "Don't even *look* at her. Remember, you agreed to all this."

She nodded her consent to whatever fucked-up game they were playing and, with that, he pushed her face back onto his cock, moving her closer to his pelvis.

His muscles tensed, but at the last second, he pulled out. Grabbing the nymph's arm, he smashed her into his chest and spread her legs apart before shoving himself inside her, not caring about her comfort.

With a perfect view from the side, Saevel slammed into the whore like he was trying to break her in half. The female let out breathy gasps, her discomfort forgotten.

Imani pretended to be bored, rambling on in painful detail. "The only other information you might find interesting is his sudden interest in the Draswood. He asked me about my high sentinel, the fortifications, the population size and density. Apparently, forces the queen sent into the Draswood were sent back in mangled pieces, thanks to Ellisar."

Holding her hips from behind, Saevel pounded harder. The movement of his arms and the muscles in his abdomen were fluid but savage as he used her until he finished.

It made Imani wonder how the youngest Niflheim prince fucked.

Imani bit her lip as the pressure spread from her belly upward. It tightened, and she clutched her chest when it locked around her heart.

Her whole body was practically going up in flames now, and her shadows writhed and cried in pain—no, hunger.

She pushed any thoughts of Kiran away.

Seeing Tanyl tonight would be imperative—as soon as possible after this charade ended.

Unable to continue speaking, she stared. He had to know Imani's hunger and fury were raging, her nerves shredded, yet he wasn't concerned, not even sparing her a glance. Willing the prince's attention to her, she kept her glare focused on him while he ran his hand through his damp hair.

His finger made a flicking gesture toward the door. "Leave."

The nymph stumbled out of the room, not even bothering to get dressed.

As the door closed, Imani couldn't help herself. She sent all the tendrils of her available soul draw at Saevel, demanding his attention, feeling equally pathetic and powerful when he wrenched his eyes to her.

They sat in prickly silence for several minutes, and still, his face gave away nothing—no flash of desire. He'd sent her into a state of feeding-crazed, but Kiran's binding held strong. He couldn't touch her or even get close to her.

"Give me my answers so I can leave," she said.

He took another step closer and picked up a shirt lying on the back of a chair, smoothly slipping it over his head. "Tanyl met with several people earlier this week. Did he mention it? Any nights he acted strange?"

"You're not getting anything else until you tell me what I need to know."

"Hmm, yes, a deal is a deal. It seems hard work pays off, even if you're on your back."

"Get to it then," she snapped.

"The next assessment is a hand-to-hand fight between the two hundred remaining witches." He paused. "There are no rules, except all participants must kill at least one person and survive until the end."

Imani understood perfectly. It would be a melee, and it would be every witch for themselves.

"You better be telling the truth," she snarled. "If I find out this is bullshit, I'm going to Tanyl, regardless of whether or not you tell the queen my secret."

He shrugged. "There is some honor between my brother and me, but you'll know the truth in a few days."

He was right. She had what she needed and had fulfilled her end of the bargain. Resigned, she sighed and moved to leave. "Well, if you'll excuse me, I have a true heir apparent to see."

"You have no idea, do you?" Saevel laughed hollowly.

Imani whipped her head toward him.

"Do you think we are the only ones using you?"

"I don't care if he is. He's going to be the next king, and I'm going to be queen consort."

"Tanyl?" he scoffed. "*You* have a better chance of taking the Crown and not as a bloody consort." He chuckled darkly. "It will go to someone else, Imani. A female."

"You're a fool and insane."

"Yet, it's often the madman who speaks the truth."

Did he think the same about his brother?

"Besides, as the son of a current monarch, I believe I know more about it than you."

"Being crowned by the Fabric isn't only about being marked highbred and exerting raw power, you know," she said. "The Fabric must deem you worthy to rule with the realm and the people in your heart. Why should I believe you? You're a strong shifter, but nothing more. You'll never measure up to your brother when it comes to magic. Who knows? Maybe Kiran will inherit the Throne despite all your scheming and plans together."

He threw his head back and laughed for a long moment before quieting. "It would be foolish of you to presume to know what my brother or I have planned, elf witch. There's a war coming, and it's not between our two kingdoms. It's far bigger."

The icy timbre of his voice made her flinch and woke up her magic. It rose to meet his, and words she hadn't planned on saying tumbled out of her mouth. "I can't say for sure, but I think Tanyl plans to kill the queen in hopes of inheriting the Crown."

Saevel tilted his head to the side in the same predatory way Kiran did. "That," he said with a smug grin, "is the best thing you've brought me yet."

The truth hit her hard. He didn't even need it.

"Information you already had," she muttered, pressing her fingers to the bridge of her nose. Revealing Tanyl's impending matricide was a new level of treason. Why was she so desperate to prove herself to these princes? If Tanyl found out about this sordid agreement, it would put her in more than a precarious position.

"But made more credible by the cunt between your legs. Your princeling has ambitious plans and is making some dangerous alliances right now."

"What kind of alliances?"

Saevel gave her a flat stare before smiling again. "My brother is incredible at his job, you know? You're perfect. I've already said too much to you, and I can't even be mad about it because you're so lovely to look at. Tanyl actually might spill all his secrets to you." He pointed to the door. "Now, go. I have work to do. Not all of us can be whores."

Seconds later, Imani was hustled out of the room by a servant and stood in the hallway.

Already seeing red, the manservant's death vision was less intense than others she'd received. However, a clear picture of him slumped against a wall with a vacant expression while lying in a pool of blood formed in her mind. Shaking her head, she tried to forget it.

"This way, my lady—"

"I know the way," she bit out as she stormed down the hall in search of Tanyl. Tears welled in her eyes, remembering her only friend had betrayed her and had gotten her into this mess with the princes. How could she have been so stupid to trust her?

But soon, these bargains would be meaningless. She was closer to Niflheim than ever before, and she'd find the Drasil there, even if it killed her.

CHAPTER 28

Someone shook Imani awake.

"Wake up," Tanyl muttered. "You're coming with me."

Imani lifted her head, bleary eyes unfocused on the ancient stone walls. "Why?"

"Get dressed," he said, tossing her clothes at her.

Anxiety churned in her stomach as she put on her dress and reached for her heeled boots. He said nothing while she laced them up. Once she finished, he grabbed her arm and dragged her down the hallway, a dourness marring his handsome face.

"Tanyl? What's going on?" He'd never handled her with such roughness. A lump formed in her throat. Did he know about her alliance with Kiran?

After the close call a few nights ago, it was all she could do to keep herself from trembling at the thought. Paranoia was driving her mad.

With his gaze hard and fixed ahead, Tanyl steered them outside the servants' entrance. He dumped Imani in a waiting coach, climbed in the other side, and then they made their way to the bottom of the hill, to the larger square. Fog hung low over the crowd, which wasn't uncommon in the capital.

Tanyl escorted her from the coach like a gentleman, leaving her hand cold. This morning, a soft plume of smoke mingled with the white haze.

Tanyl remained stone-faced as he placed his hand on the small of her back and helped her to a raised platform. Other nobles, including a few high sentinels, stood and sat around the queen, but none of them spared her or the prince a glance.

Imani cast a cold eye over the monarch, who sat like a cat who had gotten the cream on her throne.

"Why are we here?" Imani asked under her breath.

The Essenheim heir didn't answer.

Annoyed, she stole a look his way. His furious eyes were fixed on the pyre, a familiar wood pile to her. Executions occurred occasionally, but this was different, and Tanyl had brought her for a reason. It was the first time they'd been seen in public together. Why would he take the risk?

Drizzle began to fall from the thick clouds above, and a breeze born over the dark depths of the Neshuin Sea rolled in, slanting the rain like pinpricks into her skin.

Tanyl's hand went to her back again, and he raised the hood of her cloak over her head to protect her. As the heir, he had the right to sit under the canopy. Unfortunately, it meant enduring the wretched queen, and Tanyl held similar sentiments as her. In fact, his revulsion for his mother seemed to grow daily, and right now, both preferred the rain when the alternative meant sitting by Dialora.

Peripherally, Tanyl stiffened at what was about to happen below.

Royal guards escorted a figure to the front, and the moment froze for Imani as she mastered her shock at the scene unfolding in front of her. An eternity passed between each heartbeat when they peeled back the cowl of the prisoner.

Tanyl's breath came faster now, hissing through his teeth as he white-knuckled the wood before them.

Imani's stomach lurched, and she slammed her eyes closed. Spots of darkness and light flashed behind her eyelids.

No. This couldn't be happening. Eyes still closed, she stood closer to the prince, holding on tighter to the railing, knowing she might fly over it and into the crowd to stop this madness if she didn't. But, if she did, she'd only be executed alongside him.

Imani forced her eyes open. She would take in every second of this, even if her insides seized and her heart gave out.

Master Selhey stood, ready to burn to death, with a blank expression.

He hadn't been to their lessons for several days, but Imani, too distracted by the assessments and her research, had thought little of it.

As the executioner announced the crimes, Imani shook with all the emotions she hadn't experienced at the last burning. Because Aralana had deserved death; her master did not. Indeed, Imani *liked* Master Selhey. Quite a bit more than most people in her life. He'd been kind and helpful to her since arriving in Stralas and, as elves, they had a kinship with each other.

The queen stood with a delicate, raised hand and quieted the throng of bloodthirsty onlookers. Tanyl joined her at the edge of the platform.

"This witch is accused of using violent magic, causing the recent ground quake, and he has been found guilty. But, unlike our neighbors to the south, we have protected our lands from the destruction of magic by swiftly punishing those who seek to break the law. Dangerous magic and the witches who wield it are enemies we must root out and destroy. As your queen and protector, with my heir by my side, we will show them no mercy."

Tanyl nodded woodenly, and the crowd cheered.

Imani's hand curled into a ball as she imagined it punching the queen's face. She knew exactly what was happening here—Master Selhey's only crime was standing up for the truth about magic.

Among the shouts and jeers, the fire burned below. But, unlike Ara, Master Selhey didn't stay silent.

When he began to burn, the male wood elf let out a howl, chilling her worse than the frigid rain pelting her face. He'd never even raised his voice, let alone sounded so anguished. It rattled in her bones. With horror raging inside her, Imani hugged herself.

Soon, his entire body went up in flames. Black smoke from his body lifted into the wind. Ashes danced onto the flagstones.

The queen's eyes glowed, reflecting the firelight, and all the while, Imani's teacher—her friend—burned alive.

Like a snap of frigid wind, Dialora's gaze shifted, and her piercing eyes bore into Tanyl and Imani with a warning—a warning for the only other people who had questioned her recently.

While the crowd thinned, Imani stood frozen. She stayed until they doused the smoldering flames and cleared away the remains. Flesh hung from the bones, charred and black, but the rest of his features—twisted in horror as they were—were entirely distinguishable, at least to her.

The spirit lingered above the square, and for a moment, it recognized her. But she was not inclined to feed off Master Selhey's soul, and so it disappeared.

∽

WITH HER SECOND ASSESSMENT LOOMING, Tanyl and Imani stayed silent in the coach on the long meandering way up to the palace. Her muscles permanently tensed, unable to unfurl from attack mode. Everything burned—Imani's chest, her muscles, her skin.

Folding her arms across her chest, Imani hit the prince with a knowing look. "So, the rumors about her opinion of you are true?"

Shouts from the streets below and the sounds from the horses drifted into the coach as they both stared at each other.

"Indeed. My position as heir apparent is precarious at best these days." Tanyl leaned forward, bracing his elbows on his knees. "She's been quietly planning for me not to inherit while keeping me prepared for appearance's sake."

"You've also been playing both sides," Imani probed, hoping for some intel.

He quirked a brow but didn't respond directly. "Time is running out. You've seen Niflheim's power firsthand, and it's only multiplying."

"Even if the royals are immune, we can find a way to use magic to overpower their army."

"It used to be true. Not only are they taking out a chunk of our best magic wielders with their assessments, but they've been breeding the immunity into their ranks for the past hundred years. They use this army to control their magical population, but they will also be used against us when the time comes." He lowered his voice. "We won't be able to use our magical army as effectively against the immune shifters. We need help."

"Do the rest of their breeds possess as much magic as ours?"

"No, but as you know, it's atrophic magic—far more deadly." He laughed with derision.

"I'm going to be blunt and ask for the truth, Tanyl. Rumors say the prince is a twelve-mark. Is he?"

"You're referring to Kiran? Such a serpentine bastard ..." He trailed off, shaking his head. "It's highly likely since his father made him First Witch, despite despising his youngest."

"He wanted a female elf."

"Correct. Magnus would have much preferred a daughter with a powerful soul draw he could use or another high-bred shifter since he believes magic is beneath him. Anyone using magic over physical strength is lazy and unworthy, and he propagates an anti-magic culture. How powerful Kiran is will never matter because the king and Saevel use their shifted forms to keep him on a tight leash."

"The king sounds like a savage."

"He's a proficient, master level witch and the strongest shifter in existence."

"Why haven't they attacked us, then?"

Tanyl shrugged. "We aren't sure. The Throne grapples with a struggling economy and uprisings. His subjects almost succeeded in assassinating him a few times."

"But we're weak and exposed," Imani muttered. A twinge of guilt surfaced over betraying Tanyl in her impossible agreement with Kiran.

"I couldn't agree more. However, our magic is far more stable—one of the reasons the assessments were designed to take out our most powerful witches. They must expend far more resources and effort to maintain control of their magic. Keeping borders secure and people safe is far harder in Niflheim. It's a constant battle to fight the breaches from sealed doorways, slips turning into rifts, and the like."

"How can they possibly control those events?"

"The First Witch uses their Order to highly regulate the use of magic."

"Kiran," she finished for him.

He nodded. "The king was smart to name him First Witch. While he doesn't like his son, he knows Kiran is more useful alive than dead."

"Besides controlling their magic, he wants Kiran to breed a high-bred female elf for an alliance with their elves."

"I've heard the same," Tanyl confirmed. "Their drow elves are the most magically powerful in Niflheim, and they are the Throne's biggest civil threat. My guess is Magnus needs to find a way to ally with them before starting a war with us."

"Why couldn't he marry Kiran off for an alliance?"

"Their female elves are as rare as ours, and none of the powerful elven families have one to offer the king. A high-bred royal female would be enticing enough for the elves to come to an agreement with Magnus."

"Breeding him? Gods, the king sounds like a bastard," Imani said, pinching the bridge of her nose.

"Kiran isn't much better. He's a self-interested prick who will find every secret, every weakness, and any opening for him to exploit. I'm pretty sure he has leverage on most of the nobles in Niflheim, and if anyone can keep their rebellions in check, it's Kiran. Plus, he controls his magic wielders like slaves," he muttered. "They forbid even simple spells without the right permissions, restrictions, and permits, and making money from magic is taxed beyond belief. Kiran is the first archmage witch the royal family has produced in a century—"

"You're joking?" Imani couldn't hide the surprise in her voice, but she bit her lip, knowing he had to be a twelve-mark now.

"I wish. Kiran's so obsessed with being accepted by his father that he takes any scraps he can from him, and no magic—and I mean *none*—happens in the kingdom without Kiran knowing about it. The Serpent can't help but meddle, and somehow, Kiran engineered a massive web of ingenious detections, practically built into the Fabric itself. Maybe it is. It's like nothing we've ever seen. Massive enchantments, defensive spells, wards, and manual detection, too, through a network of spies, informants, and enforcement troops. We think it covers the entire kingdom."

"He truly is mad."

Tanyl let out a derisive laugh. "And to think, you've barely seen the real him here. But he's sane where it counts. That slippery elf is a formidable, brilliant witch, not to mention a conniving nasty piece of work like the rest of his brothers."

Horror crept up her spine as she thought about how easily Kiran had killed the naiad nymphs, how they must treat their people, and how Essenheim could not stand against them. "They can't be *that* powerful compared to our magic." Her kingdom held the power of the Fabric, whereas they did not—the Niflheim Kingdom never compared to their magical power.

"Meira, I'm telling you the truth. *They are*. They will be formidable once they get a handle on their internal problems."

"You understand the snake better than anyone I've talked to about him."

"I've made it my business to learn as much as possible about all the Illithiana brothers." He paused. "A reminder: the Serpent can blend in and strike when the time is right."

Imani let the words sink in. She had resisted believing it, but now it was all but a certainty. At some point, Niflheim was going to attack Essenheim, and they would probably win.

They needed the Drasil.

"And that's not all. There will be a regime change soon. Magnus won't live much longer. His sons are circling the Throne like vultures."

It had been decades since the last power transfer, but Tanyl was suspiciously sure of his assertion. It reinforced her theory about Tanyl's plans with his mother.

"When he dies, she follows," Imani stated.

"Yes, but my mother won't relinquish power without a fight. She might have something planned … The Crown is easy to put on and hard to remove." He sighed. "We might have a few months, at most, when it happens. History tells us it usually takes a season. The moon's phases might control it. We don't know." He sat back and crossed his arms, glaring at no one in particular. "We need the Drasil."

A wave of frustration nearly blinded her, especially since she had thought the same only moments before. "You don't think I know the advantage the Drasil will give us? You think I don't know my role in this relationship? Trust me; I'm clear on my role."

He stared vacantly, as if deciding his following words. "That's not all you are to me," he said softly. "I see how you act around the rest of the Court and the other apprentices. You have a fierce heart and choose your real friends wisely. You listen more than you talk. You're always watching and thinking. I can see the clever mind working in your pretty little head, and you adapt flawlessly. I could take you to a high council dinner or a gambling hall on Kesen, and you'd fit right in." He turned to her and canted his head to the side, studying. "But most of all, you have a shrewd ability to get what you want."

He was surprisingly accurate. No one had ever said anything like that to Imani before, and it made her feel *seen* for the first time ever.

"I'm trying to say you're not like the other courtiers or witches here, and I *like* having you by my side."

She didn't know what to say to that admission.

He sighed. "I have you in my bed, but I know I'll have to work harder to earn your trust. I don't expect you to believe me right now. I probably wouldn't if I were you," he added. "But my mother is in a precarious position, and when her reign comes to an end—which I know for a fact will be soon, whether Magnus lives or dies—I hope, by then, it'll be easier for you and me to be a team. Something feels right about us. I can't explain it, but I listen to my instincts."

Imani let herself imagine what being by Tanyl's side as queen consort would be like for a moment. She liked it. She liked it too much. But it was a foolish dream if she couldn't survive the second assessment and learn more about the third.

"Don't put too much stock in it. I'll probably be dead then," she said thickly, a lump forming in her throat.

Tanyl reached for her face. "You will live. I know it. And when I am king, I will find a way to bring you home, I swear." He brushed his rough thumbs over her cheeks. "In the meantime, you know you are the only one going down there I even remotely trust."

Guilt tore at her insides. Gaining some of the prince's trust was no small thing, and she was playing him behind his back. Yet, what he implied momentarily shocked her.

"I'll be caught," she whispered.

"They won't suspect a thing, my beautiful little spy," he said, a dangerous possessiveness layered in his voice. Maybe a command.

Silence fell as she mulled over his words. What a mess she had found herself in. Bound to this untested young prince on the brink of committing matricide while betraying her whole kingdom and under the thumb of his cunning, dangerous enemy.

But she wasn't a victim. While both princes controlled her, she had made the choice and still had one here.

"I'm not even a master witch yet, Tanyl," she whispered. "They won't let me near anything important." And if they caught her? Well, she didn't think the Illithianas treated spies mercifully.

He gave her a boyish half-smile. "You could have access to anything you wanted if you put your mind to it."

It would never matter if she were a master or not. Her value came from her precious elf cunt, not her intelligence or magic skills. She'd always known this happened to vulnerable female elves—people used them for their own means—but she never thought she'd be one of them. Ara had warned her this would happen, too. She kept proving she was always right.

Still, despite his blatant manipulation, she needed to take this offer seriously. She couldn't outright deny her prince and future monarch. Besides, despite it all, she was starting to consider Tanyl a friend.

"Let's revisit this if I survive," she said evasively. "I'll have two conflicting bindings to deal with then, both resulting in debilitating pain, if not death. I'm a high-bred witch and female elf, Tanyl, but not much else."

"You know you're more." He studied her through hooded eyes. "Once I'm king, I will fix the mistakes she made with this shameful treaty. We'll need master witches like you at home in Essenheim, and I will *not* give up on getting you and the others back." He grabbed her hand and kissed her wrist.

She gave him a small smile but spent the rest of the ride trying to sort through her thoughts. She was relatively sure Tanyl *did* care about her and his witches and wanted to keep them safe. Maybe a part of him did feel something for her, too. Maybe he really did have plans for their future.

But the moment he stepped out of the carriage, it was as if she were a stranger. He exited normally then had the driver bring her around the back end to the servants' entrance. Whispers and rumors would start immediately if she'd exited with him. It angered her to be considered his dirty secret again. Once his mother died, would things change?

Despite agreeing with the queen that he had no real backbone for truly ruling, Tanyl understood exactly how politics worked at court. He'd planned for their little entrance—for her to be seen as nothing despite her feeling something *real* from him.

Indeed, he was full of plans, like Saevel had said.

Tanyl appeared to be more of a player in this game than she'd assumed.

CHAPTER 29

Mere hours later, Imani stood outside with the others for the second assessment. A biting cold evening wind from the Neshuin Sea whipped through the courtyard where they stood, waiting for the princes.

When she'd left her chambers earlier, light black veins had pulsed up her hands and arms. She'd pulled her sleeves down to cover them. It worried her how much her dark atrophic magic—her shadows—pushed for freedom right now.

Master Selhey's execution had done what Ara's hadn't—anger and grief feverishly pumped through her. She was tinder, ready to ignite. Despite the constant wall of control she had brought up around her magic, she stood in the frigid gardens, clenching and unclenching her hands, struggling to keep her signature as contained as possible. Whispers flicked her ears back and forth, and her magic purred in her blood.

Unlike the rest, she knew what was about to happen.

People hushed and parted when the Niflheim royals strode into the crowd. Their advisers and master witches trailed close behind, including the female high naiad witch from the other night. They ascended the viewing platform.

Imani bristled at their relaxed demeanors and luxurious setup. All of them planned to watch this assessment like bloody entertainment. Too many innocent Essenheim master witches had died in the past few days, weakening their kingdom further, and she was fresh out of patience for the slaughter of her fellow magic wielders.

Saevel laughed at something Kiran had said. He smiled in return. The sight made her practically gag. Sweat covered her back as she forced herself to observe their every move.

The princes stood up to address those gathered.

More massive than any other male, Saevel didn't hide one inch of himself. Like his shifted beast form, Prince Saevel's presence overpowered the space around him. Yet his expressive green eyes continued to hold intelligence, hinting at a far more complex man than some animal.

Unlike his brother, Kiran hid well. His jacket, elegantly fitted in his usual black, indicated a lean yet strong body beneath. It fit his muscular shoulders perfectly. Holding his wand at his side, the younger prince appeared lazy as he scanned the crowd. He nearly smiled, an entertained little grin begging to be set free in both corners of his mouth.

Everything about Kiran felt wrong, and yet, so much about him intrigued her. He'd easily be the most fearsome yet exquisite creature anywhere he went, if not for the illusion he constantly wore to mute his soul draw and give the impression of mediocrity. It disguised a beautiful menace she didn't understand.

"The first assessment tested your willingness to obey execution orders without question," Saevel said. "The second will test your ability to fight for us in battle. Today, we'll see your ability to survive in the chaos while proving your loyalty to your new kingdom by killing your brethren."

His words hung in the air, emotionless and final, with a heavy silence falling. People shifted their feet and glanced around, wondering who was living their last hours in this world.

"Well, well, well. No objections?" Kiran taunted them with a dazzling grin. While it was undeniably beautiful, his mismatched eyes held a haunted viciousness that spoke of imbalance. They pierced through the participants wildly while he stared head-on, daring anyone to return his gaze.

Many averted their eyes, but Imani wouldn't shy away—she stared right back. What precisely did those endless black depths house?

A troubling sensation lit up inside her again. Barely there, it gently pulsed deep inside her. A desire that wouldn't abate—a constant yearning skittering below her skin. She pushed it away, determined to resist any thrall Kiran attempted to put on her.

Not waiting for a response before jumping off the platform, he prowled forward into them, intent on gleeful harassment. "Any noble objections? Does anyone want to die for their kingdom before we start? Speak up. I want to kill someone," he shouted with dark laughter, bounding further into the crowd. Barely breathing, the witches only observed. He pointed at a slender nymph. "You? Hmm?"

She trembled under his gaze, whimpering.

He rolled his eyes. "No? Fine, you'll be dead two minutes after we start, anyway."

He was probably right.

Lunging in a blur toward an older shifter, Kiran got in his face, making the man flinch. He bared his teeth, two slightly longer than others —fangs like most elves had. Imani's were minuscule in comparison.

"How about you?" Tilting his head to assess the shifter, Kiran barely waited a minute before grabbing another man by the shoulder, throwing him roughly to the ground with a manic expression. Laughing to himself, he pointed his wand at the man's chest. "You?"

The man shut his eyes in fear.

"I might kill you now for being such a pathetic coward." Kiran cast a spell, making the man writhe in the dirt, then stalked forward to leer at more people.

He was more unhinged than she'd seen before—terrorizing people at random. He cornered another two witches, tossing one to the ground. A nervous tension permeated the space.

"Anyone? Is anyone brave enough to take me? Come on!" Spreading his arms wide and snarling, he waited.

None came.

But Imani was *highly* close to volunteering. Indeed, she practically trembled now with a commanding urge to strip him down to his bones and destroy the sneer on his face. Now that they were acquainted, some sick part of her wanted to tug at the layers of magic coating him to reveal the real Kiran. Why did he make her react this way?

Her emotions were running high. One minute, she wanted to punish him for this melee—for killing more witches—and the next, she wanted to get inside him, pick his brain, stand close, be near him, and lean into his touch.

He made her feel crazy with his many facets drawing her to him. But she wouldn't give in. She would keep her head down, pass this assessment, and focus on the next one. This was a distraction.

Without moving an inch, the inky darkness permeating her signature briefly rattled its prison to flare out at Kiran in response to his call—his threat. Before she could stop it, her veins darkened further.

In the deathly quiet, all heads snapped to her immediately, including Kiran's.

Tilting his head, Kiran let her see his sharp teeth. A strange, purr-like rumble came from his chest, and his green eye glimmered. He would have relished it if she tried to break through her own self-imposed prison by challenging him here. The prince had purposely pulled on her magic signature to create a scene, goading her and enjoying it.

Shocked by her loss of control, a quiet yet furious growl escaped her throat, wordlessly expressing her displeasure at his audacity.

He grinned, absolutely delighted.

The image of Kiran's inner beast filled her mind. Terror ran up her spine, and her stomach dropped seeing his perfect smile.

What am I doing? This male elf possessed a lethal power that promised death, and she would not be dying today, if she could help it.

Embarrassment heating her skin, she tore every bit of her magic back inside with surprising strength before bowing her head in submission. All the veins had cleared. She prayed they would remain clear, and the prince would shove off.

Today was not the day she'd lose control, no matter how badly Kiran wanted to see it. No matter how badly she wanted to show him what she could do.

Kiran's chuckling broke the tension like thunder announcing an incoming storm. He braced his hands on his knees, laughing like a man possessed. "Great news, brother." He stood while clapping his hands at the witches. "Any noble or stupid Essenheim witches are dead or will be soon, those cowards. The rest are exactly like us." He swept his wand wide above his head.

A burst of Kiran's magic spread across the visible sky. Effortlessly, like breathing, he cast forth vast swaths of invisible wards. Like the first assessment, they were jaw-dropping in their strength as they wove and melded together, rippling the air. The energy thundered in her chest. The magic stilled, locking them all in his mighty, impenetrable fortress again.

He made his way back to his brother, cackling to himself.

People gave him a wide berth, averting their eyes when he strode past. All noise ceased. Unease coiled tighter inside her when she didn't even hear the damn birds chirping. The Prince of Snakes had made his point and squashed all hope of rebellion. Those who remained would either be too weak to live or pragmatic enough to serve the Niflheim Kingdom.

Moments later, the sun dipped below the horizon. The mood among the Essenheim witches changed from tense to downright unbearable.

All manner of nymphs, shifters, and pixies stood around her. The two male Norn elves were still alive, and Esa stood alone near her people, wings fluttering. Most of the remaining witches were probably far more adaptable to physical magic than her, but she'd been putting a strategy together the past day.

Melees, as an assessment, were nothing more than a barbaric blood bath, in her opinion. Like executions, combat, or other tests featuring death and brutality, their Order had stopped using melees hundreds of years ago. People still died during ascension assessments, but it had become far less common. Or so she assumed.

Both princes stood next to each other at the front.

Saevel raised his hands. "It's time." He paused for effect. "My brother tells me only the most cowardly or savage witches of this kingdom remain."

Kiran flipped out his wand again, playing with it in his hand before pointing it threateningly at them all, a serpentine smile spreading across his face. "Indeed, brother, and by the end, we'll only go home with the savages."

"Good," the Niflheim heir boomed. "Now, a reminder of the rules. There are two hundred of you. The melee ends when a hundred are dead. So, each of you must kill at least once."

"No exceptions," Kiran added, "or you'll be executed."

Lifting her chin, Imani's eyes took in the stars. The Fabric's lights danced, and the torches' amber glow lit the courtyard.

Jerking her head from the peaceful sky, Saevel's hand signaled the start. Before she could drop into a fighting stance, Prince Kiran raised his wand, and fire shot down the middle of the courtyard. Bursting forth into the darkness, Kiran's ropes of flames spun and twisted around the courtyard, herding them in like cattle in a field.

The flames were a mile of pure power from the Fabric, separating and coiling themselves into suspended rings of heat and ash, like floating funeral pyres taunting those within its clutches. A wall around them exploded upward in one whoosh of movement, almost reaching the palace rooftops. It hemmed them into the courtyard, bordered by the gardens to the southside and the cliffs to the sea to the north. Finally, they stopped. Raging columns of infernos towered tall and stood in severe warning to the helpless, trapped witches.

Kiran took in Imani's reaction with great interest, but she pointedly ignored him.

Beyond the crackling sound of the fire, people screamed. Some screamed in fear, some in bloodlust. The world moved in slow motion.

Cracking her neck, Imani tried to stay calm despite her heart pounding like a war drum.

One of the male Norn ducked to avoid two errant spells and charged for her.

Her hand tightened. There wasn't time to ask what the elf was doing, but fear didn't even register as he attacked. A Norn wouldn't hurt her.

Seconds later, he threw her to the ground. "Do it as fast as the first assessment," he grunted as she lashed at his chest. He dodged and moved to attack her again.

"I don't want to kill you," she said, drawing out her wand.

Imani could hold her own against him, but if any elf had magic, they were powerful and well-trained by the master witches in the Draswood. Yet, he appeared intent on losing.

Admiration threatened to choke her as she rolled out of his feigned kick.

"You don't have to do this for me," she whispered.

Sadness shone in his eyes. It made Imani angry, although not at him. With a feral cry, she slashed for one of his ankles, but he deftly stepped aside like she knew he would.

"Let me fight you for real," she shot back. Winding up for a hard left hook, she swung.

The elf caught her fist in his mighty grip, and she screamed in response, kicking him in the chin. His neck snapped back, pale eyes glimmering with surprise.

"You don't need to protect me," Imani repeated.

"You know the power you can wield. If you survive the assessments, you'll be one of the only witches in a position to *do* something."

"Spoken like a true man who only sees value in one thing," Imani growled as they both faked a punch and a block. "I'm not as powerful as you think I am."

"Prince Kiran hasn't stopped staring at you since we began. You intrigue him," he said, glancing over his shoulder. "Now, *that's* power."

The weight of the prince watching fell on Imani's back. She didn't need to turn but did, anyway, involuntarily seeking Kiran. Her eyes found his. Imani stared, feeling something heavy and uncomfortable in her chest.

Unflinching, Kiran's expression appeared unreadable. But when the male Norn grabbed her wrists from behind and slammed her chest into a nearby tree, the prince stood and clutched the railing in a vise-like grip.

"You're seeing what you want to see," Imani hissed over her shoulder. "It means nothing." Kiran didn't want her to die. He needed his pet to live to "continue providing value," as he had so crassly stated during their first meeting.

"Possibly." The elf gripped her wrists but let her twist away.

He didn't believe her, but this conversation was over. Kiran watched them too closely.

"Take out your wand and attack me for real. Kiran will never believe this farce," she said through gritted teeth before slamming her elbow into his face. The elf held his bloody nose, muttering a string of elvish curse words. But a second later, he drew his wand, and a blast of magic froze her limbs. Imani fell hard into the tree.

Now, this was getting serious.

Imani and the elf pretended to try to kill each other for several minutes. Her magic in combat had improved not only from assessment training but also from when she worked with Esa. She'd been practicing independently, every waking minute she wasn't searching for the Drasil. Her enchantments and illusions were two brands with some advantages while fighting against another witch.

Eventually, he gave her a minuscule nod.

Tension tightened her muscles. The crushing reality of what the elf wanted her to do made her heart pound. She had no problems with this man and did not want to kill a fellow Norn. The dread of such an act weighed heavily on her.

He nodded again, glaring at her. But still, she didn't move. There had to be another way.

A loud screeching tore her attention away from the male Norn, and the sights and sounds from the melee reminded her that she was in the middle of a bloodbath. Imani wanted to live through the night and all the nights ahead. She still had a lot to do in this realm, and looking around, she didn't think she'd last long without help.

With a resigned deep breath, Imani accepted his sacrifice. She took the opening he gave her and cast a now familiar spell.

The same severing enchantment from the first assessment forced his head clean off. It rolled unceremoniously across her feet. Hot, sticky blood sprayed onto her chest and face. Smearing it out of her eyes, she leaned against the tree, panting. Another master elf dead—this one at her hands.

From the center of the melee, gnashing teeth, growls, and spells rang through the air while dozens of witches fought for their lives. Mere yards away, the bodies of fallen witches—mainly sprite pixies and leimoniad nymphs—twitched. Between shouts of pain and blood squishing in the grass, the crackling crunch of bone echoed in her ears as the shifters chewed through the corpses.

With the madness unfolding around her, there was no doubt in her mind the male elf had made victory far easier for her tonight.

From the viewing platform, she could hear someone announcing the number of witches remaining. The princes stood on, evaluating everything everyone was doing. Their tiny smirks and shared whispers with each other made a fierce protectiveness stir in her chest.

Imani's eyes locked on the dead Norn on the ground again. A pang of horror and regret tore through her insides. It mixed with the potent fury and adrenaline blazing through her nerve endings. Her lip curled in disgust aimed at herself and the Niflheim princes.

I will make them pay for this sin someday, she thought with an agonizing internal scream.

Grasping her wand tighter, she shut her eyes. If she stared too long, she'd lose control of her shadows.

Hide. Run and hide, Imani yelled at herself. She didn't think she could control her magic in the wildness. How many more witches would die if she didn't? Cowardly as it might be, she wanted to slip away and hide in the dark corners, if she could.

When she scanned the courtyard for an escape route, chaos assaulted her eyes—witches tearing into each other, hacking through limbs with magic, half of them using their shifted forms.

Before she could pick a direction, a massive arm slid around her waist. "Thinking of hiding like a pretty little coward?" A massive leonine shifter was instantly behind her.

Imani recognized him right away. Aiden. He had attended the Neshuin New Year party with her and their group.

He leaned in close, as if reading her mind, his body warm against hers. "I'm sure you remember me. And now that I've caught you, I wouldn't be so stupid as to run. The princes won't like it at all."

Dammit. Imani slammed her eyes shut, not missing the warning in his nasty tone. She had paused too long and left herself open. While her soul draw the first night had made him desire her slightly, his heartmate binding would make it challenging to compel him.

Aiden emanated a distinct dislike for Imani. His eyes had bore into her during their daily combat training sessions for the assessments. He didn't like women who even remotely threatened him.

Two choices were in front of her—either she stayed to fight Aiden or ran and risked him catching her, anyway.

He towered over her, all muscle. Blood dripped from his mouth like he'd shifted and torn through several people. She didn't like her chances, and Imani didn't have much pride when it came to staying alive. So, she went invisible and ran.

Momentarily surprised, Aiden let her slip out of his grasp. His bloodred shifter eyes thinned at her invisible form. He couldn't see her, but he could probably smell her. The savage male grinned in her direction and charged forward.

Throwing herself into the fray, she darted through the garden's center. He was on her heels.

Pushing her legs harder, she dashed away from the shifter, like a phantom, and lost him at the tree line around the perimeter where the borders of fire ended at the gardens. For some reason, Kiran had kept the fires away from the gardens at the edge of the training field. It would be the perfect hiding spot.

A familiar form rose in the night like the moon. Stalking toward her, an imposing shadow of a man appeared with his wand raised. With the flick of his wrist, he let an intimidating wave of magic pour from his silhouetted form.

Kiran.

He stood still among the chaos.

An inhuman roar rumbled from the male witch before another stream of fire burst to life. As if there wasn't enough heat from the other fires he'd lit, a sword of blazing flames surged forward from him, cutting through the darkness.

Kiran forced any stragglers, including her, back into the melee. Over the din of the duel, over the sounds of people ripping each other's throats out—bits of which littered underneath her feet—Kiran cackled, an elated laugh mingling with the ensuing mayhem. The sound hadn't been entirely him. Something profound and unnatural layered his voice, like discordant notes playing along with a sad but beautiful melody.

Imani ground her molars hard. For some time now, she'd thought she had imagined the unholy part of Kiran rearing its head from inside his eyes at times. But now, she *knew* it was indeed there. What could he shift into?

While it fascinated her, she needed to stay far away from it.

She cast another illusion spell around her and glared at the flames before turning back around.

Off to the side, a male pixie launched himself into the air in a blur of black leather and teeth. Esa stood firm against him, wings fluttering and murder in her eyes.

They circled each other, spells flying back and forth. The male turned and grabbed Esa's collar, snarling, "It's people like you who give pixies a bad name."

But instead of attacking, he screamed like a banshee when a substance exploded into the area. Particles filled the air, getting sucked into their lungs like powder.

With the shields locking them inside, Esa's pixie dust couldn't dissipate as fast as usual. The garden filled with a thick poison. Even through her blurred vision, she could see the Niflheim princes perfectly protected behind Kiran's ward.

Imani had read what some kinds of pixie dust did to a person, and she wouldn't let Kiran see her fall apart. Luckily, she'd cast the invisibility illusion, but the dust made it impossible for her to concentrate enough to run away from the platform. Instead, she grasped onto trees and bushes—really anything—as she stumbled deeper into the courtyard to find a stealthily hidden place to collapse.

She came upon a bench with a wall of fire raging behind it, located quite a way away from the main melee. The heat was intense, and nausea hit Imani like a wall. She dropped to her hands and knees.

The landscape around Imani contracted. She couldn't tell what was up or down or how to see straight. The sounds of the world around her had grown increasingly bloodthirsty. Everyone was screaming. Esa stood crying in a pile of blood.

This was nightmare pixie dust.

A tunnel of blackness spread across Imani's field of vision, dimming the light from the fires. Ignoring it, she tried to keep her eyes open, but it turned dark around her. She snarled at the blindness.

Out of control, Imani's veins blackened entirely. Inkiness seeped from her signature. Ripples of black burst from her skin, encasing her body in a swirl of night. She must have appeared as a pure shadow while her magic embedded into her signature and surrounded her. For a few moments, all Imani could see was blackness while the shadows battered the pixie dust out of her system.

With a choke, she retched up multicolored bile and magic remnants.

After several seconds of heaving, her vision began to clear, and she called the shadows back. They instantly snapped back inside, invisible again.

The rapid response surprised her, and she flexed her hands, checking for signs of blackness. But there was none.

If anyone had observed Imani in her shadowed form, they likely attributed it to the hallucinations of the dust. She hoped she was far enough from the princes to be unseen.

Swiveling her head, she clutched her wand tight and searched for the next threat. The courtyard had become quiet except for a few moans and errant shouts. Some people crawled and writhed on the ground, still overtaken by the pixie dust, including Aiden. Unaffected by her own magic, Esa stood to the side, trying to catch her breath and wiping the gore off her face.

At least a hundred Essenheim witches lay dead. It appeared to be over.

Imani dragged herself to her feet then started the gruesome walk back to the platform. Blood and mud slopped onto the ground.

A pixie woman was in pieces to her left, and the head of the Norn elf she'd killed earlier lay to the right. Battered and smashed, it was unrecognizable after sustaining damage during the melee. Nevertheless, she gingerly picked it up, intent on memorizing his last moment.

Starlight glinted off his silver hair that was so much like her own. Blood leaked from the bulging lifeless eyes, and bones gleamed white where the skin had ripped off his skull. Only tendons remained around his once beautiful mouth, exposing blunt teeth and elvish fangs.

She wrapped his hair around her fist.

With the head swinging in her hand, Imani stomped to the courtyard's edge. Burning flames still raged across the courtyard, blocking her inside.

She narrowed her eyes to slits as she chucked the Norn elf's head as hard as possible at the Niflheim princes.

A snap of Kiran's wand blocked it.

One shrill, furious scream erupted from deep in her chest while he grinned at her like a smug madman.

CHAPTER 30

Stars blinked through the windowpanes lining the stairs to Tanyl's apartment as Imani's heeled boots announced her arrival with each step. She could see the dancing ribbons of the Fabric pulsing across the night sky in a spectacle. She'd miss them when she went to Niflheim.

Imani walked with confidence, holding her head high as if she lived there, imagining for a moment that she was queen consort and lived in these rooms. The whole palace had fallen into an unsettling calm in the days after the melee had ended, and with no one in the halls to catch this little display, she let herself indulge.

Death was always possible during assessments, but she thought such a large amount would warrant more comments. The Crown said nothing, however. Imani guessed they actively worked to sweep it under the rug because courtiers related to the dead witches slowly returned home. Any master witches who spoke out against the assessments were assigned a new job away from Stralas.

Unbelievable.

The horror of her gruesome crime against the male elf should be eating her alive, but her mind had never been quite right. In horror's place, the need for justice and revenge settled in her bones and heart instead.

While going down the hallway, Imani's mind wandered to the night of her second report. It had come and gone faster than she had anticipated, and much to her ire, Kiran had given her a pittance of information. All he revealed was the nature of the assessment—paired combat—and she'd learned nothing since.

Combat with magic was still her weakest skill, and a one-on-one fight in front of an audience meant she couldn't run and hide. After she fell out with Esa, they hadn't been practicing like before, and she didn't have a strategy yet. She needed more information. Without leverage to gather more intel, the days dwindled toward her execution rather than victory. In the past day, Imani had focused her waking hours on preparing for the final assessment or gathering information on the Niflheim princes. At this point, she desperately needed to uncover *anything* meaningful for more details on the duel.

The guards usually stationed outside Tanyl's rooms were in deep conversation at the end of the hall. Imani quickly hid herself under her invisibility spell and, for the first time, commanded a tiny tendril of darkness to slip under the door through all Tanyl's wards and locks. His spells were particularly nasty tonight. She sensed a new silencing enchantment, which was too powerful even for the prince to cast. Had the First Witch put a new ward over the prince's rooms?

Still, it didn't stop her shadows. She smiled.

Moments after stepping inside, she dropped her illusion, but a guard made her jump in surprise. There were normally no guards inside Tanyl's rooms. He kept them outside for a semblance of privacy.

The man stood with his hand outstretched, halting her. "No visitors tonight. Prince's orders. Go back where you came from," he said.

Exhausted and running on too little patience, she brandished her wand and pointed it at him in an obvious threat. The hallway darkened as her shadows pressed against her signature, thin tendrils silently snaking out to wrap around his limbs and neck. "Prince Tanyl is expecting me. Do you want to test my magic tonight? I'm under the protection of the Niflheim princes and don't mind letting some of my power free tonight if needed." Imani murmured a spell, and his windpipe constricted.

The guard's eyes widened. Nervously, he glanced down the hallway then swiftly moved to the right. She loosened the spell. He coughed.

"I'll be checking outside for a minute, and you better be telling the truth about being expected."

She almost rolled her eyes at the empty threat, but Tanyl certainly wouldn't like such defiance against his guard or her slipping by the others unnoticed, even if he had invited her. Still, her patience was razor-thin these days.

Tanyl's living room was usually a calm and quiet sanctuary, so she was surprised to hear tense voices spilling into the hallway through the silencing charm. While not quite an argument, the heated dialogue made her ears twitch back and forth. The voices grew louder—one measured, the other hissing.

Now, it was an argument.

Who would Tanyl be having such an intense conversation with at this hour? It must have been unexpected—Tanyl cleared his schedule on the nights he spent with Imani.

"You have no right to demand more witches," the Essenheim prince yelled.

Imani positioned herself behind the wall and cast her invisibility illusion again. She melted into the shadows, unseen.

Tanyl swore, and someone laughed.

Her skin prickled. Melodic yet mocking with an edge of sensuality, she knew that laugh.

Peering around the wall, she shouldn't have been shocked, but her mouth still fell open at the sight in front of her.

Tanyl and Kiran sat in two chairs positioned near the fireplace, angled toward each other. Tanyl's features contorted into a furious glare, his body so rigid he appeared seconds away from attacking. Across from him, Kiran sat like a lion. He lounged languidly in a chair, one ankle on his knee, as if chatting with a friend—or a child. His hands were steepled, and he displayed a maddening grin. As always, he was dressed in executioner clothing, wearing a black shirt perfectly fitted to his hard chest and torso. Tanyl, in blue pants and a white shirt, was a stark contrast.

Magic swirled in the air from both men. Tanyl's burst from him at erratic moments, while Kiran's remained constant, the invisible coils slithering around him like a cloak.

If the intense new wards were any indication, neither prince wanted anyone to know about this clandestine meeting.

Leaning forward in his chair, Tanyl lowered his voice. "Why do you think you can renegotiate?"

"Happens all the time in politics, I assure you, Tanyl," Prince Kiran said, his tone condescending.

The male still hadn't left his casual position, but Imani could swear he was fighting a smirk. "It's quite simple—"

Tanyl slammed his fist on the table, and it echoed through the room. "*Simple*? Your demand is not simple. We've complied with every detail in the agreement." Tanyl's voice had a hard edge to it.

"Tanyl, please. I hate being interrupted. Besides, you're smarter than this. Are you going to force me to spell it out?"

Not waiting for a response, Kiran smirked and plowed on. "Fine! Since you've been *such* a pleasant host, and I enjoy reveling in my brilliance, I'll indulge you." His voice sounded too alluring, too smooth, as he braced his arms on his knees with a wicked gleam directed at the Essenheim heir. "You promised us at least fifty of your best witches. We only have two elves remaining—I'd hardly call that sending your best. You lied about their delay. They aren't coming. Therefore, you owe us more witches for the next assessment, elves or not."

"It's not our problem your ascension assessments are killing your candidates."

"It's not *our* problem the agreement didn't protect you if your people disobeyed orders." Kiran paused.

With Tanyl so clearly backed into the proverbial corner, the princes stared at each other momentarily.

"Do I need to remind you of your kingdom's precarious position right now? Despite this transgression, my brother isn't asking for much, although he'd be well within his rights to do so," Kiran murmured, acting like a good little lapdog.

Liar, she thought. The dynamics and aspirations of the Illithiana family were far more complicated than most people assumed. Indeed, she'd seen firsthand how Kiran influenced his brother; Saevel relied on his counsel and took his guidance seriously. Dare she say the influence bordered on manipulation?

But besides what she'd observed with her own eyes, she'd still learned significantly few solid facts about the youngest Niflheim prince, and the additional rumors weren't helpful.

She swallowed, keeping her magic signature from responding to her emotions. She needed to keep it locked up tight lest the princes sense it.

Kiran continued steepling his hands, letting the silence permeate the room. He basked in it. He'd won. Tanyl knew it. Imani knew it.

Imani held her breath as Kiran inclined his head in amusement. The Serpent Prince liked playing with his food before he devoured it. Imani could admit that never knowing what the Mad Prince might say was infuriating yet somewhat enjoyable. Kiran liked the bloody game more than the outcome.

"You look like you might cry, Tanyl." Kiran pretended to pick at his nail. "I'd be happy to give you another moment to compose yourself before you agree to the addendum binding."

"Fuck you, Kiran," Tanyl snapped.

Kiran gave him a fiendish look, as if nothing delighted him more than those words.

"You've left me no choice," Tanyl conceded. "I'll support the request for renegoti—"

The hairs on her arms stood up as a burst of chilling magic flattened her against the wall. Any warmth evaporated, and she could hardly breathe as the coldest magic she'd ever experienced whipped through the room.

Tanyl's voice abruptly cut off, and a dead silence fell. Inching herself forward, she stole a glance into the room. Confusion overtook her face, mouth gaping.

The Essenheim heir sat frozen in place, his mouth hanging open still. But it wasn't only Tanyl. The clock stood still, and even the flames in the hearth appeared solid and unmoving. Indeed, the whole room had frozen in time—except for one thing.

Imani had read about this rare magic before—cadence magic. Unless the person was the caster, cadence magic stopped time for everyone and everything as long as the witch could hold the spell. But it didn't originate in the Mesial Realm.

Kiran had been gifted magic from the Under. Indeed, she wasn't the only witch with mixed brands, although she was reasonably sure they weren't illegal in Niflheim.

Kiran sat glaring at Tanyl, white-knuckling the sides of the chair. Not one hint of mirth remained on his beautiful face. Instead, pure hatred overtook his body.

Imani filed this away as another fact about the prince. She had no idea what he truly thought about anyone else—not her, not his family, not anyone. But it was clear how he despised Tanyl, and it was a profoundly personal hate.

Furthermore, he possessed astounding magic.

Imani's mind reeled as she fought against what her body knew was happening with what she thought to be impossible. Were other Niflheim breeds—and elves—gifted this miraculous magic, too? Tanyl had said creatures from their slips might be getting through. Were they breeding with beings from the Under? If so ... Imani shuddered, imagining going up against them. They had no chance if Niflheim even sent a handful of witches like Kiran.

She was certain no one in Essenheim had knowledge of the prince's cadence magic and would bet all her money Kiran wanted to keep it quiet. If Essenheim knew Niflheim possessed such power, it would change everything.

This magic was a significant discovery.

She might be able to use this against him, but the secret was so profound Kiran might kill her on the spot, as well. It was risky. She needed an incentive, not a threat.

Bringing a shaking hand up to her mouth, Imani shut her eyes and tried not to breathe too loudly. It was hard when her heart pounded. Even a tiny inhale of breath might be heard across the room by Kiran's elven hearing, especially with the profound absence of sound and the fog of her breath hitting the frigid air.

Imani dared another glance into the sitting room.

Out of his chair, Kiran stood at a desk, rifling loudly through papers, searching for something frantically—a sly fox in the hen house.

She blinked. As fast as Kiran moved before, he sat again, careless, like nothing had happened, like he hadn't performed the miraculous. He murmured another spell with his wand, and the room roared back to life.

"—ation tomorrow," Tanyl continued, oblivious.

They sat in prickly silence.

"Smart decision," Kiran said, his venom-coated smile growing wider. "Now, there's something else I want from you—"

"There are many things I want from you, Kiran," Tanyl grumbled.

"From *me*? What could *I* have that you want? How fascinating. I'm certainly curious," Kiran said conversationally, crossing his arms before dropping the feigned cheerfulness. When he spoke next, his voice was flat and emotionless. "I propose a trade. An answer for an answer."

The Essenheim heir pressed his fingers to the bridge of his nose. "Fine," Tanyl sighed.

Barely a second passed before Kiran bit out his inquiry. "How many masters in the Order practice divination?" Prince Kiran went absolutely still and fixed his gaze on the Essenheim heir. Her ears moved again, sensing a desperate undertone from the elf.

She glanced down at her divination brand—well, her sister's.

Tanyl scoffed. "If you're trying to see if you'll be monarch, try something else. Not even our best master witch could cast such a spell for me."

Kiran chuckled with him, like they were old friends. The sound made her skin crawl. "As transparent as ever. Can you find me someone or not?"

Taking a quiet inhale of breath, Imani tried to calm her response, knowing *she* had a divination brand. She could help Kiran if he needed something, which was an incentive she could work with to get more information on the final assessment.

Anticipation buzzed through her limbs, her magic tingling, and the fire dimmed no matter how hard she tried to hide her excitement. The sitting room darkened.

Both men's heads whipped toward the doorway.

CHAPTER 31

Kiran clicked his tongue. "I see you let anyone barge into your rooms, Tanyl."

A chair scraped on the floor. Tanyl would find her soon.

Kiran remained seated, apparently not in any hurry to discover her.

With a loud sigh, she lifted the veil of her glamour. After another pause, forcing them to wait, she sailed into the doorway's light.

Imani eyed Tanyl with arrogance and surveyed the room, praying she could pull off the lie she had just arrived.

Tanyl leveled her with an off-putting glare. "Why are you so late?"

Her mouth thinned. He was taking his bad mood out on her.

"Where are the guards? What about the wards Kiran placed over the door? You can't simply walk in here," Tanyl said with an air of frustration. "Go wait in the other room for me."

Imani shrugged, hiding her irritation at his tone. Instead of obeying, however, she did a slow perusal around the room. "Don't want anyone to see us together?"

Tanyl's expression softened. "I don't mind if people see us together … not anymore."

She pursed her lips at the heir apparent. What had changed? What kind of game was Tanyl playing with her?

"So sorry to interrupt your princeling party," she said as she tried to meander to the desk to peek at what Kiran had found earlier.

As if he didn't want her near the papers, Kiran chose to stand then. Like a shifter hunting prey, he closed the distance between them with rapid steps.

Imani angled away, trying to relax, but the predatory elf rounded on her, making it impossible.

His snaking signature invaded her senses, bringing heat to her cheeks. While the malice he exuded should have made her blood run cold, all her cells cried out internally to have him as close as possible. Pushing, whining, and begging, her magic was so furious she resisted his draw.

A familiar shudder went down her spine. But it didn't feel like normal hunger. Instead, it was something else entirely. Something *primal*.

Wilting inward, giving in, Imani didn't have the energy to care how his magic controlled her. In fact, she liked the sensation so much she couldn't stop herself from leaning closer and letting her own soul draw out to play. She couldn't deny there was an attraction between them—an allure.

Looming overhead, Kiran forced Imani's chin up. Her magic stirred along her skin with his gaze on her. His eyes twinkled as he peered down. She'd delighted him with the display of power.

Kiran stared back at her with those mismatched eyes that she found less and less terrifying. A certain beauty lingered in them. One eye shone pure black, as usual, but the other pupil dilated hugely. She got lost in its bright and mossy green depths for a few seconds. What would Kiran be like with two such eyes?

Unable to blink, Imani was held captive by his gaze. Like how other elves were caught in her soul draw, he was utterly, horribly mesmerizing, and while Imani didn't know if she wanted to kiss or punch his perfect-looking mouth most days, she could admit she found him beyond intriguing.

These were dangerous inclinations. She tried to push them away with Tanyl in the room.

"My, what an enchanting creature you are without all the glamour," Kiran purred, pretending he hadn't already seen her without it. He turned to Tanyl. "You lied to me about her, Your Highness. So territorial." He raised his hand to Imani's face. "But I can see why. This is the reason you didn't want me feeding from her—you have her for yourself already."

"Back away from her, Kiran." Tanyl slammed his fist on the table again.

Kiran ignored him and continued staring down at her. He tilted his head as he studied her. A too-long stretch of silence passed.

"'Don't want anyone to see us together?'" he repeated her words with a low sneer only she could hear. "And people say *I'm* manipulative."

She hummed something that was almost a laugh then bit her lip instead.

The prince of the Niflheim Kingdom trailed his fingers across Imani's neck and the scar on her collarbone, a possessive touch, making her practically lightheaded. A copper taste flooded her mouth as she bit her cheek to remain still and unflinching.

She didn't know what to think about it. Part of her loved it, but the other part wanted to swat his hand away and demand he stop toying with her. Kiran made her feel out of her skin—insane, like him.

As if reading her mind, Kiran merely grinned pure menace, pure madness. He said nothing, but his fingers still moved idly.

"I *said* stop touching her," Tanyl demanded, practically shouting. Yet he made no move to shove Kiran away.

"Why should I? I hear she's nowhere near exclusive, Tanyl," he drawled, abruptly dropping his hand. "You might be an idiot in politics, but females, too? Anyone who thinks you're next in line to be king is out of their mind."

Hearing the lies he spun, Imani's blood heated. Before she could lunge at Kiran, Tanyl's words caused her to halt.

"You wouldn't know anything about being an heir, Kiran. You're pathetic."

Kiran rolled his eyes at the dig. "Oh, there's an insult I hear twice weekly. When did you become so desperate, Tanyl? It's disgraceful, to say the least, especially for someone who thinks they will be king."

"I know more than a snake like you." Tanyl's lip curled in distaste.

"At least I accept what and who I am. Can you say the same about yourself?"

Hearing the sharp bite in Kiran's voice, her magic fluttered inside.

"Leave. Now." Tanyl's jaw clenched so hard Imani thought it might break. But despite the magic coming off Kiran, the elf prince's insolence in Tanyl's own home, and how Kiran had touched her, the heir still didn't move to attack. Instead, a stark unease entered his eyes, gaze shifting rapidly between the pair of elves standing in front of him.

"And here I thought you were such a good host that you might want to invite me to stay," Kiran taunted before throwing a lazy wink Imani's way. "I hear your gorgeous little Norn elf is open to entertaining audiences during sex." He was obviously referring to her recent meeting with Saevel.

Arsehole.

"Get out of here." Tanyl raised his wand, but the emptiness of the threat lingered.

Kiran turned toward the other prince. His face was the picture of indifference, blatantly daring Tanyl to proceed with his threat. "Or what?"

It dawned on Imani that Tanyl *couldn't* attack Kiran. It might be construed as an act of war.

Imani's patience broke. Leaning up, she pressed her wand into Kiran's throat. "Or he'll let me wipe the ugly grin off your face," she whispered with a snarl against his ear.

Kiran might be a twelve-mark, but her confidence in magic use had improved, and she wouldn't let him terrorize Tanyl like this any longer.

A warm, calloused hand slipped into hers. Kiran's thumb traced a possessive circle across her skin. "The little elf has you wrapped around these tiny fingers, doesn't she, Tanyl?"

She tried to rip her hand away, and he chuckled.

"She's delightful. I can see why you want this perfect creature for yourself."

"I am not a belonging either of you can own." Imani snatched her hand back and pressed the wand harder into his flesh.

"Such a disobedient, wild thing to threaten a visiting royal. Not to mention *Meira* simply barging in here uninvited."

His emphasis on "Meira" served to simply hold more over her head.

"I was invited, you bastard," Imani shot back.

"I am the product of royalty, thank you very much," he huffed in mock insult, his amusement still written across his features.

"A fact I'm sure you need to remind people of regularly," she said coolly.

Tanyl pointed to the door. "You told me what you wanted, and I agreed. Right now, you have nothing else I want except for you to leave. I'm sure you have some more bidding to do for your brute of a brother."

Kiran merely laughed again. "As usual, this was an *utter* pleasure. But you're right; my brother's bidding isn't going to finish itself," he said cheerfully before strolling toward the hallway.

With his hand on the door, he halted. After a thought, he made his way to stand over her again. Imani took in a sharp breath.

He inclined his head to study her, an expression chilling in its insanity. A low growl came from his chest—more animal than man—and he roughly grabbed her face. Holding firm, he rubbed his thumbs in small circles across the soft skin of her cheek. It raised the hairs on her arms.

Unable to move, she froze as the knot in her chest tightened under such scrutiny. Kiran's magic skimmed her skin in a seductive caress of power, filling her head and chest and slithering down her belly and back. A shiver of desire ran down her back and pooled in her core.

This male witch had an arsenal of magic she didn't understand. Power rolled off Kiran, compelling her as only an elf could. It murmured constantly.

Finding a sliver of composure, she grabbed his shirt in frustration. "Whatever game you're playing with me needs to stop," she hissed.

A secretive smile spread across his face, reminding her how he still owned her, and with a gentleness at odds with his nature, Kiran brushed a few hairs off her forehead.

Then Kiran turned to Tanyl, his hand lightly resting on her cheek. "I guess I *do* have something you want quite badly, Your Highness."

"Leave!" Tanyl roared again, still unwilling to attack the prince, despite the threat.

"You know, you're lucky I even let you see her like this—in her true form—without breaking your *bloody* neck."

"Don't you dare hurt him," Imani whispered up at Kiran, still fisting his shirt.

Leaning closer, he lifted another stray lock of hair from her shoulder and rubbed it gently between his fingers. "I won't, my darling. At least, not tonight," he whispered.

The low purr of his voice made it impossible for Imani even to consider replying to such a statement. Instead, she merely stared at Kiran like he'd lost his damn mind. She *was* losing her mind around, as if she were turning into him.

For a moment, a breath, they stood alone in an inescapable net of familiarity, loathing, and curiosity.

Tanyl's voice broke through their private space, invading it. "Step away from her."

Kiran's hand on her face tightened, eyes still locked onto hers. "Enjoy your final days with my perfect elf, Tanyl." His tone was no longer the casual, darkly amused one she had expected from him. It was deadly serious. "Soon, you won't be allowed anywhere near her."

"My final days with Meira? You could never deserve her in a million years. Run along, Snake," Tanyl said.

Kiran pulled away from her and clapped once. "That's the most honest thing you've said all night!" The elf prince silenced himself and let the total weight of his disconcerting gaze land on Tanyl. "But the fact remains. We are leaving this kingdom soon, and afterward, I will *never* share her with anyone ever again."

Imani wanted to tell Kiran she belonged to no one but couldn't. His words were valid. She *would* belong to him. If she didn't die attempting his assessments, she'd work for the Niflheim Kingdom ... and Kiran.

"Enough of this. Step away from her and leave," Tanyl commanded, his voice laced with the promise of violence. "The day I rip your throat out can't come soon enough."

The room plummeted to freezing, and Kiran's mask dropped. His face twisted into something more beast than man, and his mismatched eyes appeared even more insane—wilder.

"The day I die will be because I decided it, and when that happens, it certainly won't be *you* who does the honors," he said, deep and all-consuming—the voice of royalty.

Images of his death assaulted her, and his words made her blink in surprise. Did he already know the truth?

But Kiran's irreverent expression returned as he shoved the unhinged force deep inside him. The room thawed, and he sauntered out as if nothing had happened.

Still shivering from the pressure drop, Imani rushed to Tanyl and wrapped her arms around him.

"I'm sorry I couldn't do anything," he murmured into her hair. "I can't touch him without risking a confrontation."

"I know," she whispered back.

Tanyl held her shoulders and bent down. "Do you understand why they call him the Mad Prince?"

"Oh, I understand," she said, laughing darkly, still lightheaded from the volatile storm of emotions stirred up by Prince Kiran.

Kiran had lost his mind. Imani had lost hers, as well.

CHAPTER 32

Imani paced until she wore the carpet down before retreating to bed when the heaviness of her limbs and eyelids grew unbearable. A storm brewed outside. It had been a restless evening, and she feared it would also be a restless night.

Clear as day, her name flitted in and out of her ears. Irritation sparked in her chest, as it wasn't time yet to wake. The night had not yet released her from its deep slumbering spell, and frustrated, she tossed and turned, tugging the covers over her head to try to drown out the voices.

Finally, she sat up with a groan at her shadows whispering her name. Despite the warm blankets, she shivered. No, not a chill—it was a familiar magic near her door.

It had to be him. Kiran's audacity knew no bounds. How dare he? She hadn't expected he would be on time. Keeping her waiting would have been a game to him. But she hadn't expected him to be *hours* late. She contemplated ignoring him, but she couldn't. Gaining his agreement with this bargain trumped her pride.

Slow embers burned in the hearth, and her shadows flitted around the room, flashing light, then dark, then light again as they danced and twirled between the table and her dressing room.

Letting out a quiet, frustrated groan, she grabbed her wand and the heavily embroidered robe her sister had made for her.

Unhurried, she shooed her shadows away. Her control of her magic had increased, but the darkness simply followed her everywhere like a piece of her.

The sconces pulsed and walls darkened immediately when she passed by them. She flung open the door.

Kiran paced at her door, preparing to knock.

Imani pinned him with a bland look and crossed her arms. With her hair untamed and coming loose from its braid, she was hardly intimidating. In a thin, white nightgown, her glamourless face and nightclothes made her feel naked.

Taking him in, he was in worse shape. An involuntary thrill shot through her at seeing him in such a state.

Tense and oddly disheveled, Kiran held his wand loosely in one hand and ran the other through his messy hair. Someone had unbuttoned his shirt so far she could see the fine hairs trailing down his abdomen. His pants had been hastily thrown on, and numerous pinpricks of blood dotted his forearms and hands.

It occurred to her that she liked this version of him more than any other.

Had he been in someone's bed earlier? Where had the blood come from? Anger at how he'd kept her waiting spread through her chest.

Her robe fell, exposing her shoulder. She tugged up the sleeve and scanned him with narrowed eyes. He could see her breasts through the thin fabric if the robe slipped again.

His scrutinizing gaze searched her in return. He lingered on her chest and mouth, but with a jerk, his eyes snapped overhead to the space above the doorway.

"Why are your rooms not protected?" he asked in a low voice.

"Kiran," she snarled in greeting, grabbing his arm. "You're truly remarkable."

The door closed on its own while Kiran cast defensive magic around them before rounding on her. Jaw tight, he stared. She stared right back, uncomfortable around this uncharacteristic behavior.

"You don't have this place warded at all," he said through clenched teeth. "How bloody stupid can you be to sleep here like this? I can't believe Tanyl lets you stay in this room with nothing. *Any* witch can walk in."

"If they come in uninvited, they won't like the result. Besides"—Imani smiled mockingly—"what my prince *lets* me do—or not do—is not your problem for the time being."

A crack of thunder boomed outside and made Kiran jump. He dug his palms into his eyes, groaning.

Imani blinked, taken aback. "What's the matter with you?"

A beat of silence passed. "I don't like storms … the lightning, really … and I don't know how long I can keep doing this," Kiran murmured to himself, mussing his hair more.

Imani gaped at this nearly vulnerable behavior from him, and she sympathized. The lightning from the Fabric event she'd caused haunted her dreams. Most nights, she could vividly see the destruction of the orchard like it was yesterday.

"Doing what?" she pressed.

"Nothing! I'm doing absolutely nothing," he shouted, his expression darkening.

"Keep your voice down," she snapped.

"I had no idea you slept alone like this, Imani. You *need* to take more precautions."

"How dare you come into my rooms, telling me what to do? I don't work for you yet, Kiran, so allow me a few more days of freedom, Your Highness," she shot back.

"You don't understand—"

The room flashed with a bright white light from the lightning then dark again.

He scraped a trembling hand down his face and pressed the palms of his hands into his eyes again.

Imani had a distinct urge to comfort him. She slowly removed his hands from his face, raising a tentative hand. They were still shaking.

"It's only a storm, Kiran. It will pass. We are safe. I'm safe."

He stared at their clasped hands for a moment then shut his eyes. But, a second later, he snatched his back. "You're without any wards protecting your room or—"

"I'm *done* having this conversation with you," she cut him off. "My protection is not your concern until I'm entirely your pet to control."

In response, he barked a low laugh, muttering something in his elvish dialect she didn't understand.

Rain pounded against the window as Kiran wandered around her room, picking up her things randomly. He paced while mussing his hair further, picking up a book and some parchment on her desk before glancing at the furniture. Still uncertain, she didn't stop him.

Kiran *seemed* calmer. But his hands trembled, and his chest heaved as he took several deep breaths. How terrified did the storms make him? Or was something else bothering him? Maybe both? Anyone could see how tired he was right now. Imani sensed it in his magic, too. The snakes in his signature writhed in agitation. He didn't have his glamour on, either.

She admonished herself for caring. After all, he was the Prince of Snakes, a true master of deception. However, Imani's lies were also stacking up, and she was about to turn the tables on him for something she wanted. Now who was the schemer?

For all his faults and madness, sometimes Kiran and Imani were quite similar.

The thought made her shudder.

Another crack of thunder rattled the windowpanes. Imani's insides twisted as he sharply inhaled and scrubbed his hands up and down his face, scratching at the stubble growing in.

"What's going on with you?" Her words came out softly. She reached for him but pulled her hand back, stopping herself.

He shot her a contemptuous look. "Are you worried about me, darling?"

As always, he'd unsettled her again when she thought she might be starting to understand him.

"I couldn't care less," she hit back. "But you barge into *my* room hours late, berating me, acting strange—even for you—which begs the question."

"Trust me; I wouldn't be here if you hadn't asked me to come. Your note said you'd make it worth my while, but if all you wanted was to inquire about my well-being, I'm leaving," Kiran said, his voice tight.

Imani shoved the hair back from her forehead. She might be small and a new witch, but everyone had a fear—or a want. Learn those two facts, and she could hold power over anyone. All it took was information.

"You're not going anywhere. I want something from you, and I know you have some nasty secrets—worse than mine." Imani stepped closer, forcing herself to stand as tall as possible.

Kiran didn't back away, even when they were chest to chest. Instead, he dropped his chin and played with the loose hair framing her face. "Tell me what you *think* you know, my darling."

"Tell me about the divination spell you need." Her body tingled with the pleasure of commanding such an arrogant bastard.

The elf prince shrugged lazily, his response revealing nothing. "What makes you think I need a divination spell?"

"Please. Let's drop the pretense. I heard you in Tanyl's room last night."

He frowned. "I don't believe you. I cast the silencing charm around Tanyl's rooms myself. Besides, even if I did need this spell, I'm not asking *you* to make it for me."

Kiran didn't know just how easily she could slip through his wards.

Imani plowed on. "Why? You know I have a potential master level divination brand, and you know I value discretion."

He reached for her hair. "I know you *stole* a divination mark." He wasn't jumping at the opportunity to admit anything, let alone agree to her help.

More silence fell as he continued twirling her hair around his finger.

When Kiran didn't immediately respond, the pit in her stomach dropped further. The weight of failure suffocated her, getting heavier by the second.

"Your time is up," he said, dropping her hair.

If he was going to be difficult, she had to play her only other card. She would have preferred to go with an incentive, but the threat was her best chance of surviving, and she wouldn't waste it.

"So interesting you mention time," she said.

Those words broke the dam. Kiran's face contorted in ire, and magic filled the room. Flames stood still in the fireplace, like before, and the flickers from the scones froze. She waited for him to say something, but his eyes simply bore into hers until she swallowed hard.

Victory must have shown on her face, but her confidence shook as his cool gaze took her in. Imani had no idea why his magic wouldn't work on her, but she was infinitely grateful it didn't. Maybe her shadows were protecting her again.

The border of bright green rimming Kiran's eye flared.

"Think about your next words carefully, Imani," he commanded.

The words tumbled out of Imani without a thought. "I suppose this means you're not as powerful as you thought. I might fail in outing you, but I could certainly try."

He didn't like hearing that one bit. He clamped his hands around her throat. He forced her eyes up to his with a squeeze.

"You don't have to try." His grip on my throat eased until it was more of a caress. What was he doing now? Was this a game? "You don't know what you do to me."

Imani took in a ragged breath, wanting to cough at the pressure. But somehow, she met and held his insane eyes, dilated to an impossible size.

"Blackmail me again or utter even one word about my magic to *anyone*, and I'll show exactly why you're in over your head as I break this perfect little body a hundred different ways. Each one will be more gruesome than the last."

He dropped his hand but didn't walk away. His intoxicating signature surrounded her, the scent overpowering. They locked eyes in a standoff. His eyes, filled with rage before, softened and briefly flitted down to her hands, and she followed his gaze. There was faint darkness flaring from between the fingers of her clenched fists. Not like smoke, but like—

"What do you want?" he interrupted her thoughts, oblivious to the magic seeping out of her.

"In exchange for this spell *and* keeping your nasty secret, I want answers to two questions," she said.

The male elf stayed silent but watched her with dark expectation.

She shivered and crossed her arms again to cover her hardening nipples. "First, I want to know more about myself." She took a deep breath, unsteady at revealing one of her biggest secrets. But she wanted the truth so badly she would take the risk, especially with so much leverage over him. Besides, something hidden under Kiran's layers made a tiny, minuscule part of her want to trust him.

With a flourish of her wand, she ripped away the flesh magic hiding her heartmate sigil. She tore up her sleeve to reveal the red stag on her arm, and there it sat next to her glamoured High-Norn leaf sigil.

"I have a heartmate," she whispered. Then, with a delicate gag, she covered her mouth before turning to the wastebasket and throwing up a thin snake. This one's ashes fell into the basket, much smaller than the one from Ara's flesh magic spell.

Wiping her mouth, Imani ignored any embarrassment. Kiran would know what had happened. He practiced flesh magic.

She peered into his eyes again, undeterred. "I know *who* he was, but I don't know *what* he was. I've never seen this sigil." If she learned his breed, she'd learn her own, too.

Kiran grasped her hand and ripped it toward him, studying it, transfixed by the sigil. His thumb rubbed small circles on the red stag.

"*Was?*" Kiran asked without stopping his ministrations.

"He's dead."

Her answer made him shoot his eyes up to hers. A storm of unreadable emotions swirled in his green eye. "Are you sure?"

"Absolutely."

He swallowed and dropped her wrist. "And the second demand?"

"You'll tell me exactly who my opponent is for the third assessment."

Kiran let his gaze slide over Imani for a full minute. "I can give you the opponent's name after you complete the spell."

"And my heartmate's sigil?"

"I can't tell you much about it."

Her eyes flew open in disbelief. "You don't know?"

"I don't know."

He was convincing—Imani had to give him that—but she couldn't accept that as an answer.

"You're an archmage witch, and the bloody First Witch of magic in your kingdom," she bit out, impatient, "how do you not know everything about your kingdom's sigils and their related breeds?"

"I *do* know everything about my kingdom's sigils. But this …?" Kiran grabbed her wrist and shoved it in her face. "I can only tell you this red sigil is *not* from my kingdom. Ours are blue, like Essenheim's. This is from the Under realm."

The walls caved in on Imani. Saevel and Kiran had kept their brands glamoured since arriving in Essenheim, and Malis's had been flayed. She'd never actually seen a Niflheim brand.

"What …? What are you saying? He's from the Under realm?" Her heart pounded against her ribs.

"Indeed. Your heartmate is not from this kingdom or Niflheim," he said.

"How can I be sure you're telling the truth?"

He shrugged. "You can't. But believe it or not, I'd like to know more about this sigil, as well."

"Have you seen one before?" Imani asked.

"Yes. But beyond seeing it before and knowing red brands come from the Under, I can't tell you anything about this particular sigil." Truth rang in the prince's words as he studied her. A gut instinct told her he was being honest. Maybe they were starting to trust each other.

Kiran cleared his throat. "Now, do we still have a bargain for the other information?"

Imani's voice had disappeared, but she managed to nod.

Her whole life, she'd ignorantly thought Niflheim brands had to be another color. How could they be the same blue color as Essenheim brands? The kingdoms' magic was so different from each other. Her brands were much more illegal than she'd initially thought. They didn't even come from the Mesial Realm.

Again, she and Kiran had more in common than not.

"You have a brand from another realm. So, it's red, as well?" She was grasping at any information she could learn.

He smirked with a hint of evilness in it. "Not part of our bargain, little elf. You already know too much."

So, what the fuck kind of elves were she and Malis? Malis had acted like he'd been from Niflheim, but maybe he was born in another realm and grew up in Niflheim? Perhaps he was lying? Imani's head spun with confusion and possibilities.

It struck Imani how she wished Ara were alive. Her mind kept coming back to the night in the jail when her grandmother had summoned her to provide answers, but she never had. Bloody Aralana had to know the truth about Imani's heritage her whole life. After all, the sigil would have been glamoured since Imani had been born.

But Ara's secrets were an untouchable mountain Imani would never climb now. This distraction wasn't needed; she needed to focus on the final assessment.

She turned back to Kiran. "Tell me about the spell."

Kiran sighed, a loud, exasperated sound, and took a folded paper out of his pocket. "Truthfully, I should hire someone else to cast this magic, but it's bloody impossible to find a master witch who practices flesh magic divination around here, especially one with discretion. It will reveal someone's heartmate, and I want to keep quiet who it is—even from my brother. I don't think you have the skills, but I'm running out of time and options. I suppose I can let you try." He handed it to her. "I don't need to threaten you any more to get my point across. This stays between us."

"I can cast divination magic just fine," she muttered.

Unfolding the parchment, a lock of light hair—blonder than her silver but similar—rested inside.

"Since you're an annoyingly well-read person," he said with a ghost of a smile tugging at his mouth, "I'm sure you know divination magic either seeks to predict the future or reveals the unknown in the present."

"Yes, yes, I understand." She waved her hand impatiently.

"This is the latter." He inclined his head toward the paper and picked up the lock of hair, holding it in front of her face. "All we need to cast it is a physical piece of one person in the pair. In this case, a simple lock of hair will do."

"Is this the male or the female's hair?"

"The female's."

She lifted the hair to examine it more. "And whose heartmate do you want to identify with this spell?"

His response was instant. "None of your business."

Was Kiran searching for his own heartmate?

Was he ... lonely?

Imani tried to imagine Kiran with a heartmate. Would he protect and love her? Would she be as cunning as him? Would he be affectionate, like she'd seen other heartmates be with each other?

Maybe he had a soul in there somewhere after all, and yet ... his behavior constantly suggested otherwise. As did the creature who peeked out from behind his eyes.

It didn't matter. She had no idea what he wanted with this girl's heartmate, but it was probably nothing good and likely had nothing to do with him. Tanyl said he liked to hold secrets over people, and this fit the bill.

She slit her eyes at him while slipping it into her robe's pocket. "How will I know it worked?"

"The spell, when created correctly by someone with divination magic, will project an image of the other heartmate into a person's mind." He brushed some tangled strands of hair off her face. "You might actually earn a modicum of respect from me if you can create this spell."

Too startled to question why he was touching her, she shut her eyes briefly when he dropped his forehead to hers. They remained there for a moment. The only sounds in the room were the crackling fire and pattering of rain.

It struck her that she might know more about Kiran and his secrets than anyone else in the castle right now, and she'd successfully manipulated a deal out of him.

A ruthless sort of pride bloomed in her chest.

"Try not to kill yourself, my darling," he whispered, lips lightly brushing her brow.

Lightning flashed and lit up the room, and he was gone.

CHAPTER 33

Imani would give this mysterious divination spell to Kiran, even if it killed her. She *needed* the answer to the third assessment. Her curiosity about who he wanted it for would have to wait. She would deliver him a perfect final product.

Although a small part of her wanted to see the man's face, too.

She plaited her hair while repeating the different incantations. Some would work better than others. Still, unfortunately, her knowledge of divination was limited, and with a finite amount of hair, she didn't have the liberty of making mistakes while creating this spell.

It was a blatant overexaggeration on her part to claim she could perform this magic fine. Casting this flesh magic divination spell would be more complicated than she'd let on. Some witches created spells similar in structure to others, but none were ever truly the same. The power of the witch and their own personal essence ensured nearly all spells were unique, even if they had the same results—made for use by even non-magic users. Anyone could say the incantation, use the spell, or drink the potion created by the witch, and it would trigger the Fabric's power. It was what made magic so coveted and feared in Essenheim.

She clenched her teeth and lit a fire in the hearth. Flames crackled and grew. The reflections danced in her eyes as she waited for the heat to increase.

Using fire as a medium would work to her advantage because it would be fast and powerful, but divination spells behaved so prickly, so fluid. Imani preferred more precise magic.

Cursing, she flicked her wand hand. She only had a few hours before Kiran arrived, and Imani needed to focus on the task.

She got to work by holding the parchment and hair in her other hand. The first steps were easy, yet it took an hour of tedious concentration and a steady stream of controlled magic.

Acting beyond her command, tiny invisible roots of her essence and magic flowed outward from Imani's chest, coaxing the fire into a steady burn. A tendril of warm, silken magic from the fire brushed against hers and gently tried to twine itself around one of her wisps of magic. It was working.

When the waves radiated from the fire, her arm shook and sweat lined her forehead. She smiled at her work, but once she put the hair in, she would need to control and channel it into the smoke—a tricky endeavor.

Ripping her wand away from the building spell, she split the lock of hair in half with one clean cut, not wanting to use any less in case she needed more. She dropped it into the flames.

Things happened quickly once the strands caught fire. Instantly, magic burst inside the room, coating it in hot, suffocating heat. Stunned, Imani waited a second too long to grasp control again, and once she did, it overwhelmed her senses and filled her body.

Groaning, she sensed the spell falling apart. Working fast, she quickly grabbed the rest of the hair to try correcting the spell, and when the time came to drop the hair in, she didn't hesitate.

Tugging the burst outward into her wand, she murmured the unique incantation she had picked out for this spell and pushed it back into the flames. This time, it was even more potent. The fire let out a loud crack and burned blue.

The room was alive with magic. Faint whispers of it steamed off her skin and mixed with the smoke. For a moment, dizziness whirled her vision. She gripped the arm of a chair and took a deep breath, pulse racing. With one final uttered word, pain rocked her.

She sank to her knees. Imani whispered the spell she had created, and the weight of the room crushed her body. Each breath filled her lungs with boiling, sharp glass as if *she* were now the medium, not the fire.

It was too much ... she was going to kill herself.

A pepper and smoke smell permeated the room. Intense magic, indeed.

Frantic, Imani crawled to the desk and grabbed the parchment, scribbling down the version she had created, repeating her incantation like a prayer.

Tingling magic skimmed over her body. A good sign. Her breath came in short pants, waiting. A knot formed in her stomach at potentially seeing Kiran's face in her mind among the blankness. She tried and tried to cast the spell to see the man.

Did it work?

Darkness took over before anyone appeared.

Cold, crisp air filled her, lifting her slightly off the floor. She breathed it greedily as her ears popped and the pressure in the room relaxed. Lolling her head back, she stretched her gaze across the room where a female nymph stood with her wand outstretched.

The woman marched forward and grabbed her arm, roughly pulling Imani up. "Are you trying to kill yourself? Or alert the entire city you're pulling from the Fabric?" She shouted at her some more, but Imani barely registered the words. Who the hell was this nymph? Imani racked her brain.

Now, as she stood upright, she realized this was one of Kiran's advisers. Imani had seen the Essenheim naiad speaking and laughing with Kiran during the assessments.

This witch was a traitor to Essenheim, and Imani disliked her immediately for that fact alone.

Imani pushed away and braced herself against the wall. Dizzy. She was so dizzy. She'd lost control at the end. Her lungs felt painfully constricted, and each breath sounded labored. Her chest burned, and her head hurt, but she was otherwise all right.

"You stupid girl. You used fire?"

"It's an excellent medium. I've worked with it before." A lie. But Ara and Meira had used it with ease.

"It *is* an excellent medium. But you"––the nymph's eyes roamed up and down Imani's body––"are too slight to channel through it alone for flesh magic divination." The nymph's eyes flashed as Imani pressed her hand to her ribs, and the woman shook her head, tsking. "He should've never trusted you could perform divination *just fine*," she said, throwing Imani's words back at her.

Kiran must have told her about their conversation, which pissed Imani off.

"Move away from me. I did handle it fine," she snapped, wincing at the pain coursing through her head.

"Clearly."

"What are you doing here, anyway? Kiran was supposed to meet me." Imani righted herself, her eyes focusing more. "Go," she ordered, pointing to the door. "I made a deal with Kiran, not you."

The woman stood inches from her, her dark glare penetrating Imani. "You're serious?"

"Deadly. I'm not handing this spell over to some witch—"

"I'm not *some* witch." An amused grin spread across the nymph's beautiful face. "Kiran is busy, so as far as you're concerned, the prince and I are one and the same. You can call me Master Heirwyn." She put out the palm of her hand, waiting. "Now, hand over the spell, and I'll give you the answers you seek."

This was a new revelation. The nymph witch was obviously close to Kiran and wasn't afraid to throw her power around, and her being a traitor to Essenheim still didn't sit well with Imani. Faint anger stirred deep in her chest, and maybe some sort of jealousy.

With narrowed eyes, Imani thrust the spell toward the woman.

"The spell took? You saw the man?" Master Heirwyn snatched the paper from Imani's hand. "The female's heartmate?"

"Cast it yourself. I saw the poor bastard," Imani lied, tapping her temple, "right here." She prayed her bluff worked.

Imani bit her lip and waited as the nymph shut her eyes and read the spell under her breath. When they opened again, the gleam in her eyes confirmed it had worked. It was hungry. Greedy. Like the woman wanted to put a collar on Imani and force her to do tricks.

"Impressive."

A thrill of excitement shot through Imani after hearing the praise, and then she wanted to slap herself. She shouldn't preen after scraps of compliments from people. Disgusted, she went right for her answers.

"Who am I facing in the third assessment?"

"What do you know about the breed?" Master Heirwyn put her hand on her hip, waiting.

Imani's fingers pressed into her temples, attempting to stop the raging headache inside. "Nothing. Kiran never told me a name, let alone a breed."

"Pairs will publicly duel to the death, using magic and physical strength. And there's one rule—no blood. Each witch must be practiced and precise to ensure no blood is spilled—"

"Yes, yes," Imani cut her off. "More sanctioned and permissible murder. Kiran explained those details. Tell me about my opponent."

"He's a high leonine shifter named Aiden."

Imani was silent momentarily before muttering, "How is this even a fair fight? He's not a master but certainly one of the strongest and biggest new witches here."

"Indeed, he is," she said. "You will be forced to channel your best magic and overcome your shortfalls to kill the other person and trigger the master brands."

Should she trust this traitorous nymph? One who betrayed Essenheim to live in their country and work for the Niflheim royals? Imani had no choice. She had no other leads.

"This is bullshit," Imani cursed. Her body was still shaking from the aftershocks of magic.

"Get used to bullshit if you survive, which is unlikely because even I'm inclined to think the princes want you dead with this pairing. No one will go easy on you in the Niflheim Kingdom." The nymph's magic signature surrounded Imani's. "As an Essenheim breed who's lived in Niflheim a long time, a bit of advice—"

"Save it. This deal is complete," Imani spat, motioning to the door. "Leave."

"I'm trying to help you, girl." Master Heirwyn's chuckle was a low rumble as she moved to stand over Imani. "You made this mistake once, but never find yourself bargaining with any of the Illithianas ever again." Her gaze darkened. "Especially Kiran. He's more like their father than any others have ever been or will be. You've seen a sliver of what he's like and capable of."

It took every ounce of her strength not to shrink away from the high-bred witch—her power was formidable—and yet, the condescending warning, while probably true, sent Imani's temper flaring.

"Are you threatened by me?" Imani managed to rasp.

In a disconcerting reminder of Ara, the nymph threw her head back and laughed. It was a cackling, spiteful sound, heating Imani's face. After a deep breath, she quieted and regarded Imani with arrogance.

Imani's shadows itched to rip the flesh from her pretty face.

"Wake up, elf witch," she continued. "Pray you don't survive the assessments, or you'll wish you'd died when you arrive at Kehomel. You're beyond naïve, possessing magic you have no business wielding, batting your big, beautiful eyes, and assuming you know how this realm works. You don't. And if you're smart, you'll fulfill your end of this deal with Kiran and slink away from his sight. Because if you end up any more tangled with us, we will drain you of life, shredding you into something you don't even know, and eventually, you'll be in so deep with binding magic you can't get out. Like your grandmother."

The nymph walked to the door. Her movements were painfully graceful, a perfect reminder of her predatory constitution. When she threw a glance over her shoulder, Imani could have sworn she wore a victorious little smirk.

CHAPTER 34

The foreboding sound of feet crunching through the blanket of fallen dead leaves was Imani's death march.

She longed to devour a soul more than usual. Death was all she could think about, but she'd fed from Tanyl yesterday, and even in the dark, spying eyes observed the witches.

The dull roar of a crowd grew in the background until it drowned out the spirits' taunts. Unlike the others, tonight's final ascension assessment would be public.

Entering the cells below the outdoor fieldhouse made Imani think the whole city had come out for the spectacle.

Clad in black fighting leathers, like everyone else, Imani looked around the tent, taking in the remaining participants. The third male Norn elf was there. After Imani had killed the other Norn, he'd kept his distance.

Nearly all the survivors were male, and spectators placed wagers against the four remaining women. It shocked Imani there weren't fewer females remaining. Nida and Esa were competing, and the fourth was an unfamiliar redhead.

Strangers betting against the women filled Imani with a sick sort of glee.

She found Esa sitting with her wand between her teeth, lacing up her boots. Those fools should be afraid of the female pixie, in particular, and despite their rift, Imani would relish Esa's victory.

Esa surprised Imani with a curt nod. *Give them hell*, her eyes said. Imani returned it in silent understanding with a tilt of her chin as Lore swept into the room to loom over Esa.

His face hardened, clearly in a dark mood. How did he manage to be here without competing? Especially since he seemed ready to kill *everyone*.

With her wings hidden tight behind her, Esa stood, looking deadly, too.

Lore planted his hands on the wall on either side of her head, bracketing her in, and positioned himself tightly around her, hiding her.

Esa's face contorted into a sneer. Her head cocked to the side while saying something to him. Despite being so much smaller, Esa was still somehow even more impressive, at least to Imani. More surprising was how she didn't push him away. In fact, Esa angled herself closer and allowed his hand to skim her arm lightly.

A nerve ticked in his jaw while Esa laid into him. A quiet tension built, but Esa didn't relent. Lore didn't, either. Instead, he blinked then laughed without amusement.

She pushed at his chest, not moving him an inch, which only made him smile down at her. Her mouth moved again, but he cut her off with a raised hand and pointed at Esa's chest. Whatever he said made her scoff dramatically.

Shuffling forward, Imani slyly caught the tail end of Esa's insult.

"You think this means you're worthy?" she hissed, grabbing his hand, the master brand gleaming. "Unlike you two, I *never* needed it. I never have, and I *never* will."

"You're infuriating," he snarled, ire flashing across his face as he lifted their clasped hands to his mouth, lightly kissing them. "You think I care about any of it when I have you?"

"You think a brand means you have me?" Her voice was low and venomous. "You've got *fuck all*."

As if sensing eyes were on them, Esa glanced up and tried to push

Lore away again. It only made him pull her closer. Flustered, Esa managed to shove him off and storm away.

"Bloody fuckin' hell," Lore groaned to himself. Rubbing his hand over his bristle-heavy chin, he worked on composing himself. Mismatched from his blue hair, the shadow of dark stubble added to the strength of his jaw and the sharp lines of his face. His narrowed gaze landed on Imani.

"What are you looking at?" Lore snapped. His violet eyes were aglow with anger. His hair was a tousled mess. Not bothering to let her respond, he stomped out of the room after Esa.

Arsehole.

The bells sounded again, calling them outside. A heavy silence fell as the witches wove through the pits below the arena and trudged out under the scaffolding to the benches lining the edges.

Thousands of eyes landed on the participants.

A few weeks ago, Imani had walked down here to see the field-house, but she had never seen it so full of people and from this angle.

Noise, magic, and emotions swirled in a cloud of thick smog. At least some Essenheim subjects didn't find this practice barbaric. Would the Order bring back dueling to increase their goodwill?

Stone bleachers rose all around her, much more extensive and higher than she remembered when packed with people. Many stood on the steps, along the wall, and above it. The wood stages and platforms typically lining the center of the ring had been removed, and a smooth dirt floor had taken its place. The rain had been sparse the past few days—not since the storm—so the dirt remained dry instead of a mass of wet mud.

The Illithiana princes sat in the center box seats on one end of the ring. Imani seriously considered if they had any deity blood in them because they seemed like gods.

Although Kiran was the more handsome of the two, with their fine clothing, both appeared impeccable. But even more alluring was their magic.

Clawing and snarling, their signatures freely rolled off them. A tugging sensation in her chest stole a little of her breath. Her whole body responded to the power, simply *wanting* to be near them. It made her think about the other four brothers and what all six of them were like together with their father, the Niflheim king.

She shuddered, both excited and terrified by the thought.

Kiran sat with his fingers over his mouth in amused indifference, surveying nothing and everything. Sitting beside him was the elegant Master Heirwyn who had visited her the other night. They moved their heads close together, conversing privately. Kiran laughed with a rare, genuine smile.

Imani narrowed her eyes at the sight.

The queen and Tanyl sat in the more ornate box directly across from the Niflheim royal family. No one laughed or spoke, which made sense. For all intents and purposes, the event was an embarrassment for them.

Saevel stood, and the audience grew calm and still.

"We value strength over magic in our kingdom," he boomed, the deep rasp of his voice echoing throughout the stadium. "The third and final assessment will test the witches' magical skills, mental fortitude, and physical ruthlessness in combat."

With a flourish of his wand, he sent fireworks into the air, signaling the start of the first match.

~

VIOLENCE AND DEATH permeated Imani's keen, elven sense as the evening wore on. They were nearly through the night, and Esa was taking on a high satyr witch.

The pixie witch's terrestrial magic kicked dust up in a constant swirl. Esa hammered him with blows from her fists and magic, but she could never hurt him enough.

Surrounded by all this brutality, a stirring grew inside Imani. She smothered the emotions as she readied herself for the awaited duel, needing all her strength for what she had planned.

The shifter probably assumed Esa was an easy kill. The pairing of the slightest participants with two of the largest did not go unnoticed by Imani. Victory—and staying alive—would be a challenge for the females, and even the unshakable pixie appeared ragged and animalistic as her match wore on.

Seconds ticked by, and the noose of death tightened around Esa's neck.

It was close to ending. Indeed, Lore appeared to be losing his mind next to Tanyl. The male sprite was an arsehole, and Imani didn't understand his relationship with Esa, but it was clear he cared for her. Imani's heart hurt to see such a powerful witch be so helpless. His pain also made her nervous.

What would he do if Esa lost? The thought was concerning.

Bursts of dirt flew high above, forcing Imani's eyes up again. The shifter whinnied loudly, circling below, taunting her. Esa flew into a corner of the ring as if in retreat.

People booed, assuming her imminent loss, and Lore roared, tearing his hair out. He had chewed his lip to shreds, and blood coated his mouth.

An end would come soon, either way.

Onlookers cheered or shouted, their eyes on the horse. Imani's eyes were drawn to the dirt and the unnatural way it moved. It churned like the sea, forming subtle but distinct waves.

She inched forward in her seat, her mouth gaped in anticipation; it was clear Esa wasn't in retreat. Instead, her friend had been working —yet waiting—in complete control the entire time. Some magic took longer than others to cast.

The two combatants stood in limbo for seconds. Then, arms rising, Esa clutched her wand in both hands above her head. Her thin, nimble Draswood heated, an orange ember appearing on the end.

With a lurch, Imani's power pressed harder against her skin, as if responding to Esa's magic. She doubled over, clutching her belly. No longer contained in her veins, fingers of black ink spread subtly out from her skin. With her jaw clenched, Imani imagined strong, invisible hands shoving the power back down where it belonged. If it exploded here, they'd demand her death.

When it quieted to a background whisper and disappeared altogether, Imani's shoulders sagged in relief as the pressure dropped in the stadium.

In one movement, Esa took control of all the air. All of it was sucked out of their lungs.

Imani choked, grabbing her throat.

A force shuddered the ground. Separating her hands, Esa sent it outward. Gravel flying around appeared too slow, floating unnaturally. Loose earth coalesced into five giant moving columns, moving like puppets.

Yes, Esa.

The pixie's spell put pressure on the structure—a massive creaking sound groaned through the building. Imani and a hundred others rose to their feet.

But it held.

Like the magic of all master witches, it appeared effortless. Her brother had trained her well, far better than Ara had trained Imani.

A gleam of pure pleasure shone in Esa's wide eyes while the slight movement of her wand commanded the storm across the arena floor. Her cold, murderous gaze reminded Imani that she wasn't alone in the horrors she'd seen in this world. What had Esa been through that had led her to this moment?

The sight also reminded Imani how people underestimated the pixie's true strength.

Twisters of dust and debris boxed the satyr into the corner. With a push of her hands, Esa lifted the air again. The magic blew out of the arena, where it presumably dissipated.

A whistling from above forced their heads skyward.

Mangled, the shifter's corpse dropped from the sky. It slammed into the ground with an unceremonious splat, but no blood shone on the corpse.

The pixie's wings gave out. She dropped to the ground on her knees, tucking her wings tightly behind her, and then mayhem erupted.

Esa roared as the new brand seared into her skin, and an onslaught of new magic imbibed her being. Trembling, she ripped at her face in the most undignified way. It reminded Imani of the day on the river when her brands had formed, except worse.

Yet, when Esa quieted, the mob merely murmured in hushed whispers. Imani understood why. Esa looked incredible—insane, yet beautiful.

After a moment, Esa stilled and stared at her hands in her lap with her wand discarded at her side. Despite the chaos, Esa didn't care one bit. The pixie hated the Crown and the Order, and the master brands and everything they stood for. But she put on a masterful show.

Such brilliant yet terrifying magic. A true master witch, whom the Fabric honored, walked out of the building.

The spirit of the victim swirled and flickered in confusion over Esa's head, trailing her as she left. Hunger tore through Imani, and her hands shook with black tinting her veins and tendons again.

They called Imani's name next.

CHAPTER 35

Unsettled by the lingering souls of those killed, Imani's magic tried to break free from its cage as she stepped onto the gravel to face her opponent. They snarled in response. Her shadows of death hungered to claim Aiden for themselves. A knot of nervous energy settled in her gut.

The spectators chanted, jumping up and down, their fists in the air, and Imani scanned the mass of hungry people. They screamed for *her*, and she fed off the overwhelming energy of the crowd, enjoying their bloodlust.

With a deep breath, she revealed herself. Lifting her chin, she ripped all the glamour away. In a moment of clarity, her entire body burst into glittering life. Elf magic pulsed from her like never before. A deafening cacophony overwhelmed her senses as the crowd responded, shrieking. Their shouts were barbaric and bloodthirsty. Her soul draw pulsed, sucking them all toward her.

Putting on a show like Esa, she sauntered forward. Locking her face into a neutral expression, she let the draw distract the spectators while dimming the *other* dark magic in her signature. They weren't ready for her illegal magic—her shadows—and hand-to-hand fights, like tonight, would be the most challenging test of her control. She needed all her available advantages.

With her marred face, large bright blue eyes, and luminescent skin, Imani imagined she was a sight. Maybe beautiful. Definitely horrible. But either way, it blinded everyone, pulling anyone not mated into her thrall.

She could feel it *all* now. Their eyes were fixed on her like an obsession. The thought was liberating and intoxicating.

Although her illicit magic still pulsed against the restraints she'd placed on it, she wasn't afraid of the crowd. No one could charge past the barriers, despite the catcalls, whistles, and shouts directed at her. Kiran had fortified them himself—she sensed his magic signature all around them.

Imani had thought about her strategy for a few days now, although anything she tried would fail. She'd seen Aiden's death and wasn't the one to kill him. But she had to try.

A familiar sensation slowly took over, one that had taunted Imani for years.

Unlike other Norn elves, she had a fixation—death, death, death—and the obsession with feeding on an entire soul had nearly driven her to madness when she was a little elf. She'd accidentally ripped her grandfather's soul from his living body the day she'd killed him as a child before devouring it. She hadn't needed to take the whole thing, only a piece, but she had lost control. It had shocked and horrified her parents because, although Norn could presumably do it, it was unthinkable behavior—and no one lost control. Yet Imani couldn't stop herself, even after the sadness she'd experienced from her grandfather's death.

But, lately, since the emergence of her shadows, the urges had been riding her harder than ever. Why the temptation had always been so much harder for her to lock down than any other Norn remained a mystery. She used to hate herself for it, and maybe part of her still did.

Today, she'd give in to the desire. Her grandfather's death had been an accident, but this would be intentional. After all, to most people, it would seem as if she were simply breathing near him, and a soul draw wasn't illegal. There would be no blood involved, either.

Imani palmed sand over her sweaty hands, digging her heels into the dirt.

Prince Tanyl and his mother watched on from the troupe box. The queen was perfect and delicate with her light hair and the long, thin branches from the Crown of Life growing out of her forehead, but she seemed only slightly interested in the duels. Her son looked like the pinnacle of the leimoniad breed—a powerful, handsome male nymph, wearing a striking fur cloak, his sandy hair adorned with a circlet. Tanyl's hands were steepled, and his narrowed, sky-gray eyes stayed locked on her from above.

At the opposite end, Kiran's face was without his characteristic amusement. Arms crossed tight over his chest, he leaned back with an eager, discerning look on his sharp features. His chest seemed broader than usual, and he wore no cloak. Were Niflheim truly as cold as they said?

Saevel sat unmoving, forward, with his arms on his knees, watching Aiden. Unlike his Essenheim counterpart, the Niflheim heir apparent wore no circlet today, but his status was undeniable.

Aiden wore the same fighting leathers and sandals as her, but they couldn't be more opposite otherwise. For the two of them to fight to the death was practically comical.

He was gigantic compared to Imani, with thick corded legs and arms as solid as a tree trunk.

Elegant yet tight, functional braids held Imani's silver hair in a complicated knot. The arches of her elven ears were evident to all, as was the crack of scarring down her porcelain skin. Nevertheless, she was determined to die looking like herself.

The only thing they had in common now were the matching wild expressions on their faces.

Saevel lifted his hand, and silence fell instantly. "The female High-Norn elf will take on the male high leonine shifter," he said.

As customary, Aiden bowed to Imani first.

She returned the gesture. But she lifted her wand on a whim and pointed it at Aiden in the ultimate signal of disrespect.

Twisting his hand, Saevel signaled the start. Everyone fixed their gazes on the elf and the shifter.

Choruses, cheers, and screams twisted people's faces, and piercing, shrieking whistles spewed from their lips. The queen and the princes bore down on the two of them. The weight of their gazes was immense enough to make her skin prickle.

Aiden's scowl deepened, and she went invisible.

Confusion flashed on his face. It sent delicious pleasure through Imani, but he recovered quickly and charged with a loud, angry incantation.

Barely a second to respond, she bolted to the left, moving right before he flung his first attack at her. A force of water flew by, mere inches away from her face.

They were simply warming up.

He would shift soon. Otherwise, she could use her soul draw on him.

It didn't matter. She was reasonably sure she could still drag his soul out of him in shifted form, but a small part couldn't be sure.

Under pressure and unsure, Imani's instincts grew sharper. Still invisible, she went on the defensive for a while. She didn't have a defensive brand, but she held her own. There were now dozens of enchantments and illusion spells she could use. Imani needed time to analyze his fighting style. She'd find his weaknesses, anticipate his moves, and adjust. Although her soul draw raged, he never once looked her in the eyes. Imani silently begged him to—if he did, she could take control.

Damn the heartmate binding he and Nida had. It would make it harder to get his attention.

Mud sprayed them both as the leonine threw magic at her relentlessly. Each time he did, the crowd grew louder and more savage. Soon, wet dirt caked their clothes, and each intake of breath sent pain through her chest. Her shadows clamored to be released. But she quelled them as Aiden ambled off to the side to catch his breath.

He stood unfocused while he tried to resist her thrall. It called to him, making him sloppy. His eyes fluttered open and shut as he fought for concentration. His breathing became slightly labored. His arm muscles trembled from the effort of holding his wand upright. It gave her confidence.

The onlookers were a blur of color as she parried fast.

"You can't continue like this," she shouted to Aiden. She needed him still enough for her to focus on looking into his eyes.

She shifted her gaze to the stands where Kiran observed with amusement twisting his features. It spurred her on, and she bared her teeth at her opponent.

But Aiden didn't stop. Like in the melee, he could smell her. Chasing her back, he moved closer, crowding her with his size.

A deep, guttural roar ripped from his chest, and then a massive lion stood before her. She'd never seen him shift before. Not even at the melee. The animal's sheer size and sudden ferocity were enough to send her stepping back.

Disappointment sank in her stomach.

Shifting was smart. Even though he couldn't cast magic, Aiden could resist her draw in this form, and it would probably be more challenging for her to latch on to his signature.

He herded her, massive paws lashing out and blocking any attempt to evade, even while she was invisible.

Her fear spiked to an unbearable level as he pushed her deeper into the darkened corner of the arena. Frantic, her thoughts raced as she struggled to find a way to move close enough to this beast without getting killed.

Aiden must have sensed how close he was to drawing blood and backed off. It was a tricky rule the Niflheim brothers had devised. The witches' magic would have to be precise, perfectly controlled, and powerful enough to kill someone without bleeding.

Pacing around her, he opened his huge maw and roared in her face—a booming sound laced with animalistic ferocity. It rattled her bones, yet a determined will to survive rose to the surface inside her. It cut through the other noise and clutter. She'd been void of magic all these years, but now she had an arsenal.

In a blink, all the barriers she'd mentally constructed broke. The entirety of her power ripped through her core as the confines holding the darkness shattered, blackening her veins. Luckily, hidden underneath the mud, no one noticed.

Covered in grime, she stood in her true, *raw*, shadowed form, uncaring to hold even the invisibility illusion over her body anymore.

No, no, no. Now wasn't the time to lose control.

The world blurred around her again, and she threw her head back, unable to catch a breath. Chest heaving, trying to keep the shadows from releasing their dark force, she pointed her wand upward and called the energy back.

A flash of lightning crackled above, and people started shouting and pointing at the darkness churning above. They all grabbed the railing and craned their necks to see better.

Moving like a shadow, she didn't waste time. She pushed off the wall, shouted an incantation, and flew at the lion. Her magic was free, but the threat would disappear if she could kill him quickly.

Across the arena, Aiden rumbled a warning growl.

Imani's spell built again when he moved toward her. Wisps of shadows burst forth and blew through the fieldhouse like gusts of wind. Those watching closely might be able to tell she was casting magic, but Imani wasn't sure. The shadows started cornering the lion, ready to coil themselves around him and cut off his air.

She stole a glance at the troupe boxes.

Tanyl's face was unreadable. The queen glared. Saevel laughed. Kiran's brows snapped together as he looked down at her.

Trembling, Imani tried to call the shadows back again. Slinking backward, they listened, but it was slow, and tendrils of smoke covered the ground around Aiden.

Kiran stood now, gripping the railing. His once-bored features were now twisted in anger, and for one horrifying second, his entity revealed itself, snarling in dire warning. Warning for *her* to stop. Of that, she was sure.

Imani threw what little strength she had left into dragging her shadow magic back into her signature. But in her weakened state, it had little effect. Barely contained within the shell of her physical body, every image and scene of fright and foreboding, shame, shock, misery, bloodshed, and agony—it all came to a head—and the storm above was too much for her to handle.

Her control wavered again. Inky magic surrounded her. Her hands were now entirely black, and ghastly fingertips left her body and whirled around the corpses off to the side. She stared at Kiran's face, the horror all-consuming, as power poured off her, forming thick columns of shadows that rose into the sky. The still-invisible red ink of the brand on her arm burned as she flipped her wand and raised her hands. The magic above them was vast and thick, swirling into menacing clouds.

Something awful moved inside the cloud—an evil entity. Imani remembered the first time the magic inside Kiran had reared its head. It reminded her of that.

Releasing her darkness—the mist-like substance of death—was something the world wasn't ready to see and could never unsee. It would spray blood on her if it eviscerated Aiden. She could use the shadow magic but not the darkness.

The leonine shifter paced anxiously, sensing the unease in the air. Groaning, roiling clouds of Imani's shadows coalesced in a crescendo directly above them. Thankfully, it appeared as if a storm brewed, and people covered their heads with coats and hats, expecting rain.

Aiden roared and batted his massive paw at her, risking blood to demand she step back. Moving forward with her wand aimed at his chest and her little fangs bared, she was ready for the whole stadium to watch her devour his soul. She would end this now. Once she killed Aiden, the threat would be gone, and the darkness would return to her.

With his eyes on her in fear, she tugged at his signature.

A boom sounded, and thunder rumbled dangerously above them. It made both Aiden and Imani tip their heads up. The lightning came in wild bursts, one after another. A feeling of falling surrounded them as the ground fell away.

The reality of their surroundings shifted, not unlike when her parents had died. Among the splices of the world, moving pictures of what appeared to be another realm flashed in front of her. It had to be. Imani had never seen anything like it. These bits and pieces were terrifying. It was as if a thousand eyes stared at her.

Souls. Alive. Some dead. Some didn't belong here. Some didn't belong *there*, either, didn't belong anywhere. The beings all spotted her and immediately shouted, demanding her attention and pulling her.

So many dead. As if they fed from *her* and threatened to collapse her body.

It lasted only a second.

A fierce pull grabbed her in the chest—a painful snap. Whipping her gaze to the side, Kiran stood up from his seat, his body rigid, holding his wand. Rage and abhorrence heaved up his shoulders, all directed at her. His lips curled, hands rolling into fists, as if her attempt to save her own life had sent him over the edge of sanity.

His mismatched eyes penetrated the fog of chaos and mud, and Imani jolted as their gazes locked. Both irises glowed like fires raging in the distance, grabbing onto her, yanking her back to reality, and filling her lungs with air. Indeed, something about his reaction hit her head-on. A small part of her needed whatever controlling magic he used on her signature.

Self-preservation kicked in. The situation was far too dangerous, not only for Aiden.

Her magic brewed a Fabric event. She had to find a way to pull back her darkness, or they would all die. She couldn't let any more damage come to the magic of this world because of her.

Fighting for control, she summoned any bit of strength she possessed to pull her magic back inside. Arms spread, screaming, it slammed into her all at once, knocking the wind out of her lungs.

She fell to the ground, coughing, laying on her back.

Shouts and murmurs broke out into the crowd, confusion reigning.

The clouds cleared, and the Fabric danced above them once again, stars twinkling as if nothing had happened.

Aiden drove toward her. He was half-shifted, something she'd never seen before, and the disturbing sight could only mean one thing in her mind—he was now over the edge, ready to destroy her by any means possible.

Dragging herself upright and barely breathing, she jumped up and veered left, smashing him with her fist. It was like hitting concrete.

Groaning, she fell backward, slipping in the mud. Imani cursed her magic when her head hit hard against the ground. Disoriented, it took her longer than she wanted to stand.

Aiden didn't waste time. Needing access to his magic again, he shifted back into his skin and roared as if he'd been playing a game before but now was ready to kill.

He whipped his wand from his pocket, immediately pummeling her with magic. The rain he created hit her like needles, and she tripped in the wet dirt again.

The water started coalescing around her. Building it into something larger, something far more dangerous, he aimed to drown her.

She tried to crawl away, but he grabbed her ankle.

She struggled against him like an animal caught in a trap. She went wild, kicking, screaming, thrashing, pushing out as much magic as she could whisper without losing control.

An undeniable sense of loss crashed over her.

Flickers of pure dark still escaped her weakened body, and the torches they'd lit in the stadium dimmed and brightened repeatedly. She took the deepest breath she could and ripped it all back inside. The darkness fought harder against her, but she would not let it out for anything.

Her downfall wouldn't be long now. Without her shadows, darkness, or a miracle, Aiden would kill her soon. She had maybe a few more minutes to act, or she would die.

Her own death swirled around her. Aiden sensed it the second the threat disappeared. He tilted his head to the side in recognition of her weakness and twisted her arm to pull her up. Imani didn't even see him coming when some combination of his magic slammed her against the wall.

An inhuman screech came from her, one she'd never made before. While not deep enough to kill her, blood dribbled down her chest from a long gash across her collarbone.

He had barely missed her artery.

Eyes wide with fear at what he'd done, Aiden didn't blink or move.

The whole crowd grew utterly silent while the red mixed with the mud on her pale skin.

CHAPTER 36

Not one person had broken the rule ... until now.

A mix of rage and surprise shone on Aiden's face at the sight of her blood. Tense anticipation swirled in the air.

"You did this on purpose, elf witch," he said, ready to rip her apart. "You and your dark magic."

A growl cut through the silence before he went in for the kill. In an instant, the Niflheim heir loomed over her. His speed seemed impossible for such a large man. Saevel let out a snarl, deeply more menacing and more predatory than anything else from the night.

The hairs on her neck rose.

Not daring to move from the ground, she watched with disbelief as the scene from her vision unfolded.

"It was an accident," Aiden sputtered. "Things got out of hand, but—"

"It was not an accident." Saevel curled his lip and held the other male by his throat with one hand. "Thought you could get away with it, huh?"

Just as her vision had foretold, the prince dipped his head, and whatever the shifter was about to say ended in a gasp. Before Imani could register the punishment, the shifter fell. Dead. His body hit the ground with a heavy *thud*, and his heart followed, smacking into the mud.

A shrill scream—Nida, most likely—erupted from the chambers below while chanting and shouts broke out in the audience.

Unable to look away, Imani surveyed the body. Bones, tendons, and flesh hung out of his throat in a gnarled mess, with dark red liquid spreading in a halo around him.

Saevel stepped back with a savage expression as Aiden's body twitched, the last bits of life leaving him. He nudged the corpse with his foot, turning it over with a wet *plop*. Blood pooled on the ground, dark in the twilight.

Above her, the crowd surged to their feet, booing. Most had come to see a duel to the death. This had simply been an execution. Even worse—she hadn't received her master brands.

Imani resignedly held up her hands, studying them with profound disappointment. There could be many theories why, but it was probably because she hadn't accessed her whole arsenal of magic or demonstrated control of it by killing Aiden. Proving control over powerful magic was vital, but holding back was not.

Tilting her head up, she saw Aiden's spirit hovered. The shadows Imani commanded earlier still clung to it. Unlike Master Selhey, whose spirit had disappeared of its own accord, this one called out in silent anguish, unsure where to go or what to do at the sudden ripping from its corporeal state.

"Leave," Imani told the spirit, pointing her wand at the sky.

Much to her surprise, he did.

Good. If he hadn't, she would have eaten him right then and there.

From the corner of her eye, she saw Kiran jump down from the box, sauntering over.

A slow clap made her snap her gaze to him, and he grinned maniacally. "Incredible! I'm in absolute awe over your performance." The jacket he now wore whipped in the wind as he moved to stand next to his brother.

Saevel was a murderous beast, but Kiran was utterly insane.

Imani's heart pounded wildly in response to Kiran's intense eyes on her.

"Hmm," he said, "maybe you should have practiced magic more instead of trying so hard to be beautiful tonight."

This prick.

As if hearing her thoughts, something malignant flashed over his face, and he winked. "Now, my brother and I will discuss whether to let you move on or fail."

Her mouth dropped open. "You can't be serious."

His handsome, joyous face was next to hers. Those mismatched eyes glinted even in the dark, daring her to fight him. "I am. You're done for the day, little elf. But you delivered the entertainment of the evening, no doubt."

Imani raised herself on her elbows and wiped at the blood, mostly smearing it across her chest. Her fingernails were caked with mud as she dragged herself into a standing position. Defeat sagged her shoulders. Had she won, the pleasure would have been indescribable.

But she hadn't. Once again, her life depended on other people's decisions.

"I should win by default," she hissed so only the princes could hear.

The Serpent Prince tsked, now close enough she could breathe him in. Lightheadedness came over her as Kiran leaned in, smelling her hair. "I like the scent of blood on you." His voice dripped with condescension.

His gaze landed on her neck as another rust-colored droplet ran down and onto her chest. Kiran stroked it with his fingertip then licked it. The delicate skin at the corners of his eyes crinkled when he shot her a mesmerizing smile. "My brother told you all the rules before we began. Were those pretty little ears listening? While the person who drew blood is executed, the winner is determined by us afterward. Since you couldn't adhere to the other rule and kill—"

"I might have killed him if he hadn't intervened," she argued, motioning to Saevel. It wasn't true. She had been about to die, but she was desperate. Kiran had made the rules, and he had made them purposely vague. This was her life on the line!

"Liar," Kiran breathed. He stole a glance over his shoulder at his brother.

Saevel paced behind him, blood still on his mouth and hands.

"I'm not lying," she said through gritted teeth.

"Do Norn elves have inferior hearing abilities? I said *leave*."

There could be no mistaking the threat in his tone. If Imani kept pushing, it might get her killed. She couldn't afford any foolish decisions, so she shot him a look she hoped said, *fuck you*, and with a quiet, tiny, frustrated growl, she stormed off.

Once in the shadows, she peeked back, unable to shake the suspicion the cut hadn't been an accident.

Workers rolled corpses and stacked them together in preparation for the burning. It was dirty, morbid work.

She wasn't sure how long she stood there. The bodies weren't catching her attention; it was the souls floating restlessly above them. While most were shades of white, gray, or black, one appeared to be flickering and forming into something red above its host.

Below the soul, the witch's hair shined dark red, while her eyes were white. It was the fourth female in the duels.

Someone dragged the woman up off the ground, her head lolling against the hard dirt, and tossed her into the pile. She landed on a jumble of arms and legs and stayed. Her matted red hair flowed from her head, tangling with another body. Imani imagined her asleep, as peaceful as a newborn babe relaxed in its mother's arms.

Another body smacked against the dead woman with a *thud*, pushing tight into the larger mountain of corpses. Now, the only visible part of her, the crimson hair, was a piece of life shining among the grotesque flesh.

The red apparition in the shape of the beautiful witch came into focus. With shaking hands, the woman cupped her cheeks, lifted her shimmering head, and let out a silent scream. Her eyes locked on Imani's in a final, mournful howl no one else could hear.

With a whoosh, the mass of shadows swirled up around Imani, trapping her in an invisible storm. They swept around her neck and down her arms, soft like a breeze, and dozens of voices whispered, clamoring together into a cloak of shimmering smoke.

And Imani was tired of holding back. Tired of denying herself. So, she did the only thing she could and breathed deeply.

Each soul dove inside her broken, bleeding body, feeding her until they existed no more.

∼

Weariness enveloped her as she carefully limped into the bedroom and shut the door to her suite. On edge, invigorated from feeding, emotions raging, she wanted to throw things, destroy her furniture, and set something on fire. Instead, she cried until it hurt … until she was only a husk of her body.

Not only had she not received her master brand, but she would need to go to Tanyl and ask him to bargain for her. He had more power in this instance, and she hoped he would be motivated enough to save her life. She trusted him enough to at least try.

She didn't particularly want a master brand, but she'd worked so hard and sacrificed so much, and it had been her ticket to Niflheim if she had won.

She would never know, and it didn't matter. What mattered most was survival, and her family's safety.

Wiping her eyes, Imani eventually tore the clothing from her body, desperate to throw everything away. While feeding had helped, it hadn't magically cured her body, and she hissed at the pressure undressing put on her wounds.

After somehow shimmying out of her leathers, she lifted her nightgown over her head, wincing, then carefully slipped on her robe.

A knock made her jump, and she froze.

More knocks turned into bangs. "Meira, it's Tanyl."

The clock showed an hour past midnight. The feast would be ending, and while he might want to check on her, he'd never been to her rooms. A sense of wrongness settled in her bones.

Another shout and hiss came from him. It made her smile, remembering the wards Kiran had cast the other night. Tanyl had tried to enter without her permission.

Not willing to show her face in the harsh light of the hallway, she shadowed herself more then opened the door a crack. "Yes?"

He took it as an invitation and barreled inside. "Who placed these insane wards? You don't have a defensive brand. And what happened out there?" He ran to her windows, pulling all the drapes shut and shrouding the room in even more darkness. When the prince turned around, his eyes widened at her ghastly appearance.

Her reflection in the mirror over the hearth stared back at her. Crusted red blood stained her chin, mingling with her black scar. Where the blood hadn't splattered, her skin was translucent, with black and blue bruises spread across her arms, thighs, abdomen, and chest. A deep throb ached across her chest where the cut made movement difficult. Imani suspected she had a few broken ribs, too.

Live or die, she fought well with such a battered body, and she didn't want his sympathy or disgust. She was strong and proud of her determination.

"The definition of a win appears to be up for discussion," she muttered, rubbing the tension in her neck. "Have you heard anything about their decision?"

"No. The princes plan to announce the outcome tomorrow morning."

"At least I'll have a few hours to—"

He shook his head and grabbed her shoulders, shaking her. "Listen, Meira. Do not leave this room tonight. Keep whatever wards you have in place, and do not open the door for anyone except me."

Imani narrowed her eyes. "What aren't you saying? I should be safe until morning at least."

"You won't. Something else has happened." He raked his hands through his hair, tugging at it gently. "I have no idea what she has on you, but my mother is hearing evidence tomorrow, supposedly proving you killed a merchant named Malis and caused the Riverlands' Fabric event with the dark magic from tonight. She claims you released atrophic magic, causing the storm over the stadium, and if she deems the evidence about the murder credible, she'll use you to send a message to the entire kingdom and the Illithiana family. The Crown won't wait before taking you into custody, and you'll be swiftly and publicly executed––deal with the Niflheim Throne be damned."

Her thoughts raced. What evidence? Her magic might have left remnants—the harsh, peppery smell—but it would have been only enough to identify it as atrophic magic, not even sufficient to differentiate if it was flesh magic. She had left her cloak there, but it hardly proved anything. Everyone had cloaks. Losing one didn't mean she had committed those crimes. She had checked the manor and had been alone. Maybe someone had seen from the orchard? If so, they'd waited a long time to come forward. Why now?

And her magic? The whole crowd had seen it, sure, but could they prove she had cast it, and that the event hadn't been an unnatural phenomenon?

Did it even matter? If the queen wanted her dead, she would be dead, and the secret about her shadow magic was out.

"I don't believe it," Tanyl assured her, running his hands up and down her arms in comforting strokes. "That wasn't any kind of magic from a spell. It would be impossible to cast, especially for a new young witch."

Imani almost scoffed and corrected him. It was certainly possible, and she hated how he underestimated her. But she couldn't reveal too much. She had to protect her siblings.

Tanyl continued, "Something is wrong with this situation, and I will do everything possible to stop it tonight. But my mother might not listen to me, and if so, it also means you can't come back to Essenheim while she still lives."

"It could be decades." Tanyl planned to kill his mother, but Imani didn't know how or when.

A burning urge to touch the queen and learn the truth of her death reared inside her.

"I see it in your eyes—the wheels of your sharp mind are spinning something into a plan. I know you're probably already plotting something," Tanyl said, searching her face.

Imani looked up from the floor. "I have no idea what you mean." She hadn't yet had time to plot, but she would get there.

"Please don't do anything rash. Stay here," he repeated, shaking her shoulders. "It's too dangerous to wander around without protection right now. The whole country knows what happened in the Riverlands, and all people are talking about are the high-bred females from the duel tonight, especially the elf and the storm. If my mother thinks the person responsible is slipping out of her grasp, she might take you into custody even before hearing the evidence."

Powerless to control her life, the walls closed on her. Her fate rested in the hands of powerful people, all singularly focused on their own dangerous plans.

"Thank you for speaking with your mother for me." She paused. "Tanyl, if anything happens to me, please look after my siblings," she whispered. This situation called for it, despite how much she hated begging in general.

He pulled her close. "It won't be necessary, but I will," he said, kissing the top of her head. "Now, don't leave this room tonight." He turned away, his tone cutting off any argument.

The sickness in her stomach worsened when the door clicked closed, but she believed Tanyl. He cared about her and would do what he could. Still, it didn't matter. The Essenheim heir wouldn't be influential enough to protect her against the queen. After all, she was entirely guilty, and if they had proof of Malis's murder, it was probably damning enough for them to convict her circumstantially. Given the dire situation, not even the heir apparent could protect her against the Niflheim princes. Besides, he was preoccupied tonight. She needed to handle this alone before Dialora arrested her.

Dragging her hands down her face, she composed herself mentally for what needed to be done. One vile option gave her the best chance at protecting herself and her family, and it wouldn't happen waiting around in this room for Tanyl.

CHAPTER 37

With her mind made up, a cold, determined fury replaced the white-hot anger as she prepared to throw herself at the mercy of the Illithiana princes. It didn't matter which one. She'd attempt to bargain with whoever she found first. If they disagreed, she'd unleash her darkness.

No matter how she spun it, this option, however awful, still gave her the best chance at survival. Both would likely kill her if she attacked, either by Saevel's shifting or Kiran's magic, but maybe they would be cowed enough to agree or curious enough to keep her alive for longer.

If she died by their hand, at least she had some semblance of control over her life and death.

The manservant, Jai, showed her to a bedroom. Instead of breezing coolly inside with a mask of indifference, as she'd planned, she was caught immensely off guard by the sight in front of her and stood awkwardly, blinking in surprise.

There was no sign of Saevel, but Kiran lounged naked on the bed.

Despite feeding earlier, searing heat spread from her belly to her chest as she watched on unapologetically. Imani truly understood then why people hated and even feared her kind so much—feeling a soul draw consume your body was a blissful torture.

At least males couldn't use compulsion. No one knew why male elves hadn't evolved to possess the particular skill, but Imani was eternally grateful.

A green-haired trow pixie, naked with her wings spread wide, crawled down his body, moving her mouth around his cock.

Imani's breath picked up, and she clenched her hand around her wand. Insane thoughts swirled around her mind, wishing it was her on the bed instead.

In the tangle of arms and legs, *another* pixie crawled up his body, leisurely kissing up his throat with blue hair Imani would recognize anywhere. What was Esa doing here ... *again*?

Did Kiran and Esa have some agreement around feeding like she and Tanyl? It could mean emotions were involved, but it could also only mean business.

Still, she was at her wit's end. With his draw controlling her, shocking rage quickly replaced her surprise. A sudden, base urge to tear out every blue strand of hair from Esa's head rose in Imani. Her lip curled in feral disgust as her magic urged her on. *Kill. Kill. Kill.*

The fire dimmed, and the scones shrank to nothing. The light in the room flickered in and out for a few seconds. Unbound and wild, shadows clouded her vision. Tears burned her throat, and Imani hated them—hated this glaring weakness.

This. This was exactly what her grandmother had meant when she'd said Imani was a monster. This was what Meira had meant about Imani potentially losing control again. It had simmered for months now, rearing its head since her magic had returned, but exhaustion and Kiran's draw had to be sending her into a tailspin.

Fighting the magic to stay inside, she clamped down on it with considerable effort and stood frozen, staring daggers at the bed, unable to leave. Unable to stop torturing herself.

The other female kissed Kiran's mouth. Imani stifled a low snarl threatening in her chest.

Snapping his gaze to her at the sound, Kiran's unnatural eyes glowed in the dim light. He tilted his head to the side while they stared at each other for another moment. His mouth tipped up into a tiny, infuriating smile.

After everything she'd been through tonight, being toyed with ripped away the last of her patience. Imani was finished with this nonsense. She turned on her heel to take her chances with Saevel. Any binding Kiran had cast on him had lifted when the assessments had ended, so she could touch him now. Have sex with him, even.

"Everyone out."

The soft command from him stopped Imani halfway to the door.

It wasn't meant for her.

With a slow turn, she slid her eyes shut as she took a few composing breaths.

He made her so crazy and enjoyed it. He was an infuriating person. Imani despised him in one breath and, in the next, couldn't turn away from his cold, beautiful face. Yet she still couldn't find it in herself to hate him entirely.

There was more to Kiran, and she hoped to use information about him to make a deal.

Crossing her arms, Imani stood tall and narrowed her eyes to slits as the pixies gathered their belongings.

Esa eyed her, too, and when she slid past Imani, murmured, "Be careful."

Imani didn't reply.

The door clicked closed, and then the two elves were alone.

Imani managed to mask her emotions, giving him only a mere delicate arch of a brow. She took in the shadow of facial hair from the past few days and sharp but subtle points of his ears. Kiran's cheekbones were brutally jagged, like he hadn't eaten or slept properly in weeks. Being a conniving bastard was hard work.

Standing before him in her robe and soft white nightgown, she hadn't bothered with her appearance beyond bathing. Bruises covered her body, and the cut down her chest was still raw. Both garments covered her down to the floor, but her breasts were on display, and the thin material clung to the outline of her body. The only glamours she wore were the flesh magic illusions to cover her brands and a light illusion over her scarring and disfigured fingers. The rest was bare. Pale elven skin, bright eyes, signature, soul draw—all of it showing.

Let him look. Even battered, she needed every advantage tonight.

Kiran's eyes roamed hungrily over her as he eased his pants back on, somehow making the movement graceful. The illusion magic he cast over himself was gone, too. Without it, Kiran was more like an elf than ever before. Shirtless and watching her, his undeniable beauty sent her adrenaline surging.

With no glamour, his elven draw—the sensation torturing her since the first moment she had laid eyes on him—tugged on her again. She rubbed the tension on her forehead, trying to stay calm despite the discomfort. Without the other women near him, it was easier to ignore.

Spinning in a tight circle, a wave of magic rippled from the center of the ceiling outward to the floor. "I hope these are stronger than the shields you cast outside," she sneered, jerking her chin toward the door.

His grin was lazy. "I was so disappointed to learn you could break into all the princes' rooms. I enjoyed thinking I was special."

She let out a loud sigh but didn't reply.

"I suppose you're here to convince me not to end your existence?" he asked, throwing her words back at her with cruel mirth.

"He broke the rules, so I should win by default, in my opinion," she said bluntly.

"*Your opinion? That* couldn't be more irrelevant," he said, trying not to laugh.

"So, you've already made your choice?"

"We're still undecided. But I'll repeat it … what a stunning performance. Although the display of atrophic magic was risky, and dangerous, it was smart to remove your glamour. The beautiful high-bred female is all anyone is talking about tonight."

"I guess it means I'm more difficult to murder now."

The glee in his expression only increased. "My brother and I couldn't care less about how popular you are here."

"Fine. I want to strike a deal. You hold my life in your hands, and even if you didn't, I can't stay in Essenheim." Imani cleared her throat. "I was a fool to let so much of my dark magic out—people saw it."

"So? People are idiots. Most master witches wouldn't even recognize such magic. Besides, it didn't look like you wielded anything. You have absolutely no control over it, so anyone who thinks you cast dark magic is foolish."

"Unfortunately, the queen isn't an idiot. And even if she didn't recognize it, she knows an opportunity when she sees one. I might be arrested as early as tomorrow."

A slow smile blossomed on his face. "Now, that's interesting."

"I need you to let me win. What do you want in exchange?"

"I'm not sure there's much left for you to whore out."

The words stung, but they were true.

Imani considered blackmailing him by threatening to reveal his magic. But Kiran had warned her against doing it a second time, and she anticipated he'd kill her instantly if she tried again. Instead of a threat, an incentive was probably the best course of action.

"Name your terms," she murmured. The words were poison on her tongue.

"Imani, my darling, you are either the bravest female in this realm or the stupidest." Leaning against a chair, he leisurely ran his hands over the fabric. "As it stands, I'm not sure if you have anything I particularly want at the moment, whereas Saevel—"

"Yes, Saevel wants sex from me," she cut him off. "I won't lie; I would offer it to him in exchange for my life. But I found you first, so here we are. It's your lucky day."

"Because you're such a slut?"

"Because there's *always* something to be traded," she said brusquely. "Now, what can I offer to save myself?"

"For what you're asking, I want something precious in return. Far more valuable than your used cunt."

She let the insult roll off her. "Then stop stalling and tell me what it is."

A second later, he was mere inches from her. She almost flinched at his closeness.

"I love this," he murmured, distracted as he played with her braid. His warm fingers trailed across her cheek and lifted her head, catching her chin in his grip when she turned away. "Desperation somehow makes you lovelier." He leaned in, his mouth barely an inch away from hers, and winked like this was all some joke to him.

"You have five seconds to decide or—"

"Or *what*?" He laughed and released her chin with a shove.

Anger, frustration, and fear pulsed from her. The room darkened ever so slightly as she stopped herself from stumbling.

A terrible silence followed.

Tilting his head, Kiran studied her as he rested his hands on his hips. Imani steeled her gaze at him, demanding his answer, not wanting him to have any reprieve from her.

His responding grin was both magnificent and eye-reaching. It told Imani all she needed to know. He was about to ask her to do something terrible, and she could not say no.

"I'll give you what you ask," he said loudly, clapping his hands together. "I should warn you this will be a horrible bargain for you."

Relief rushed through her.

"Tell me," he crooned, dropping his voice. "Why does a beautiful Norn elf want to go to my despicable kingdom?"

Imani scoffed, hoping to hide the truth. "You said it yourself—I'm trying to save my damn life—"

The prince put up a hand to silence her. "Wrong. Or, at least, not entirely correct. You *wanted* to be chosen the first day. In truth, I didn't want to waste a pick on you, especially since, at the time, I had no idea Esa had put you in place with Tanyl. But my brother is impulsive, and you used your nasty soul draw on him. Ultimately, I didn't care much at the time because choosing you enraged Tanyl." His eyes narrowed in calculation. "But now? I want to know why."

"This is ridiculous."

"Is it? Before we showed up, you had a comfortable life here and could have kept it. Indeed, Tanyl seems genuinely in love with you …" He trailed off, his gaze on the ground as some private torment consumed him. "And that's a powerful position to be in. Something I know you crave."

Those insane eyes fixed on her again, and there was no hint of him mocking or bantering this time.

"But instead, you put yourself through torture and pain, and now you're here, begging me to save your life instead of Tanyl. So, tell me why," he said, his entire presence commanding her attention as only a prince could.

The man was too brilliant for his own good.

"There are answers I need there," she said eventually.

"What answers, my darling?" he pressed. His voice was soft but no less demanding.

Imani shut her eyes, trying to think of a lie as warm hands landed on her face. Kiran traced slow circles on her cheeks, his eyes imploring her with a look she hadn't seen before.

She had an irrational desire to tell him the truth for a moment. Despite what she knew about his character, despite his actions and how he treated everyone, including her—

Imani stopped, silently admonishing herself for the pathetic line of thinking. She could never trust anyone regarding the Drasil, *especially* Kiran.

She ripped up her sleeve. Although she'd removed the flesh magic illusion and hadn't had time to cast another, a weaker one dissipated over Malis's sigil at her command. "He and I will never be anything, but this sigil means there are things I need to learn about myself in Niflheim."

"I told you the sigil isn't from my kingdom."

"I'm not going to get any answers waiting around here," she shot back.

Even as the words came out, they surprised her. Lies mixed with a bit of truth.

"No, probably not," he agreed.

"What do you want from me?" she asked.

"There's a place in a remote territory of my kingdom few can access. If I save you"—Kiran trailed off, a cruel, assessing expression back on his face—"then, when I ask, you must come with me to this place without hesitation."

"And when we're done, it disappears like other bindings?"

He didn't hesitate. "Yes."

"Why me?" Imani gaped at him, unable to fully comprehend the insane idea he proposed.

"To gain access, I simply need someone bound to me to tag along."

"You want a binding between us then? What is this place?"

"No more questions, little elf," he snapped. "I don't need to share these details to keep my promise."

True. Kiran had revealed probably as much truth about his intentions as she had, and besides, she had much more to lose and far fewer options. She chewed her lip while silently debating her response.

Kiran crossed his arms, leaning against the door. "You said anything, Imani," he sneered. "Agree so we can cast the binding and sleep before dawn. We'll make it a flesh magic one, of course."

Casting *another* flesh binding made her heart stutter. So many powerful bindings—the one working for Niflheim, one with Tanyl, and now a third with Kiran—would put her in an even more dangerous position and strip her of more freedom. And to strike one with Kiran? The man was a liar, a brilliant sorcerer, a madman, and a murderer.

But freedom didn't matter if she was dead. So, what choice did she have? For her life and everything else, she would do it. She'd beg, whore herself out, murder some more, perform evil magic—she'd do all of it. Imani had work to do and didn't want to die today or tomorrow.

"Y-yes," she stammered. "I agree."

His fangs appeared as he bared them at her. The grin was friendly one moment and predatory the next.

"I'll need to talk to my brother if we agree to let you win," he said lightly.

The knot inside her stomach tightened. All her instincts told her to run from this bargain, this man, and this place. Yet, she couldn't.

Weeks ago, she'd anticipated Kiran would back her into a corner. Imani now stood in said corner. But she had put herself here.

As he left the room, a small, tiny insignificant voice of doubt chimed quietly in her mind, and she seriously considered if she'd be better off dead.

CHAPTER 38

He burst back into the room nearly an hour later.

"Immmannnni," he called in a sing-song voice.

The shadows coiled and writhed at the sound of her name, and she turned to find him standing in the doorway. He seemed broader somehow with his chilling demeanor radiating a wild determination.

It was Kiran, but something about him was different. When she met his eyes, a shiver ran down her spine. Gone was the light mocking amusement she'd come to expect. Something far more dangerous had taken its place. The corner of his lips curled, and she shrank back from his face. His features gave nothing away, but both his eyes were nearly black. There was so much darkness swimming in them, and the unpredictability and penchant for cold violence truly scared her the most. This could go *extremely* wrong for her.

A razor-sharp smile formed on his face. "It's done. My brother agreed."

"Does he know about this little binding between us?"

"Yes," he said instantly. A threat simmered beneath the words.

Dragging his hand over his mouth, he slid his gaze over her, swallowing hard as if he wished to say something else. But he held back from it and, a second later, made his way across the room.

"Before we do this binding," he continued in the same flat tone, "I need to be absolutely sure you understand the terms. Not only will you be required to accompany me, but you'll also serve our kingdom like all my witches until we terminate your service or your life ends. You won't get any special treatment, nor will you speak about our agreement."

"In other words, you'll be my master, and I'll be your slave?"

An uncomfortable silence greeted her question, and she immediately wished to take her words back because Kiran's expression couldn't have been more vacant.

"Slaves aren't paid," he deadpanned after a minute.

"So, why do I need a binding? Order me to go there with you." Her fear built in a slow, tense crescendo. Her unglamoured skin must be a sight.

He rolled his eyes. "I already told you we must be magically bound to enter." Without sparing her a glance, he held his wand in his teeth and rolled up his sleeves.

"What will you make me do once we're there?" she asked as he bit into the flesh on his arm.

"Nothing. Your role is to help me enter—that's it." His blood gushed into a bowl. "Assuming it all goes to plan, the trip will take a few hours for you."

A sense of trepidation tingled her senses. *I can read you better than ever*, she thought. She knew he wasn't being honest, if not entirely.

She sighed, realizing the Niflheim Kingdom's First Witch needed a sacrifice. Someone willing to agree to a powerful binding with him to go to their death. No wonder he hadn't found anyone before her. He needed an expendable tool, and not many would agree to bind themselves to Kiran for something like this.

"So, what now? You're—"

"No more questions." His tone left no room for argument. He turned away, humming to himself as he walked across the room, over to the desk in the corner, ignoring her like she was nothing more than a piece of furniture.

Ambling over, sickness swirled in her gut, but she tried to appear uninterested. Murmuring several words in his elvish dialect, he conjured bowls and herbs out of thin air, and various other magical items. Floating flames appeared at his command, bursting with warmth. Her frantic brain only discerned about half of the herbs and tinctures.

A pinch of black powder and dried sage forced the mixture to swirl. It thickened after adding a dash of the tincture and several grains of chalk. Glancing up to see the white smoke rising from the table, wrinkles appeared on his forehead in concentration. He put each item inside a circle made from salt and six floating flames, ready to spell them. Kiran then lifted his hands, infusing his alchemy magic into the substances before the cup lifted itself and poured its contents into a large bowl. In one smooth motion, he cut his other wrist with his fangs and let more blood cover the top layer. Red liquid poured from Kiran's arm.

Indeed, with all this blood, the flesh magic he planned could only be one type.

"This is a blood burning," she whispered, picking up a dried leaf. It had a musky scent.

"Very good," he said, still humming in elvish while preparing the materials.

Highly illegal, she'd only seen it performed once before. Both people in the binding had mixed their blood with the magic then consumed the substance. The person's essence would latch inside the other, supposedly tied to the signature and the body.

It was also a powerful aphrodisiac.

Nasty, invasive spells like this killed people. There would be unforeseen consequences with this type of deep sacrificial magic.

"These are almost impossible to perform." She averted her eyes, pretending to study the ingredients.

As his capable hands worked, she had no doubt he'd done this before. Maybe several times. Even while performing several complicated spells at once, he worked with practiced efficiency. She remembered all the binding brands covering his body. How many people controlled him?

Or... how many did he control?

Kiran muttered another incantation, but it was barely even a whisper, and she couldn't understand the words. He seemed outwardly relaxed, despite the taxing magic he was doing. The rough way he grabbed his collar and unbuttoned his shirt told her how tense he might be, but he didn't let it slow him down.

A knock sounded at the door, but neither moved to answer it. They needed privacy.

For all the time Kiran had spent observing her in the assessments recently, she hadn't seen him perform any significant magic since the first day. They had yet to come close to seeing the full extent of his capabilities. He was a mesmerizing witch to watch up close—an artist, really.

"It's difficult to burn the blood properly," she continued. "Most of the time, it smokes off or thickens too quickly to be viable, or the blood is incompatible. If you try to drink it, you either die, become sick, or lose too much blood from repeating it." And this magic needed a lot of blood. "The bond will be strongest if we're more compatible. Being elves should help, but …" Imani trailed off.

A sudden shadow darkened the door, and Kiran and Imani whipped around to see Jai standing there. His eyes widened at the scene unfolding before him, no doubt recognizing the magic they performed.

Imani remembered Jai's death scene in her mind. He'd been slumped over in a pool of his own blood.

Kiran and Imani exchanged a glance. "I told you to cast better wards," Imani muttered.

They could hope he kept his mouth shut but, as if reading her mind, Kiran shook his head. Imani agreed with him. She had lost all faith in everyone—even her so-called friends—keeping secrets to themselves. Unless they were a close family member—the only people Imani would consider trusting these days—they'd use them sooner or later as leverage.

With Kiran elbow-deep in blood and smoke, she glared at him. It would be up to her to kill Jai to remove any witnesses. It had to be done. Even Tanyl was difficult to trust entirely. However, a part of her did think she could learn to trust Esa again … and maybe Kiran, if he let her in more.

She at least trusted Tanyl enough to care for her siblings and Kiran enough to perform this binding.

Months ago, she would have balked at such an act, but this was too important. No one could find out. So, tonight, she snapped her wand out, froze Jai's body, and slit his throat clean through. Lifting the spell, he fell down the wall, blood covering the front of his shirt, eyes wide.

It only took a minute for him to die. Once he did, she enchanted his body out into the hallway and propped him up against the wall, placing the knife in his hand.

There. Now it was a suicide.

The act left her oddly unfazed. Imani blankly walked back into the room and shut the door. This time, Kiran pointed his wand at it and cast even more defensive spells. She didn't think *anyone* would be getting in there tonight uninvited. He'd been sloppy before. How badly did he want her to agree if he forgot simple defensive spells?

"So"—she shuffled to stand beside him—"you better know what you're doing with this flesh magic binding, or we're both dead."

"True. But when used to enhance a binding, it's unbreakable," Kiran said eventually, so quiet she almost didn't hear him. He covered a mix of plants in a bowl with a few drops of a tincture. "It will take several months to cure, but a blood burning like this one will create a powerful bond between the two people."

It wouldn't be unbreakable once she had the Drasil. No magic would be unbreakable to something so powerful. But Imani kept it to herself.

Fangs snapping out quickly, he cut another deep cut across his forearm. His face remained impassive, not acknowledging the pain from the wounds. He barely looked at her and said little as he brewed the dried flowers.

"This is a root binding, too." Imani frowned, the complete understanding of what he was about to do disturbing her even more. "What's the ramification?" She turned to him, heart hammering. "Death?"

No response.

She crossed her arms and stared at him expectantly, but he still didn't answer.

"Gods, the ascension assessment binding wasn't a root. Not even most *heartmates* choose bindings this extreme," Imani added.

Again, his silence was all the answer she needed.

The magic in root bindings planted deeper inside someone the longer it remained in place. The blood burning and the death ramifications ratcheted up the intensity of these bindings considerably. Imani pushed her hair off her face, feeling real fear for the first time in a long time.

Actively working to break her promise might cause the magic to tighten around her throat. It might constrict her chest, stop her heart for seconds, or cause blackouts. She would never be able to break or lessen magic like this, even with the Drasil. It would be part of her, like an organ. When complete, the spell would never entirely disappear, like other bindings.

He had lied to her earlier.

"I suppose it's a perfect choice," she mused, trying to mask her anxiety. "Blood burnings are highly regulated here. Only the Order is sanctioned to perform them after a strict application process."

"You know a lot about magic," he stated. "Most people here lack the curiosity to understand its properties beyond anything but transactional truly."

"My, my, a compliment." She preened a bit but managed to keep her face blank. "You don't know as much about me as you think you do."

"I know enough," he said.

Before she could respond, magic filled the room. It was thick and smokey, suffusing the air. The heady effect was immediate.

He closed his cut with his wand then gently pulled her closer while her mind drifted. Imani mentally detached herself as he cut and bled her. The magic seeped into her body.

Kiran pressed a soft kiss to one of her wrists then waved his wand over it, his healing magic sealing the cut. Then he did it again to the cut on her chest and the bruises across her face. After, he swiftly stripped his clothes.

Hugging her arms around her waist, a tremor racked her body. Limbs heavy, she could barely move, transfixed as he stepped out of his pants. Her head might have floated into the clouds from all the magic in the room.

He stood in front of her now, practically naked. Imani started to smile dreamily at him but somehow stopped herself. The magic gripped her, amplifying her attraction to him.

Kiran narrowed his eyes at her. Lifting her hand, he let out a quiet shudder as she moved her fingers lightly up his arms. His skin, a shade more golden than hers, was warm. Trails of sparkling emotions across his skin appeared at her touch.

In a daze, she kept up her movements. He overpowered her senses when he was this close.

Looking up, she was surprised to see his eyes slide closed. Her hands were comically small compared to his, but she ran them down his chest to the trail of hair leading to his undergarments.

Kiran stood perfectly still for a moment. Imani could not read him. She could not understand what was going on in his mind right now.

The striking combination of virile elf and shifter blood gave him a sharp, rugged beauty, incomparable to others. She was glad half-breeds weren't illegal in Niflheim because there was no contest. He was the most attractive man she'd ever seen.

Why did he hide this perfection from the world? She didn't understand. In many ways, he hid more than she did.

Something frightening and possessive passed between them.

And she liked it.

With a deep inhale, her nostrils flared, and Kiran bit into his bottom lip. This was more intense than the binding with Tanyl, and it should have terrified her.

Kiran held her face, frantic yet soothing, before dipping his head to nuzzle her neck. A thrill shot through her like she was drowning, and she moved to trace lightly down his abdomen again. But he sucked in a breath before she could finish and snatched her wrists, painfully squeezing.

She yelped, surprised.

Glassy eyes lifted again to meet hers. Any trace of desire was gone, leaving only wickedness and a vacant expression hinting at something swimming beneath Kiran's mind and body.

How did he switch between personalities so quickly? One second, he was passionate and sarcastically amused. The next, he was cold with malice. She couldn't keep up. Imani could never get a read on him, and it infuriated her.

In one smooth motion, he removed her robe, tossing it on the floor. "Take the nightgown off."

She carefully slipped off the straps of her nightgown, letting it pool around her feet. Holding her wand at her side, she took several deep breaths to regain control.

"The magic tonight will draw us together. It requires us to feed from each other, which could also lead to sex. But let me be perfectly clear; I would never touch a dirty whore who's been with that piece of shit, Tanyl." Kiran's tone was befitting a prince, snobbish and cruel, like she was a small-minded little girl and he was far superior in all ways.

In her mind, she'd known this fact: he despised Tanyl. But the slap of his words made her jerk, and for some reason, she didn't understand.

A deep ache of hurt burst forth in her chest, as if he'd physically struck her. How was he resisting the magic so easily and she wasn't?

"Well, *you* might be the biggest hypocrite in the world," she supplied thickly, masking her pain with barbs. "You'd be lucky to sleep with a whore like me. But you'll never know since your diseased cock is one fuck away from falling off."

A swift movement between them startled her. He had her robe in his hands again, and she held her hand out for it. Conjuring, another skill to add to her growing list of his confirmed magic.

He threw it at her, hitting her in the face. "Try not to be a slut for a few hours. We have work to do." He glared at her as if she were a revolting pest he wanted to forget after killing.

She stood there, frozen. Half in anger, half in embarrassment. Tears from both humiliation and hunger threatened to spill from her eyes. Seething, her hands shook so violently she could barely wrap the garment around her while vaguely thinking this might be the worst night of her life.

CHAPTER 39

Kiran performed the next phase of bleeding efficiently. Cutting into her flesh, a line appeared between his eyes as he trailed the various scars lining her legs. They bothered him. He tried to hide it, but it flashed in his expression.

Let him be disgusted. Despite the sting of his words earlier, Imani wasn't ashamed of doing what she had to do to survive. If it made her a whore, so be it.

She curled her lip in a sneer. "Don't act like your body is as clean as a newborn babe. We both know yours is even worse than mine."

He glanced up at her, unreadable, but didn't reply.

Heating the first layer of blood with his hand, it smoked. Breathing it in, the spell produced a peppery smell and humid heat, preceding intense magic.

They were close to being ready to perform the binding. It was hard to say how Imani understood through her dizzy head, but a sliver of fear rushed down her spine.

She blinked.

Magic exploded into the room.

Not nascent or atrophic, this magic was something else entirely. Primordial and otherworldly, it caused her heart to pound in her ears.

An unbridled ferocity from Kiran's signature called to every piece of her existence, throwing her over the edge of awareness.

Against her will, Imani's magic came to the surface. The rush was so powerful it knocked the wind out of her. She sank to her knees, too weak to stand anymore.

Kiran dropped down next to her and handed over the cup of their blood for her to drink. Lifting the cup to his mouth, he motioned for her to do the same. She quickly tipped all the liquid into her mouth, and it fell to the back of her throat. She swallowed the thick, warm substance. It burned like fire all the way down into her belly.

Steeply and rapidly, a force shot her signature into the ceiling. The spell filled the entire room with a stifling, carnal air and blackened her veins. As she fought them back, a tunnel overtook her vision. Her magic wanted out—all of it.

Her body slipped backward. The cup fell from her hand and shattered. In the next instant, she found herself on her back.

Kiran straddled her and dug his nails into her arms. "Let it go, Imani. I want to see it. I know you're fighting your own nature. I know there's darkness in you, desperate to get out. It calls to you, and you're suffocating when you resist."

Her eyes rolled back at his predatory touch as she obeyed. It felt good to stop fighting, finally. The magic threw itself out in an inky mess into the room, colliding with the rest of Kiran's and their blood magic. The room darkened to a black void as if all light had been snatched instantly. Glass shattered somewhere, and wood splintered at the force. She couldn't see her hands in front of her face. She couldn't see the floor beneath her.

She pressed her fingers into her forehead, but she couldn't focus, couldn't get a firm grasp on anything. Yet, somehow, she kept a tenuous hold on her oppressive magic so it didn't destroy the room. It responded to her pull, but barely.

After another surge in her power, he relented and ran his hands up and down her bare arms. Pain and pleasure warred inside in equal measure now, but the touch helped her regain control. His warm hands tracing small circles on her skin sent shivers through her.

Dim light returned around them.

Eyes fluttering, she almost slipped into an exhausted sleep.

"Stay awake a bit longer, my darling." His throat strained, and he held her face with his hands.

With barely a thought, Imani loosened her hold on the magic, letting the whirls of shadows move in twisters throughout the room. It was nice but strange to have them roaming free.

His hands fell from her face.

When she glanced at Kiran, he stared open-mouthed at them. Confusion and awe shone in his eyes, and he grinned. Her dangerous shadows had exploded into darkness earlier in front of Aiden, and Kiran'd had to help pull her back from a terrifying Fabric event. She assumed he'd be threatened and furious with her for being so careless. And yet, he appeared to love it or at least, appreciate it. Why did he appear so excited and amused? Did he know what her magic was?

Whether he did or not, somewhere in the recesses of her mind, she relished it. Celebrated unleashing the power and controlling it in front of him. More than anything, she wanted to let it tear through the room in all its destructive glory.

"Are you not afraid of my magic?" she asked, grinning back at him lazily, uncertain why she smiled like a fool, yet she couldn't stop.

As thick columns of black clouds swirled around them, Kiran smiled down at her like a brilliant dawn morning, but his eyes showed no kindness.

"Mine—this is mine," he whispered to himself, his eyes unhinged as they stared into hers.

Somehow, she found herself agreeing or, at least, unable to argue.

Kiran twined his fingers through her hair and yanked her head back until she stared at the ceiling. "When did you last feed?" The frantic question tumbled out of him.

She shook her head, wanting to sleep.

"Focus on my voice, Imani. Let me see those perfect eyes," he whispered raspingly as he pinched her chin, forcing her eyes to open again.

Imani spiraled into madness when concern slipped into his features.

"There you are, darling," he sighed, leaning his forehead against hers.

"Tonight," Imani mumbled, trying to clear her head.

He was desperate to finish this binding with her, and if she couldn't deliver, she might not wake up again.

His fangs came out again, and he ripped a massive gash in his arm like he was angry at something then let it gush into his cup. "Good. We'll risk it."

"Risk what?" She was still bleary-eyed as she stared at him and gently stroked his arm.

His pupils blew wide, a menacing black overtaking them both. "I can't help but hate you."

Confused, Imani wrinkled her brow. Hate her?

But, with a shake of his head, he refocused and grabbed his wand from the floor next to him. The blood heated again, smoking. He pressed her wrists hard above her head, holding her tight to the floor.

"Stay still," he ordered before quickly pouring the blood into her mouth.

Practically gagging, she let out a slight cough but managed to keep it down.

He drank the rest, and then he brushed his lips over her ear as he initiated the binding. Again, her muscles locked in the now-familiar connection.

With his strange dialect and her broken elvish, she didn't fully understand the words—a stupid position to be in. She should have told him to cast it in the common tongue, but it was too late now.

Kiran's melodic voice anchored her as he proceeded with the binding.

Everything fell away. Imani's belligerent magic, once screaming and clawing to protect her, now purred in bliss. Instead of pain, the ache throbbed like pleasure. As he continued, she fisted the fabric of her robe, listening to it chant in her head and chest like a drumbeat.

More, more, more.

When she opened her eyes again, he gazed back at her with such intensity that it startled her.

Leaning in, he pressed his mouth to hers but didn't kiss her. "Repeat it for me," he murmured.

Dazed, she gave him a slow nod as he fed the words to her. His hands moved soothingly all over her skin. Her mouth had a mind of its own as phrases she had no control over stumbled out in a whisper.

Imani managed to translate a few of the pieces. First, he had her pledge what she thought was loyalty to the Throne, the king. The second binding was the promise to follow him somewhere when asked.

A surge of crisp white stillness speared Imani through her core, driving back the irrational fear and the sticky black cloud of death. Brilliant healing magic inside her chest spread out through her veins, clearing her spirit of darkness and hopelessness.

They were nearly done, and then the final words to seal the binding tumbled out of Kiran's mouth. *"Aomagho ruya."*

The words sent a magic rush through her, and she whimpered. Catching her breath, she pulled him closer, and their eyes locked in terrifying clarity. Warmth spread between her ribs.

Deep in her most hidden corners came a whisper of familiarity. Of sameness. Belonging. The promise of rare, undiluted power matched her own in its ugliness, cruelty, and beauty. A tingling caressed her body, and she craved it like a fiend. Based on the look in Kiran's eyes, he did, too.

"Aomagho ruya." The words came out slowly as Imani attempted the correct pronunciation.

Kiran groaned, rubbing his nose against her cheek and neck, which caused a strange, unwelcome kind of nervousness to twist in her stomach. Again, this was too familiar to what had happened with Tanyl and his binding, except much worse.

But before she could question anything, the magic forced another wave of power through them, and a burning heat melded their bodies together.

Hands moving all over her, he wrapped his arms and legs around her, clutching her tight, almost painfully. Equally desperate to be close to him, she buried herself against his chest and dug her nails into his back.

Tears streamed down her face. The pain focused on the center of her being. Imani had never experienced flesh magic or a binding—or indeed *any* magic—this powerful.

It consumed her.

But the magic affected him, too. He tensed, hissing through his teeth and digging his fingers into her flesh where he held her.

A final roar of power blasted inside her skull, and the spell locked into place.

The room cooled as the magic dissipated.

But, simultaneously, something wholly primitive reared its head deep within Imani. It was like the spell had snapped the cords of her restraints—a violent need for Kiran's soul. An innate sense of needing to own every part of his essence roiled through her entire being.

He said they would need to feed from each other, and he was right. Now that the binding was locked in place, she was starving for him.

Clutching his shirt, she tried to move closer. She could practically see his essence glowing inside his chest and floating around his body. As if it equally wanted *her*.

But he pushed her away with a snarl, low and unnatural in response.

CHAPTER 40

Blackness dotted her sight. Streaks of pain burst forth again from fighting the need. Her throat grew tight with a cry fighting to escape. She reached for him, but his eyes darkened.

He snarled at her in a warning and pushed her away. "Not yet. It's too out of control."

She held her breath, gritted her teeth, and tried to focus enough to fight back. Magic slammed against her, pushing her, raging at her, demanding she feed from Kiran. Resisting it tore her up inside. The longer she fought feeding from him, the tighter her body grew, threatening to unfurl explosively as the urges added to an increasing mania.

"Why are you stopping this? I can't. I can't bloody do it."

"Fight it. You made this choice. I'm not immune to this magic or pain, either. We *need* to wait a bit longer." Kiran's jaw clenched. His eyes, face, and signature radiated equal parts rage and unease, a strange combination for the elf prince.

"Where is she?" he muttered, his jaw clenched tight, glancing at the door.

Imani wanted to laugh and cry at the same time. The physical repercussions weren't nearly as bad for Kiran. Neither her body nor her magic was as strong as his. Although she'd fed, she was exhausted and injured.

Feeding from Kiran was all she wanted, and if she did, she'd want to have sex with him—badly. Maybe he was making them wait because it would be easier to resist the sex. Who was he waiting for?

But part of her was grateful. She couldn't sleep with Kiran in such a state of vulnerability. She shouldn't sleep with him *at all*, even though she could admit to herself now how she wanted to. Boneless, she fought against a whimper. Imani couldn't sound weak or out of control in front of him. She wouldn't give him the satisfaction.

His gaze narrowed on her as if he didn't like the flash of pain she showed. But he made no effort to help as his expression turned impassive and stony. He was right; Imani had made this choice all on her own. But he didn't have to behave like a complete bastard while she was in pain. *That* choice was his.

With a nasty sneer, Kiran dissuaded Imani from any passing notions she mattered. The bleak reality of what this was—and wasn't—and how little he cared crashed into her again.

Good. Imani needed the reminder. And the truth that she might die later from this binding gave her enough strength to speak clearly again. A strangled cry rose in her throat.

"I hate you," she bit out.

"Trust me; the feeling is mutual right now," he snapped.

However, if she wanted to survive this, and he refused to let them feed together or have sex with each other right now, she needed him to touch her at least.

He knew it. He didn't like it but came to the same conclusion because his expression morphed into something animalistic.

"Imani," Kiran's deep, melodic timbre filled her ears while she screamed unabashedly, begging him to stop, hating her powerlessness. Darkness licked her skin, but staring into his strange eyes sent soothing waves rushing through her.

The pain dulled.

"You were warned many times not to bargain with me, you stupid girl," he ground out, clutching her against him.

"I will find a way out of this binding," she seethed, trying but failing to keep the lust from her words. Damn this magic for making her want him so badly.

Kiran wrapped his arms around her without warning again, yanking her against his hard body. "You will fail. I long to see your face when you finally understand my power over you."

His utter confidence silenced her. But was this another façade?

It took her a few heartbeats to gather her wits and school her face into a mask of indifference. The trembling eventually calmed, but it didn't abate the hunger entirely.

Kiran pushed the sweat-drenched hair away from her face. His pupils were blown wide. "You're the most perfect female I've ever seen. And Tanyl was right … I don't deserve you." A flicker of surprise flashed across his face at the admission. But moments later, it was gone. "I knew you would cause so many problems for me."

Exhausted, she let her forehead fall against his chest.

His heart beat erratically. He hid it well from her, but as he said, he wasn't immune. Neither of them would survive if he lost it now. She'd needed him to touch her, and he probably needed the same. Damn this magic.

Barely moving, she lightly pressed a few soft kisses to his chest, trying to calm him. If it did anything for him, he didn't let on. But his trembling slowed. For a while, they didn't move.

Sensations of being torn open persisted, but they lessened to a dull ache as the root binding created a layer of magic in them, steadily searing tighter and tighter, mooring together. If they couldn't feed and fuck at the moment, they needed to be close as the magic worked itself through them, binding them.

Her eyes flew open when his mouth brushed against hers. Then his teeth nipped her bottom lip. A soft, surprised gasp escaped her mouth. He gave in, and she was relieved. A part of her hated him, but not enough to stop wanting him at this moment. Maybe it was the magic. Maybe it was something else, but she lifted her hips instinctively.

He reacted immediately, losing control, kissing her with a need they both possessed.

The world quieted, and the pain dulled. Coherent thoughts slid to the back of her mind as she threaded her fingers through his hair.

It was soft but thick, and she liked her hands there. The sound of their breathing echoed through them, the only sound she cared about.

Pulling away, an expression she didn't understand came over his face. Afraid he might stop, she reached inside his pants and wrapped her fingers around him. He was hard in her hand.

Touching him only marginally muted the yearning clenching her stomach. Her body begged for relief. She only needed a little ... just a taste to get her by.

Like slipping through his wards, wisps of her magic twined and twisted into his signature. Waves of pleasure from the intimacy were unleashed. Even from a mere brush of initial contact, she sucked in air, grasping the depth of his power.

But it wasn't enough, not even close. Imani needed to go deeper, feed, and be close to Kiran. Layers and layers of the Fabric itself were woven into his existence and welcomed her inside, exuding a lovely brightness—

There.

A thread of sparkling warmth trickled from his signature.

Snatching a sliver, she devoured the tiny piece of his essence before it receded inside the cage he'd built around his heart.

The amplified magic churning inside her set off a chain reaction, settling something into place inside her, answering a forgotten question she'd asked long ago.

A current of power blasted through her middle. It was his. Or hers. Or maybe a combination of their magic. It merged into one stream, a collision of dark and even darker, granting them a bridge.

A bliss of sensations skittered across her skin, and her mind went blank again. *Is this what the heavens beyond the Under feel like?*

The binding strengthened as the spell's roots grew deeply, embedding themselves in her signature and body.

For a moment, the massive well of power trapped inside them roared like a tidal wave about to crash on some unsuspecting town. It gathered, gathered, gathered, and—

Rearing back and pushing himself into a seated position, a fierce growl built in his throat. His magic exploded around him, like a mix of heat and ice. She stilled in anticipation, but nothing happened for several moments.

He gaped at her, on his knees, and she didn't know how to react to it or him. It was as if whatever magic he'd performed spooked him.

Moving to straddle her, he wrapped his hand around her throat and held her in place. Closing the distance between them until their lips brushed, his angry eyes peered into hers. "And they say *I'm* manipulative. If you try to feed from me again, Ara's punishments will be like pleasantries between lovers compared to the pain and horror a witch like me will inflict. Do you understand, little elf? If you were anyone else, you'd be dead already for what you tried to do. So, I won't tell you again. I told you we must wait to feed until the spell calms down, and that's a command."

The telltale tightness wrapped around her throat as he'd exerted his power over her again. Sinking her nails into his forearms, she drew blood. The binding choked her more, and she coughed. Kiran let out a string of curses in elvish as his lips wrenched back in a snarl that was every bit the dark, savage elf he was.

Imani coughed and sputtered, glaring at him. "You will never fully control me," she choked out, trying to breathe through the binding magic around her throat. She was stupid for trying to hurt him, knowing the binding would hurt her, too.

"I will in all the ways that matter." Shadows moved around them, but Kiran never even flinched. Instead, he grasped a handful of hair, unaware or uncaring Imani's magic still poured out of her in an uncontrolled stream. Acting on all instinct, his green eye turned wild. "Now that you took from me, I'm going to take from you."

She didn't even know how a drow elf like Kiran fed. Was it the same as her? However it was, she would endure it with dignity.

Painfully wrenching her head back, he bared her neck to him and nuzzled his nose down her skin. Then his signature swirled with hers, poking for a way in. She opened herself a sliver, and he shoved himself through.

It was the same.

How much of her soul he took from her, she had no idea. She shut her eyes and let him, even as he went against his own words not to feed yet. It was only fair since she'd taken from him, and although she hated it ... it was heaven.

A sumptuous, heavy feeling coursing through the binding sparked a primal knowledge that this wasn't just about satisfying a pang of physical hunger.

He cupped her breasts, and she let out a gasp of pleasure. The silky strands of his hair fell through her fingers as she ground herself up against him. He groaned.

But then he let out a growl of frustration.

Dropping her to the floor, she grunted. A furious madness stared down at her. He didn't use the binding but waved his wand, muttering a spell.

And her body was frozen.

Imani had experienced this spell before—from Ara. And it made her hate him even more.

She writhed against his power as it stifled the air, holding her rigid in place. All her muscles tightened, and she could barely get a breath out, as if he'd locked her organs, too. She hated being so powerless in front of him.

A deep rage simmering inside her threatened to boil over. Then flashes of intermittent darkness and light intensified in the room as Kiran's magic lifted from her. Imani stripped away his spell over her and sat up with a lopsided, cruel smile. Shrouding him in shadows, her black magic slithered around him, waiting for Imani to cast the final command and bury him in the darkness.

Kiran's eyes widened in surprise at her fighting back against his magic.

"You should've used the binding if you didn't want me to fight back." Derision coated her voice. "Let me be clear: I possess something out of your reach entirely. And you will *never* truly own or control me."

The little piece of her mind that had fought off Malis's magic, *that* piece was hers to give, and no one could take it. And a part of her magic was as strong as Kiran's, or stronger, because she could strip it away.

The binding protected them from hurting each other, but could her dark atrophic magic bypass it? It could bypass his wards and his cadence magic, after all. It had bypassed Malis.

Maybe it was because she lay naked and exposed, maybe because she was half-starved and delirious, maybe she liked hurting people, or because she lay beneath a remorseless, spoiled prince. Whatever the reason, an icy rage descended on her, and she could not stop it. While she didn't want to kill him, she wanted him to hurt. And he was right; she barely had a shred of control over her shadows.

With a growl from deep inside her chest, a void of her magic sucked the air from the room. It moved violently, blanketing the walls and floor in pure nothing again, as the inescapable darkness engulfed him.

A loud crack shattered in her ears and rattled her chest. The binding strangled her.

She shrieked in horror, wrapping her arms around her middle as her heart wrenched. It was like being separated from her body. Strange screeching, and scratching, and incoherent whispers surrounded her, growing louder the longer her inky magic ran wild through the room.

They couldn't overpower such a strong binding. She should've known.

Come back, she ordered them.

But the pain continued.

Pretending they weren't about to perish, she tried to drag herself to Kiran, thinking for some insane reason she could save him if she could get to him, touch him. But she collapsed. The energy she spent attacking Kiran, the binding, the emptiness caving in her chest—Imani could have sworn she was dying. She probably was.

The room faded as a different sort of darkness enveloped her.

In the moments before she lost consciousness, Imani could have sworn a massive shadow—not her own—grew up the wall above and roared.

The room went silent.

CHAPTER 41

With heavy lids, Imani tried to wrench her eyes open, despite the grainy texture. She tried to swallow, too, but her tongue stuck. She coughed. Her lungs burned as she shot up from the bed she'd been placed on, trying to catch her breath.

Her vision came into focus like a curtain being drawn. The ceiling above the bed became sharper, and the room stopped spinning.

Moving her head to the side, she saw Kiran lay beside her, awake and watching. Everything inside Imani bloomed with heat when their eyes met.

Exhaustion etched Kiran's features, but his expression eased when she looked at him. Something else still played in his glassy eyes. Something like concern.

Half-asleep and still dazed from the spell, she reached her hand up to his face. The man was a bastard, to be sure, but the blood of another elf was something she didn't want on her hands. At least, not yet.

He heaved a sigh, dragging a hand over his thick, dark hair. "I thought you were dying."

The low, melodic tone from Kiran's voice affected her even more this time, and she fought the urge to purr in response. A noise she'd never made in her life. Her overwrought body relaxed, oddly at ease now.

Kiran eyed her closely, absently rubbing his hand against his chest. He must have also sensed the same pressure there from the binding.

"I thought I killed you, too," Imani whispered thickly.

It was obvious now, but the binding was too deep and would prevent either of them from killing the other. Even her shadow magic couldn't breach it. Kiran might have gotten hurt, but the blow would never be deadly.

His features morphed into annoyance. "Sorry to disappoint."

At his flippant words, she was hit with the absurdity of where she was. In bed with *Kiran*? They were lying far too close together.

Distance. She needed space from him.

She threw her legs over the bed and found she was dressed in her nightgown again. A quick glance around told her they were not in Kiran's room—this was somewhere else entirely in the palace.

Her robe lay discarded on the floor. Snatching it up, she wrapped it tightly around her then headed to a narrow, tall window. Blinking and shaking her hands out a bit, she ripped open the drapes, taking a moment to compose herself.

Dark clouds moved quickly as a storm brewed overhead. It was still the middle of the night. She nearly shuddered in relief.

Cracking her neck, Imani tried to remember how she had gotten into this room. Flashes of the magic they'd cast ran through her mind, and the bargain she'd made with a blood-burning binding assaulted her.

A warm hand gently curled around her neck, and she stiffened. As if checking for injuries, Kiran ran his hands over her braid and face, his other hand running lightly up her arm like he had every right to touch her. Even the way he stood and the position of his body next to hers was unmistakable in its possession.

She let him, even though she didn't understand why.

"Where are we?" she whispered.

He pulled his hands back to his sides. "I brought you to Master Heirwyn's rooms when you wouldn't wake. I needed ..." He trailed off and rubbed the back of his neck. "Well, I needed her help."

Confusion clouded her mind. Kiran needed help?

As the magic wore off, he acted more strangely. She needed to leave.

Without a word, she shrugged him off and turned away. Slipping her wand from its pocket, she cast her illusion.

Nothing happened.

She glared as she tried again.

Nothing.

Panicking, she pulled her left sleeve up to examine her brands. She took in a sudden breath at what she found.

A detailed meshwork of red lines was now burned into the skin on top of her left hand. They crisscrossed over her scarred, previously unbranded skin and up her arm. The brand was *massive*.

Whipping back around, she found Kiran leaning against the wall with a ghost of a smile on his face. Something like masculine pride emanated from him. A corner of an identical brand showed on his hand, the rest covered by his sleeve.

Imani simply stared at him, unblinking, unmoving.

Powerful bindings often manifested in apparent locations to identify a bound witch quickly and deter frivolous, unnecessary magic. But not even her binding brand with Tanyl—appearing on her abdomen and lower back in a swirled design—was this blatant.

Once a person ran out of skin, it meant their bodies reached the limit of magic it would allow.

Almost no one ran out of space anymore, but she remembered Kiran's shirtless body was covered. He probably only had a few places where any new bindings this large could appear. This must be one of them.

A marking like this would need to be glamoured if she wanted to avoid questions, magic not all had the luxury of doing. She was lucky.

Her chest tightened as a wave of fear crashed into her. "Kiran, where is my magic? Why can't I cast?" She marched over to him, intent on violence. But this time, the binding tightened her stomach, twisting more as she moved closer. Right in front of him, she doubled over, cursing root bindings. It had gotten stronger while she'd slept.

Laughter echoed ominously in the room while she winced at the pain and hunger—insatiable hunger. He kept laughing at her, and she covered her trembling lips with her hands, waiting for it to pass. A binding like this was unprecedented.

A mess of emotions churned inside—conflict, screaming with hate, rage, want, need. Saints, she was *starving*. She needed to feed for her strength to return.

At least the heady effects of the binding were lessening now.

A long, thick silence fell between them as she backed away, breathing hard until the pain dulled a bit.

"Tell me what you did to me and my magic," she said again through gritted teeth, rubbing her chest furiously. "Is this the bond between us or—"

"What are you fucking talking about? The binding where you're the servant of the opposing king or some imagery *bond* you think exists because of it?" He looked down his nose at her, void of any spark or concern. Only cold, cutting depravity played in his eyes now. It set her teeth on edge.

"I'm relieved to see you alive. It's more than I can say for others who've done blood burnings with me." He sighed. "And it would have been incredibly inconvenient to find a replacement."

Humiliation flooded through her, pinking her cheeks. It was all obvious now that she was one of the many people he had already controlled. How many times had he manipulated and trapped others in the same way? Based on his brands, the number was too high for her to comprehend.

Replaying the events, she could see it now—all games and lies, him moving her where he wanted, controlling her, making her weak—

A scream sat at the back of her throat, but she gave him a nasty smile instead. "You lied to me, and you'll regret it someday," she said, barely above a whisper. Her voice came out harsh and cold. Still, she wished it sounded colder.

"I highly doubt it." He chuckled. "I regret many things, but this will *never* be one."

"You made an enemy of me today. I will return the favor at some point," Imani shot back.

"*Made an enemy?*" He threw his head back and laughed.

Clenching her fists so they didn't shake, anger rooted her in place. All she could do was watch Kiran laugh.

"Fortunately for me, I have a lot of enemies," he said, finally managing to compose himself. "So, I couldn't give a fuck about one more."

She gave him the finger. But he merely grinned like a proud cat who had caught the mouse.

"Yes, I lied. You know all I needed was a Norn elf desperate enough but also magically powerful to agree to such a binding, right? I was lucky to find one people wouldn't miss much. When I return, I can't afford anyone asking questions about my trip."

"My siblings will ask questions."

Pity crossed his face, but he ignored the comment. "I already told you the spell requires feeding afterward. It's settling more, so we should complete the ritual. We didn't take nearly enough before."

Being here for one more moment would surely kill her. Or Kiran.

"I need to leave and meet Tanyl. Goodbye, Kiran," she said curtly, barely throwing him a glance over her shoulder on her way out.

Moving at a speed she didn't think possible, his hand shot out, capturing her jaw.

"You're *never* feeding from him again. *Never* fucking him again. Am I clear, Imani?" He applied pressure until her mouth opened, tipping it up, the command of the binding practically choking her.

She mirrored his glower while attempting to call her shadows forward. "I tire of your demands, Your Highness." Her jaw tightened in his grip. "But fine, I won't fuck him until I find a way out of this binding."

A menacing unkindness danced in his eyes as he studied her. The dark emotion in his lingering stare made Imani's knees tremble. Imani had to endure it because her magic was a barely lit ember burning inside her—a wisp of smoke, as if someone had blown out the candle of her power. Even the whispers couldn't soothe the mounting panic. For one terrible moment, she thought he had enchanted her magic to be locked again, like Ara had done.

"I swear, if you've taken any of my magic, I will—"

He pushed her jaw out of his hands. "Calm down before you

almost kill yourself again. I cast an echo shield, which might briefly dull some of it. Once you're rested, it'll be fine." He paused. "I think. I've never cast one before."

"You *what*? I *never* agreed to have you cast any more magic on me beyond the binding."

"Well, good thing I'm so generous. Otherwise, you might be dead. You should be thanking me." Kiran laughed, rolling his eyes. "It's a powerful, useful illusion spell. Until it weakens, it allows you to hide or call forward your magic at will, including your pesky shadows and nasty soul draw. So, you won't have to remove and recast your illusion each time. And, unlike your illusion, no one can remove it. Except me."

"Your arrogance is astounding. You don't think there's a witch more powerful than you?"

He chuckled. "It has nothing to do with how powerful I am. This spell is different. It reflects a person's own magic back to them. It doesn't matter how powerful they are; they won't sense anything besides themselves unless you want them to. At least, until it weakens in a few months, at which point maybe I'll cast it again for you. Maybe I won't." He crossed his arms. "You're welcome, by the way, you ungrateful—"

Before he could finish, Imani pointed her wand at his chest. "Will you shut the fuck up?" she snapped, not caring her wand was useless against him.

He opened his mouth to speak but stopped, staring down at her arms.

Currents of power vibrated under her skin. Her brands brightened and burned.

"Hmm, my magic is waking up," she murmured, baring her own minuscule fangs.

Kiran glared at her wand when she pressed it harder into his flesh. "I told you it would come back," he grumbled.

"Excellent. Now, out of my way." She tilted her head to the side like he always did, her shadows gathering around her like a halo. "I hate repeating myself."

"You're adorable when you're trying to be me." A sinister smirk spread across his face. "You could never be me, though—villains don't bargain, Imani. I take what I want and refuse to settle for anything less. Besides, I don't know where you'd go. You need to feed to ease the root binding, and Tanyl is off limits."

The air grew thinner, and the light grew darker. After a moment, the door opened. Master Heirwyn sailed inside, oblivious to their standoff. She stood near the edge of the bed and fixed her gaze on Imani.

"Let's go," Master Heirwyn said in her commanding tone.

Giving the prince a sideways glance, she saw how Kiran's eyes drew a lazy trail down the length of the naiad nymph's body. Flawlessly built, the nymph witch had the perfect hourglass figure, and although she was obviously older, she'd aged beautifully. The conclusion only made Imani hate the woman more.

"As fun as this has been, darling," Kiran said, turning to Imani, "you and I both have another commitment we can't miss now."

"Move. I'm leaving—without you. I'll figure out my own feeding. Maybe your brother would be interested now. Your binding has disappeared after all."

"My, this night continues to be quite humiliating for you." He stepped closer, threading his fingers through her hair, tilting her head back. "See, I correctly assumed you'd have difficulty accepting your position in our kingdom."

"What position?" she asked through gritted teeth, trying to remove his hand.

He brushed his mouth against hers, even while she fought to turn her head away from his seductive lips. "An elf whore with a magical cunt, one I control," he said simply. Kiran's mouth turned up into a cruel smile.

Before she could respond, he grabbed her arm and pulled her out the door after the nymph.

Magic burned wildly through her veins, her anger pulsing from head to toe. But she couldn't hurt him—the binding prevented it entirely.

She hated it even more now that the truth about him was in the open. People hadn't been exaggerating when they'd called him a bastard and a snake.

"Where are we going?" She tried to tug her arm back, but he held her firm.

"Back to my rooms so you can feed. I've taken care of everything so we can finish this binding properly in the safety of my rooms. There's more security there."

"Who will I be feeding from?"

He ignored her question.

"I wouldn't have sex with you if you were the last elf in the realm."

"As I said before, good thing I refuse to sleep with Tanyl's whore then."

"Then who is it?"

He rolled his eyes. "Saints, you're annoying. Master Heirwyn will supervise to make sure nothing … goes too far. It's why we couldn't feed earlier. We shouldn't have done it without someone else in the room. Now, I'm ordering you to come with me."

Her throat constricted before he had even finished the sentence.

CHAPTER 42

A strangled sound came from her throat. "You bastard."

He sighed. "The first binding—the one where you pledged loyalty to me and our kingdom—means I can make you do anything I bloody want."

"You know," she grated out in a whisper, "this seems like a great time to mention I'm about to be implicated in the murder of the Niflheim-bred merchant in our town, and since you're obligated to fulfill our binding and keep me alive, I don't mind admitting every word of it is true. Do you know what was left of him? Nothing. My shadows completely obliterated him. So, trust me; I am not an elf you want to be ordering around like this. Unless you want me to unleash them again on you when this binding is complete."

He leaned closer and lowered his voice as they kept walking. "I'm not afraid of your magic anymore."

"Ah, but you admit it *did* scare you before we agreed to this binding." Smugness imbibed Imani's voice.

He shot her a flat look. "Call it more of a morbid curiosity." His mouth brushed over her ear. "And I've known about your crime for months, my little murderess."

Imani jerked her head back in surprise. "What do you mean? With what proof? How could you have anything the Crown would legitimately consider?"

The nymph witch trailed behind them, an unreadable expression as she observed them.

Ignoring Imani's anger, Kiran continued pulling her toward the balcony around the inner atrium. They stopped, and he glanced at her arrogantly. "You're right. The queen would never give me an audience for any conversation whatsoever. But rumor is the evidence the queen and your precious heir will hear from your sister tomorrow will be extremely compelling."

Imani's stomach turned over, and she honestly thought she might pass out. "What are you talking about? What is my sister doing here?"

"Meira decided she couldn't take your lies anymore. She arrived yesterday and told them how you likely attacked the merchant after your grandmother's burning, how you came back smelling of smoke and covered in ash, how you lost your cloak—the exact one they found near the remains. Oh, and she *also* told them how you've been lying to the Order and the Crown, hiding your true magic and identity."

Imani pressed her hand to her fluttering chest to calm her racing heart. Her mind careened out of control with possibilities. She didn't believe Meira would do this to her. Not her sister. *No.*

Imani could barely get the words out. "How did you force her to say those things? What did you do to her?" Her voice cracked, and she fought tears again for what felt like the millionth time tonight.

"*Me?*" He touched his chest in mock offense. "See for yourself." He led her to the railing and made her look down at the people milling about below.

She froze. She couldn't move, could barely think.

Indeed, both Meira and Dak were below. Meira spoke to two witches from the Order and didn't appear under duress. Dak waited patiently, sitting nearby, sketching.

Imani's chest cracked open. Deep down, she knew Kiran spoke truth.

Imani wished she could crawl out of her skin. She wanted to scream, claw her heart out, and throw it at her sister.

Kiran tsked. "They do appear to be more high naiad than you, but I think you'll find them easily in the crowd—"

The prince cut himself off as Meira came up the stairs with one of the master witches.

Kiran let her out of his grip so abruptly that Imani almost tripped, stumbling toward her sister.

She stared at Meira floating up the stairs, hardly breathing, hardly seeing. Meira's severe gaze stopped her in her tracks.

Imani's heart raced, and tears gathered in her eyes.

The master witch blinked in surprise but politely stepped back to provide them privacy.

Meira glided toward her, displaying far more poise and calm than Imani was capable of right now. Her blank expression never wavered. Imani couldn't read it. She barely recognized this spiteful, icy witch in front of her.

How long had Meira been pretending? When had she changed?

It didn't matter. She *had* changed, and it broke Imani's already horribly ruined heart to see the bare truth now.

"Why did you do this?" Imani rasped as fat, stray tears fell down her cheeks and lips.

Meira's big blue eyes filled with tears, too, but her lip snarled in frustration when she spoke. "You betrayed me first, and once I learned the truth, I was *sick* of living life with your selfishness and lies. Because instead of keeping your head down for us and focusing on getting home, you've been searching for that *fucking* wand and acting recklessly in pursuit of a myth. For yourself." She paused. "But you go after what you want, *and so do I*," Meira said, her voice dropping low.

Meira had never spoken this way, but despite the strange coldness in her demeanor, Imani understood perfectly. She knew her sister, and Meira wanted only a simple life with her own children. She had always tried to bring them together as a family.

Besides, there was truth in those words. Imani *had* lied to her sister about the murder and many other things. The choices she'd made had taken her away from her siblings and closer to the wand. Those lies and Imani's entire existence threatened Meira's dream, as had Ara's execution.

But Imani had made mistakes before, and they always forgave each other.

Not this time, it seemed.

Once Meira had learned what Imani had done, she'd probably sought to sever herself from those black spots, making it clear what side she was on—her own. She'd have to stay here and take the ascension assessments, but afterward, if she survived, she'd be an unmated female, alone with one younger sibling almost grown up. Without Ara or Imani, she'd be able to return to the Draswood with Dak. She'd be able to find a mate. Maybe even her heartmate.

It all made sense now.

"Did you tell them the truth about my identity then?"

"I did. They know it all. I refuse to lie for you anymore."

Her heart ached fiercely. The fact was more fuel for the queen to put on Imani's impending pyre.

"You will regret this someday," Imani snarled.

"Will I? How does it feel to know you're truly alone now?" Tears now fell freely down Meira's cheeks, as if the insults hurt her more than Imani. Meira could always be the hero and the victim, and how well her sweet sister played her role.

The words—same as Ara's—gutted Imani, and she stepped back a few paces, carefully keeping her glare locked on her sister. "I love you more than anyone, but you would have sent me to my execution with no mercy. So, while I might be *truly alone*, I'm going to console myself by burying you alive and dancing on your grave," Imani stated, her voice and fists firm.

Meira flinched, a flicker of fear passing in her eyes. It soothed Imani's pain somewhat.

Turning on her heel, Imani returned to the prince's side and lifted her chin to meet his gaze. Kiran stared back with evil triumph shining in his eyes, and the smile that formed on his lips was pure mania.

Crazed, self-deprecating laughter burned in her throat, but it faded as her mind traveled further, realizing how deep this deception went. Kiran had known Ara. He had known Malis. He'd known of Imani before even coming here. How long had this plan of his been in motion?

And then it hit her.

She brought her hand to her mouth to keep from screaming.

The Serpent Prince had planned this *weeks* ago, when she'd stood on the balcony as a High-Norn elf. The only one here at the palace. His attention had been on her initially because he'd been suspicious about her identity. While Imani had been pretending to be Meira here, Kiran had known the truth, and all he'd needed was proof, which he had gotten, to create a situation where she'd have no choice but to go to him and bargain for her life.

Which she had.

He could get anyone to agree to anything with the correct information—leverage. He didn't need just someone to bind to him; he needed a *female High-Norn elf* for the binding, and he'd found one.

And he had also needed Meira to help.

"The queen would never let you roam the kingdom freely. How did you leave the castle to visit Meira? How did you convince my own sister to betray me? How did you know I killed Malis?" Imani whispered.

"I knew someone had killed him when he never returned from Essenheim, so before I came here, I went to investigate. I can roam more freely than you think. And I found remnants of books, notes, and maps. He left all his work, unfinished—why? The Malis I knew would have only done that if he were dead. The Crown must have done their own investigation, and once they found Malis's bones, or what was left of them, they started searching for a murderer, not a missing merchant." He rubbed the stubble on his chin. "You should have cleaned those up, my darling. Your magic doesn't destroy quite everything. It could have been anyone else, but you left your cloak—another mistake, I'm afraid."

"But how does it prove I killed him?" she asked.

"Your sweet sister confirmed it was yours. She also confirmed you were suspiciously late and covered in blood and soot when no one else who attended the execution had been."

"It doesn't mean I killed him."

"It doesn't matter to the queen—or me, frankly. It's enough to say you did."

So, while he wasn't the one who had brought her lies to light in front of the queen and Tanyl, Imani was sure he'd offered Meira exactly what she wanted—the heartmate spell she herself had cast. By dangling her heartmate and the freedom she'd always wanted to return to the Draswood in front of her, he'd set the wheels in motion for *her* to do it—to have her own family.

He had probably even found a way for Aiden to break the only rule in the assessment.

In all her overconfidence, Imani had naively convinced herself that she had figured him out and understood how he thought more than others. But he had backed her into a corner from all angles, and it dawned on her that she didn't honestly know the prince.

Imani paused to see if, by chance, he'd take it all back—admit she was wrong, say she had made a mistake, to explain how he hadn't been lying to her from the moment they'd met. But his gleeful expression told Imani beyond a shadow of a doubt that she was right about everything.

"You can lie to the rest of them, my darling"—he sighed—"but I collect secrets better than anyone you'll ever know."

Hearing the truth in those words terrified her.

"You shouldn't trust anyone but yourself, Imani." Kiran shoved her forward, but she could barely sense her surroundings. Every step reminded her she was prey caught in the jaws of a viper.

She thought she'd been keeping up all this time, making her own choices. She thought she was clever by trusting only a small circle of people. But she'd been following every course Kiran had set before her. Everything leading up to this moment had been a trap he'd set up, one she had walked right into.

Imani stole a look at him over her shoulder. And his infuriating *smile* told her all she needed to know. The man was good at getting what he wanted. He was *beyond* good. It was breathtaking.

People had tried to warn her. Esa and Tanyl had both emphasized how Kiran was more dangerous than people realized. But, unfortunately, even among the false rumors, some were true. And Imani hadn't listened.

Like Malis and Esa, she had been an easily tricked fool. Her overconfidence, not to mention how many people she'd been trying to please, like Tanyl and her sister, had made her sloppy. It was a wonder Imani still drew breath. Her stupidity should have killed her ten times over already.

Hysteria built, and she couldn't breathe enough air into her lungs. Whispers raged around her as she lost the last shreds of her sanity. Indeed, she barely noticed as Kiran deposited her inside his bedroom.

"Who am I feeding from then?" Her voice shook.

"Why does it matter? You have so much *experience* that I'm sure you'll be fine whoever it is."

His countenance was half-arrogance, half-smugness, and she knew it would be him.

"You want us to feed from each other still?" Despite his betrayal, the thought didn't disgust her as much as she wanted it to. It had been divine when they'd fed earlier, and she wanted to do it again. A darkness inside him called to hers, even though she wished it didn't.

Her eyes found Kiran's again. The heat in his gaze nearly burned her.

"It seals the binding deeper. We shouldn't have started earlier without someone to supervise. As I said before, I'm not sleeping with you. But it must be me, or the binding won't work."

"You sure were interested earlier," Imani shot back.

"It was the binding magic and your fucking soul draw. Do you think I want this? Do you really think any of us—me, Tanyl, my brother—actually harbor any emotions for you? Tanyl might *think* he loves you, but trust me when I say you're nothing more than a tempting honey pot, trapping people—end of story."

"I get it." She ground her teeth together. Would anyone ever truly be able to love her with this soul draw? Malis was dead, and everyone else was simply under her spell.

"And as I said before, I'm sure as shit not sleeping with some whore Tanyl touched. You have what you need. I have what I need. Which is why we will have an audience so this doesn't get out of hand."

At that, Master Heirwyn breezed in, all light, beauty, and power.

Kiran grabbed Imani roughly and nipped his teeth against the delicate flesh of her throat before whispering, "I told you this night would be more humiliating for you."

CHAPTER 43

Imani despised another person witnessing the intimacy of her feeding. His earlier words still stung. He had said she was *nothing*, and she certainly felt that way now.

Tears filled her eyes as anger tore through her insides, causing a sob to build in her throat. Imani couldn't move, couldn't do anything except let a few tears fall down her cheeks while standing in her nightgown and messy hair. Probably looking precisely like the elf whore they all considered her.

After a few seconds, she forced her composure because Imani had few options now. She could run away and face his wrath, and probably be killed for disobeying the binding. Or Imani could fight Kiran instead of feeding from him. But already weak and defeated, she didn't like her chances.

So, what choice did she have? None. Absolutely none.

Knives cut her every breath as she hardened her resolve, fortifying herself behind an impenetrable wall as she decided she wanted to live. If Kiran wanted them to feed from each other, she'd at least get something out of it. The best way to fight pain was with more pain, and she had much to ease at the moment.

A soft hand ran up and down her spine as Kiran pulled her closer. He was hard against her belly, and a sick part of her liked knowing he was as attracted to her as she was to him, even though they didn't actually like each other.

Imani thought she might pass out when Kiran pressed his lips against her throat, kissing the pulse racing there before his tongue traced against it.

He gripped her neck tighter, pulling her closer. When he spoke, his voice was more menacing and crueler than ever. "Are you done with your pity party? Because I'll only repeat this once, elf witch. I control you now. Understood? Mind and body. You are now my little pet. So, start behaving, or I may decide you're never waking up from this nightmare."

As fast as he'd grabbed her, he let go, and she stumbled backward without his arms to support her. He glared at her with an unreadable look. Contempt? Desire? Both?

A rush of frustration hit her. Why did he have to be so unreadable?

She tried one more act of defiance.

Imani pointed her wand at the nymph witch. "Make her wait outside. I don't want anyone here."

"None of this tonight." Kiran wrapped his arms firmly around Imani's waist as she lunged to cast a spell at Master Heirwyn.

Imani groaned, struggling, but he held her tight against him as more of her braid came loose, strands falling over her eyes and forehead. Finally, she stilled.

"Let go of me," she said, her voice flat.

He did, turning her around. They both glared at each other.

"I absolutely adore these territorial displays from you," he murmured.

Imani opened her mouth to protest how it was absolutely not *that*. Well, it wasn't entirely that. Something about someone watching her feeding partner *did* make her territorial.

But Kiran's hands moved up to her face, silencing her. Lightly holding her cheeks, a dark, malicious expression shone on his face as his forehead dropped to hers. "I need you to behave tonight, darling. This will be over soon."

They were both free of glamour in his rooms, so Kiran's soul draw pulled on Imani. Or did it? The beast in his eyes stirred a strange base desire inside her, natural and unnatural in equal measure.

A wrinkle appeared between his eyes, and his breathing picked up; otherwise, he was strangely quiet. Hair fell across his forehead. Imani wanted to push it back and feel the silky strands between her fingers again.

He drove her mad with confusing emotions. Not to mention he was lying when he said he didn't want to have sex with her—she was absolutely sure he did.

She wanted power over the handsome, cruel prince, even if it was superficial.

Staring him dead in the face, she pierced the prince with a sultry gaze as her soul draw locked onto him. "Let's get this over with then." She let her robe pool at her feet and lifted her nightgown over her head.

His eyes raked over her almost naked body. Glazed, they sparkled with the promise of aggression.

A crackle of shadows moved below her skin, and she flexed her hands as the darkness shot around the room, extinguishing the candles to wafting smoke and the hearth to smoldering embers.

Feeding didn't require either party to be naked, but she wanted him to suffer. She wanted to make this difficult. While his soul draw held a bit of a spell over her, Imani's despair still lingered beneath the game she was playing with him and gave her purchase to fight his allure.

"Oh, and Kiran," she added, undoing her braid as she moved closer to him. "I'm starving and going to eat the shit out of your soul."

Much to her surprise, he threw his head back and laughed.

She fought her own smile. Something was calming about taking control of her fate after this day.

Imani swiped her tongue over her lower lip and stripped off his shirt. She couldn't help but admire his chest again.

Meandering away, she moved to sit on the bed. It would feel good, and she did need to feed, but focusing was difficult. Waves and waves of her stupidity kept overtaking her. She'd underestimated Meira's resentment and the rumors about Kiran. And now, she was stuck here, wanting him, feeding from him, but also hating him. Her emotions were a maelstrom inside her heart and head.

But she needed to accept the reality that she had underestimated a great many people, and now her only option was to move forward—alone.

Meira viewed her as some wild beast to be put down. For gods' sake, her sister *knew* they would hear her witness testimony and swiftly execute Imani like they had Ara. She still had done it.

On the other hand, the male stripping his pants in front of her thought of her as a stupid female elf whom he could treat as his plaything before marching her off to her death. Imani had been a little brown mouse, and he had been the snake, coiled and ready to strike.

They both wanted to use her for what *they* wanted before she died.

Deep down, a part of Imani admired people for their ruthlessness and willingness to take what they wanted, like Ara and Kiran. Despite being a woman and despite being an unwanted prince, they weren't afraid to be strong.

She used to be such a person. The old witch had accused her of not accepting who she was the night before she'd died, and she'd been entirely correct. Imani had denied the essential part of herself for years, especially recently. Controlling it was not the same as denying it. Trying to do what her sister had asked her—to make Meira *happy*—went against her instincts. She should've listened to herself when warning bells had gone off about making friends in Stralas when Meira had suggested it. What an absolutely fucking stupid idea that had been.

Ara had understood the urges were infused into Imani's body, infecting her essence. Her obsession with death lived in her blood and bones. Unless someone drained her dry and ripped her to pieces, Imani would never be rid of her desires. Instead, she'd fought her natural inclinations for the past decade. Could she be such a person again? Did she have enough control now to let the ugly part of her out to play?

All witches were in danger of being trapped for their power, and her kind grew up hearing stories about elf witches, especially females, who were captured and enslaved for their magic. For their cunts.

Throughout her whole time at the palace, she had come dangerously close to that fate, and it horrified her. She had to crush the emotions further down inside her at the moment. It wouldn't do for Kiran to see her hurting.

She never wanted to be controlled like this again—never. If she didn't find a way out of this, Ara would be disgusted.

With a deep breath, Imani forced herself back to the present.

Kiran marched forward and ripped her bralette away, flinging the whole thing to the floor. She gasped.

With darkness and desire emanating from him, he watched her like she was a goddess. Then she wasn't thinking about anything but the present.

Imani bit her lip as he took one of her breasts in each hand, kneading gently. He leaned down to lick at her nipples, and she moaned as he pinched one, sucking on the other to make it hard.

He gave her an impish smile. "You're sensitive here," he said. He teased her, scraping his teeth against the extra-sensitive undersides of her tits, sucking the top of one. Imani clenched her core at the dizzying sensations.

But he was taking his time, and her mind was all mixed up. It kept wandering, wallowing in self-pity.

Her grandmother and Riona would shout for her to stop feeling sorry for herself, to get up and go back to work. Ara would never let her give up, forcing Imani to learn from her mistakes. In fact, letting any of them win sent a sensation of pain through her signature, magic, and body like she'd never experienced before.

She dragged her nails down his back to push away those emotions, but it didn't help.

Esa had been correct; Kiran was far more dangerous than anyone had let on. If he hadn't already been born a madman—which he had—his family and kingdom had certainly twisted him until he'd transformed into one.

Her nails dug into his skin painfully when he rubbed a rough hand down her soft belly. When his fingers found the waistband of her underthings, she whimpered aloud.

He pulled back and gave her a cocky grin, making her hunger surge. "You're easy to rile up, you know."

Imani pressed forward. "Keep touching me."

He obeyed, still under her thrall, and moved his calloused hands down her thighs. She tried to lose herself in the sensations, to forget how deep the depths of Kiran's magic and insanity went. She tried to ignore the humiliating truth—it was *him* she was doing this with after everything he'd done.

Another wave of his need from his draw hit her. A primal need to rip out his throat for this entire evening was a living, breathing thing inside her, but at the same time, desire warred inside her. She clenched her fists, fighting the conflicting feelings.

Imani wondered—honestly wondered—who was the real Kiran? Did he even exist anymore beneath all the games, gambits, and glamour?

She would find out.

He was much broader and more muscular than he let people see. Savage like a shifter while still possessing dark, elven features.

When his gaze snapped open and locked onto hers and stayed, a jolt of emotions slammed into Imani's chest—a mess of anger, frustration, lust, and longing.

They were both playing a game. He'd orchestrated this entire display for *her* earlier before she had any idea they'd bargain with each other.

The thought didn't calm her. If anything, Imani was *more* out of control. It meant he might have thought about her as much as she thought about him, needing to unravel his mysteries.

Without a word, he lifted her up, and she wrapped her legs around his waist.

"Let's do this as fast as possible," she whispered, trying to fight the sensations he created inside her.

Imani went first. Leaning forward, she shut her eyes and breathed in the scent of his neck. His magic signature surged at her soul draw. Nuzzling his neck, her signature gave him a gentle tug. Then she pushed her way inside.

Imani did what she'd been craving—she breached his magic signature and reached deep inside his being, straight to the core, letting the power it emanated fill and strengthen her. It was pure, untainted energy to Norn.

As she pulled it out and into her own body, his magic pulsed to life inside her, and the pressure came again. Only, this time, instead of controlling her, it empowered her.

He kissed her flesh, suckling her breast, and then he nipped her hard. She whipped her head back.

"Enough," he whispered.

Indeed, he had only allowed her to take a sliver of him. Oh, but what he allowed was beautiful. It tasted pure. It tasted like secrets, too. What was hidden inside the core?

Spreading like warmth through her veins, her energy increased ... the world was sharper.

When she slid down his body to stand, Kiran's eyes were nearly closed with bliss. "You are a dangerous creature," he murmured. It was the most honest thing he'd said to her all night.

Imani tilted her head in surprise. "You've never fed from a High-Norn female, have you?"

With his eyes rolling back, he shook his head. Oh, he liked it.

She let her soul draw wrap around him, cocooning him in comfort.

A second later, his eyes ripped open. His bright green eye rapidly bled to black, perfectly matching his other. "My turn."

Baring his elongated fangs for Imani, he ran his nose over the column of her neck and breathed deep, like he couldn't get enough air into his lungs. She could feel him slip inside her magic signature and tickle her soul inside her chest. He was careful, taking his time and only partaking in a sliver. Imani wanted to stay suspended in such a lovely feeling for all eternity.

Finally, he pulled away, panting, eyes glassy.

They stood still, catching their breath for a moment. Her whole body trembled in pleasure, and she hated him for it. Hated how much she loved it.

Pushing her tangled hair off her face, she retrieved her underthings and nightgown, repulsed with herself for these confusing sensations.

He started laughing at her. Imani didn't understand why, but did he need a reason? He was the Mad Prince.

When she turned back to him, her eyes were clouded with shadows. "One day, I will enjoy making you kneel before me, begging, even if it's only once," she whispered.

His eyes sliced like knives into her soul. "That day will be a long time coming. For now, I'm your king, and you'll kneel before me if *I* so desire it."

"You're nothing if I'm the only one kneeling before you, and I doubt the current monarch's unstable snake of a son will *ever* truly take the Throne, so I'd let go of that dream."

"What do you know about my dreams?" Unglamoured, his magic signature was menacing as it snaked around him, silently snapping and snarling at her. Fangs still out, he shoved her against the wall. "You're a pawn in this game and my family's plans ... and you don't even know it."

Kiran might be a handsome prince, but underneath his arrogant tone, a hint of longing and insecurity he tried to hide surfaced.

"If I'm a pawn, so are you," she sneered. "If the rumors are true, then your father *hates* you. So, why would he confide his plans to you at all? How could you, of all people, know anything about his plans? It's laughable."

"You couldn't even fathom the relationship my father and I have, so don't presume to understand."

A tense silence fell until someone clearing their throat startled them. Their heads ripped toward the door.

Master Heirwyn's voice was flat when she spoke. "Kiran, we have work to do. Wrap this up."

He gave her a curt nod then turned to Imani. "Don't linger in your rooms. Get to the traveling party as fast as possible, or the queen will arrest you and there's nothing I can do."

She nodded.

"Leave me, Lady Aowyn." His voice was low and had an air of viciousness.

"Gladly." She tugged her nightgown on and barely shoved on her robe before storming from the suite.

Anger like she'd never known burned through her. But she was also invigorated. Because the longer she was around Kiran, the more she learned. And he was every bit as mad, insecure, and desperate as the rumors said.

A vicious look spread across her face. Kiran might *seem* unpredictable, because no one understood how he worked or his endgame.

They didn't understand Kiran, the man.

Only the prince.

CHAPTER 44

The sun's rays pressed against Imani's eyes for the last time in months—maybe years.

Rolling over, she stared listlessly at the ceiling, uncaring how her chest hurt from bruised ribs or the root binding ... uncaring the queen's guards could grab her at any minute. In fact, now that Imani was out of the safety of Prince Kiran's rooms, Dialora would be on her way. Imani was wasting time, wanting to enjoy the sun a bit longer.

Any remaining shreds of responsibility toward her family deserted her. Now, the bits of her fringed sanity flew off into the distance, almost too small to be seen, and the darkness of insanity careened inexorably toward her in an attempt to splice her world permanently.

Feeding from Kiran had been the best part of her horrible night. His soul didn't leave her wanting. It was quite beautiful, all things considered. And she must admit a small part of her was slightly disappointed they didn't give in to their desires.

It was disgusting—he was a madman—but she wanted Kiran. Plain as day. At least she could admit the confusing truth to herself now, which had been building for a while. It felt good to get it all out in the open.

Defeated, her shoulders slumped as her head dropped into her hands. "God, how stupid could I be?" she whispered.

A loud banging on her door interrupted her thoughts.

"Open up, by order of the First Witch and Her Radiant Majesty the Queen."

She padded to the door and pressed her ear to the wood. The men let out shouts and hisses of pain as they collapsed to the floor, presumably injured.

More yelling ensued, but Imani smiled.

No one was getting in here unless she or Kiran allowed it.

She'd been angry then, but now she couldn't be more grateful for Kiran's defensive magic around her rooms.

Still, the intrusion meant she had no more time to waste.

She whipped out her wand and started flinging her things around the room into a pile on the bed.

Her grandmother's voice echoed in her mind as she scurried around the room—it always did in all her moments of failure—and a memory of Imani bleeding on the floor, wanting to give up, surfaced with stunning clarity.

"Do you think this is over? Nothing is over until you're dead, Imani—and even then, the saints will bargain with the willing."

Was Imani going to let one setback ruin her plans? Ruin her chances to find the Drasil? Was she so weak she couldn't handle a few complications?

Her base nature roared to life inside her soul in a shocking rush. Deep inside, Imani had always known this day would come, and her biggest mistake had been believing her own lies. She'd been pretending to be someone she wasn't. Her sister was right, and Ara had been right, too. She was alone—utterly alone. At six and twenty, she had no family and no freedom. But she would have a future, even if it killed her.

Outside her room, it was oddly silent. But the guards would be back soon, probably with the First Witch, if the wards needed to be stripped away by someone as powerful as Kiran.

Like a wild summer storm, she ran around the suite, gathering the last of her things and dumping them into the small trunk. Fury blackened her heart, but Imani forced herself to keep going.

A stark sadness struck her when she picked up a pile of the clothes her sister had made. After a moment of indecision, she folded them neatly and packed them away. Imani loved the dresses, even if she hated her sister. It would be a damn shame to waste them.

With a slam, she dropped the lid closed then engaged the locks. Imani whipped out her wand, casting a few illusions and protective enchantments before sending the trunk into the air and sweeping from the room with her own invisibility spell cast. Servants typically performed this task for her, but she couldn't risk it falling into the wrong hands. Imani would take no chances when it came to the queen now that Dialora was indeed coming for her.

Oddly enough, no soldiers waited outside. She'd assumed there would be at least a few to subdue while they waited for the First Witch to arrive.

But a crowd had gathered over the atrium, whispering and watching something.

Perfect. She had gotten lucky but wasn't going to question it.

Keeping a rapid pace, she made her way to the back stairs. On her way down, she consulted the paper left in her room and memorized the instructions for departing, including the coach she'd been assigned.

Outside, she took a deep, calming breath with the traveling company in sight. A quick glance to her left, however, made her do a double-take.

The two Niflheim princes stood surrounded by their royal guards. A few whispering words passed between Kiran and Saevel, the arrogance clear in their expressions. Was this what everyone was on about?

Kiran wore black, as usual. The early morning light glowed around the handsome elf prince like a halo. It reminded her that they both only had a few more days in the sun's warmth.

She swept her eyes over him again, taking in the muscle twitching in his throat, the twist at the corners of his mouth, and the unruly waves of hair falling across his forehead. He pushed them back with one hand, unsheathed his sword with the other, then let himself smile maniacally.

Curiously, Kiran's fearsome elven features were more on display today, too. What moments did he choose to lighten his illusion? It was subtle, she'd noticed it the second she'd discovered he was glamouring himself. The magic came on and off like clothing he slipped into when needed.

It would be one of the first things she tried to learn about him, along with the rest of his magical brands.

While she could appreciate the view, the appearance of Kiran's beautiful face only served to cause her more anger. If anything, it was an intimidation tactic and nothing more, and she wouldn't let him have such power over her anymore.

Before she could study him further, Kiran moved stealthily through the guards and simply … disappeared. No matter how hard she scoured the lines of horses and milling people, she could not find him again.

A moment or two later, she reached her coach and secured the trunk to the back. A commotion drew her gaze away, toward the palm-framed yard and boulevard leading to the main palace gates.

Mouth gaping, she took in Tanyl sparring with Kiran. *This* was what had all the courtiers pausing their days to stare.

Seeing Tanyl's form was a practiced ferocity didn't surprise her, but he was running on emotions, and the Niflheim prince was as cold as stone, and as equally trained. With a simple sword, the way Kiran moved, twisted, and leaped between the blows he delivered was, unfortunately, spectacular.

Imani was hard to impress when it came to combat without magic. It was true what Esa had said—powerful witches tended to be lazy fighters who wouldn't stand a chance without their wands, and high-bred nobles fought with rules and honor that would make them an easy target for dirty fighters like Imani.

But, to her surprise, Kiran didn't miss the opportunity to strike a fearsome but low blow into Tanyl's side with his fist. Doubled over, Tanyl didn't see Kiran move to trip him, either.

Tanyl stumbled, and Kiran slammed his boot into the other prince's back with a snarl. The Essenheim prince fell to the ground, kicking up a cloud of dirt.

Prince Kiran Illithiana would do anything to win a fight, even getting his hands dirty, which shouldn't have impressed her, but it did.

Tossing his sword at Tanyl on the ground, Kiran held up both his hands, as if to say, *Well, is that it?*

"Someday, Kiran"—Tanyl bared his teeth, his tone low and threatening—"I'm going to kill you."

"You can try," Kiran said, flicking his gaze toward Imani.

She froze.

"But until then, little Princeling, you can trust I'll keep her safe and alive. Hmm ... I can't wait for the day I possess everything of yours." He paused. "And don't even think about trying to talk to one of my witches again. Don't even *look* at them."

Kiran's gaze zeroed in on Imani with intensity, his magic tingling across her skin.

Imani swallowed, her pulse fluttering against her neck. How could he see her? Her trunk was already tied to the back of the coach. She was nonexistent.

Tanyl shouted something in response. Kiran threw his head back and laughed. When he stopped, amusement glinted in his strange eyes. Then he shrugged and sauntered away.

Cursing herself for getting distracted by him again, Imani grabbed the carriage door and thrust herself inside.

The second she was settled, the door opened. Startled, she snapped her head to the side and narrowed her eyes.

Tanyl slammed the door shut behind him and dropped onto the seat in front of her. He was one of the three people she desperately didn't want to see right now.

When she regarded him, the innocent look he wore like a mask fell from his face, turning him from the picture of impish charm to something more intriguing altogether. Something darker.

Straightening her back, she forced a blank expression onto her own face. "Tanyl."

"Imani," he said evenly, piercing her with one of the coldest glares she'd ever received.

"What was the fight about?"

Tanyl's face twisted in frustration. "I said I wanted to talk with you

—only *talk*—and he goaded me, said I could if I could beat him. I couldn't refuse. It's another one of his games. It meant nothing, Imani, so forget about it."

It meant *something*. Kiran didn't do anything for nothing—he was making a point. But she didn't argue.

"Hmm, how nice it is to hear you say my name," she murmured, trying to hide her trepidation.

"I should kill you. My mother certainly wants your body tied to the stake. Despite what I told Kiran, she *did* send me to retrieve you for your crimes," he said with disdain. Even through his chilly demeanor, a flicker of hurt passed Tanyl's eyes as the words left his mouth.

Imani ignored it and waved her hand dismissively. "Please. He was a Niflheim loyalist, and besides, it was self-defense."

"Seemed premeditated to the group listening to your sweet sister's story."

"Ah, yes, and what else did my sweet sister tell you?" Imani hissed.

"You'll never be able to set foot in this kingdom as long as my mother is queen. Especially with what she fears is dark magic that you possess."

While Imani had expected this outcome, it still cut to her core. To leave Essenheim willingly, searching for the wand, was one thing, but to be forced out and on the run from her beloved home was devastating.

"And when you're king?" Imani rasped out after a full minute of silence.

"If you come back empty-handed, then yes, you're a traitor to Essenheim, and you'll be dealt with accordingly."

Imani swallowed, reading the deeper meaning behind his words. While Tanyl was furious, he was more upset Imani had lied to him.

Her face softened. "We've always discussed how it's more likely to be hidden here, but you know I'll bring you the wand if I find it. I'm bound to our promise."

"Indeed, thank the gods for that, since you're such a pretty liar. But I'm talking about something else—information."

Her stomach dropped, remembering their conversation from a

few weeks ago. "Tanyl," she whispered, "how do you expect me to get anything without getting caught and killed?"

"If you ever want to come home, then you'll figure something out."

"What information do you want specifically?"

"Anything you can learn about their magic and Kiran's." Tanyl's cold eyes cut into hers with an intensity that made her cringe.

"How will I get this information to you?" Imani asked, picking at a string on her dress, growing increasingly furious by the second. "We will all be spied on, but Kiran knows about you and me. He's going to keep a special eye on me, likely."

"Not my problem," he said, the picture of indifference. "Get creative. I don't care. Use his attention on you to your advantage."

She had half a mind to tell him Kiran was probably the only unmated male she couldn't manipulate with sex, but she clenched her jaw and stayed quiet. Losing her temper would only reveal her vulnerability, and Kiran was a weakness she needed to keep silent.

"Fine," she mumbled. "But it still doesn't answer how we'll communicate without getting me killed in the process?"

"The Illithianas use a fleet of low and common bird shifters to communicate across their kingdom," Tanyl explained. "Ingenious, and something I intend to bring here when we are united as one again. We're lucky to have one in our pocket who's found a way out of the silencing binding they force on the shifters. He'll go by Ren, and when it's time to send updates, he'll find you. So, be prepared at any given time."

"And he's loyal to the Crown?"

"You let me worry about it, but yes, he is. Although, he's a low-bred shifter." The same cold look fell upon his face. "I have a feeling you'll be getting access to much more than he's been able to, little elf."

She wanted to smack him. "How long will I be in your employ?"

"Hard to say. But realistically, you'll probably be there until we are strong enough to overtake the Throne." He paused and smiled. It wasn't kind. "Or until you find the wand and can free yourself. In which case, know I will welcome you with open arms."

Trusting Tanyl anymore would be stupid.

He paused. "This is how you show your loyalty to your kingdom, Imani. Otherwise, you truly are a traitor."

She stared at him, unblinking.

His penetrating gaze still fixed on her. An exacting, imperial gleam in his gray eyes made her think of Kiran, as if she were under a lens. Tanyl's gaze lacked the wild menace of Kiran's, but she still wanted to claw out his heart and stomp on it to get some hint of emotion. Anything would be better than the frigid indifference he now wore so well.

"And if I decide I won't have any part in this?"

Bracing his elbows on his knees, Tanyl leaned forward. "Imani, if you choose them over us—if you decide never to come home or never send us what you will no doubt learn—I will personally light the fire around your body when you're captured and let it burn until there's absolutely nothing left. Not even bones."

"I could be there for *years*," she said through gritted teeth. She hadn't planned on needing that long to search for the wand, but he didn't need to admit it.

In one smooth motion, he grabbed and shook her shoulders. "You better pray it doesn't take years. We don't have the time, and I don't plan to let us grow weaker before moving. Things are already happening to make this upcoming conflict inevitable."

Flinching, she tried to push him away. "Get off me."

"I want to hear you agree to all of this," he growled in a tone she'd never heard him use with her. His conversation with Kiran was the last time he'd been so forceful.

"Get your hands off me—" Imani cut herself off at the sound of the carriage door opening.

Esa and Nida stood outside, eyes squinting in the sun. It was higher in the sky, although not even midday, but it was hot enough for Imani's anger to break her out in a sweat.

"My, my, what do we have here?" Esa asked in a lilting voice.

"Nothing," Tanyl grunted, shoving his way out the door. Wearing that cold half-sneer she'd never seen before, he smoothed his clothes and hair before striding off without another word.

Imani glared at his back. Tanyl hit hard and fast when someone betrayed and attacked him—a part of him she'd never anticipated. For a fleeting moment, Imani wished things could return to how they had been. The fact remained—she still liked Tanyl.

But their old relationship was gone, shattered by her lies, and it wasn't returning until she had the wand in hand. Even then, was Tanyl lost to her for good? Maybe. Imani didn't care at this point if it meant she'd have the wand in her hands, but she still couldn't deny the pang of hurt in her chest at losing another friend.

A terse silence settled around the three women. She and Esa hadn't exactly been friendly with each other lately, and despite Nida's sweet personality, Imani had killed her heartmate, even if indirectly. The female shifter wasn't about to forgive her any time soon.

"I must say I'm a little surprised to see you here this morning," Esa murmured. "Impressed, too."

Imani didn't deign to respond.

Esa was sly and unbothered as she climbed inside. "Who did you have to fuck to get them to spare your life?"

Imani wanted to open her mouth and scream her shadows at the pixie for assuming she had. Although, in most instances, Esa would probably be right.

Whispers murmured, and magic pressed against her skin. It wanted out. She wanted it out, too.

Imani faced the tiny pixie, her teeth clenched. The whispers built in her, feeling as violent as the one she held in last night against Aiden. The one she'd made herself sick shoving back down, so sure it would have been as horrifying as the first time with Malis.

Nida rubbed her temples. Then, with a fierce glare at odds with her beautiful face, she exited the coach, marching off to presumably find another one to ride in.

Probably for the best.

Esa ignored her and plowed on. "You could have avoided this mess if you hadn't held back. You should've killed Aiden when you had the chance."

Taken aback, Imani's mouth gaped. "Held back what? He was bound to win, even after I gave him everything I had."

"Don't lie to me. I saw the magic. It was barely there, like shadows, but there was *something*. And even now, this whole carriage is steeped in shadow. What have you been hiding?"

Pointing to Esa's chest, Imani's lip curled. "You know nothing about my magic."

Esa tilted her head to the side. "I might know something. And I'll repeat it: I'm on your side."

Imani arched a skeptical brow, and her mouth thinned. She *wanted* to have Esa as a friend again, but Kiran had told her not to trust anyone but herself. Ironically, sane advice from the Mad Prince.

"Are you? Because I will repay each person according to what they have done," Imani said in a dark voice. The words tasted like violence. They felt like destiny.

It cowed Esa into a contemplative state, her violet eyes studying Imani before briefly flitting to the window.

Imani shut her eyes and leaned back against the plush seat, effectively ending the conversation. It had improved her spirits to hear Esa was on her side, but she wasn't in a forgiving mood at the moment.

In the darkness of her mind, she committed Meira's and Kiran's faces from earlier to memory. She would never forget those looks—like they won, and she had already lost.

If they thought *this* meant she had lost, they didn't know her. As far as she was concerned, both had drawn first blood, but they were merely getting warmed up.

Despite the iron-clad control over her soul draw that she'd developed because of Ara, she was still herself deep down in her bones. Accepting this person, the good and the bad, was the only path forward. Denying it was like asking someone to live without a beating heart in their chest. Ara had been right all along.

These offenses wouldn't go unchecked. It wasn't in Imani's nature to acquiesce without a fight, especially not after being betrayed, left for dead by her own sister, and forced into a gilded cage by a mad prince before he finally sacrificed her in the dark bowels of his kingdom.

Crazed laughter burst from her, and Esa watched her warily. For a moment, Imani probably resembled Kiran in all his madness.

With her hand pressed to her mouth, she quieted but couldn't stop smiling. She wasn't grateful to Ara for much of anything, but she did have her to thank for her hardened heart.

With that thought, Imani was steadfast in what she needed to do. She wasn't going to cry anymore. No. While grief still permeated the edges of her heart, the rest of her was now fucking *furious*. She focused on manifesting her desired future.

And such a wicked, ruthless future awaited her, too.

The last piece of advice Ara had given her that night stuck with Imani the most. Accepting everyone would soon hate and fear her did make things easier. It also reminded her how a person couldn't accomplish anything without power, which required sacrifice, focus, and ruthlessness.

Even from the grave, her grandmother influenced her.

That was power.

She might not be a threat right now, blindsided and weakened, backed into a corner, but she could become one. She'd watch. She'd listen. She'd bide her time. She'd regroup in Niflheim, let them all bask in victory while she found her footing again. And the Drasil.

All the while, she'd learn everything their hearts truly desired, every secret, every wish, burying herself so deep into their skins they would question their sanity.

Then she would rip it all away before finally letting them die and consuming their souls.

THANK YOU

Thank you so much for reading The Elf Witch. As an indie author, reviews are critical, and I ask that you consider leaving one on Amazon or Goodreads.

Need more Imani, Esa, Kiran and Tanyl in your life? Sign up for my e-newsletter at www.jacquelyngilmore.com for deleted scenes that didn't make it in the book.

ABOUT THE AUTHOR

Jacquelyn Gilmore writes fantasy and science-fiction romances about villains. Her stories aim to push readers to enter new, terrifying worlds. She has over a decade of professional writing experience, a bachelor's degree in English literature and an obsession with anti-heroes. Jacquelyn lives in Austin, Texas, with her partner, Josh, and dog, Boomer.

COMING SOON

THE PLOT OF THE SIX SAINTS SERIES:

THE SERPENT PRINCE (Book Two)

THE OTHER HALF OF THE END SERIES:

DREAM IN THE ASH (Book One)

ACKNOWLEDGMENTS

First, I want to thank you—the reader. This could never have been possible without you picking up this book and taking a chance on me. I know it's risky to start a new series by an unknown author, but thank you for entrusting your time and attention to me. Thank you for getting excited on social media and sharing your love. From the bottom of my heart, thank you.

To my beta readers, your honest reactions and constructive criticism were invaluable. Thank you for taking time out of your day to read and honestly share your thoughts on *The Elf Witch*.

To my editors, you helped create *The Elf Witch* into the book it was meant to be. I would have been lost without your guidance and direction along the way.

To Beautiful Book Covers by Ivy, I'm still in love with this cover (and the rest) and couldn't have done this without you.

To my ARC/Street Team, you are an incredible group of humans. Thank you for cheering me on, shouting from the rooftops, and loving these books so damn hard.

To my friends, thank you for listening to me ramble on about the highs and lows of writing this book (and all the others). Your patience knows no bounds.

To my husband, thank you for putting up with this madness and supporting me in every way.

Printed in Great Britain
by Amazon